THE MARBLE KISS

Jay Rayner was born in 1966. He grew up in North London before going to Leeds University in 1984 to read politics. While there, he gained a grounding in journalism through his work on the city's weekly student newspaper. He returned to London in June 1988, and has since gone on to work for (among others) the *Guardian*, the *Mail on Sunday*, the *Independent*, the *Independent on Sunday*, *Cosmopolitan*, *GQ* and the *Observer*, and has been a regular presenter on Radio 4. In 1992, he was named Young Journalist of the Year in the British Press Awards.

THE
MARBLE
KISS

JAY RAYNER

PAN BOOKS

First published 1994 by Macmillan London

This edition published 1995 by Pan Books
an imprint of Macmillan General Books
Cavaye Place London SW10 9PG
and Basingstoke

Associated companies throughout the world

ISBN 0 330 33094 2

All the twentieth-century characters in this book are entirely
fictional save for Professor James Beck and Signor Giovanni Caponi
who appear, if briefly, as themselves in Chapter 6. Any resemblance
to real people, either living or dead, is purely unintentional.

1 3 5 7 9 8 6 4 2

A CIP catalogue record for this book is available from
the British Library

Typeset by Intype, London
Printed and bound in Great Britain by
Cox & Wyman Ltd, Reading, Berkshire

FOR PAT
WHO WILL ALWAYS BE MY EDITOR

ACKNOWLEDGEMENTS

I am indebted to Richard Fremantle, art historian, writer and resident of Florence for more years than he cares to admit, who shared with me his knowledge of the city and its people, and his expertise both on art restoration and the Renaissance. A number of the ideas in this novel come from *God and Money*, his own book on that period. Not only did he allow me to steal those ideas; he even read the manuscript afterwards to check I had got them right. Without his enormous contribution this book would not have happened. All mistakes, of course, remain my own. Further thanks are due to Jonathan Freedland, who read the manuscript and made incisive and tactful suggestions as to how it might be improved. I would also like to record my gratitude to: Professor Gino Corti of Florence, for providing translations into Latin; Clare Margetson, of the *Guardian*, for providing translations into Italian; Claire Rayner for her impeccable advice on matters medical; Bruce and Barbara Marshall for their hospitality and the loan of their view of the Tuscan Hills which enabled me to finish the book; Dame Ruth King for her patronage; my editors at the *Guardian* and *Cosmopolitan* for their patience.

My agent Rachel Calder provided unending support and encouragement, even when there weren't any books for her to agent. Likewise, Bill Scott-Kerr, my editor at Pan, was there whenever I needed a whine and kept me on the editorial straight and narrow. Finally I would like to thank Jo Frank, now editorial director of Simon and Schuster, who, in another incarnation, got the ball rolling in the first place.

'As the doctors say of a wasting
disease, to start with it is easy
to cure but difficult to diagnose;
after a time, unless it has been
diagnosed and treated at the outset,
it becomes easy to diagnose but
difficult to cure.'

MACHIAVELLI,
The Prince,
1513

PART ONE

CHAPTER ONE

Her groans did not so much put him off his task as punctuate it. They gave him a strong if irregular beat to follow, a gut-driven rhythm that pumped out through the night. They echoed around the empty halls and stairwells, bounced off the stone floors, slipped out of the windows and away up the chimneys only to be lost, at last, on the wind and the rain that beat down outside. At first she would manage only a moan, a quiet wheezing thing that she seemed to be expelling through gritted teeth. Then she would pant for a few seconds, huge solid breaths drawn up from the very pit of her stomach, before moaning once more as though the effort of all that panting had just been too much.

He learned to ride these waves of agony, his stroke slow during her periods of moaning, gentle even, as though he wanted to nurture the pain. He did not, after all, want to be hurried to a conclusion. Not now. Not tonight. This was a moment to be savoured. In time he would have the opportunity to produce the grand finish, the grand display; for now he should be patient. When she began her panting, deep, dark breaths that rumbled up from far below, he would increase his speed, working his wrist hard over his flesh, tugging until the skin became taught. But when, later, as though in sympathy, the thunder and lightning broke over the castle walls and her panting and moaning gave way to more exotic screams of agony, he had, at last, to rest. While he considered himself something of an artist where these pursuits were concerned, skilled and well practised (he had indulged in each and every one of the seventy-three rooms

3

in the castle, including the pantry) he felt sure he could not maintain the speed that the intensity of her pain demanded without producing that grand finish somewhat early.

Old Father Sadini, his face drawn down by time, had told him it was a sin. 'Dear Bartolommeo,' he had said slowly, as though even his jaw were a martyr to gravity, 'My dear, dear Bartolommeo. Have I not been your faithful confessor these fifty years, a loyal and trusted servant?' There he had stopped, his thick-lidded eyes examining the prince's face for the twitch of the lip or the lift of the eyebrow that would signal the sinner's acceptance of his priest's moral authority. Bartolommeo would always oblige. In return Sadini had dredged up the look of deep sadness that he reserved for just such eventualities, the times when he was called upon to receive the details of his flock's more grievous misdemeanours. It was a solemn little face, lips puckered, nostrils flared, designed to be striking without being too austere.

He ploughed on: 'Have I not listened patiently? And have I not told you before? Have I not said? Of course I have. Of course I have. And I know you have listened. But I will say it once more because you are my Lord protector and have treated me well these long years.' (Never shy away from a bit of flattery, he had told his younger students once; it couldn't do any harm.)

Another little pause, a silent overture to the main event. Finally the lesson itself: 'You cannot allow your seed to waste itself on the ground so. You especially. A prince's seed is a precious seed to be saved, to be cared for, like that of the greatest oak, the mightiest tree, waiting . . .' But then his words had stopped, strangled by wicked imaginings, as though the glorious thought of all that regal fiddling and fumbling had somehow managed to bury the dry store of moral certitude that he had forever believed lay at the very centre of his being.

Ah, but what did Sadini know? What could he ever know? 'I am Bartolommeo dei Strossetti, Lord of this city,' the prince muttered to himself as he lay in his bedchamber on this stormy February night, examining his erect member. 'A prince cannot help it if he is blessed by such potency.' He gently stroked his length. 'It cannot just be allowed to go to waste, to stand there unattended. I must be allowed my release.'

He listened for the sound of his wife in the room below, waiting for the thick groans, the sign that her contractions were coming once more. There could, he reasoned, be no greater symbol of his glorious potency than what was coming to pass down there. The shouting and the pain and the effort. Childbirth was a wonderful thing, he decided. Her screams were notes in a glorious hymn being written in praise of his power.

'It is,' the prince said out loud as he gripped his penis once more, 'the good Lord who has made me what I am.'

Indeed, but what the good Lord had made him was no longer such a thing of beauty. Bartolommeo dei Strossetti, prince of the city that took his name and its surrounding lands, the eighth generation of Strossettis to occupy the throne, lay atop the royal bed, nude and desperately unlovely, this late winter's night. If he propped his head up a little and gazed down the length of his body the effect was tolerable: a solid chest, flat stomach, even rather noble feet. Save for the heavy varicose veins that trailed around his calves, dark sea-green swellings that broke the line, it was, from that position at least, a body that well became an aged prince.

From above, however, the geography was somewhat different. A life spent in pursuit of comfort through the brazen pillage of the royal kitchens had left him with a collection of permanent trophies: lumps of fat had lain claim to his hips and thighs and now spread away from him across the bed like some enormous ripe Brie. His flesh was grey and pallid, the colour of sweating veal. The only healthy glow he could muster this evening was at the very end of his penis. His glans shone out like a beacon, by turns bright red and deep purple, the hapless victim of a good half hour's over-enthusiastic attention.

There were those around the castle who claimed to remember a time when the prince had been a truly beautiful thing to behold; loyal servants these sixty odd years who, like Father Sadini, had somehow neglected to die of old age and so continued to live for want of anything better to do. Back then the prince had been the proud owner of a solid jaw, they would say. Eyes of sparkling blue, hair thick and black, a full pair of lips, ever moist, lips that seemed to be preparing to separate at any moment so as to swallow the head of an incompetent subordinate. And tall. A good six foot. A giant. Oh, they would say, he was a grand sight. Masterful. Bold. Now, of course, it was all gone, lost in a tangle of greasy jowls and drooping flesh.

The dramatic looks of his youth were remarkable, not just because they became a prince so, lending a certain gravitas to his more outrageous bouts of princely posturing but because, in truth, the various members of the Strossetti family had never been fêted for their prettiness. Generations of active inbreeding had seen to that. While their little principality, tucked away in the rugged Apennine mountains of north-western Tuscany, was known across all of northern Italy as a place of great natural beauty, the members of the House of Strossetti that ruled it were more famous for their long, flat foreheads and their penchant for slobbering when they became excited. They were, in short, ugly as sin.

When the family had first wrested control of the principality in 1296, replacing the name Arzanna with their own to enforce their authority, cousin was betrothed unto cousin to secure the blood line. It was, the first prince had reasoned, merely a matter of expediency. Later, however, it became more a necessity. Despite the premium placed on a good marriage within diplomatic circles, few ruling families in the region could bring themselves to marry off their children to a Strossetti, whatever the political gain. Politics, they argued, was one thing, torture quite another.

And so, over the years, the gene pool had slowly shrunk. With it had gone many of the Strossetti limbs. Generation after generation of Strossetti children were born with club feet and hare-lips, their twisted flesh and strange bulbous eyes testament to the suffocating atmosphere of family. The indignity would not last long. Most of these children would die of some digestive disorder or other when they reached early adolescence. Those who managed to survive often turned out to be insane; most were slavering maniacs who spent their adulthood talking to trees or, with a discreet nod to Greek tradition, trying to murder their mothers.

It was said that, for the last four months of his life, Bartolommeo's grandfather, Prince Annibale dei Strossetti, had been chained to his bed to prevent him running amok, a difficult imprisonment to maintain on account of the madman's constant resourcefulness. He would regularly free himself and appear naked on the rooftops of a warm summer's evening, limbs akimbo, screaming that he was a mighty eagle and could fly, before being wrestled back to the bed and the chains. It was a sad and truncated life. He met his death proving that he could indeed fly, if only downwards and not for very long.

Thus it had been impossible to keep their hereditary problems from the people of the principality. Around the narrow streets of Strossetti it had become something of a joke that the ruling family had taken to economizing; the town idiot and the prince were now usually one and the same.

The forty-two-year rule of Prince Bartolommeo dei Strossetti had come, therefore, to be considered a golden age. He was sane and, although now going to seed, physically in one piece. He had the correct number of limbs and all were of the proportionate length. He had once been handsome, remained reasonably fair in matters of justice – he always took pity on the deformed – and was not a bad businessman or diplomat. Indeed, under his careful control the people of his principality had become relatively wealthy.

Though, given the opportunity, Bartolommeo liked to take the credit for the prosperity his subjects now enjoyed, he knew full well that he had been aided by a simple accident of geography. Certainly he had exploited it well, bringing to bear whatever diplomatic skills he had acquired over the years. But still, he knew that had it not been for the line of steep, rocky mountains that ran in an arc from the north-west to the south-east, enclosing this mountain city like a grand shield carved from the very earth itself, the ambitious merchants and craftsmen who ruled Florence some hundred miles away would long ago have overrun them. He needed only to study history to see that. Let the past be your teacher, he always told those who were willing to listen, let the past show you the way. The town of Pistoia, perched just eighteen miles from Florence, had fallen a little over 130 years before in 1351. Pisa, just thirty miles to the south of Strossetti, had, after many furious battles and campaigns, been taken in 1406.

But Strossetti had been entirely defendable from all sides. Bartolommeo's fondness for wandering the rooftops to admire the view or for taking long walks along the ridge that began but a few hundred feet above the castle was not, therefore, born of some poetic instinct that lurked deep down in his soul. It was more calculating than that: he knew that the glorious view was also the key to his glorious rule. And so, over the years, those men who had taken their turn to sit in the Signoria, the Florentine republic's government, had wrapped themselves in their crimson coats of office, with their neat little ermine cuffs, musing on all the possibilities and options and solutions. And regularly they had come to the same conclusion: it really wasn't worth spending the money required to hire enough Swiss mercenaries to assail the principality.

Instead they made deals, paying premiums to the House of Strossetti in return for the right to cross its lands to the natural harbour of Marinella di Sarzana fifteen miles further west, a valuable port on the Mediterranean. It was simply a mercantile deal, nothing more. Other cities could fight each other; Florence and Strossetti would trade. Occasionally there would be arguments, of course. Aren't there always in such forced marriages? Sometimes Florence would try to get away with paying less; other times it would flex its muscles and accuse the smaller town of siding with one or other of their enemies (and they had many). But Bartolommeo's even ways would usually win the day, and all would return to normal.

Only one cloud hovered on this sun-licked horizon. Though Bartolommeo had escaped the more obvious maladies common to his family he had been cursed with a new one: infertility. His whole life had been dedicated to one troubled end: retaining the independence of this land of sickly princes. It was not easy being sandwiched here between the sea and Florence, forever playing off different warring parties in search of small advantage, but he had succeeded, and succeeded in style. Yet if he was infertile there would be no heir and if there was no heir there could be no succession. Who would rule Strossetti then?

There had once been a brother twenty years Bartolommeo's junior. The brother lived still though the people of Strossetti did not know it. At the age of fourteen Piero dei Strossetti had, like his grandfather Annibale before him, begun to exhibit the symptoms of acute schizophrenia. He would babble and shout and scream about the messages blown to him on the wind, the voices from above that told him he was the Christ. He would wake Bartolommeo at dawn and tell him, wide eyes staring, his tongue slobbering from a mouth awash with froth, that he must repent, that he must be cleansed. 'Come with me, my brother,' he would say. 'Come with me and we will do it together.' And he would lead him to the rooftop from where their grandfather had jumped thirty years before, babbling and screaming once more at the early morning sky. At last, exhausted by his crying, he would fall into a deep sleep, and Bartolommeo, ever patient, would carry him quietly back to his room.

When Piero was fifteen his elder brother determined that he should never be succeeded by this madman. As it happened he was sure it would not arise. Bartolommeo was convinced he would soon be a father. It was, he reasoned, only a matter of time. He and his young wife Camile were making sure of that. But better to remove Piero now while it was possible, while he would not be missed. Better safe, he would say, than sorry. The rumour of the mad Piero's death soon went round the town; he had tumbled from the tower or fallen prey to infection or been poisoned by a viper. The means of his death mattered little. The town knew he was dead. They said it was a tragedy.

But Bartolommeo was only a determined prince, not a ruthless one. He built a fort, five miles from the city of Strossetti, in a worthless valley of rock and scorched brown scrub ignored by farmers and soldiers alike, a single-storey construction of high sandstone walls that turned to a shimmering gold each evening as the setting sun burned itself out over the hills. It had only one level – to save the mad prince the inconvenience of hurting himself – and a garden of delicate lilies and orchids, pear trees and olives. Here Piero passed his days in contemplation of the sky, shaking his fist at the devils who stalked him from behind the clouds, oblivious to the world around him. The people of Strossetti were told by Father Sadini that three men had died in the construction of the fort.

'Was it not a sad thing,' he said by way of a sermon one Sunday morning, 'that these spirits should remain, that they should stay and they should haunt the place of their death? Is this not truly sad? Believe me it is, the greatest tragedy of all.'

The wild screams that came from within its walls at night, as Piero fought in vain to chase away the voices in his head, convinced them the old priest had spoken truths. The fort remained undisturbed; there would be no succession from that quarter.

But there was another threat, one that was without doubt even more serious than having a madman who enjoyed talking to the clouds sitting on the throne. Many, many years ago a Strossetti, who had mercifully been spared the excesses of deformity that plagued her brothers and sisters, had been wed to the third son of a well-to-do mercantile family of some political import from Florence. It was, the Strossettis had reasoned, a perfect way to keep an eye on the ambitions of its expansionist neighbour. But history had worked its wicked trick once more, turning solid advantage into political uncertainty; the House of Strossetti now found itself firmly tied to the powerful and ever more ambitious House of Medici. Because the succession passed through the female line, Lorenzo de' Medici would have the only viable claim on Bartolommeo's beloved city should he fail to produce an heir. Accordingly, the self-styled ruler of Florence, who grew ever more eager for land and possessions as the years passed, watched the Strossettis' efforts at reproduction with growing interest.

'When he calls me cousin,' Bartolommeo said to Cesare Scorza, his most trusted aide, one day, 'Lorenzo makes it sound as if he has rights to my soul. Oh Lord, matrimony can be a wicked mistress.' Scorza, well tutored in the ways of diplomacy, let his gaze fall to the ground and said, 'My Lord, when the blood line is secured such threats will be rendered mere family pleasantries.'

But the prince's earnest belief that he would eventually be a father proved unfounded. However much he and the sweet Camile played and rolled and danced around the royal bed she still would not become pregnant. 'What dreadful sin have you committed,' Bartolommeo said to his wife one night, as much in frustration as in anger, 'that the Lord has chosen to make you barren? By your foolishness you risk everything I have worked for.' And he had stormed from the room. In the absence of the means to prove that it was, in fact, he rather than she who was at fault the poor Camile agreed that she must, indeed, be a sinner and had fallen into a deep depression.

Not long after, she was found floating in a lake close by the castle, her white linen nightdress stained a sickly orange brown by the clay that caked the bottom of the pool. There were those in the royal household who whispered darkly about Bartolommeo then. Politics could make you do desperate things, they said, terrible, awful things. Bartolommeo, they decided, had done one of those terrible things.

As it happened, he hadn't. Later he admitted to himself, if no one else, that had he been strolling around the lake just before dawn that fateful morning and had he come across his melancholy wife, shivering in her thin nightgown while she tried to fill her lungs with muddy water, he would not have waded in to save her. Oh, he felt saddened by her death of course. At times he missed her badly, cursed the Gods for their wicked ways. But, as the pain and grief began to subside, he accepted it was all for the best. Killing her would have been completely out of character, he reasoned, far too mucky and complicated a task for one such as he. But he must have an heir. Camile had made the ultimate sacrifice for the future of Strossetti. Lord protect her sinning soul.

Then, many years later, had come Joanna; the beautiful Joanna, the fragrant Joanna. The fertile Joanna? No one could tell with any certainty. Olive-skinned and petite, she had captivated the scout sent in search of a new bride from the moment he had set eyes upon her. He had thought of trying to marry her himself, heading south instead of north, but realized he would never get away with it. But still, what a beauty. High, fine cheekbones framed a small but perfect nose which turned up just at its tip, as though the shape were almost an afterthought. Her eyes were set large in a tiny face and of a rich green; they seemed to burn holes into your soul when she but glanced at you. She had a tight mouth whose lips barely moved when she spoke, as though the words she mouthed, each one less than a twitch of the lips, were a pout or a kiss proffered only to you. And when she was listening, those eyes wide with wonder, her mouth would be only just open, the slightest flash of pink, moist tongue, small but perfectly formed, resting just within, waiting for the right moment in which to lick you into submission.

In Siena, where she was born, they said her beauty was so divine that when first she had visited the hilltop town of San Gimignano the towers of brick that spear its skyline had all bowed down to kiss the ground before her; that when she stepped upon a lake shore, fish threw themselves on to the grass so that she might sate her hunger. Her voice, they said, was as soft as silk, like an angel's breath upon the air; when she sang, the lark would fall silent out of respect. But then the people of Siena had always loved myths and fairy tales.

Yet for all those stories that danced upon her shoulders, the tales that came before her, there were people in Strossetti who did not think she was right for Bartolommeo. The daughter of a wealthy goldsmith, she was not of the highest stock, they said. But neither, said Bartolommeo, were the Strossettis. At first only a family of loyal civil servants, diligent and efficient, they had grown powerful and bored and restless until they had finally determined to take the throne for themselves. That did not give any of them the right to get too precious. Joanna, just sixteen years old, had the advantage of youth. She would provide an heir. That was all that mattered. Her beauty was a bonus. So it proved. Within a year she was pregnant and, though Bartolommeo had been concerned that it took longer than he expected, he was still overjoyed to find himself, in the autumn of his years, on the brink of fatherhood.

He lay on his bed listening once more to her groans of agony from the room below. Childbirth certainly was a wonderful thing, he thought, but such an effort. And didn't it go on? At least later there would be time for drinking. There was that to look forward to, something to cling to during this long journey through the night that he had to endure alone. Oh, the burden of kingship. But for now it was back to that which he knew and loved best, that which he cared for most deeply. That which truly understood him. He gripped his aged and gnarled penis with his right hand and set about his work with vigour. What bliss.

When Joanna's contractions had first begun Bartolommeo had been as excited as never before. He had waited around the bottom of his young wife's bed watching, shifting his considerable weight from foot to foot, as though expecting the new Strossetti to make an entrance any moment. 'This,' he said, 'will be my greatest act,' as he stared obsessively at his wife's vulva, looking for the slightest sign that something was about to happen. Joanna was in too much discomfort to inform her husband that she had the monopoly on great acts this evening; in any case he would not have understood. Eventually he was sent from the room by the nurse and, after many hours trudging round the rooftops, ears alert for the slightest hint of a baby's call on the air, had retired to his bedchamber, his bed and the comfort only he could provide for himself.

But now, many more hours later, there was a new intensity to the sounds from downstairs. Joanna's groans were deeper and harder and they came every few seconds. Over the top of her exertions he could hear the nurse and her maid Claudia urging her on, encouraging her to push, to try, to shove. With renewed enthusiasm Bartolommeo worked his wrist harder; the grand finish was at hand. Onwards went Joanna, onwards went Bartolommeo, together pushing through the dark night. Further they went, harder, onwards, faster together, onwards, onwards, harder, harder, shoving and pulling as one . . .

Bartolommeo came as his wife's last groan cracked open the house, the rare synchronization of a child's birth and its father's ejaculation. There was silence for a moment. And then, just as the mother's cries had faded away so the child's rose up, sharp and shrill, cutting through the stormy night. The new Strossetti greeted the world in full voice. Bartolommeo lay on the bed for a moment, proudly watching his semen seep into the danker recesses of his navel. With a large sigh of pleasure he heaved himself off the bed, pulled on a thick gown and made his way downstairs to where the new arrival was, he felt sure, waiting to greet its father. He did not knock.

Joanna was propped up against a pillow, panting, the young maid Claudia by her side, holding her lady's hand. The princess managed a slight smile for her husband and nodded towards the nurse who stood at the end of the bed. Bartolommeo turned towards the older woman, eyes open wide in question.

'My Lord, it is a boy,' the nurse said as if in answer. She handed over the tiny bundle.

'A boy,' the prince repeated. 'A boy. At last we have a son. What a marvellous night.' He looked at the thing in his arms, pink and creased, a little blood and mucus still clinging to its forehead. And this is our future, he thought. So small but so important. So terribly small and vulnerable. This is the link with what has been in the past and what will come in the future. This is our salvation.

Only then did he hear Claudia's voice. She had been calling to the princess for some time but he had been consumed by the sight of the child. My lady, she was saying urgently, an edge of desperation shattering the words, my lady, what is it? Bartolommeo turned to his young wife. The eyes that had directed him to his son only minutes before now seemed to have glazed over. She was gasping for breath, panting heavily, a slight blue tinge spreading across her upper lip. Claudia was holding her hand and screaming at her. Do not leave me now, she was saying. Do not go. The nurse pulled back the sheet that had been covering her legs and hips and gasped.

The blood was spreading out across the bed, pouring from between her thighs, away and under her calves, great thick puddles gathering in the rumpled bed sheets. It flowed down her calves to where her heels indented the mattress. And still it came, more and more blood, as though the young girl's body had been punctured, the life flowing out and away from her. The heavy breathing subsided to become but the slightest wheeze, until she barely breathed at all. The haemorrhage was mercifully quick. Joanna managed but one word before consciousness left her. She looked into her maid's eyes and, in barely more than a whisper, said only, 'Promise!' And with that, Joanna dei Strossetti, but a week off her eighteenth birthday, died.

There was a cold silence in the room, broken only by Claudia's sobbing and the wind and rain knocking at the windows. Bartolommeo stared at his wife's body, lifeless against the pillow. He squeezed the bundle in his arms until the nurse, fearing that the night would end with a double tragedy, the new-born child crushed in his father's arms, took him away from the prince. As he handed over the new Strossetti, Bartolommeo began to mutter. 'She has served us, served us all. She has made a sacrifice beyond any that mere mortals can demand. Surely she has, the greatest sacrifice it is possible to make in this world. Never has there been anything like it before in these lands. And she loved me, loved me for what I was. What I am.' He fell silent and then, his face creased with anguish, said simply, 'Oh no.' He closed his eyes, as if trying to shut out the sight before him so that he could think clearly. 'There will be a memorial to this princess,' he said. 'One as great as she was herself. Nobody will ever be allowed to forget the name of Joanna dei Strossetti.'

The nurse rocked the new-born baby in her arms. Claudia sobbed.

In a room far from the princess's bedchamber, far from where the prince now mourned, down dark corridors where few ever walked, beyond damp corners where the sunlight never touched, a man wept silent tears. He allowed the drops to fall upon the collar of his tunic, to drip from the simple horn buttons that ran down its front, but still he made no noise. Anybody outside the door would have heard only the thick, damp breath from his nostrils, like water boiling away in a hiss. But there was no one outside the door this lonely night. And, he knew, there never would be anyone again, no one whose presence he would welcome. The corridors remained dark. Thus would they ever be. He walked to the window and, grabbing hold of the heavy oak frame, wrenched it open. The wind and the rain exploded into the room, blowing aside papers that had been laid on his desk, sending huge drops of water on to the stone floor, soaking his bed, drenching him. All this was of no importance now. He raised one fist at the sky and screamed from the very pit of his stomach.

'Why did you take her from me? Why, oh Lord, did you do it?'

The night did not reply.

CHAPTER TWO

The shimmering blue tubes shone out above him, like some enormous mechanical intestine. He sat forward in his chair and squinted at the neon sign to check all the tubes were working. It was only a detail, but a good one: crumbling old town façade, new façade intact. He nibbled his bottom lip. He could use this. It would need work, of course, a little tweaking, but the contrast stuff, old and new, that was good. He opened the red notebook on the table in front of him and, at the top of a blank page, wrote the words 'Strossetti Case'. He underlined them three times and added the date. Beneath that he scribbled 'neon, Repubblica, crumbling façade'. He read them over, laughed, picked up the cigarette that had been lying on the table before him and lit it. He inhaled deeply and began looking around the square again.

He couldn't help feeling he was pulling a fast one. There was something so intrinsically dishonest about it, as though he were claiming powers and skills for himself that he did not have. But it was so easy. And so satisfying. Still, it was a kind of trickery. Ah, but that was the business, wasn't it; continuous sleight of hand, the creation of expertise from nothing, a game with mirrors. He read the four words over again: 'neon, Repubblica, crumbling façade'. What did he have to feel guilty about? He was only doing his job.

It was a scam he had learned from an old Asia hand, a grizzled *Washington Post* correspondent he had come across in Kabul while the press corps had sat out that miserable Easter getting only halfway drunk and watching the empty streets,

19

waiting for the advancing Muslim Mujaheddin to overrun the city and lock away even the weak Afghan ale they had been able to get their hands on. On a hot, still afternoon, when even the flies had shut up shop for the day, the American lectured him: 'Young man,' he said, in a thick growl rubbed dry by years of Asian cigarette smoke, 'correct me if I'm wrong but does not your editor scream at you for detail every time you file your copy?' His pupil nodded. The American continued. 'Detail they want, always detail. Every day you are searching through your notebooks for some little shitty bit of detail which will give your copy edge, the real minutiae, the things that give sense of place.' He spoke the last three words as though they were proper nouns, upper-cased and proud.

'And it's never there. The more you look the less you find. In the end you're reading travel books, magazines. You're stealing details. You become obsessed by the small things. And is it tiresome? Sure it is. So what you do is this.' The old man snorted, withdrew a notebook from his top pocket, opened it and stabbed one nicotine-yellowed finger at a blank page. 'Whenever you get somewhere – Time Square or the Champs Élysées or the Gobi Desert – wherever, doesn't really matter where, what you do is you take out your notebook and you make a list of details. Three should do it, maybe four. The small and the pointless. The number of lamp-posts in the square, the way the grass grows through the paving stones. The temperature of the sand at noon. Then you do your story. Sprinkle these little nuggets of information liberally through your copy and I guarantee that, within a month, your editors will be lauding you for your fabulous eye for detail. They will come up to you and they will say, "Boy, you have one sharp eye on you, you know where to look." '

So it had proved. He had been praised by every department head on the paper. They had lectured him in their offices. They had whispered conspiratorially to him in the canteen, engaged him in intense discussions on style in the thick fug of the local pub. He had this eye for detail, they said. That was what made him different. That was why he mattered. Not everybody could do it. It was a talent. Treasure it. On this warm Florentine afternoon in early June, Alex Fuller, feature writer and sometime follower of the world's bloodier conflicts for the *Daily Correspondent*, could be found taking their advice: he was sitting at an outdoor café table in the Piazza della Repubblica studiously having 'An Eye For Detail'. It took real concentration, real effort to spot the truly insignificant. He was breaking down the dilapidated square before him, dismantling the pieces that gave it its sooty grandeur, its sense of style, and turning it into a linguistic Airfix kit, to be reassembled at some later date, deep in the heart of his word processor.

And yet it was not literary ambition that drove Alex on but the need to bear witness. There was virtue, he said, in being the man on the hilltop with the view. 'But what's the point in being there if you don't tell anybody about the things you have seen?' he would ask his friends. 'The moment is paramount. You have a duty to let as many people know about it as possible. If you keep quiet it might as well never have happened.' Words were not to be treasured for themselves, he said. They were only a means to an end. All he wanted was to tell the story the way it was.

Alex was the king of the anecdote. If there was silence around him he would pour out words to fill it up. If conversation had begun to stutter he would stitch up the holes from his vast store of tales, the stories he had covered, the stories behind the stories he had covered and the ones he had never been able to pin down. He adored an audience, loved to see the pub crowd clasping their pints, leaning forward over the table towards him, lips tensed on the edge of a smile in anticipation of the next grand yarn: of the zoo keepers who, surrounded by a raging civil war, were forced to eat the exhibits; of the mutinous Soviet soldiers in Afghanistan who dreamed of a future elsewhere and so tried to trade their weapons for English lessons from the press corps; of the elephants, kept as working animals in a Sri Lankan village, who became so aroused they toppled over, mid-coitus, crushing three of the villagers' homes. Alex liked the bawdier tales. He declared himself an enemy of euphemism. 'It's the key to good journalism,' he would say with a half-smile. 'If they were fucking, say they were fucking. We should always be exact.'

He tried not to judge as he worked his way through the twists and turns of his darker narratives, but invariably he failed. You could always tell where his sympathies lay, from the turn of his lip or the lift of a hand, or the way he would drop his eyes to the ground when he described some grotesque event in which he felt he should, in some way, have intervened.

'So you see,' a story might end, 'they really felt they had no choice.' And he would look away to study a dead part of the room, disappointed that his tale had reached its conclusion without the end he had hoped for, even though he had known from the beginning how it would turn out; as if he had hoped that in the retelling he might have been able to give the story the ending he always wished for. Those who resented the huddles that gathered around Alex, beneath their stagnant clouds of cigarette smoke, said he was an egotist, too in love with the deep sound of his own voice. His friends would defend him.

'Sure, he likes to entertain,' they would say, 'but tell him a good story and he'll listen,' and it was true. He would sit, shoulders hunched, elbows rested on his knees, sucking the life from his cigarettes, eyes slightly narrowed, chin lifted. Listening. 'So tell me,' his expression would say. 'What did they do? Tell me the end of the story.'

He feared quiet more than anything else. If he was conducting an interview and his subject should happen to fall silent he would dive in head first with a question, raw and ill-formed, anything to bind the gaping wound in the conversation: 'How long did you cry after your daughter died?' or 'Do you think you were to blame for your wife's adultery?' or maybe just 'How will you ever forgive yourself?' Later he would always curse his words, blushing at the thought, just as later there would be moments when he would have cause to curse his actions. But when he would finally come to look at his notes, he would find that the single ill-considered question had paid off. He always got an answer of sorts. He knew well that silence could be helpful too, but Alex had to discipline himself to use that.

It was not so much the enthusiasm in his voice that forced his subjects to speak, as his appearance. Despite his twenty-nine years on the planet, the skin around his eyes had refused to mark or crease. His time spent waiting and smoking in fractured third world airports might well have left its mark on the rest of his six-foot frame – a slight roll of fat already clung to his belly; there was a droop to his shoulders that came from too much boredom – but there was still a boyishness to him that could be unnerving. The eyes were fringed with rich, black eyelashes, so long and full that at parties women would sometimes try to lean close to him surreptitiously, to check they weren't false or weighed down with mascara. And when he smiled a single dimple appeared in his right cheek. Some found the combination bizarre or unsettling: a well-built man with a dark, intense brow and calloused hands who was also irredeemably pretty. Others found it irresistible. Neither could refuse him an answer.

Did he know about his looks? Oh yes, he knew. He gave thanks for them and cursed them in equal measure. Sometimes, he said, it could be useful to have the face of an innocent. Sometimes it made people talk. But at other times people ignored you, because they could not see you as a threat. 'Nothing should get between you and the story,' he would say. 'Unfortunately I always seem to get in the way of mine.'

Alex picked up his notebook and fanned himself with it, to beat a little of the heat away from his face. He stopped and looked again at the page where he had been writing. He had the neon lights. That was good. That was perfect. He looked up at them. The sign was an advert for *La Repubblica*, the Italian daily newspaper, each letter a round-edged, authoritative lump. He looked at the name of the square: Piazza della Repubblica. Now there was an idea. The corporate sponsorship of streets. For an appropriate sum you had the name of your company slapped on every corner, the perfect marriage of commerce and architecture. How about Nabisco Avenue? Exxon Drive. Du Pont Plaza. He put his cigarette down in the ashtray to his right and scribbled some more. He should add that in, a little joke, ill-formed but worth nurturing.

Just a few other details. Two more should do it. A tired old pigeon alighted on his table, the bare flesh of its chest just visible through a fast-disappearing cover of feathers. The bird eyed up his coffee. Alex counted; two toes instead of three. Must be the taxis. Lots of them around here, lots of pigeons too. Nice animal angle, wildlife in the city and all that.

One more detail to go.

He was foraging around in the canvas bag at his feet for another packet of cigarettes when the man appeared at his side. From that position he had to check out the stranger by sections as he uncurled himself to sit upright, as though putting him together, a shattered mosaic of features. With his nose that close to the ground he could see the dust on the man's suede desert boots and the way the hem of his elephant cords turned up an inch so that they bulged uncomfortably where the seams met. As Alex rose up, unopened cigarette packet in hand, he took in the thin leather belt that kept the trousers only just in touch with the man's narrow hips, past the copy of *Art Scribe* magazine that he held beneath his arm, past the frayed cuffs of his jacket sleeves until, at last, he could look him in the face. There was a pause while they considered each other.

'I'm Alex Fuller,' the journalist said eventually. 'And you must be Professor Kelner.'

The art historian looked at the cigarettes. 'You shouldn't smoke,' he said. 'You haven't opened that packet. Don't bother. Put it away.'

To his peers he said: 'It's a bullshit story. No real meat. But it's a bullshit story in Florence. And I would rather be in Florence for a week on a bullshit story than in London for a week with a phone stuck to my ear.' His peers nodded.

To his editor he said: 'It's a story about art and expertise, a battle of wills. Who has the greater right to criticism, who has the greater right to pronounce? Of course there are wider questions there as well. Like, how do we care for our art treasures? How do we fund it? I find that sort of thing fascinating. Don't you? I think it's a vital issue and one we should be covering. One we have to cover.' The editor nodded.

He came across the yarn while scavenging through the news-in-brief columns of a pile of specialist magazines, through the detritus that gathers at the bottom of every page, the staff movements and company mergers, the product launches and legal wrangles. Alex swore by his specialist magazines; if there had been a magazine called *What's New in Cheese and Onion Flavour Crisps*, Alex Fuller would have bought it. As it was there was a magazine called *Meat Trader Weekly* and he'd already bought that. It was money well spent. He had travelled the world on his dog-eared cuttings, a scandal here, a mystery there. Such curios, the peculiar footnotes in everyday life, secured his reputation. He wasn't just good at watching people kill each other in strange corners of the globe, they said. He could find weird stories and deliver them too. He found the Florence story on the international pages of *The Lawyer* maga-zine. The details were few and far between, but an hour on the phone and a trawl through the cuttings library had provided him with enough information to sell it to his editor.

Eighteen months previously Signor Salvatore Falchi, the Soprintendente of Art in Strossetti, responsible for the upkeep and restoration of the many great artefacts in the mountain town and its surrounding villages, had decided that the tomb of Joanna dei Strossetti, situated in the west wing of the city's Cathedral of San Martino, was beginning to show its age. This was not unreasonable; it was now well over 500 years old. The huge lump of marble, carved by the Early Renaissance master Antonio Rafanelli and completed in 1487, was turning black. Joanna dei Strossetti was, the Soprintendente said, still a breath-takingly beautiful woman, a gorgeous woman, but there was now dust and grime caked on to the fine wisps of her hair; the warm glow of the stone had been dulled by centuries of woodsmoke and pollution. It was, he said to the local press, like seeing a woman you love dearly go to seed. Something would have to be done. He would see to it.

The Bank of Massa nearby, ever mindful of the law demanding they put some of their profits towards the upkeep of state treasures, agreed to pay the cost of the restoration. In turn the Soprintendente hired Andrea Conte, a leading Florentine restorer, to execute the work. The son of a respected local painter and a familiar figure around the city's art scene, Conte issued a statement before he began the job, telling the world, and Florence in particular, that he had always loved the sculpture of Joanna. He considered it one of the most exquisite pieces in the world. It would, he said, be a great honour to restore her, a veritable labour of love.

Thus, one crisp November morning he arrived at the Cathedral of San Martino, bearing as much tubing and rubber padding, as many bottles of chemicals and packets of salts, as one could ever hope to see. He informed waiting journalists that Joanna dei Strossetti would be restored in time for Christmas. She would, he said with a flourish, be reborn at the nativity as became an angel. The little huddle of journalists had scribbled and laughed knowingly and shaken the great man's hand. And with that he entered the cathedral, raised four high walls of canvas around the sculpture so that she was hidden from view, set up burning white lamps within, the light seeping out through the ragged holes in the curtains, and set to work.

Reports of how long he took over the job varied. Some said he was there every day, dawn till dusk, cleaning out every last crevice himself, others said he made only rare appearances.

Whatever the truth he kept his promise. On 23 December Andrea Conte removed the canvas and declared the work complete.

Professor Robert Kelner did not see the newly cleaned Joanna until four days later. A professor of Renaissance art history at the University of California, Los Angeles, and a visiting lecturer at the Florentine Institute of Early Modern Sculpture, he had been spending Christmas with his Italian wife's family at his house in the old Tuscan hilltop village of San Casciano only ten miles south of Florence. The day after Christmas he received a frantic telephone call from a former student. Something terrible had happened, the young man said. The professor must come to see the tomb of Joanna, really he must. It was vital he came soon. Forget Christmas, this was more important. His student knew the American would come; Robert Kelner was widely regarded as the world's leading expert on Rafanelli, an artist who was so slow, so diffident, indeed so bloody-minded, he had only ever produced six works. Happily, each of them was a masterpiece. Every curve of stone, every line, held in it the very essence of the classic Renaissance.

Kelner's student promised to alert the local press that he was coming; unfortunately the local press, weighed down by its Christmas hangover, was not particularly interested in being alerted. On that damp late December morning there was only one journalist present, a sulky young trainee with long greasy hair and a constant scowl which was not improved by the cigarette that laid claim to her lips that morning. The tobacco did not endear her to the historian who sniffed the air when he entered the cathedral and shook his head when he saw the girl's lip extension. She was averse to being there; she was equally averse to asking questions.

It mattered little; she did not need to say anything. Kelner did all the talking. For a few moments he stood before the tomb, the mellow orange glow of devotional candles dancing out across the stone before him, and said nothing. Later he said it had been one of the worst moments of his life. He felt as though it had been his skin that had been removed, his very soul that had been stripped bare. For a while he gripped the wrought-iron barrier that surrounded the tomb. 'What,' he said eventually, 'has the man done?'

'I was right to call you then?' his student asked.

'Right? Of course you were right,' the professor said sharply. 'But what has he done? What has the man done? Where is my Joanna? It looks like he plunged her into an acid bath. This tomb has been here for more than five hundred years. Five centuries, dozens of wars, it survived all that, and then this man comes along and in a month, one month . . .' He was silent again. Then once more he said, 'What has the man done?' Nobody tried to answer.

'The patina has gone, all shape, all form. All the subtlety has disappeared.' He took a deep breath and walked around the tomb, assessing the damage from every side, from every angle, peering into the deep dark holes of her eyes. 'Young woman,' he said finally to the journalist who had retreated into the black shadows by the wall to sit and smoke. 'Get this down.' She put the cigarette back between the lips, puffed a cloud of smoke into the air around her and raised her pen. 'We must beware the evils of restoration,' Kelner said grandly. 'We cannot replace these works of art. Once they are gone they are gone.' He waved one hand across the prone form of Joanna, like a teacher dismissing his class. 'I fear this piece is gone for ever. It looks like it has undergone an industrial cleaning. The man responsible should be ashamed.' He was silent again. The trio stood motionless, the student and the journalist watching the older man, unsure of what to say, for fear, perhaps, of making him weep. Kelner broke the silence. 'Let's go,' he said. 'There's nothing more to see.' He returned to San Casciano that day ablaze with fury. He ranted and raved at his wife; he wrote letters to art journals and professors. He drank an awfully large amount of wine and then he fell into a deep alcohol-soaked sleep.

The reporter did a far better job than anybody would have dared to expect. Her story appeared in the Strossetti paper two days later. Three days later it had graduated to the nationals. Kelner was quoted verbatim. His claim that the tomb looked as though it had been dumped in an acid bath was afforded special attention. *La Nazione* finished their story with a quote from the restorer. 'I am consulting my lawyers,' Andrea Conte was reported as saying. 'This is a very serious matter.' Kelner had laughed when he read that. He kept one hand flat on the newspaper and, turning to Fiammetta, his wife, he said: 'What does the fool think he can do? Sue me? I am the expert. I am the one that knows. I'd like to see him try it.'

Fiammetta merely sighed. 'I suspect we shall soon know what he is going to do,' she said.

The writ was delivered a week later, by a dark young man in a raincoat, who hunched his heavy shoulders against the beating wind and the rain, stood in the open doorway of the house and said: 'I suppose you were expecting this. Well then, here it is.' He handed over the envelope, shielding it from the weather with his chest. He did not wait for Kelner to say anything. The young man shook his head sadly, raised his eyes heavenwards as if to say 'we are all in this sad business together' and backed out of the house into the storm, his head bowed. 'Goodbye then,' he said, looking up. Then he turned and walked away down the drive.

The writ was simple and straightforward. Kelner was cited for defamation in print and ordered to present himself at Florence city court within twenty-eight days, when the preliminary paperwork would be drawn up. The injured party was cited as one Andrea Conte, occupation: art restorer. Lawyers were found. Meetings were held. Discussions were entered into. It was all to no avail; Conte would not budge. The case was expected to take just over a year to come to court. 'This is a very serious matter,' the restorer told *La Repubblica*. 'That is why this so-called expert is charged with a criminal libel. The judge can send him to prison for three years if he wants to. That is how serious it is. He cannot be allowed to say those things about me. It offends me both as a man and a craftsman.'

In the Florentine art world, so small and compact that the walls which once enclosed the city might still define its scale, the self-styled guardians of the icons of Western civilization – the restorers and the curators and the historians, the cash-rich buyers and the cash-poor critics, the Ladies who Lunched and the men who sometimes Lunched them – rubbed their hands together with glee and settled in for a glorious spat. In a city where people live by force of expertise alone – their knowledge of what makes one piece of stone better than another, what makes one tattered canvas more important than another – the prospect of two men claiming they both knew more was just too delicious. It was a terrible business, they said to each other, an awful business. That an argument over a work of art should end in court. Shame. Pity it would take so long to get into court.

'I am happy that we're going to court on this one,' Kelner

told a press conference in Strossetti soon after the writ was issued. 'I am the expert. I must be allowed to criticize. I can make that point in court just as well as anywhere else.' And then he was photographed by the tomb of the Joanna, looking mournfully over his love, one hand stretched out towards her beautiful marble face. The picture, grey and grainy, appeared in *La Nazione* one Monday morning under the headline 'Professor Defends Princess'. The look on his thin bony face said 'how could they do this to her?' But it also said something else, something far more painful. It said 'how could they do this to me?'

For the first few minutes Kelner did not talk. He sat arranging the heap of papers, files and books that he had produced from his case into a neat pile, carefully aligning each edge so that they formed a cube on the café table between them. Alex watched him work. The American was smaller than he had expected, a slight man, seemingly built only of bone and tendon. The thick, tortoiseshell glasses gave his face extra width but it remained a collection of defiantly sharp features, weasel-like in the extreme. The only compensation that softened the effect was the eyebrows, solid and bushy, which formed into little tufts pointing outwards and upwards, like the horns of feathers of an owl. Kelner's hair was wiry, receding at the temples and flashed through with wide streaks of grey. Despite its length – at the back it drifted around his collar – it stayed resolutely off his forehead as though it knew its place were out of the way, up there somewhere, keeping that precious mind warm.

The hands that arranged the documents so carefully were designed around bulbous knuckles, as if it were the point where they flexed that was important rather than the fingertips which did all the feeling. The fingers worked as one limb rather than as separate actors in an ensemble, shuffling and patting and aligning. On the top of his growing cube the historian placed a glossy book bearing a photograph of the tomb of Joanna dei Strossetti, her tight lips dead centre of the cover. Beneath her chin were printed the words 'Robert Kelner'. Here then was the point: this pile of documents was the historian's informal curriculum vitae, a store of ideas and theses, propositions and references that this upstart journalist would have to challenge. It was positioned on the table as a barrier; Kelner had built a wall of learning in front of him, its very neatness, its compactness a symbol of the clarity of the great man's thoughts. Don't tangle with me, it said, don't even think about it. I know what I'm talking about.

But still he did not talk, save to order himself a large vermouth. Then he sat back in his chair so that his shoulders disappeared behind the pile of books. Finally he said, in a tight east coast American accent, 'I expected your paper would send someone with more experience.'

Alex tried his reassuring smile. 'You mean someone older?' The historian nodded.

'I'm not sure I need to give you my credentials but, if it's any help, I have been on national newspapers since I was twenty-three.' Kelner raised those eyebrows. 'That's six years,' Alex said, answering the unasked question. 'In any case,' Alex went on, 'it was not a question of the *Correspondent* sending someone. I found this story. I thought it was worth covering. If it hadn't been for me nobody from Britain would be here.' Kelner put up his hands in a sign of mock surrender. His drink arrived and he took a long sip. He smiled for the first time, a weak thing that barely broke the line of his cheeks, but a smile none-theless. Alex decided to press on.

'I always think it worth just going over the biographical details first, so if you don't mind . . .' He picked up his notebook and flicked back a few pages. He began to read quickly. 'You were born in Boston, the son of Jewish immigrants from Poland who came to the US in the 1930s. Your father ran a printing company. Your mother helped run the business and dabbled in art. After the usual run of high schools you attended Princeton University where you read history, the first member of your family to go on to higher education. You graduated Magna Cum Laude and afterwards you obtained a position as an assistant professor in the art history department of Ohio State. Ohio State? Is that right?' Kelner nodded.

'You met your Italian wife Fiammetta there, and you have been married to her for twenty-seven years. Two kids, one of each. After Ohio you moved to Princeton and then to UCLA where you have been for the past fifteen years, first as lecturer in Italian and Greco-Roman art, now as department head, and also for the past seven years occupying the honorary chair of Renaissance art. You live in Santa Monica and, when you can, in San Casciano. Last year you spent a sabbatical year at the Institute of Early Modern Sculpture here in Florence, where you are a visiting professor.' Alex stopped, turned over a page and without looking up said, 'You are fifty-four years old.'

Kelner sniffed. 'Fifty-three,' he said.

Alex repeated the words as he crossed out the figure in the notebook and wrote in the new one. 'Apart from that everything else is correct?'

'You've done your homework,' the historian said. 'I'm suit-ably impressed.'

Alex smiled, so that his cheek dimpled for the first time. 'Professor Kelner, there will always have to be an element of trust here. I hope you will be able to trust me.'

Kelner nodded once more. He drained his drink and ordered another. 'There was in fact one mistake, but you can be forgiven. I had a son, past tense.'

'I'm sorry,' Alex said. 'It just wasn't in the cuts, it . . .'

'Don't worry yourself. It was a while ago. Well, a little under two years ago.' The historian stared at his drink.

'I know this may sound like a very obvious question,' Alex said, 'but I think it's as good a place as any to start. Can you tell me how you felt when you first saw the tomb of Joanna dei Strossetti after it had been cleaned?'

Kelner placed one hand on the book which topped the pile in front of him and said, 'Have you ever seen the Joanna?'

Alex shook his head. 'No, I only arrived here this afternoon.'

The historian managed his slight smile again and, with a flourish, pulled the book from the pile as though it were a piece of vital evidence.

'This,' he said, 'is a monograph, published two years ago by a press here in Florence. The pictures are by a Sienese photographer. I wrote the text. It is solely an evaluation of the Joanna.' He opened the book to a double-page photograph of the tomb. 'I think you should see what she looked like before. That way you may begin to understand.' There was a solid emphasis on the word 'begin'. He obviously didn't expect the Englishman to advance beyond that. He turned the book around so the journalist could examine the picture. The young girl was dressed in a single long tunic, buttoned down the front, the narrow collar extenuating the delicate line of her neck. Her arms were crossed over her chest, the hands laid flat, and her hair was dressed with a garland of flowers. Alex looked at the face, the smooth cheeks, the lightly lidded eyes. He was captivated by the mouth, its tightness, as though it kept something locked away, some beautiful secret. She seemed to be more asleep than dead. He looked down to her feet, where a dove sat nestling by her ankles as if awaiting a signal from his mistress. She had been, he realized, a tiny woman. Yet she seemed to possess some greater strength that went well beyond her small frame.

Kelner reached over and waved a hand towards her head. 'See here?' he said. 'See how the grime has gathered around the hair, see how it gives definition. That is how Rafanelli would have intended it. He would have known that is how it would age. He would also have known how the patina would change. You can barely see it here, unfortunately. Do you know about the patina? The patina is what changes a piece of stone that has been attacked with a hammer and chisel into a piece of sculpture with a sense of life. It is the skin of the marble, the sense of depth and volume.' Kelner leaned forward and slammed the book shut under Alex's nose.

'All that is gone now. There is barely a patina there any more. Conte has stripped the thing clean.' He held the book in both hands, and studied the cover. Then he looked up. 'So you ask how did I feel? I felt as if something I loved had been utterly destroyed.' Alex had been taking notes. It was his turn to look up.

'But surely it's still there? Surely it has only been damaged? It still stands in the cathedral.'

'Certainly,' Kelner said. 'The lump of stone is there, or part of it at least. But the essence has gone, the thing that made that lump of stone the Joanna. When someone dies you don't tell a relative who is grieving that the body is still there so there's no need to weep. You don't tell them to keep the corpse in the bed beside them for company. You know the soul has gone. There is no point. It is no different with a piece of art that has been killed.' Kelner gripped his glass, emptied it and said, 'Conte is a murderer, nothing less.'

The historian sat back in his chair, his elbow propped on the arm of his seat so that the empty glass clasped in his hand waved slightly in the air.

'I can see you think it is not that important,' he said. Before Alex could answer, a waiter was at their side. He offered the historian another drink. Kelner accepted.

'It wasn't that I thought it unimportant,' Alex said. 'It's just that . . . Perhaps I underestimated the strength of your passion for this piece.'

Kelner let out a long, sharp, booze-driven laugh. 'Passion? I wonder if you understand the word. Joanna is not just some artefact to be fêted and then discarded when she becomes unfashionable. She's not just a curio.' He leaned forward and pointed an index finger at Alex, the gesture all the more dramatic because his fingers had, up to that moment, seemed incapable of making a solo appearance. 'Joanna is a woman, a beautiful woman who has made grown men weep. She is one of the most beautiful women in the world.'

An interesting use of language, Alex thought. The historian was now talking in the present tense as though Joanna were, at this very moment, in some other part of the city, tying up her silken hair in its garland of wild flowers, buttoning her tunic in readiness for the night ahead.

'When we talk of passion we talk of love,' Kelner went on. 'Let that be the way. Love is the right word. I have loved Joanna for two decades. This is not some game. It's not some crass academic exercise.' He reached for the new glass of vermouth before him. 'This is real.' He took a large gulp.

Kelner slumped back in his chair, back behind his shifting tower of academia. The journalist hunted for a joke, something light to cut through the air between them.

'Tell me, Professor Kelner,' Alex said eventually, 'does your wife know you feel this way?' The historian glowered for a second, stared at his drink and then knocked back what was left. He remained silent for a moment more, staring at Alex as though the young man had asked him to confess to some terrible crime, the very thought of which offended against human decency. 'No,' he said sharply, 'she does not know.'

The neon sign on the rooftop high above them was now at its brightest against the sodium-burned night sky. Alex looked up at it and began trying to count the number of tubes in the sign so as to avoid eye contact with Kelner who was now staring drunkenly into his lap. He kept losing count. Finally he gave up and looked over at the professor who was once more holding the book and staring at the picture on the cover.

Alex closed his notebook and shoved his pen into his inside pocket. An obsessive, he thought. I've come this far for an obsessive. No, it's worse. I've come this far for a drunken obsessive. An uptight, drunken, academic obsessive. The worst bloody kind. He reached for the packet of cigarettes he had discarded when the professor had arrived, removed one and lit up. Kelner did not appear to notice, even when Alex exhaled a plume of blue-grey smoke in his direction. The journalist sighed deeply. What in Christ's name am I doing here? he thought to himself. Why did I bother to come?

CHAPTER THREE

They could hear the man at work long before they could see him. It was a dull repetitive thud at first, a growl of a noise that they felt in their stomachs and at the base of their spines and in their knees rather than heard on the air. At the brow of the hill Cesare Scorza brought his horse to a halt and, with one upraised palm, ordered the boy to do the same. They sat in silence, tugging their thick woollen cloaks around their shoulders against the wind, warming themselves with their breath, and listening for the sound once more. It was sharper up there, a bright, high metallic crack that echoed around the stony crevices of the valley below. Scorza shielded his eyes from the thin winter sun and looked down the slope.

A forest covered the valley floor, stretching far up to the escarpment on their left. The path they had followed petered out a few feet away but reappeared, he could see, just beyond some large boulders which lay where the slope levelled out. A little further on, blowing towards them from among the trees, was a plume of smoke, sometimes steady, at other times pulled apart by the strong breeze so that it floated away in all directions across the forest. They would press on. The hill had been in the way, Scorza later told the boy, as they rode their horses towards the source of the banging. The earth had swallowed up the sound, he said, soaked it up, just as it had the rains that had drenched these lands only two days before. The boy nodded and broke his silence to say only 'I see', and then fell silent again. He was tired and cold, just a little saddle-sore and certainly in no mood for a lesson on the miracles that the earth could perform.

They followed the path, the sound growing louder all the time. Occasionally the rat-a-tat-tat would stop for a few seconds, a short pause for breath, before taking up again, cutting its way through the thick forest that lay to the left and the right of them. Soon the path through the pines widened, so that there was space for a lush grass verge on each side. There were no flowers yet, of course. It was too early in the year for that. Another month or so maybe. The path curved round to the left, opening up further as it went, spreading itself wide, until finally it gave up any pretensions to being a path at all and became a wide clearing. In the middle sat the house.

It was a ramshackle affair of rough-hewn grey stone. On the left was the main building of two floors, heavy wooden shutters still enclosing the windows of the upper level, as if someone up there was still sleeping. To the right was a single-storey building with no windows but a pair of wide, double barn doors that were open to the afternoon air. The beating rhythm came from within. Scorza and the boy dismounted, tied their horses to a pine post by the barn and made their way inside to introduce themselves to the man whose careful hammer and chisel work had led them there, and whose careful hammer and chisel work they now wished to employ.

The air made them choke at first, clouds of marble dust mixed with wood-smoke catching at the back of their throats and burning the insides of their nostrils. But it was at least warm. At the far end was a wide hearth enclosing the fire. Lying flat along the length of the room, positioned right in the middle, was a large piece of rough-cut marble, eight feet long, five feet deep and the same across. Leaning over one end, his thick black curls hanging forward so that the ends flicked across his wrists and obscured his face, was a thin man wearing a solid leather waistcoat and heavy woollen breeches. He did not look up.

'We are looking for Rafanelli,' Scorza said, when he had become accustomed to the dim light within. 'Antonio Rafanelli.' And then, in case they had not yet found their man, he added: 'The artist.'

'Hmm,' the man said without looking up from the stone, repositioning his chisel and hitting it so that a shower of marble splinters flew up around his wrists. 'And who might "we" be?'

'Cesare Scorza,' the visitor replied, 'and his stable boy.'

'Cesare, eh? A Roman?' The artist hit his chisel again with a solid thwack.

'No,' Scorza said. 'Though the son of one. My father was always rather sentimental about the city of his birth. I come from much closer by, from Strossetti, fifteen miles to the west. From the court of the prince.'

Now Rafanelli straightened up. His hair fell back from his face, to reveal his long, sharp features: the nose that was so fine it all but had a crease along its leading edge, the cheekbones that rose up to the line of his red-rimmed eyes, and the jutting chin that gave the impression the man had actually modelled himself with the chisel he held in his left hand and the mallet he held in his right. He was thirty, maybe a little more. He squinted at Scorza through the dust and the smoke.

'Are we a nobleman or a bureaucrat?' He looked his visitor over and, without waiting for an answer, said: 'Not a nobleman. Too proud for that. A bureaucrat I would say. A handsome bureaucrat though, well preserved for his age, lovely grey eyes. One day his hair will match them, though not quite yet, I think.'

Scorza smiled and said, 'It is indeed my honour to serve the prince. I am his chief adviser.'

'Then,' said Rafanelli, with a display of self-conscious

formality, 'I suppose it is my honour to welcome you. Would you like to warm yourselves by the fire? The wind on the hills can be vicious this time of year, can't it? Cuts through even the thickest of clothing.' He stared at the boy, extended one hand towards the hearth and smiled a small, slightly toothy smile. The lad made his way over. 'There is a little wine in the jug and some bread, I think, in the basket by the side. Even some cheese. I hope you will not mind if I continue. I have made some progress this afternoon.' But he did not continue. He stood watching Scorza for a while as he followed the boy to the fireside. The prince's representative could not help but feel uncomfortable under the artist's gaze. It felt, he later decided, as though the man had been examining his body, watching how each muscle worked, concentrating on the frame rather than the person; assessing each joint, each tendon, trying to work out just how it would be cut from stone, as if the Lord were a respected rival when it came to the shaping of flesh and blood, whose work should be judged carefully.

Finally Rafanelli returned to his sculpture, laying the chisel against the rock and hitting it so the head slipped half an inch along the face of the marble. 'Now,' he said, 'you asked for me by name so I can assume you were not just passing through. We are not, after all, a great distance from Strossetti. What can I do for you?'

Scorza stood up from the fireside and wandered over to the other end of the marble slab. He rested one hand on the stone and said: 'We have a commission for you.'

'A commission indeed?' Rafanelli did not look up. 'A commission. What a grand day this is. Now who would ever dare propose Rafanelli?'

'Your former teacher, Caltuccio. He gave me an audience

today. He has decided to pass his last years in Strossetti.'

'So I heard,' the artist said. 'How is the old man?'

'Ailing. He may not last long, but he has his faith in the Lord and has led a virtuous life.'

'Hmm, indeed. Yes, I had heard he was not in good health. Mind you,' he laid a heavy thump on the chisel, 'he never was. There was always something wrong with him. I could never get it out of my mind that Caltuccio was badly finished. You know? That none of him really worked the way it should.'

'He did not seem to like you much either.'

Rafanelli let out a high-pitched giggle. 'Oh good. Tell me, what exactly did he say?'

'He said . . . Well, he intimated . . .' Scorza stopped, gathered himself and said slowly, 'that you were not the best there is, but all the others are dead.'

Rafanelli giggled again. 'How sweet. And probably true.' He lifted himself from his work and sat on one edge of the stone so as to face Scorza across its length. 'It is good to see that his humour can be dry. Though I tell you this . . .' he pointed at the visitor with the tip of his chisel – 'it is the only thing that ever is.'

'I beg your pardon?'

'Didn't you know?' The artist flicked his long black hair over his shoulders. 'The old man is incontinent, always has been. Was forever pissing his breeches. Never apologized. Not once. Just did it, in a steady drip, drip, drip all day. Terrible business. I assume you visited him early rather than late?' Scorza nodded. 'How fortunate you were. In the summer the smell could be awful.'

Scorza took a sharp breath. 'That is no way to talk about a master.'

'Believe me,' Rafanelli said, taking up his tools again and leaning forward over a portion of the stone further towards his visitor, 'it is no way for a master to behave.'

They did not speak for a few moments now, the silence broken only by the crack of the chisel on the face of the stone and the noise of the boy slurping his wine. The shape of a head could be seen emerging from the rock, and the shoulders too, though only just. The rest was raw and unsullied, except for the small patch where Rafanelli worked now. But if he looked carefully, Scorza imagined he could see the rest of the body trying to escape the bonds that nature had placed upon it; the solid rocky prison that the earth had created around whatever lay within. 'What is this to be?' he asked eventually.

Rafanelli gritted his teeth as he worked, throwing his whole bodyweight behind his chisel. 'An image' – crack – 'of' – crack – 'our lady.' He got up, took a step backwards and, with a shrug of his shoulders, said simply: 'Aren't they always?' He looked at his handiwork. 'It is for the Cathedral of Pistoia, commissioned by some wealthy merchant or other, desperate to atone for his sins, I have no doubt . . .'

'Why are you working here? It is a long way to Pistoia. Would it not be better to carve in the place where the finished work will stand?'

'Oh, the stone came from close by.' The artist casually waved his mallet back over his shoulder as though the marble quarry were somewhere in the corner of his house. 'The rock will be lighter once it is carved. Why go through all the effort to carry it there now when it will be easier later? And besides, I do like to make a grand entrance when I have finished. After all the effort I have put in. You cannot make a grand entrance with a lump of rock.'

'If you were to take our commission we would expect you to work in Strossetti, though, as it is Prince Bartolommeo, you can expect more than adequate remuneration.'

Rafanelli was chiselling again. 'You have not told me what the commission is.'

Scorza paused for what he imagined was dramatic effect. It went unnoticed. He said: 'The House of Strossetti has suffered a great loss. The Princess Joanna has died in childbirth and the prince has decreed that she shall have a mausoleum carved in her honour. It shall, he says, bear her full image so that those at court should never forget her and the sacrifice she has made. She bore him a son who will succeed him eventually.'

'Oh,' the artist said casually, head still bowed. 'So that's it, is it? How long has our little princess been dead? I do so hate working with an odour.'

Scorza took a step back, as though stung. 'Sir. Please.' Rafanelli looked up surprised, saw the look on the older man's face and apologized. 'The princess has been dead two days,' Scorza said. 'So there is, you see, a certain urgency. The boy is here to carry your tools and supplies. I assumed that if you took the commission you would want to make a death mask now rather than later when the body has, ehm, when the body has started . . .'

'To decompose? Yes. You are absolutely right. It is a tiresome effect. The eyes sink back after just a short while and, well, they never look quite the same again. Makes every single last one of them look like they died from great shock, as if they had laid eyes on the devil himself. Once that has occurred you can only extemporize and the family are rarely satisfied. They always tell you you've got something or other wrong. So, if you're going to be immortalized speed is of the essence.'

Scorza pushed on. 'As you mentioned the question of speed, I must ask. I have been warned that you have a tendency to slowness.'

Rafanelli glanced up from his chisel. 'The Lord's work cannot be rushed. We are carving stone, not moulding clay. Is there a reason why speed is important?'

'The prince is an old man. It would be of little point if he were to die before the tomb were finished.'

'That old, eh? And she a mere girl, if she was of childbearing years. The sly old goat. Maybe we should make this a double booking then. It is so much easier to get the essence of a person if you can catch them while they are still alive. I could do the prince at the same time, have them lying side by side, maybe even holding hands, something like that. What do you say?'

'I am told you can breathe life into the dead. That, after all, is why we are employing you.'

Rafanelli held his hands up and wiggled his fingers. 'You may trust me. I am touched with the glory of God. These hands are the very hands that carved Eve. At the Lord's direction, of course.'

Scorza was not sure he liked the man's sarcasm. He liked the way he eyed the boy even less. But he was good. There was no doubt about that. He was very good. And they needed a good sculptor, not a courteous one. A combination of the two would have been pleasant, of course, but they would have to settle for this. Scorza suggested they set off that afternoon. They would reach the castle shortly after nightfall. If he didn't mind working by candlelight, Rafanelli could make his death mask that night. The artist agreed.

Death. Why did life always have to end in death? Wasn't there an alternative? Some other way to end things? You couldn't just shrug off death. You had to be sad. You had to weep and cry and wail. It was one of the rules. That was the way it was. Couldn't there be another way, one which was happier? One which was less complicated?

Claudia leaned back against the door of her lady's bed-chamber and wept, long deep sobs that shook her body from the ankles up. She screwed up her eyes, bit her bottom lip, and let her body shake, her eyes leak and her nose seep. It had been two days and still the pictures in her head wouldn't go away, the black dreams and wicked shapes that came to her at dead of night. Her mistress lying back against the pillow there, silently pleading for help, for anything. And then there was the blood. So much blood. All of it sort of pouring everywhere. It couldn't be stopped. Nothing could stop it. But why couldn't it be stopped? Why?

Claudia looked over to the bed. The thick woollen sheets that had covered the mattress had been removed soon after Joanna had died, but the mattress still held the stain, the mark that Joanna had left as her life quickly slipped away from her. Soon they would come and take the mattress away too. It couldn't stay there for ever, all bloody like that, for everybody to see. When it happened the nurse had tried to mop up the blood that had splashed, thick and red, on to the flagstones. But all she'd done was spread it around further. She'd had other things to do, a baby to care for. And now here was Claudia, loyal Claudia, trusting Claudia, here with her water and her brush to scrub away the mess her lady had left on the floor.

The strange thing was it seemed as if Joanna had known it was going to happen. Really it did. Well, of course, Claudia said to herself, her sobs now settling down to light hiccups, she couldn't really have known. Nobody does. But still. The things she had said before. And the letter. She slipped her hand into the pocket of her smock and pulled out the little package, turning it over, looking at the seal and the name on the front.

It had happened only a few hours before Joanna went into labour, perhaps three at the most. In the room below the prince's bedchamber, that evening, the two women were sitting on a divan. Claudia remembered it now as though it were happening again. She saw it clearly when she closed her eyes, pictures rolling through her head, sharp and distinct. The princess was lying back in her maid's lap, a look of something approaching contentment gracing her near-perfect face. Claudia was slowly rubbing Joanna's temples, her fingertips tracing delicate circles around the skin beside and above her mistress's eyes, humming softly under her breath as she worked.

'If patience is a virtue,' Joanna said to Claudia quietly, 'then pregnancy is a virtue too. It is nothing but waiting, preceded by nothing more gracious than vomiting. It bores me.'

'Don't fret,' the maid said. 'It will be over soon, all of it. You'll see. You'll wonder what the fuss was about. And then we'll laugh about this.' She stopped her massaging for a moment. 'In any case motherhood hangs well on you.'

Joanna snorted. 'Motherhood just hangs,' she said. 'There is nothing more to it. Motherhood is all downwards. These days I merely have to think of an orange tree and I feel tired. All that fruit to support, all that weight to hold up. Everything hangs. My breasts would be by my knees by now were it not for the fact that my belly had reached there first.' Claudia giggled and went back to tracing her circles. They were silent for a moment. Then Joanna reached up and took her maid's hand in her own.

'Claudia,' she said. 'I have a job for you. A task if you like. I know you'll do it for me. You're loyal like that, aren't you? You're my friend. You always have been. I know you will be now.' Joanna squeezed her maid's hand; Claudia could muster only a simple 'yes'.

'In the first drawer of the cabinet by the door there is a letter bearing the Strossetti seal. Bring it to me.' Claudia gently eased her mistress's head from her lap, went to the drawer and found the letter. It was sealed with a heavy lump of wax, embossed with the family coat of arms, a mess of sticky red ridges. On the front, in Joanna's delicate hand, was written what she assumed was a name. Claudia returned to the divan with the letter and repositioned herself beneath her mistress's head. She tried to hand over the letter. Joanna waved her away.

'I don't want it,' the princess said. 'It is written. It is for you now.' Then Joanna took her maid's hand again and squeezed it hard. She stared dead ahead and said, 'Claudia, if anything should happen to me when . . . when the child is coming. If I were . . . If there should be any problem, you are to keep that letter.' Claudia tried to remonstrate. Nothing could go wrong, the maid said. Nothing would go wrong. She would see. Honestly she would. And then they'd be laughing about this. Really . . .

Joanna silenced her. 'Sometimes I think it would be better if I really were not here after the child were born. So much simpler.' She laughed quietly and then let out a short hiss of breath. 'We must stop this . . . this sentimentality. We are short of time.' She hesitated for a moment and then, with renewed confidence, gave her instructions. 'If I should die during or after the birth of my child you are to keep the letter. Then on the eve of the child's fourth birthday you are to take it to the man it is addressed to. Make sure it gets there and is read by no one else.' Claudia looked hopelessly at the writing.

'My lady, I cannot read this. I, ehm, do not have power of reading.'

'Of course you can't. Silly me. Forgive me. It says Lorenzo the Magnificent. You know who he is? Head of the House of Medici? Of course you know. You shall take it to Lorenzo.'

Claudia looked at the strange lines on the front of the envelope. She knew who he was. Who could fail to? She squeezed the bottom corner of the envelope with the ball of her thumb. There was an object inside, something small, hard and square.

'He will know from what is inside that this letter is genuine,' Joanna said. 'Do not open it. Promise me this.' She squeezed her maid's hand. 'Promise.' The word rang out like a call to arms: promise to do my bidding, it said. Promise to protect me, to stand up for me. Promise to be loyal. Promise to remember me. Claudia promised. She would do as her mistress wished.

'But what,' Claudia blurted out, 'but what if the child dies too?'

'Ah, then, it will all have been for nothing.'

Claudia was woken from the pictures in her head by the sound of voices and horses' hooves in the courtyard below. She went to the window and looked down. In the pools of light cast by the lanterns, she saw Scorza climbing from his horse, giving orders. She could not see the man behind him but assumed he had something to do with the arrangements for the care of Joanna. Now she was dead, there were lots of people coming, people who had never known Joanna. Strangers, who had been hired to do one thing or another by the prince. They were interlopers, these hand-wringing, smarmy tradesmen who were only doing it for money and had no right to be here. Claudia took a deep breath and turned to look at the pail of water and the heavy brush that lay alongside it. At least this would not be the last service she would perform for her mistress. At least there was still the letter to deliver.

Scorza led the way down the steep stone steps to the crypt where Joanna's body had been laid out. It was cooler down there and dry, the air thick with the smell of dust and old cobwebs and ash that had not been shifted in years. Joanna would start to decompose down here eventually, of course, but it would take much longer than up above. It was fortunate she had died in winter. In summer the result would have been desperate, even here in the mountains. Even now she would have to be embalmed as soon as possible.

They turned into a long corridor, their footsteps echoing loudly off the heavy, slab rock walls. Ahead, by what seemed to be a doorway, Rafanelli could just make out a figure slumped on a chair. Scorza swung the lantern that he carried before him casting a rich, buttery light that sent huge shadows creeping up the walls and along the floor, as though reaching out to touch whoever it was sitting down there, among the dust and the darkness.

'Vincente,' Scorza said quietly, touching the sleeping figure on the shoulder, when they reached the corridor's end. 'Vincente.'

The man awoke with a gasp. 'Who? What? What do you want? I'm looking after her. There's no need for anyone else. Leave us.' His eyes were red-rimmed and bloodshot and he was obviously blinded by the glare of the lantern so that he could not tell who the two men were.

'Vincente, Vincente, it is all right. It is only me, Cesare.' Scorza held the lamp up to the side of his face so that the sitting man could identify him. But the light sent sharp black shadows into the crevices of his face and the depths of his eye sockets so that he looked, for a moment, not unlike a gargoyle. The man recoiled with a squeal. 'Vincente, please . . .' Scorza turned to Rafanelli. 'He is Joanna's half-brother. Or was, I suppose. He has been sitting here like this for the past two days, protecting her, he says. But from what, only the good Lord could tell us.' Scorza turned back to the young man and talked to him as though he were going deaf. 'You're protecting her? Is that right? Making sure?' Vincente nodded, jerkily, as if he were still trying to shake himself awake.

'This is Rafanelli,' Scorza said, holding the lantern up to the artist's face. 'He is the sculptor. He has come to immortalize your sister.' He tried to soothe the young man. 'Really, Vincente, you have performed your duty but you should sleep now. Go to your chamber and lie down. You cannot stay here like this.'

Vincente jumped up, rearing out of the darkness, and thrust his head close to Rafanelli's, like some monster escaping from the thick black shadows that clung to the cracks in the walls and the fractures in the floor. Rafanelli recoiled. 'I loved her,' Vincente said quickly. 'And she loved me. Oh yes, she really loved me. But it wasn't just normal love. No, no, no. Not boring everyday love. This was special love. The love that the Lord has given us.' He paused for a moment, and looked around himself as if suddenly unsure of who he was or what he was doing there. Then he swung his face back round to Rafanelli and, with his nose practically in the man's left eye socket, said, 'It was a secret special love and nobody will ever be able to understand, not ever, and . . .'

Scorza gripped him on the shoulder and gently forced him back into his chair. 'We know, Vincente, we know. Now, you just stay here and ehm . . .' he looked around himself for a moment – 'and guard the door. Yes, guard the door.' The two men pushed their way past as Vincente settled back down, his wild glassy stare scanning the darkness once more and settling on a point of nothingness somewhere far, far down the corridor that nobody else could ever hope to see.

'I'm afraid he has the fervour of the new disciple,' Scorza said as he went around the room, lighting the torches that hung from its walls. 'They did not meet until she came to live at court here something over a year ago – I suppose because they were only half-brother and -sister. But he became an immediate convert to her charms. We all did, in a way, but Vincente especially. He declared himself her protector and rarely left her side, particularly when she was with child. I think her death has somewhat unhinged him.' The room was fully lit now, the six torches casting a bright, flickering glare across the figure who lay, dressed only in a thin cotton robe, on the marble slab before them. Her skin had a solid, waxy sheen to it, almost yellowy in colour, so that she seemed to be part of the table that supported her, carved from marble already. There was a sickly-sweet odour in the room, but it was only slight and more than bearable.

Rafanelli stood at one end looking down, studying the length of her frame, apparently in deep contemplation. He said distractedly, without looking up: 'So, do you think they ever had each other, Vincente and Joanna?'

'Sir, they were half-brother and -sister. It would have been a wicked sin in the eyes of our Lord. It would also have made a cuckold of the prince.'

'Oh, I know,' Rafanelli said, his eyes still on the corpse before him. 'That would have been part of the appeal, I would have thought.'

'You have the manners of a pig,' Scorza said.

The artist looked up, with a broad smile. 'You are, of course, right, dear sir. It comes from spending far too much time alone. No social graces whatsoever. I have the manners of swine and the hands of an angel which, in my trade, is a lot better than the other way around. I'm sure you will agree.' Scorza knew that no reply was wanted, so gave none.

'To work,' the artist said. He walked round to Joanna's left side, lifted one arm and peered at the underside. He gave a little nod. 'She did lose a lot of blood, didn't she? Usually the blood in a body drops to the bottom when the life goes from their soul and you can see large purple marks where it settles. But look, here, there's a little staining but nothing like you would normally see.' Scorza tried to remonstrate with the man but he ploughed on. 'No, this is important to our task tonight. Come, look at her face . . .' He had moved round the table and had stopped as though genuinely struck.

'Her features were so . . .' he swallowed – 'so complete.' He leaned a little closer. 'I know very little of the attractions of women. They have never seemed to appeal . . . Did other men find her attractive?'

Scorza coughed. 'Yes, many were struck by her beauty.'

'Yes,' Rafanelli said. 'I can see that would be so. But look here, it is a pity. Because she has lost so much fluid her skin has already dropped back. We can do something about that, with wadding to fill the cavity of her mouth. We would not want the wax to flow away into her when the mask is made. The skin really is such a beautiful colour in death, is it not?' He walked completely around the table. 'After I have taken the death mask I will also make a study from terracotta, for the finished piece. You say your master would like some sort of mausoleum? A casket, I would say, a little like an altar.' He lifted her hands so that they lay on her abdomen.

'What do you think? A nice reference to how she met her death?' Rafanelli shook his head. 'But it was done some years ago, by that snob della Quercia, and I do so hate being thought of as a plagiarist, so we shall instead emphasize the spiritual side to her soul and lay her hands upon her heart.' He moved her arms so they lay across her chest. 'Do you approve?' Scorza gave a slight nod. 'We can decide the details later,' Rafanelli said.

There was a rap at the door. 'Father Corsano,' Scorza said opening the door wide so the priest could make his entrance. He was a tall, handsome man, with a short-cropped mound of dark hair and black eyes that seemed to search every corner of the room, a priest whose long black surplice made him look a part of the shadows from the corridor outside who had somehow walked within. 'Father Corsano would like to offer prayers for the soul of Joanna before we begin.' Rafanelli said, 'Of course,' took a few steps back from the table and bowed his head. The priest approached the body and laid one hand on the forehead of the corpse. With the other he held the crucifix around his neck. He closed his eyes and began to intone in barely comprehensible Latin.

After a few minutes he opened his eyes and looked down upon the body. There was silence in the room. Rafanelli and Scorza raised their heads in time to see the priest lean down and place a kiss upon the mouth of the dead woman, a full touch of lip upon lip that released a loud, echoing squelch which bounced around the room. He looked up and blushed deeply. 'I am finished here,' he said. The three men crossed themselves. 'I will disturb you no longer.' And with that he was gone. Scorza closed the door behind him and turned to the artist, who was grinning broadly.

'What,' Scorza said, 'is so damn funny?'

'Save my blasphemous heart,' the artist said, 'but wasn't that kiss a little beyond the needs of the spirit? Death becomes increasingly attractive if you get to go that colour and get kissed by tall dark men for your troubles.' He looked once more at the corpse. 'It seems a lot of men in this court loved your dear Joanna.'

Scorza sighed deeply. 'As I believe you said, we have work to do this long night.'

'Yes indeed,' Rafanelli said. 'Get the boy to bring down my bags and we will begin.'

CHAPTER FOUR

It started as a light tickle somewhere deep in his chest, a delicate nerve dance that seemed to grow and expand as he gasped for air. He stayed bent double, leaning against the hedge for support, a hand braced against each knee, and took a shallow breath, trying to put off the moment for as long as possible. But he knew it would come, and sooner rather than later. The tickle turned into an itch, became a scrabbling of claws in his throat, until the bubbling, hacking cough came roaring out, shaking him from the depths of his belly to the echoey recesses in his skull. He felt a drip of sweat begin its journey down his lower back into the crevice between his buttocks, and then another roll from his right temple where his hair was cropped shortest, across his cheek to the corner of his mouth, so he could taste the saltiness.

Alex looked down the steep gravel path to the indistinct point some 200 metres away, where the white sunlight lay shattered on the dusty ground, fractured by the branches of the trees that overhung it; the point where, a minute or so before, he had chosen to start his sprint. He coughed once more and then, through his wheezes, said to himself, 'It hasn't got to me, not yet.' He would live to smoke another day. Over the years Alex's cigarette-habit had become a war of attrition that he fought with himself, one in which he took a perverse kind of pleasure. But the battles were not between his desire for cigarettes and the knowledge that it could eventually kill him; he had long ago concluded that his smoking was a given, a fixed piece of his personality like his desperate need to fill up silences or his distrust of prudery and euphemism. The real struggle was to prove the habit wasn't having any physical effect. When he ran, he ran against the logic of his own body. The path up which he had just scrambled ran along the eastern side of the Boboli Gardens behind the Pitti Palace, the former residence of the Medici dukes in Florence. It had been a fair old hike, he decided. And he had managed it. He would live. But Christ, didn't it hurt finding out?

Alex straightened up, took a deep breath and sucked up the sweet smell of jasmine and lemon that lay in the warm shady spots beneath the trees that stood along his route. He ran his hand across the waxy green leaves of the hedges as he passed and let his feet scuff against the gravel path, gently kicking up little clouds of dust that shook themselves out around his ankles and over his shoes. He took low, easy breaths, enjoying the lazy pleasure of the walk after the run.

It was only a minute before the hill levelled out and he came across the light maroon walls of the Kaffeehaus, perched high on a shoulder of the gardens, where they had arranged to meet. He made his way to the café and found a table on the little gravel terrace at the back. What was a place called the Kaffeehaus doing in Florence? Alex looked around. It seemed no different from any of the other cafés in the city, except that the coffee was more expensive. In this city, however, that was some achievement. Still, it was Kelner's choice. He had said it suited his purpose. And the girl had said she knew where it was so why not? And there was always the view.

The terrace looked out to the north over the terracotta red roofs of the old city, the tight knots of towers and town houses, villas and palaces that crowd in around the solid bulk of the Duomo, the Florentine cathedral, as though desperate to suckle from the enormous teat of its dome. Alex reached inside his jacket for his cigarettes. He found a pack and his notebook, lit up and sat back. He took a hot drag down into his lungs and scanned the skyline. There was something about the prettiness of the city that depressed him. How could he be expected to take the place seriously when it looked like that, clad in its clothes of red and umber? Cities aren't meant to be pretty; they're meant to be exciting. You lose the prettiness when you get the excitement. The two are mutually exclusive. Where is the degradation, the depravity? How could you be bad in a city like Florence?

At least there was the smog. That was something.

'Old stones and dry bones,' he said to himself quietly. 'Always old stones and dry bones.'

'Signor Fuller?'

Alex looked up with a start, as if he had not been expecting to hear his name called. A woman was standing by his side, looming over him slightly and blocking the sun so that, for a moment, she seemed vast against the bleached sky. She walked around to the other side of the table, slipping out of shadow.

'Isabella dei Strossetti,' she said. 'I did not mean to surprise you.'

'No, sorry I was miles away. The, ehm, the view . . .' he stood up, casually waving one hand to the city set out beneath them. 'Please . . .' He extended the other hand and she shook it. They sat down.

'Yes, it is beautiful here,' she said, her accented English catching every vowel and syllable of the word be-a-u-ti-ful. 'Though I do not come here. Too expensive. It is for the tourists, I think.' She smiled, a full-face smile that stretched her tight mouth wide and creased up the skin around her eyes and made her chin jut forward just a little. There was a unity to her features that was striking: the gently turned-up nose, the full lips, the solid line of the jaw that defined the face from the bottom, and the tight crop of dark hair that defined it from the top. Even though she was small, almost petite, there was a heavy confidence to her, an imposing physicality that lay in the way she held her slender arms and her square shoulders. Alex reckoned they were of an age; maybe she was a little older, he thought. But then he changed his mind. There was something about that confidence, something disconcerting. Hell, maybe she was a lot older. He couldn't tell. Was her skin really glowing or was it just painted that way? There were always things you could use these days, weren't there? Didn't they put seal placenta in face powders? Essence of baby, extract of foetus, ingredients that were still growing for the ageing wealthy to use to prevent their skin acquiescing to time. How could you tell if someone was using those sorts of tricks? What were the signs to look for? There were no lines on her face, no wrinkles, no joins. But surely that didn't mean they weren't there. Surely, if you had enough money, you could cover them up convincingly. Christ, she even smelt expensive. Alex leaned forward to take a closer look. Perhaps that was just what aristocrats looked like.

She wore a light silk jacket of deep burgundy that came down to her hips, ending a little below where the matching culottes began, buttoned high on the waist. When she crossed her legs, knee over knee, the folds of burgundy pulled taut across her thigh and fell back at the ankle, to expose a shimmer of sheer charcoal hosiery that, like the curve of black lycra beneath her jacket, clung to her without compromise. She had dressed herself in a suit of diaphanous body armour, colour coded and sublime, a construction designed to hold the world at bay by elegance alone. Alex pulled the sleeves of his crumpled beige linen jacket down a little. His shirt was far too big for him and the aged cuffs were now adrift, smothering his hands in a sheaf of tired material. Next to Isabella he felt shabby and unwashed, as if he had thrust himself head first into the chaos of his suitcase that morning in pursuit of anything that would hide his nakedness. Perhaps he had.

She placed her bag by her feet and said: 'You chose this place?'

'No. No, it was Professor Kelner. There was something he wanted to show me here, I think.' He tapped his pen distractedly on the edge of the table. 'I hope you don't mind. And thank you for coming on a Thursday afternoon. I didn't want to drag you away from your work at the bank early.'

'You did not drag me away. We are civilized here. Early start, early stop. Not like America.'

'That's where you learned your English?'

She nodded. She would not explain any more about herself, not, at least, for the moment. She said: 'Yesterday, on the phone you mentioned you wanted to talk about the Joanna? What are we to talk about?'

Alex reached for the notebook that he had placed on the table, his badge of authenticity. 'Hmm, yes. You see I didn't know there were any descendants of Joanna dei Strossetti still . . .' He hesitated.

'Alive? Oh yes, we are alive. All of us. The old families do not die. They just go on getting richer.' She let out a little laugh, assured and certain. She watched Alex intently.

'So I thought it might be interesting to talk about what the

Joanna means to you with Professor Kelner when he's here and we could discuss the issues and turn them all around a bit and . . .'

'I see,' she said, with a slight, knowing smile. Alex was babbling. Time for short questions.

'You have met Professor Kelner?'

'Yes, once. After mass in Strossetti one Sunday, a little over a year ago. He is, how do you put it . . .? Er, *passionale*,' she searched for the word. 'A little too intense. That's it. Intense. And he has a way of looking at people. But he does at least care.' Again she did not elaborate. She liked short sentences, clean and businesslike. That much Alex could hear.

'Will you be attending the court case?'

'On Saturday?'

Alex nodded.

'Oh yes. My father is to be a witness so I should be there. The family has an interest. Obviously.'

'Obviously.'

'Yes.'

'You care about the Joanna?'

'She is something that has always been there. You care for a brother because he is always there. Joanna is part of the . . .' she waved her hands slightly in front of her as though gesturing to the whole terrace – 'part of the fabric of my life.' She shrugged. Maybe she thought it sounded silly.

Kelner appeared at the far end of the terrace, looking nervously from one side to the next, like an anorexic owl, sharp-beaked and angry. A large leather briefcase was tucked clumsily under his right arm, so that one bony elbow jutted out. The same corduroy trousers hung lank from his hips; his brown check shirt billowed, desperately trying to wrestle itself from underneath the waistband. Kelner spotted them and made his way over. They both stood up.

'Ah, Signorina Strossetti. *È un gran piacere rivederla. Com' è passato tutto questo tempo?*'

'Oh, very well thank you,' Isabella said firmly. 'But I think we should speak English. It is the one language we three have in common.'

Alex raised his eyebrows in apology.

'The English never were good linguists,' Kelner said dismissively, taking his seat, inspecting the gravel beneath it and selecting the exact spot for his case. 'Too lazy to learn another language, always too lazy. Not like your good self.' He grinned at Isabella. The smile said: 'We're on the same side, you and me.' Isabella said nothing. Alex tried a little grin of his own. Kelner was the interviewee; he had to be kept sweet. Treat it as a joke. A waiter appeared at their side. Kelner asked for mineral water as if aware he had somehow undermined his passions by boosting them with vermouth when he had met Alex the day before. Alex had the same. Isabella ordered an espresso.

They sat without talking, looking at the city beneath them, as it shimmered in the thick heat of the afternoon sun. From here Florence was almost silent save for the whine of a motor scooter nearby and the odd car horn that rose up through the smog haze to greet them, a lone metallic shout from the mute crowd below. Alex began to shuffle in his seat. He had been ready with so many questions, so many points of entry. But none of them felt exactly right for Isabella. A silence filler wasn't good enough. He needed something shaped and fully formed.

Kelner spoke first. He said: 'Italy is so proud of its cities but look how it treats them. These buildings are living things, but look . . .' He waved one arm across the scene in front of them.

'They're trying to poison them, seriously. They're trying to choke them to death. The problem is they don't like people saying so.'

Alex said: 'You mean they don't like you saying so?'

Kelner shrugged. 'Me perhaps, but others also. There's a status quo here that they don't like to have disturbed. They're so proud of their position as the curators of Western civilization. And so they should be.' He turned to Alex. 'Do you know that half of all the artefacts in the galleries of the world are from Italy? Did you know that? Did you?'

Alex shook his head.

'No. So they're the curators, the guardians. People like dear Isabella here.' He grinned at her again. 'These are the guardians. A privileged job.'

Isabella sniffed. 'Thank you so much.' There was something terribly neutral in her tone.

Kelner ploughed on. 'And then someone like me comes in and says they're making a mess of it and, well, they get upset. Isn't that true?' He addressed the question to Isabella.

'People are sensitive. That is true. But it is only because there is so much here, so much art to be cared for. They do not know what to do with it all. They are embarrassed.'

Kelner nodded. 'Perhaps,' he said quietly. And he turned to consider the view once more. 'They don't need to be embarrassed,' he said slowly, 'just to think about things a little more.' He let out a deep sigh, sipped his water and turned to look at Isabella.

'You know, you have the jaw of a Strossetti,' he said.

'Only if you wish to see it,' she replied. 'I look more like my brother, and my brother looks more like my mother than my father.'

'Believe me,' Kelner said. 'I've spent much time looking at

a jaw like yours. I have studied the tomb of your ancestor for many years. I know the form of her body intimately.' He leaned across the table to look at her more closely, pausing for a second so that the last word hung in the air between them. She pulled back. 'Believe me, I know the shape so well; the way it cuts up so squarely.' He pointed an index finger along the fine line of her jaw. 'It's very positive. You should be very proud.'

He settled back in his chair and looked away at the view once more.

'I think Isabella is much more than a jaw bone,' Alex said. He wanted to be on her side.

'Of course,' Kelner replied. 'Much more. Much more . . .' His voice trailed off.

Isabella crossed one leg tightly over the other, leaned towards the historian and said, very deliberately, 'What do you mean?'

He turned to look at her as though she had, in some way, missed a very obvious point: 'You have the privilege of being flesh and blood. You breathe. You are alive in the here and now.' His east coast accent gave the staccato phrases an even sharper edge.

'I'm glad you think it matters.'

'Of course it matters. The Joanna is gone. Our friend Conte has made sure of that. So you become all the more important.'

'I am not a museum piece.'

Kelner laughed, a rough throaty thing that barely shook his shoulders. 'You're not a museum piece in a classical sense, no. But within you, deep inside, you carry a great antiquity. You must see that. You are the link, the proof. You are the evidence. It's there in your blood. We know who and what the Joanna is because we have you in the here and now. Your family has what one can only call an exotic history. You can help people like me understand. To a historian it's more precious than any document. Believe me, it's not an insult.'

'No?' Isabella sat back heavily. 'I don't know why, but it feels like one.'

Alex scribbled the two words into his notebook: exotic history. What did he mean by exotic? Did he mean foreign? Beautiful? He would have to ask some time, but not now. It wouldn't be good to jump on the back of Kelner's questions. This spat was good copy, or could be. But he didn't want Isabella to be offended. An idea was forming in his head and she would have to be well disposed towards him even to consider it. She sat glowering at the professor who in turn stared obliviously at the view, like a sailor staring out to sea, focusing on everything and on nothing at all. It had been good to get hold of her: great-granddaughter of the Joanna, however many generations removed, real Italian nobility. And a Florentine banker to boot.

'Tell me, Isabella,' Alex said in his strongest journalist-asking-a-question voice. 'Do you feel the Joanna has been ruined?'

Kelner swung back round to the table. 'Of course it's been ruined. It's been savaged. She's been raped, hasn't she? Violated.' He was leaning across at Isabella again.

She raised one hand in resignation. 'It seems Professor Kelner speaks for me. I will just agree with him. It is easier.'

Kelner looked startled, pulled himself back from the table, placed both hands in his lap and bowed his head slightly while still looking up. 'Signorina, forgive me. I . . . I have no manners. I didn't mean to interrupt you. It's just that I feel so strongly about . . .' He looked strangely childlike, a schoolboy who had just been caught carving his initials into a desk, or throwing stones at sleeping seagulls.

'I understand,' Isabella said quietly. 'And I do agree. Joanna has been damaged. There can be no doubt about that. A brightness has gone.'

Kelner relaxed a little now. He asked Alex and Isabella if they would mind indulging him. There was something he wanted to show them both. They agreed and he led the way, along the narrow paths now crowded with tourists who had come to seek out the peace and shade offered by the trees. Alex followed just a little behind Isabella. He liked watching her walk, the gentle sway of her hips, a well-balanced motion that allowed no stutter or stumble. She kept her head just a little back as she moved, as if she were not expecting any kind of challenge, confident that whatever she might find around the next corner would be no obstacle at all.

The historian led them to a small ornamental pond. At one side stood what was left of a sculpture, a little over five feet tall. In better days she would have held an urn upon her shoulder with her left arm. Her right arm would have come across her body to rest on her thigh. The hair would have been decorated with flowers. But the sculpture was all but a ruin now. Where the left arm should have been, a thick piece of iron jutted out which must once have held the work together, now crusted and cracked with orange rust. Little of her face remained; the right eye and the beginning of the right nostril were there but the rest seemed to have all but returned to raw hewn rock.

'This is sixteenth century,' Kelner said. 'A study of Aphrodite, goddess of love. But then I'm sure you know that. Nobody is sure who the artist is. It is – or was – no masterpiece. But that's only by the standards of what's around it. It should not have been allowed to decay like this.'

'What happened?' Alex said.

'No one really knows because not all of these pieces were

catalogued. It has stayed here for centuries, been moved and dropped and broken. No one has seen fit to take it into one of the museums. It was never good enough for the Bargello. So it is lost through neglect.' He fell silent while the three of them studied the fractured rock before them.

'This is what will happen to all of it if we're not careful. The stones are dying.' Slowly he shook his head, swallowed loudly and said: 'You know, I used to think that marble had more integrity than flesh. Flesh gives up its secrets. Eventually the beauty decays, falls slack. We've all seen it.' He looked down at the ground and then, almost under his breath, said: 'I've certainly seen it.'

He recomposed himself: 'But marble, I thought, marble keeps it. The beauty is set in stone. But Set In Stone has no meaning any more. Look at her.' The trio studied the sculpture.

'And then they discover these things are happening and to make up for it they go for these grand restorations, like the Joanna. They want to prove they're doing something; they want to make the restoration exciting. But they skin the sculptures alive. They've got it all wrong because they're feeling guilty.' He turned to face his audience. It was time for a lesson: 'Imagine a child spills paint on his parents' white carpet. And they're not there to see it happen. Imagine that. He leaves it to dry in until it can't be cleaned off, until it will need to be treated with all manner of industrial chemicals. Terrible mess. But he can't let his parents see the stain. So he cuts a hole in the carpet where the stain is. That way they never see the accident. It has a logic, no?' Alex and Isabella agreed.

'Well that's what they're doing here.' He gestured towards the tattered Aphrodite. 'They're cutting holes in the carpet because they feel guilty. It's a tragedy, and I have to be the parent who comes in and tells them off. It's my job and I go to court for it.'

Kelner seemed genuinely drained of emotion now, as he looked once more at the lump of brutalized stone before them, its face blanked out by time. 'I think I've spoken enough,' he said eventually. 'I've said my piece. I hope I will see you both in court on Saturday.' And with that he turned and walked off down the path, his bony feet scuffing against the gravel to slow his descent.

Alex and Isabella watched him go in silence. And then Alex said: 'Miss Strossetti. I have a favour to ask.'

Andrea Conte, master restorer, claimed only one ambition: to spend the days of his life on the hill of Fiesole to the north of Florence and the days of his death on the hill of San Miniato to the south. The apparent modesty of his ambition, his simple desire to afford himself little else but a view for all eternity was, however, undermined by the status of the two locations he said he wished to call home. If you were able to afford a villa in the lush, quiet lanes of Fiesole, you had, more likely than not, achieved solid wealth and security. And if, in death, you could still afford to be buried in the cemetery of San Miniato, among the gargantuan marble mausoleums, the bonsai cathedrals erected by the lords and ladies of the city to celebrate the enduring nature of old money, then, in short, you had been very rich indeed.

Conte had already achieved the first part of his ambition and, from the look of things, seemed well set to manage the second. His old stone farmhouse, tucked discreetly off the Via Fra' Giovanni Angelico just below Fiesole's old town, had benefited from every one of the modern improvements that money, and a modicum of taste, could buy. The majority of the back wall had been knocked out and replaced with a single piece of thick plate glass to afford the best possible view over the olive groves to the city far below. The floors had been laid with large slabs of Carrara marble and half of the upper level had been taken out to produce a vast airy vault in the centre of the house, whitewashed and carefully lit, with a simple gallery running around its four sides. This was Conte's personal statement. It said: I've worked hard, I've made it, and I'm going to show off.

Isabella eased her hatchback to a halt by the side of the house and they sat looking at the view. The garden slipped away just beyond where they had parked, giving the impression that the restorer lived on the very edge of a sheer drop down to the city, his city. Below, in the Arno Valley, the sodium lights of Florence burnt through the dusk, an orange fire against a sea of deep blue.

'Thank you for agreeing to help me out,' Alex said, to break the silence. Not a smart thing to say but it filled the quiet.

Isabella said, 'I was curious. Remember, I do have a personal interest.' He had told Isabella that he was due to see Conte the next evening, to get the restorer's side of the story. The interview had been set up by an Italian speaker on the foreign desk back in London. But, as Alex didn't speak Italian, he would need a translator. He suggested Isabella do it. It was a double opportunity; the idea of putting together the restorer and a woman descended from the Joanna appealed hugely. And, even better, he got to spend some more time with this strange Italian aristocrat with her proud walk and her short sentences. Her brush with Kelner had made it much easier to convince her than Alex had expected; it seemed to have given her an appetite for the story, rather than put her off. She had argued with Kelner. Now she wanted to see if she could argue with Conte.

'So you want that I should meet the man who raped my grandmother?' she had said.

'I'm not sure he is a rapist. Come with me and help me decide. You don't have to tell him who you are, at least not at first. You can just be my translator.' He liked the idea of sharing a secret with her, a tiny, pointless conceit.

'That would be good for your story, I think?'

'Perhaps, but I'm sure you would find it interesting too.' She had agreed.

They left the car and went to the house to introduce themselves. Andrea Conte was waiting for them in the huge living room, with its cream-coloured rugs, its white linen sofas and its glass-topped coffee tables. It looked, Alex decided, like some art director's vision of heaven, stolen wholesale from a tacky 1970s disco movie; a paradise of bleached soft furnishings which would never need cleaning. And if they did, well there would always be some cherubim or seraphim hanging around to do the hard work. And a pile of money to pay for it.

The grand view of the city below, twinkling through the long plate-glass window at the end of the room, gave the impression that this really was some otherworldly place, a room from which to watch. In the middle, cast in the role of St Peter, was Conte himself, his broad hands raised in welcome, his teeth closed in a grin. He was as big as Kelner was small, a tree-trunk of a man who rose thick and solid from the pale marble floor to fill the room. The distance between his calf-skin loafers and the thatch of fat black curly hair, flecked with grey, standing proud upon his head, was the better part of six and a half feet.

Isabella introduced herself as Alex's *interprete*, hands were shaken, greetings exchanged. Alex asked Isabella to thank Conte for agreeing to see them on the night before the trial. The restorer simply smiled and said it was his pleasure to see them but his great sadness that it should have come to this. Heads were nodded. Glasses of Vin Santo were offered and accepted. (Never turn down a drink from an interviewee, Alex always said, even if you really don't want it. It puts the subject on the defensive.) Alex and Isabella chose to sit at either end of a sofa; Conte positioned himself at the end of the next sofa nearest Isabella.

Then he raised his hands again and, with a broad smile, said: '*Allora, di che cosa parliamo?*'

Alex said: 'Eh?'

And Isabella said: 'He's ready for your first question.'

'Oh, right. Then ask him, when did he first see the Joanna?'

And so the interview began, a strange game of linguistic catch. Alex delivered the questions clause by clause; Isabella returned the answers in gobbets. Her translations were punctuated by wild arm movements as she sought to find the right phrases, the correct words, grabbing at the air as if trying to pluck the bits of vocabulary she needed from the space above her head. Alex found himself watching Isabella's translations as much as listening to them. She had shifted her weight to the front of the sofa, was leaning forward with her arms outstretched so that the line of her left breast became clear against the material of her simple, black cotton jacket. Occasionally she would turn to talk directly to Alex but even then her eyes gazed over his head, into the shimmer of night behind him, her hands still raised, her narrow waist all the more pronounced by the way she had twisted her body.

'He says he first saw the Joanna when he was a child . . . His family used to spend summers in the mountains near Strossetti to escape the heat and occasionally they would go . . . go to mass at the Cathedral of San Martino.' Isabella suddenly laughed. 'He says that as a child he used to kiss her hand after mass.' Conte shrugged. Alex wondered whether Isabella was about to tell the restorer who she was. But no. They still had their secret.

'He had strong feelings for the sculpture then?'

'He says yes . . . he has always felt something, something like love for the Joanna. It was the first sculpture he got to know and . . . oh, I see . . . and she was the first woman outside of his family that he kissed.'

'How did he feel when he was given the chance to restore Joanna?'

'This was the greatest, ehm, the greatest honour for him. He had been worried when he heard they planned to restore her . . . because he does not trust anyone as he trusts himself . . . so when they asked him he was relieved.'

'Did you feel she was in need of a major restoration?'

'He says when he first looked at her . . . when he first saw her there was some, ehm *rovina*, what is the word . . . breaking, no, not breaking . . . decay, that's it . . . decay. Especially on the face and around the neck. But other than that it was only dirt. But . . . he says that had he not taken off that dirt it too would have started this decay.'

'What tests did he do?'

'Eh, he says . . .' Isabella pulled a slight face. 'He says he did no tests. This was not his job.'

'Did anybody else do any tests?'

'He says he does not know . . . I trusted my own, ehm, profession, no, sorry . . . my own professionalism. *Sapeva come guardare il pietro* . . . ah, he knew how to look at the stone.'

'Was he pleased with the restoration?'

Conte sat up as if he had been slapped around the chops. He looked at Isabella and then across at Alex and raised his eyebrows so that they almost disappeared into the thatch of hair above.

'Shall I take that as yes then?'

'I think you should.'

'OK. Ask him what does he say to those people who say the Joanna has been damaged?'

'He says that . . . he says that the Joanna has been changed, not damaged. There are a lot . . . of people, a lot of people who love Joanna and know her . . . one way. So they see a new Joanna and they are not sure. But she is the same. Only . . . only better.'

'Some people say he rushed the job.'

'Do you want me to put that to him as a question?'

'Statement or question. It doesn't matter.'

Conte leant forward and showed them the palms of his hands. 'He says you must understand that . . . his relationship with . . . Joanna was a physical one. He touched her . . . with these two hands. It was a relationship between his hands and the warm stone of Joanna. A relationship . . . built on love. He . . . I would not have rushed such work. I would have defended Joanna against those who would rush.'

Alex let the room fall silent for a moment, as he scribbled in his notebook. He had to force himself to stare at the page. If Isabella caught his eye he would need to speak, to say something to answer her unasked questions. She had a way of looking at him which was strangely unnerving; she would scan his whole face for meaning rather than just fix on his eyes, in a way that demanded he explain himself. But he wanted that beat, needed that sudden breath, to allow Conte's theatrical protestation of love to grow. The next question would come off the back of the silence and be all the more charged. After forty-five seconds he looked up from the page where, in truth, he had been doing little more than drawing spirals and said, innocently, 'So what does he think of Professor Kelner?'

Conte let out a thick grunt: 'Huh!'

Then he spoke. 'He says . . . he says he could still be friends with the professor . . . but he chose to say these things to the press. Do we not both care about the same things? He should . . . he should have come, ehm, come to see him so that we could debate. Instead he makes a noise so that everybody knows the name of . . . Professor Kelner. Now they know his name and . . . and now they spit on the name of Conte. Kelner says my methods are bad. I say his are . . . his are terrible.'

There was another pause. Conte was looking out at the city beyond the window. Staring blankly.

'Ask him, does he want to see Kelner go to prison?'

Conte looked down at the floor and pushed a piece of fluff from one of the rugs around the marble with his toe. 'It would be, ehm, sad . . . sad if he went to prison. But I must be given back my . . . my dignity. The professor says I use acid. This offends me both as a craftsman and . . . oh, dear,' Isabella winced slightly and turned from Conte to Alex. 'He says it offends him as a man.'

On the wall opposite where Alex sat hung a simple painting, just three lines of black which swept from the bottom left to the top right of the frame, running towards each other and away again, so that from the relationship of those three lines was formed the figure of a female nude, reclining, her left arm back behind her head. Alex had been trying to work out how the lines had been planned, how they had been fitted to the form. There was something so random in the shape of the lines. And yet there was the human figure.

'Ask him who the painting is by.' He eased himself up from the sofa and went to have a closer look. Conte was flattered by the question. He got up and went to join Alex in front of the picture, answering Isabella as he went.

'He says it's by his father.' Then Isabella added: 'His father was Carlo Conte. He was a very well-known Florentine painter.'

'So, when he went into the art world, he was following in his father's footsteps?'

'No, he says he was not good enough to be a painter . . . now he just, ah . . . he is a midwife for artists . . . Eh?' Isabella asked for clarification. 'He says he helps great artists to be reborn.'

The conversation had strayed on to the territory of family. Alex was tempted to try and let them leave the house without Isabella saying who she really was. He wanted to enjoy the pointless conspiracy a little longer, the intimacy of deceit. But he thought there might be something interesting in Conte's reaction and this was the obvious moment to test it. Casually he suggested to Isabella that she reveal herself.

She said, 'You are trying to play with me. I am not going to be part of some game for you.'

Alex was taken by surprise. 'Of course not. I didn't mean to . . .'

'I will decide when I tell someone who I am.'

'Absolutely.'

'You do not give me orders.'

'No.'

She turned back to the picture and the three of them stood

in silence studying the thick, black lines. Alex thought: I've screwed up. She would have told him by now if I hadn't been so heavy-handed. At least I've got the interview. It would have been fun to get the other stuff, but . . .

Isabella was twisting a ring off her hand. Alex turned to look. She was biting her lip with the effort as she pulled on the thick band of gold, twisting it, turning it, inching it down and down over the knuckle of her middle finger, the metal stretching her skin as it moved. Finally it came off. She handed the ring to Conte and told him to look. He turned it over. There was a coat of arms pressed into a square of the soft metal at the front of the ring. He lifted it up and squinted. He brought it closer and said, tentatively: 'Strossetti?'

Isabella grinned, plucked the ring out of his hand and pushed it back on to her finger. 'Signor Conte,' she began, '*Ho qualcosa da confessarle.* (I have a confession to make.)' She walked back to the sofa, sat down, crossed one leg over the other and folded her hands in her lap. And then, for over a minute, she explained herself. Conte rested one hand on the mantelpiece beneath the picture and listened, nodding his head every few seconds, a quick twitch of comprehension. As Isabella spoke, his brow seemed to furrow further. Finally she said the words 'dei Strossetti' and pointed to Alex who stood beside him. Conte threw back his head and let out a hoot of laughter.

'Una Strossetti. Ha.' He turned to Alex and slapped him firmly on the back.

'Una Strossetti.' He walked over to Isabella, leant down, placed both hands on her shoulders, and kissed her loudly on each cheek. He talked animatedly for a moment and then looked eagerly at Alex.

'He thinks we should all go for a drink together in town to

77

talk some more. He says he is proud to meet me because he already knows my father and would like to buy us both a special drink to celebrate, though I'm not sure what he wants to celebrate exactly.'

They agreed to go. As the three of them left the house a woman's voice bawled from somewhere deep inside, a shrill call that brought them to a halt for a moment: *'T'interessi di più della Joanna che della famiglia,'* they heard her shout. *'Dovresti andare vivere con lei.'*

Isabella translated: 'I think it is his wife. She's telling him that if he cares more about the Joanna than his family then he should move in with her.' Conte looked at them both as if to say 'Well, what can I do?' and they left.

So here was his story, Alex thought, as he sat in the back of Isabella's car on the drive down into Florence; these two men, restorer and historian, experts both, going to court to defend their reputations. Because reputation and expertise are what count in Florence. They are the common currency. And what they are fighting over is a woman they both say they know more about than anybody else. But really it's a love triangle. Two men, one woman. Except the woman has been dead 500 years. An eternal love triangle. A love triangle with a decomposed woman in it.

He felt a wave of depression fold over him. It was a story, but it wasn't his sort of story. It didn't have Alex Fuller's name on it; the drama was purely intellectual. It took place on some undefined territory between the minds of these two men. And the main character wasn't even the restorer or the historian but the dead woman. And he hated stories about dead people. You couldn't interview a dead person. History should only be the counterpoint to the narrative in journalism, he thought to himself, it shouldn't be the narrative itself. Otherwise it is no longer journalism but a history lesson and people don't want to read history lessons.

A memory, tattered by denial, dragged up by the rhythm of the Fiesole Road. Another road, dusty, somewhere hot. Too hot. Too hot to think. Too hot to breathe. The buzz of flies and the glare of the African sun and the smell of the dust. A man, tall and thin, walks towards him out of the sun so that he's in shadow. But even when he turns into the sun he's still in shadow. Black. Deep and shiny. He's holding something in his hands. A stick. Alex can't see what it is. But he wants it. He doesn't want the shadow man to have it. He wants to take it. Then confusion. Noise, loud. Christ so loud. Won't it stop? Please? Then silence. Another man lies on the ground in the dust, silent. Silenced for all time. And Alex has the shadow man's stick. He lean's over the man in the dust, turns his head over to look into his eyes. But he only has one eye. The other has gone. He only has half a head. The rest is blood and meat and the buzz of flies.

Dead people. You can't interview dead people.

Conte took them to a place called Roses, a sleek little bar hidden away on Via Parione to the west of the Piazza della Repubblica, where they served salted popcorn in bowls and the staff wore polo necks and tight smiles. They sat at the blonde wood bar, Isabella tucked in between the two men, ordered large whiskies and talked. It was simple stuff. Conte dropped in little queries about what Kelner had said; Isabella asked neutral questions about how Conte faced the prospect of going to court.

At first Alex joined in but, with Isabella's identity now out in the open, with their secret now gone, he began to feel more and more isolated. He was the outsider, the foreigner. At first, by asking Isabella to translate Alex had been able to use his lack of Italian to his own advantage: she had been forced to concentrate on him, to work for him. As far as Alex could see, he was the only reason Isabella was there at all. Conte had nothing to do with it. But now, seated at the bar with the lights down low and the interviews finished Alex had become the silent fool, strangled by language. Isabella and Conte had things to talk about. They had things in common, not least a vocabulary. Alex was just tagging along for the ride.

He turned to look at Isabella, to get a smile or maybe an acknowledgment. He didn't want much, just a sign that she knew he was there and that she'd enjoyed spending the evening with him and that she might want to see him again. But she had her back to him. He turned back to his drink and lit up another cigarette. Alcohol wasn't his drug. He stared at the liquid. Booze was for the old boys. He'd seen them, their bellies propped up on their desks, capillaries split, livers shot to hell, staring at their terminals and going on about the stories they'd done, and the beer they'd drunk, and the copy they'd filed half-cut. That wasn't what Alex wanted. He had other demons. What need did he have for another monkey on his back?

But tonight the whisky looked inviting, a refuge from exclusion. A refuge too from the mess inside his head, the desert-road memories and the blood-stained dreams. Maybe tonight a little whisky would do him good. He took a sip, swallowed and felt the burn inside his chest. He took another and this time he held it in his mouth so he could isolate the flavours. But he couldn't taste it through the alcohol. He tried another gulp, just to be sure.

As the second and third whiskies took hold, softening the muscles in his legs and making his head droop ever lower down on to his neck, he took to watching the silent images that played on a television screen set into the wall behind the bar, and smoking continuously. Conte and Isabella talked on, the restorer punctuating his conversation with little incidental touches, a hand on her shoulder, on her back, on her arm. She watched and talked and smiled. Alex slumped further down on to the bar and tried to pretend he hadn't noticed. He felt the room shift slightly.

The picture on the television changed. There was a young woman in a little black dress, pretty and muscular, leaning forward over a cello that she held clasped between her thighs as she played it. A thought came into Alex's head and he opened his mouth to speak, desperate to break his own silence, but decided against it. He turned to look at Isabella. She had her head back and was laughing, eyes squeezed up to creases. Conte had his hand rested on her shoulder. The journalist shook his head a little. He might as well say what he was going to say. He had nothing to lose. After being silent for so long, he was surprised by the sound of his own voice. 'I think the cello is a deeply sensual instrument,' he heard himself say a little too loudly, as he stared at the television, 'when it's played by a woman.'

Isabella stopped laughing, looked at Alex and then at the screen. 'Yes,' she said. 'It's all in the way she's taking control.'

Alex smiled. At last. He had her attention. All he had to do was keep it. He was drunk now. He knew it and he didn't care. He was safe, in the dark warmth of this bar, with its strong smell of tobacco and liquor. 'It's nothing to do with her being in control,' he said. 'It's the way she's got her legs open. Look at her. Just look. She's letting the cello in. Tell our friend down the other end of the bar that.' Isabella frowned at him. Alex said, 'Go on, tell him.'

Conte laughed and spoke to Isabella. She closed her eyes and sighed with irritation. 'He says he wouldn't mind being the cello.'

Better and better, Alex thought. While he had made well-formed and intelligent observations about the cello, Conte just wanted to be smutty. With a bit of encouragement he could make Isabella really hate him. That would be the end of the smooth-talking restorer. He swigged some more whisky and said, 'Tell him me too.' Alex's mouth had fallen open now as he stared at the screen. The woman leant heavily on her bow, dragging ever harder on her strings.

Isabella barked back the translation. 'He says sure, but do you think you are a good enough instrument?'

Alex sat up and turned to Isabella, with what he imagined was a look of desperate shock engraved on his face. He almost slipped off the stool.

'You two have got it all wrong,' Isabella said, furiously waving one hand at the screen, as Alex pulled himself back up. 'Look at her properly. She is the one in charge. She's holding that cello like that because she has allowed it to be there. It is not an act of ehm, an act of, oh damn, what's the fucking word? Ah, an act of submission.'

'Yeah, sure,' Alex said. He reckoned he only needed to throw Conte another line and the man would hang himself with it. 'Tell Andrea . . .' he stumbled over the man's first name. 'Tell Andrea, I once had a girlfriend who played the cello.' He burped loudly.

Isabella's face flushed and she bit her bottom lip. But still she translated.

'He says . . .' She shook her head. 'He says you're a lucky man.'

And so the conversation went on as the two men exchanged their thoughts on the many roles of the cello in sexual intercourse, its shape, and the myriad ways in which it could be held. Isabella translated, but the more she did so the sharper her manner became, the tighter her phrases. She bit her lip hard as each question and answer was fired at her and rapped her fingers loudly on the bar. His mind blanketed by a whisky haze, his thoughts clambering across each other to escape his fetid mouth, Alex was still convinced he was only encouraging Conte to be as vulgar as possible.

He sat up, pointed at the screen and said: 'When I die I want to be reincarnated as her cello.' Isabella translated and the two men hooted with laughter, a bold merry shout that rang out through the bar. Isabella slipped off her stool, picked up her bag, turned to Alex and, with a sneer, said, 'Even if you were reincarnated as her husband's prick she would not have you.' She turned to the restorer and said something in Italian which Alex took to be similar.

And with that, she left, slamming the smoked glass door behind her as she went.

Alex leant over the now empty stool towards Conte. Conte leant towards Alex. The journalist shook his head and said, 'Now look what you've done.'

Conte furrowed his brow, ran both hands through his hair and said simply, 'Eh?'

Finally, Isabella had managed to silence them both.

CHAPTER FIVE

Antonio Rafanelli lived up to his reputation. His work on Joanna's tomb advanced so slowly that the people of Strossetti, a feisty lot, given more to feasting and bawdiness than dour acts of contemplation, soon agreed the carving of the piece to be an event of such mind-numbing tedium that they quickly lost interest.

In the years that elapsed between the original commission and the work being moved to the Cathedral of San Martino to receive the finishing touches, acorns grew into young trees. Girls had time enough to pass through puberty, become pregnant, give birth, and then become pregnant all over again. The castle's baker burned down his house, twice; the blacksmith wore out three anvils; and half the horses in the royal stables simply died of old age.

Nice and slow. That was the way Rafanelli liked it. There was nothing that bored him more than a procession of eager spectators passing through his studio peering at the work, considering the stone from every angle, and then proving their ignorance by asking him how he was progressing, what he was doing and why he was doing it. Hell's teeth, could they not see these things for themselves? If he had his way, he would have chosen to carve in his house deep in the forest. There he could work without interruption, carving his stone and seeing only those he wished to see. But Scorza had made him a generous offer. How could he refuse? He would receive a healthy living while he worked on the tomb and be fed and housed by the royal household. And when he finished the task he would receive a huge lump sum in Strossetti silver which, he reckoned, could keep him for years to come.

So it was in his interest to work slowly; it got rid of the spectators, kept him in rich food and wine, and allowed him time enough to finish his sculpture of the Madonna for the Cathedral of Pistoia.

But even as studied an expert in sloth as Rafanelli – he could spend hours chipping away at a useless piece of marble just to make it sound like he was working, filling his head instead with wicked thoughts about the stable boys, smooth-cheeked and supple, who passed by his door every day – even he knew there came a time when he could stall no more. And so, three years and eleven months after he began his work, the tomb of Joanna dei Strossetti was heaved, piece by piece, on to a cart and dragged the few hundred feet to the cathedral that lay just down the hill from the castle.

The four sides of the sarcophagus, decorated with the figures of eight garland-carrying cherubs – three on each side, one on either end – were erected on the stone dais in the east wing, the obese children a nod to the cause of Joanna's death. The coffin, containing her shrivelled, linen-wrapped body, that had been kept all these years in the cool of the castle crypt, was placed inside. Lumps of lead, the thickness of Rafanelli's thumb, were set around the rim of the sarcophagus and the lid, bearing Joanna's image, was lowered down upon them supported by inch-thick ropes held by ten strong men. The ropes were then dragged out. Had this been summer they could have relied on the vicious Italian sun to perform the next task, but it was still early in the year and the sun was offering little in the way of warmth. So they improvised. Torches were lit, and the flames held against the soft metal.

At first the lead released only wisps of thick, pungent smoke that could be seen to rise high into the roof of the cathedral until they were lost in the dark. And then the metal began to melt, bubbling and bending as it went, most falling inside the tomb but some dripping down the outside, in slate grey trails. Until, finally, the lumps of lead were melted entirely and, with a dull thud, the tomb slipped shut for ever.

It irritated Rafanelli that he would have to complete the work in such a public place where the rabble could so easily wander in to watch. But he had little choice. The piece had to be assembled before he could make his last marks which meant labouring where the tomb was to stand, body already inside. He unpacked his tools, the very sharpest of chisels and the finest of files, and set to work, sharpening a line here, smoothing a curve there, digging deep into the stone in search of the final details.

He was disturbed first by Vincente who came to stand and watch just a few hours after Rafanelli had begun.

'Ah,' the artist said, as he saw Joanna's half-brother approaching out of the cathedral gloom. 'The love-struck one. Have you come to criticize my labours?'

'No, sir,' Vincente said. 'I have come only to watch.' He stood a few feet away, apparently eager not to get too close to the artist and his tools. Rafanelli stood facing him over the far side of the tomb. 'I heard you were near finishing my sister,' Vincente said.

'Your sister is finished already, dear Vincente,' the artist replied as he worked a deep line into the sculpture's hair. 'She lies finished inside, wrapped in linen. I am here only to make her in stone.'

'Do not mock me,' Vincente said. 'You are restoring life to my dear sister. I can see it in the marble.'

Rafanelli said nothing, hoping the sullen young man might remove himself if he kept quiet. For a while Vincente stood watching, motionless in the shadows, until the artist wondered whether he was hoping, by force of will alone, to become part of the cathedral's statuary; released from the burden of breathing to stand guard over his half-sister, petrified here for all time.

Finally Vincente said: 'Tell me, Rafanelli, why did you choose a life working with stone rather than paint?'

The artist stood up straight and considered the man, his head on one side, a half smile hanging on his lips. 'Because, dear Vincente . . .' he walked to the middle of the sarcophagus and placed his left hand over Joanna's crotch, so that his fingers dug deep into the point where her marble tunic dipped between her thighs, pushing down hard, forcing the blood from his knuckles until they were as white as the stone itself. 'Because . . . I like to feel my work.' And then he threw back his head and cackled with laughter.

Vincente scuttled back into the shadows, with Rafanelli shouting after him. 'Have patience, my boy. Soon you will be able to come and touch her too.'

His next visitor was Father Corsano, dark and intense, who attended daily to offer prayers for Joanna's soul. On the second day, after he had done with his prayers and his blessing, he came and stood close by the artist who was working once more on Joanna's hair, so close that Rafanelli could feel the priest's warm breath upon his neck. The priest reached out and rested the tip of an index finger upon her lips, gasping slightly at the cold touch of the stone.

'Will you labour more on her kiss?' he asked.

Rafanelli looked at the mouth for a moment. 'A little,' he said. 'I wish the bottom lip to be fuller so I must dig down and around it. But I will not do much.'

'Good,' Father Corsano said. He slowly ran his finger around the smooth bulge of the mouth. 'Those lips are . . . right.' Then he said, 'Lucky the man who touched them when once they were warm.'

Finally, on the fourth day, when Rafanelli was working on the dove which sat at Joanna's feet, Bartolommeo himself came. In the time it had taken Rafanelli to carve the tomb the prince had turned from an old man into a sick old man, who now shuffled along the cold stone floors, wheezing and creaking as he walked. A servant padded alongside, steadying him by one arm. When they reached the place where the artist worked the servant went off to find a bench. Rafanelli could hear the wood stretch as Bartolommeo lowered his bulk down upon it, the joints squeak and begin to splinter. The prince took a deep breath and said: 'Rafanelli, now you have all but completed your task I have decided we shall bless the tomb of my late wife on the anniversary of her death in ten days' time. You shall be finished by then.' It was an order, not a question.

'Yes, my Lord.'

The prince sat in silence, watching the gentle rhythm of the hammer on the chisel, listening to the crack of metal on stone.

'You enjoy your work?' he said eventually.

'We each have a task to perform,' he said simply. 'I was bound to be an artist.'

'That is God's gift?'

'Indeed. It is my duty to use those skills that I have, just as you, my Lord, are born to be prince of Strossetti.'

Again the prince fell silent and gazed at the face of the Joanna. The artist looked up and saw the old man's dead stare, fixed on the stone lids of her eyes. They will not open again, Rafanelli thought to himself as he worked, however much you wish it.

'What is it about carving stone that appeals to you?'

The artist wondered for a moment whether Vincente had been telling tales. Was this a test? He stopped his chiselling and looked at the prince. No, Vincente would never bother a man as tired and sick as this with such trivialities. His continued presence at court depended on keeping a low profile.

'My Lord,' he said, with a flourish. 'Painting is the process of addition. You are always adding to the canvas. You place upon the canvas layers of paint, forever looking for the truth by placing more and more upon it. This philosophy does not appeal to me. I believe the truth lies in taking away.' He closed his eyes and turned his face up to the roof as though seeking divine guidance. He was enjoying this speech, savouring its cadences.

'Sculpture, in stone, is a process of reduction. You are always looking for less in the stone, cutting away to find the truth within it, like a forester cutting through a thicket in search of the path. You can never add to it, only take away. From the moment the marble is carved from the hill it becomes less than it once was. I carve further and further until the stone is so much less but, I trust, so much more.'

Bartolommeo nodded. 'And stone is immortal, of course.'

'That I cannot guarantee. A sculpture is only as immortal as those who wish it to exist. It is true that it is easier to destroy a painting. But how many sculptures have been lost because there are those who do not wish to see the stone cut that way? Many, my Lord, so many. It is the hands of men who cut the sculpture from the rock and the hands of men who can break the sculpture too.'

Bartolommeo scowled at that, and growled as he cleared his lungs of the thick, green phlegm that gathered there so often these days. He pushed what he had brought up from his throat into the damp cavity of his mouth, rolled it around with his tongue and then swallowed. 'We shall see,' he said. 'We shall see.'

Bartolommeo refused to allow that fey, slovenly artist to depress him, however gifted he happened to be. What did he know about the moods of men? He made his slow way back up the hill to his chambers, there to sit and indulge himself in one of the few pleasures that still attended him in his dotage: watching his son, Francesco, at play. Joanna was the past. Here was the future, alive and happy on the royal cushion. Here was the future made from flesh, not from stone. This was all that mattered. In less than two weeks the child would celebrate his fourth birthday. How proud his mother would have been, how happy.

In truth Francesco did little playing. Mostly he just rolled around and threw the cushion at the servants. He was such an important child, such a precious child that Bartolommeo had decreed early on that he should receive only the best of everything. His every whim was indulged. Rarely did he need to walk; there was always someone to carry him wherever he chose to go. If he had normal appetites nobody knew about them. He had been fed on only the very richest of morsels from the moment he could but move his jaw and overeating was now the norm. As a result he was enormously fat, a soft, round ball of pink and white blubber, fit only to sit on tasselled cushions, kick the servants and bawl whenever he felt he was not being paid sufficient attention.

But Bartolommeo loved him. He knew full well that the boy would not reach his eighteenth birthday before his father died – the prince had lived long enough to be free of idiotic illusions – but he had already appointed a regent to act in his stead. Cesare Scorza, ever scrupulous, ever loyal, would see that right was done. What mattered was that the succession was secured, not how it happened. As the boy's birthday approached, the day upon which the soul of the child's late mother would also finally be laid to rest, a great calm came over the elderly prince. He was, at last, at peace with the world; he knew he had achieved his life's work.

When the head of the household informed him casually, just five days before the celebrations, that a maid by the name of Claudia had disappeared from the castle, it barely registered. He was far too complacent to allow such trifles to concern him. He vaguely remembered that she was once one of those who served his Joanna, but little more. He assumed she had eloped with one of the gangly lads from the town, the randy tykes who often came in the evenings to flirt with the serving girls down by the kitchens.

Certainly he did not for a moment imagine that her sudden disappearance from court signalled the beginning of the end of everything for which he had strived.

'Hmmmm.' The elderly man leaned his long, hooked nose close to hers so that the mean slits of his eyes appeared to merge into one deep black hole. She recoiled on her seat. 'Hmmmm. What is the thing we have here? What is it? Full hair and smooth flesh. Is it a girl? A girl, here at the house of Lorenzo? What should she want here? Hmmmm?' He stood up as straight as his cracked and crooked spine would allow, peered at her scalp for a moment, said simply, 'No lice. Ha,' and walked off towards the door at the end of the corridor resting his weight on the gnarled stick that he carried in his right hand, and clicking his tongue against the roof of his mouth. He banged on the door with the end of the stick. Unseen hands partially opened it and he slipped inside, kicking it shut behind him.

Claudia was alone again. Thus had it been for the two hours since she arrived here, at this grand house on the western side of the city of Florence, claiming she had an important letter to deliver from the court of Strossetti to Lorenzo de' Medici, a letter she could give only to Lorenzo himself. She was eyed up and questioned and considered for a full half hour. Men came to look at her and then disappeared back through the door at the end of the corridor. They asked her why she could not give the message to them to pass on. Lorenzo was a busy man, they said. He could not receive just anybody who came claiming they had important business. A great many people had important business. Who was she to come making such demands? And why was she in such disarray? Had she been sleeping in a haystack?

In truth, yes. She had travelled from Strossetti to the noisy, narrow, piss-stained streets of Florence on the back of a cart with barrels of wine and olive oil for company and hay for the horses to soften the ride. It had been uncomfortable and exhausting but she had made her promise and she would keep it, whatever it took. So now she sat, watching the dark wooden door, nibbling her bottom lip and saying to herself: 'So, what now? Well, what do I do?' She reached inside the little leather pouch at her hip and felt the rough edge of the paper, the soft ridges of the wax seal. She liked the texture, thick and rough. She liked the feeling of importance the letter gave her, even if it did mean being stared at by ugly, old men.

The door opened half a foot and another, younger face

looked out at her. He considered her for a few seconds and then slammed the door shut again. A minute later the door opened once more. This time the man stood filling the space between the open door and the frame, one leg in the room, one leg out. He gestured to her to come. She was too tired to be afraid. She eased herself up off the hard wooden bench where she had been ordered to sit so long before and went to do her Lady's bidding.

Seven men sat around the walls of the low-ceilinged room, silent and dull-eyed. They were well dressed and shod. Their hands, like Bartolommeo's, lacked the calluses that the common herd considered a natural feature of the human body. The only bits of their bodies these men used were their minds and up there the calluses did not show, although Claudia was sure they were there nonetheless. Their faces revealed no emotion, as if it were a luxury only the less important could afford. They observed her as they would an animal brought before them for sale: cold, impassive, unwilling to be drawn.

Standing with his back to her, staring out of the window at the far end of the wood-lined room, was another man who wore a long jacket of purple and black. He had thick, dark hair that hung in slight waves around his ears and rested just above the collar at the back. Claudia heard the door shut behind her with a clunk. The man turned to look at her.

Claudia tried to stifle a gasp. She had heard Lorenzo wasn't pretty but had expected nothing as grotesque as this. His brow stood proud above his eyes in large, rounded lumps as if he had been beaten hard around the face. His nose was slightly twisted to the left and his top lip pulled to the side in a constant sneer exposing his crooked teeth. When he breathed the noise was loud and uncomfortable, like a bristle brush dragged slowly across stone. He held his chin up slightly and considered her.

Then he gestured to a three-legged stool that had apparently been placed in the middle of the room for the purpose.

'Sit down, girl. You have come a long way.'

'Yes, sir. From Strossetti.'

'Now why would you want to do a thing like that?'

She couldn't believe he hadn't been told; she had explained herself so many times. 'I have a letter that my Lady, Joanna dei Strossetti, made me promise to bring to you.'

'Hmm. Yes. She is dead.'

'Yes, sir. All but four years ago.'

'Does anybody at the court of my cousin Bartolommeo know you are here?' She shook her head.

'Well then. Intrigue upon intrigue. What risks we take in the name of duty.' He laughed and looked around at the seven men, the audience gathered around the edge of the conversation. Obediently they laughed too.

'Come on then. Let's have it.' He snapped his fingers. Claudia reached into her pouch and pulled out the envelope. Lorenzo took it, looked at the front and then at the seal on the back. 'It has survived well these four years, I think,' he said.

'I have taken care of it.'

'Of course you have.' He walked over to the window where there was more light and cracked open the seal. As he unfolded the letter a small gold cross, decorated with a single emerald where the two bars met, dropped into his open palm. Lorenzo held it up in front of the window, letting the chain hang down, so that Claudia and the rest of the room could see it. 'Do you recognize this?' She shook her head again.

'Well then . . .' He held the jewel in one hand and the letter in the other. 'Let us read.' He scanned the letter for a minute, the silence disturbed only by the rustle of the gowns of the men who sat and watched. 'Girl,' he said, without taking his eyes off the letter. 'Did you write this?'

'No, sir, I can't.'

'No, of course you can't.' He looked at the cross, turning it over in his hand. 'And you say you do not recognize this.' Claudia shook her head again.

'Then if what we have here is genuine it is very interesting indeed. My friends, I shall read . . . a little.' He tilted his chin up again and idly scratched his neck with the hand in which he held the piece of gold.

' "I, Joanna dei Strossetti, write on this thirteenth day of February in the year of our Lord fourteen hundred and eighty-three to confess my sins and protect those who will come after me." ' He stopped and scanned the room to check everybody was listening.

' "I am content that if you read this now I have gone to meet whatever fate the Lord should have deemed be mine and though my soul be immortal, the flesh has long returned unto dust. Those acts to which I now confess were only such that the human heart demanded. I beg no forgiveness but accept my fate." ' Lorenzo straightened his back and cleared his throat; what had gone before was only the overture.

' "The child that has been born to me, who the prince my husband should want to sit upon the throne of Strossetti when he has gone, does not have the right to succeed." ' The seven men sat bolt upright, as if they had just been slapped hard across the face for slouching. Claudia bit her bottom lip until it started to bleed a little. Lorenzo smiled at her and went on.

' "I have seen the burden of kingship upon the shoulders of Bartolommeo dei Strossetti and know the terrors such honour brings. I should want no child of mine to suffer in this way.

95

Thus I have chosen to let it be known that the father of my child is not Bartolommeo dei Strossetti, but another. Though I served my husband the prince as a wife should, he was not strong or full enough to provide me with a child. Within the time that I became with child he had not been close to me as a husband should.

'"And while I served the prince, my husband, I felt no love for him. Nor could I ever have done so. My body and soul were deemed a part of the contract of kingship. My child was made not of kingship but of love and I wish his life to be lived in truths not in falsehoods."' Lorenzo halted again, nodded his head slowly and, between wheezes, said to the room, 'We have a woman of strong spirit here, strong spirit indeed. And there is more.'

'"I shall not name the father of my child. But let it be recorded here, if nowhere else, that I loved him in the way a woman can and in the way the Lord designed, whose teachings he knew well. He must remain hidden for fear of what fate would deliver him should his identity be revealed. I could not allow such a thing. The Lord shall judge us both. But, so that you know I do not write in falsehood, you will find within a cross of our Lord Jesus given to me by Bartolommeo on the night we were wed."' Lorenzo held the cross up above his head as he continued reading. '"He told me I was to keep it with me, close to my heart. If I should be separated from it then I had been separated from the prince, my husband. Now you have the jewel and my soul is at last released from its false bond for ever. The child carries no Strossetti blood and cannot take the throne as one."' Lorenzo folded the letter up and recited the next line which he appeared already to have memorized. '"The succession passes to the heirs of the Medicis as marriage demands."'

He looked at the cross in the palm of his hand again. 'The rest of the letter is merely an apologia.' The old man who had examined Claudia so closely a few minutes before closed his eyes and rapped his stick gently upon the wooden floor, deep in thought. The others leaned across to one another to discuss the meaning of these things, the ramifications and the upshot, the tactics and the rewards. Claudia remained motionless on her stool in the middle of the room, listening to the murmurs turn into a roar of wind as a lump rose in her throat. She began to sob.

'Girl, do not weep,' Lorenzo said, without a hint of sympathy in his voice. 'You have served your mistress well. And you have served my family too. The Medicis reward those who perform such tasks. You cannot return to Strossetti, that is clear. I shall find a place for you in one of my households.' He turned to an untidy heap of a man who now stood at his shoulder.

'Sinibaldo. Have the horses prepared for the journey. We should leave for Strossetti today.'

Father Sadini let the heavy lids of his eyes fall closed, and bowed his head to the floor. 'Is that not the most grievous of sins? Really is it not? That a wife should do such a thing? Such a terrible si—'

Bartolommeo turned and bawled at the priest. 'Be silent, old man.' Sadini took a step back in surprise.

'Cousin, please. He is a man of God.'

The prince sneered at Lorenzo. 'Yes, and he is my man of God. He may advise me in the church. Here I am my own counsel.' Bartolommeo returned, for a moment, to staring at the letter that he held in his left hand and the jewelled cross that he held in his right. He looked up and beckoned to Scorza to come and help him as he made his way to the large chair placed at the far end of the room. Scorza took the cross from his master to give him a free hand as he sat himself down. Then he placed it back in the old man's leathery palm. Bartolommeo snorted, spat on the floor and said to Lorenzo: 'What is this thing you do to me?'

When he was first told, earlier that afternoon, that Lorenzo and his party were close by the city walls he had laughed. 'Is he coming to wish my dear Francesco a happy birthday? There is nothing else for him here save celebration.' But later, when Lorenzo had said his 'Dear cousins' and his 'Are we in good spirits?' and had generally picked his way through the slippery language of diplomatic pleasantries, Bartolommeo's mood had changed. The prince had become wary as, with some ceremony, the Medici placed the open letter and the cross into the hands of his host. Then, as he studied Lorenzo's name on the front, Bartolommeo became confused. Why should Lorenzo come all this way just to show him a letter?

His confusion had deepened as he read, each word tugging at the very depths of his stomach, until confusion gave way to misery and misery gave way to fear. He found himself reading aloud in a low monotone as if each word and phrase were a sleeping draught, dulling his senses and clogging his throat. It was old Sadini's witterings that had slapped him awake.

'I do nothing to you,' Lorenzo said, in reply to the prince's question, 'that has not been done to you already.' The two men eyed each other silently. 'Dear Bartolommeo, I do only that which truth demands.'

'So I should believe that this is truth?' The prince waved the letter angrily to make sure all those in the room could see it. 'This vile . . . vile set of false oaths?'

'Cousin, is the jewel that you hold in your right hand that which you gave to your wife on her wedding night?'

Bartolommeo closed his eyes. What was this? How had this happened? Where had it happened? The cross was certainly Joanna's. As he had given it to her that night he had sworn to protect every inch of her young, supple flesh. And now the cross seemed to be burning a hole in his.

'And is this letter that you hold in the left written in the hand of Joanna?'

'Wicked tricks,' Bartolommeo screamed.

Lorenzo shook his head. 'Do you think so, cousin? Do you really think so? You know there's no trickery here.'

Bartolommeo slumped forward in his chair and rubbed the right side of his face with his hand, as if waking from some deep, drugged sleep. He looked up, his eyes now bloodshot from the rubbing. He said: 'They call you the magnificent. Is that for the way you scheme? Shall a Medici become a prince through treachery?'

'So you accept it is true?'

'I accept nothing. I accept nothing at all.' But deep down, beneath the bile that rose in his throat and the phlegm that clogged his lungs, beneath the red hot fury that burned behind his eyes and sparked across his brain, Bartolommeo dei Strossetti already knew he was finished, beaten by the cruellest kind of betrayal. It mattered little whether these things were true or not. Lorenzo had his own kind of truth, a political truth, rich and dreadful, a truth he could make others believe in by conviction alone. That was all that mattered.

'Where is the girl who brought you this . . . this evil?' He spat out the last word.

'Enjoying the protection of the Florentine Republic. She shall not return here.'

'Ah, the great republic. And how shall they like the presence of a prince in their midst? What shall they say?'

'It is a shame, dear cousin. You are so skilled in the political arts and yet your future is decided by that which is outside the disciplines of good government.' Lorenzo walked across the room to examine a rich tapestry that hung on the wall, as if this were just some casual discussion. He kept his back to Bartolommeo as he spoke. 'As you are obviously aware it would be impossible for one such as myself to succeed here. Thus on your death – we pray it shall not come soon – the good government of Strossetti will pass to the republic.' Now he turned to face the prince. 'Its affairs to be given the closest attention of the Signoria.'

'And of course,' Bartolommeo said, 'you control the Signoria. A prince by any other name.'

Lorenzo nodded his head and said: 'It is my great honour that there are those in the government who believe my learning is of use to the republic. But I am only ever its servant.'

'You are no more a servant than I am a . . .' the prince took a snort of breath – 'than I am a farmer of pigs.'

Lorenzo raised both hands and smiled broadly. 'I know only my own role. It is not for me to draw comparisons.'

'Do not mock me,' Bartolommeo shouted as he scrambled to his tired feet, his face reddening, a vein standing proud at his temple. 'Do not dare mock me.'

Lorenzo spoke sharply now. 'So what would you wish, cousin? This letter exists. The future cannot be what you planned it to be because the future is now changed. That is political fact. If I . . . if we, the republic, do not take over the business of Strossetti others will come and there will be conflict. That is not good government.'

Beads of sweat had broken out across Bartolommeo's brow. 'Who are you to lecture me on good government?'

'Cousin, I will leave you now. I fear the strain of today's news is taking its toll and I would not wish you to bring sickness upon yourself. You have your son's . . .' He stopped, chewed his bulbous bottom lip in thought, and then went on. 'You have the boy's birthday to celebrate. We will overnight at our hunting lodge in the next valley.'

And with that they were gone.

Bartolommeo waited until they had left the room. 'Scorza,' he said slowly. 'Fetch my son.'

After a few minutes a maid appeared at the door carrying the child, panting from the effort. Bartolommeo squinted at the mound of flesh the maid held in her arms. 'Let him walk to me. The boy has legs.' Francesco stumbled towards him across the floor, unused to the exercise. His small round body leaned forward over his podgy thighs as he ran, causing him to all but overbalance. He stumbled on until he reached the chair where Bartolommeo sat. The child wrapped his arms round the prince's calves and turned his face upwards to grin broadly at him.

Bartolommeo placed an open palm under Francesco's chin, and ran his hand gently over the smooth, pink skin, around the globe of his face, across his cheek, caressing the child's flesh. He let his palm come to rest upon the top of the child's head, feeling the soft strands of hair beneath his hand. The boy grinned up at him still, enjoying the warmth of the attention, the old man's skin against his.

Suddenly the prince grabbed a thick clump of Francesco's hair and yanked his head back on his neck. The child screeched and began to sob, but the old man did not let go. He leaned forward and looked into the weeping eyes of the boy he had always called his son. And as he stared, leaning down and down, closer and closer, until he could feel the tiny, damp breaths of the tear-streaked child against his own lips, a shiver coursed through his tired body. He remembered the night of the boy's birth, the storm that had attended his arrival; he remembered the eyes of the child's mother as the life slipped from her; he remembered his pain as he saw her hot red blood drip on to the cold stone floor.

And he knew. In the deepest recesses of his mind, in the dark space where fantasy battles with truth and the passions mark out their territory, he knew. Denial was a game for fools. The child was not his.

CHAPTER SIX

When a Florentine man wishes to trust to fate he says *tocca ferro* which, in English, means 'touch iron'. It's a nod to the dense metal that once was pulled from the Tuscan hills and upon which the Etruscans, the gifted contemporaries of the ancient Greeks who first occupied these lands, built their wealth. But there is little of the deep red iron ore to hand for the superstitious Florentines to touch these days. Instead, when a Florentine man now says *tocca ferro* he reaches for that which, in his mind at least, is equally as solid, equally a source of his power and strength; he clasps his right hand about his balls and grins.

On this, the morning of his trial, Professor Robert Kelner could frequently be heard saying *tocca ferro*. He was even managing to smile as he said it. But, though he felt at ease in Florentine society, could pass comfortably through its exotic salons generally holding his place in the carnival of expertise that attended the modern world of art history, his right hand never went anywhere near the tired old sac which hung loosely within the folds of his tired old corduroy trousers. It just didn't feel right.

For true Florentine men it is a gesture born of the unconscious, as if there is some invisible cotton thread tying the hand to the groin which could pull the one to touch the other when the moment demands it, regardless of what the women may think of them as a result. Even if he had once possessed such a thing Kelner's cotton thread had certainly now been snipped; however hard he tried to consider himself a Florentine by adoption, the two ends could not now be retied. These days he had to make a conscious effort to find his balls at all. But then true passion, he had always said, as if in unwitting defence of his cool reserve, should be an affair of the intellect, not a crude response to some primeval urge that refuses to lie down.

This humid Saturday morning, then, he stood in the old oak-panelled café on the Piazza San Firenze, rapping his bony knuckles against the marble bar, drinking his coffee and, like so many members of the accused before him, considering his chances in the case that was soon to begin in the grand old courthouse across the road.

'In the name of free speech,' he said in Italian to the little band of students who had gathered to watch their teacher go into battle, 'we shall win. Believe me, we shall win. Touch iron.' He sipped his coffee and listened intently as each of his pupils competed with the next to find a better metaphor, a sharper example, with which to damn Conte and his fellow restorers. He was the angel of death, they said. Restorers were the forces of darkness, come upon the earth to rape it of its virtue, to destroy those masterpieces within which lay the very essence of human experience. To the gallows with the lot of them. And then they shook their heads, and sighed and sipped their coffee once more. Fiammetta Kelner stood by her husband's side and said nothing.

The clatter and rush inside the café threw Alex at first. He had been looking for a little calm; a dark, warm place where he could nurse the ache behind his eyes and still the shifting liquid mess into which his brains had dissolved overnight. This certainly wasn't it. He took a deep breath and steadied himself against the door. Thank God Isabella had stormed out when she had. His drinking hadn't stopped then but it had slowed a little, particularly after Conte had clapped him on the back and left as well. But he had stayed to drink by himself, slowly and steadily, glass after glass for, oh God, how many hours was it? Who could know?

He stood up as straight as the thud in his head would allow, and then eased himself through the huddle to the centre of the room. A coffee. He needed a coffee. And a cigarette. Then he would feel better. He passed Kelner with one upraised palm in salute – as much a shield against unwanted words as a friendly gesture – and shifted, right shoulder forward, through the crowd, to the left then to the right, then a left again, a zigzag through the human obstacle course to the marble slab bar which he all but fell against.

'*Un cappuccino*,' he said to the waiter as he dug into the depths of his jacket in search of a cigarette. He lit up, breathed deeply and, after holding it for a moment to feel the smoke cling to his lungs, released what little his body would allow to go free.

'You smoke too much,' a woman said.

Alex looked to his right. Isabella was standing beside him. She had obviously been there when first he slumped against the bar. She had one toe slightly up off the ground, resting on the chrome foot rail and she held her shoulders square. She did not look up from the newspaper which she held flat against the marble before her.

After a moment's thought Alex said, 'I don't smoke enough.'

'It's an ugly habit. Why should you want to smoke more?' Still she did not look at him.

'It's like this: I know I'm not going to give up because I like it too much.' He coughed slightly, the last of the hacking spasms, this as every other morning. 'So I reckon that if I just smoke more and more, I'll eventually get to a point where my body will have had enough and it will react so badly against the fags that I'll never be able to smoke again.'

Now Isabella looked up. She nodded her head slowly as if to say, 'So what kind of prick are you?' and then returned to the paper. Silence. The waiter brought Alex his coffee.

'Miss Strossetti.' Silence. 'Isabella.' Eyes on newspaper.

'Signorina Strossetti. I'm sorry about last night.'

Silence still.

'Really, I behaved appallingly. I'm not usually like that.' Try a little confession. Appeal to her better nature. 'I don't normally drink. I'm not used to it. That's why I got so out of hand. It may sound like a feeble excuse, but it is the truth.'

She looked up, raised her eyebrows in disbelief and returned to her paper.

'I can't apologize enough. It was wrong of me. I'm sorry.' And he was. He hadn't wanted to upset her. Really. He had wanted her approval. He had wanted to be liked, to see her laugh at his jokes and his stories. But it hadn't turned out that way. It was just one of those nights, whisky-injected, liquor-driven. He began gathering up his things – cigarette packet, matches, coffee – to move off down the bar. There was little point hanging around for hard silences.

He said, 'If it's any consolation I'm paying for it now.'

'That I can see. You look terrible.'

'Thank you.'

She shrugged. 'I think the truth is important.' This time she didn't return to her paper.

'Will you accept my apology?'

Isabella gave the smallest of nods, almost a twitch. 'I may,' and she let a thin smile creep across her lips. 'I must go and meet my father now. He is a witness for Kelner. I will see you in there?'

Alex said she would. She picked up her bag, folded the paper under her arm and left.

A few minutes later he followed her. Across the narrow piazza, still in shadow this early, but already smelling of hot dust; up the steps that stretched, bleak and grey, along the front of the building; past the yawning carabinieri who stood guard by the door, their aged automatics slung slack at the hip, and into the vast, echoing depths of the foyer. It was cool and dimly lit in there, granite clad and quiet, the space so vast that even the loudest of voices seemed to be swallowed by the shadows. He was directed up another set of stairs and along a corridor, its stone ceiling over-arched like some sparse cathedral crypt, the floor laid with parquet the colour of polished conker.

Ahead he could hear a murmur of voices, high tones cutting gently through the air. He padded slowly towards it. Soon the corridor broadened out and he found himself on a wide gallery that ran along three sides of a vast covered courtyard. Along one wall were three sets of double oak doors twenty feet apart. Groups of people stood in alcoves and by pillars, both audience and cast, apparently waiting for the doors to be thrown open wide. At the far end he could see Conte standing proud of his circle, head slightly bowed to catch the chatter that flowed below his earshot. Isabella stood with her back to him a little way in from Conte, talking to an older, well-dressed man whom Alex took to be her father. The lawyers, better dressed still, sat on the benches that ran along the outer edge of the gallery, briefcases on their laps, noses buried deep inside, like grizzly bears trying to pull fish from a river's flow, the better to justify their enormous fees. Occasionally they would find a prize – an unremembered piece of evidence or a mislaid precedent – and pull it out to show a colleague who would nod supportively. Then they would replace it and search for another.

And the Florentine art experts, shabbily dressed in a studied sort of way, the ones who had come just for the hell of it, for the thrill of the case, milled around, talking conspiratorially and laughing loudly at each other's whispered jokes.

Alex leaned back against a pillar in a quiet corner, withdrew his notebook and began scribbling. More details: the smell of strong tobacco on the warm air, the tattered notices on the walls, the symbols on the coats of arms above the doors. He knew he should be talking to people, panning for quotes, but he couldn't face it. Not yet. This was easier. He looked down into the courtyard as if checking to see if there was anything exciting there, enjoying the pretence of working while actually just staring blankly into space.

'Used to be a monastery,' a woman said in a hard, east coast American accent. He looked round but there was no one there. Then he looked down and found her. She was short, round and dark with a single eyebrow that weighed her moon face down making her appear even shorter than she was. In one hand she held a notebook.

'What's that?'

'This place. Used to be a monastery. Before that there was a Roman theatre on the spot. Kind of makes sense, don't it.'

'Yes. Makes sense.'

'Who you covering the case for?' She pointed at the notebook in his hand.

'Oh, *London Correspondent*.'

'Yeah, for what paper?' She looked confused.

'No, I'm a reporter with the *London Daily Correspondent.*'

'Ah, yeah I know it. So you been here long? You based in Rome? Or isn't Bernard thing in Rome?'

So many questions. So fast. 'Coolahan. Bernard Coolahan's the chap in Rome. And no, I flew in on Wednesday. From London.'

'They flew you in from London? So they're taking this Strossetti stuff seriously. Me, I came from Milan.'

'Who are you with?'

'Hell, sorry.' She reached into the front pouch of her leather bag and dragged out a card. 'Raisa Sharpe, *New York Times.* That's sharp with an e.'

'Thank you. Alex Fuller. Sorry, I don't have a card.'

'No problem. Alex Fuller. Easy to remember. Who you talked to so far?'

Alex hated this kind of competition. Professional rivalry passed off as native curiosity, but he didn't have the energy not to play the game. 'Kelner and Conte, and one of the Strossettis. It's shaping up.'

'Yeah, you haven't talked to Falchi? Soprintendente for art in Strossetti? You should talk to Falchi. He's vital. Got more to answer for than Conte.'

He knew she'd have one up her sleeve, one he hadn't found. He just knew it.

'You've been covering this case long for the *Times*?'

'Yeah, in and out, in and out. It's big stuff this. Or about as big as it gets in Florence. Nice town but small, you know. Provincial. I only come here to visit. Still, they've got everyone out for this.'

'Big political story, right.'

'Political sure. And legal.' If he'd said political and legal, she'd have said 'and social too'. He nodded, and wondered if she might not prove useful after all.

'Anybody here you recognize?'

The American looked round. Kelner was now approaching them up the stairs, surrounded by his huddle of students and an older man. Fiammetta took up the rear. Raisa Sharpe gestured in Kelner's direction.

'See the stocky guy with Kelner? The older fella? That's Jim Beck. Another American professor. Columbia I think. Also on the restoration scene. Made a big noise about that job they did on the Sistine Chapel a while back. Kind of follows this sort of stuff. Frankly I don't think he likes Kelner much as a guy but sort of respects him for what he's doing.' Kelner and his crew walked past the two journalists without acknowledging them.

Alex pressed the palm of his hand against his left temple to try to ease the throb there. Why had he drunk so much whisky?

'Yeah, see the guy with the greased-back hair?' Sharpe was pointing to a huddle by the middle doors. 'He's interesting. Something to do with the chemical companies but, shit, I can't remember his name.' She turned to look at Alex, eager to dredge up some more information to reassert her authority. 'You know the chemical companies have got a lot of money in this. Kelner wins and they have to have this big debate about restoring things. And the Italians, they do not like debating. It isn't the way they do business. And if they decide restoring's out, then all the chemical firms have to find something to do with all this stuff they've developed for cleaning paintings. Serious business.' She was scanning the gallery once more. Alex made a note in his book: chemicals, cash.

'Up by Conte. With the tight curly hair. A little shorter than

Conte. He's a restorer. Well known. Trained with Tintori, the Florentine restorer who did that work on Masaccio's Trinità?' Alex didn't have the first idea what she was talking about. He nodded. What else was he supposed to do?

'Well that guy up there, he's Giovanni Caponi. They like to stick together, these restorers. It's sort of a . . .' There was a loud click from the middle doors and people started to move towards the courtroom.

'Hey. I think we're on. See you later.' And with that Raisa Sharpe was gone, swamped by the crowd into which she had dived. Alex leaned away from the pillar that he had been resting against, said simply, 'Oh well, sod it,' and trailed in.

He found a spot at the back of the courtroom where he could lean against the wall to soothe the kidney ache in his lower back. It was brighter in here than out on the gallery but not by much. Though the walls were painted an even white, a thick layer of yellowed grime had gathered on the outside of the high windows, draining the sunlight of its strength and giving a dour air to the room, even on clear days like this. But at least it was cool. Alex braced himself against the wall, pushed his feet against those of the people in front of him, easing out a little more floor space from the crowd, and hoped the hearing wouldn't take long.

The mood in there was not what he had expected. Alex knew about the Italian passion for bureaucracy, that the filling of government forms was a precious sacrament to which they were all devoted. He knew that the state employed a greater proportion of the population than any other country in Europe. The outward appearance, therefore, was of a nation with a highly developed sense of *res republicae*. If that were the case then the judicial process would be a vital state ritual, the trial an act of civic faith to be observed with furious and hushed devotion. But here, in the diluted sunlight of court number three the mood seemed to be relaxed, almost chaotic. At the far end was the judge, black-gowned and well groomed. He was leaning back in his seat and chatting casually with the two parties who sat in two rows facing each other across the court; Kelner to the judge's left, Conte to his right, each with two lawyers. Between Conte and the judge there was a walled platform which Alex took to be the dock. There was no jury that he could see.

Closer in, there was a low wooden wall which separated the court from the rest of the room so that the press and public were corralled off. There were three rows of plastic seats, six in each, and then some floor space. All the seats were full as was the standing room. But there was no formality here in the audience. People nattered to each other even as the judge took what Alex assumed to be the opening remarks. The crowd shuffled its feet and tapped each other on the shoulder, and wandered – as much as they could wander in such a crowded place – from where one friend stood to the next. If any of them were awed by the experience of witnessing Italian justice being dispensed, they were managing to disguise it very well.

Alex looked around. Standing down at the front in one corner, where the wooden barrier met the wall, was Raisa Sharpe, dark and compact, resting her elbows on the top of the barrier and leaning forward as if in concentration. I will have to find a translator, Alex thought to himself. And soon. He listened to the mess of talk coming from the far end, the strange latinate babble that he could make no sense of, the shape of the words swallowed up by a mass of people before him. French he was comfortable with. Arabic he wasn't bad at either. But Italian? There had never been any need to learn Italian.

He saw a woman over in the front row bend down to pick up her bag, scrabbling around on the floor by her feet. Was she leaving? She was just beginning to get up. Alex made a dash for it, shoving his shoulder hard against the crowd and muttering '*Scusi, scusi,*' as he pushed towards her. He made it to the end of the row just as she was leaving it, pushing himself back against the wooden barrier to let her pass, grinning as he did so. Then he made his way, past the knees of the other seated spectators, to the now empty chair.

Isabella looked up at him from the next seat.

'That was fast work,' she said as he sat down.

'Sorry?'

'I didn't even see her move and then suddenly you are in her seat.'

'It's called having your eye on the main chance,' he said, as he arranged his bag at his feet.

'Hmm. From last night I know you are good at thinking only of yourself.' She turned back to the judge and leaned forward, resting her head in her hands.

Alex studied her beautifully tailored back, wrapped in a jacket of fine blue cotton. She had not yet forgiven him. That much was clear. He had better stop trying to make her forgive him and carry on with the job. He touched her gently on the shoulder. It was a little bonier than he had expected. 'Isabella?' She looked round. 'I was wondering why there is no jury.'

She considered him for a moment as though, like so many women before her, she was trying to work out what it was about his eyes that she found so striking. She dropped her gaze. 'You want me to translate again, don't you?' she said eventually.

Alex shrugged. 'It would help me.'

'You have a cheek.'

Oh Lord, he thought, here we go again. 'I did try to say sorry.' He had his eyebrows raised in apology. 'And I really didn't mean to upset you last night.' Isabella nodded slowly, studying his face again as she did so.

'I cannot apologize enough.' Please don't make me beg, Alex thought. I'm not good at begging. Never have been.

'OK,' she said finally, leaning back in her seat, 'but why I help you now I don't know.' Alex leaned back in his seat so that they were nose to nose and grinned broadly at her. She hesitated, as if she were about to change her mind. Then she spoke.

'These small criminal libel cases, they never have juries,' she said. 'The evidence is too complex. So many hearings to be had. You will see. This case will not be finished today. So it is only a judge who decides.'

'The case won't finish today?' Alex felt his guts fall in disappointment. He had thought he could wrap up the story this morning, quotes and all, and then get back to London, to whatever was waiting for him there. He sighed deeply. But even as he did so, even as he realized that the whole trip would become so complicated if there were no decision here today, he felt a little twang of pleasure somewhere just in front of his aching kidneys. Perhaps he could stay for longer? A break. It appealed and he didn't quite know why.

'No, they cannot finish today. Already they are arguing over evidence.'

'Oh yes?'

'Yes. Kelner wants to call people who will say Joanna has been damaged. That is why my father is here as a Strossetti. He is sitting outside . . .' Isabella waved one hand towards the door – 'waiting to tell the court what the family thinks.'

'So?'

'Conte's people have said it is nothing to do with Joanna. Just the language used by Kelner. Whether he libelled Conte in what he said.'

'Oh, I see. It's a game of semantics.'

'Sorry, what is semantics?'

'Good question. Games with language. And the judge? What's he saying?'

'He is just hearing all these things. He will not say yet.' She stopped talking and turned back to listen. After a minute she leaned over to Alex and whispered conspiratorially so that he could feel the tip of her nose against his ear: 'The judge knows this is important. He knows people like you are watching him.' She leaned away from him and smiled broadly, a warmer expression than she had dredged up before, a smile that said, 'So you are a part of this as well now. Both you and me.'

Alex said, 'Why so important to him?'

Isabella placed her fingertips against her lips in thought. Then she said, 'Firenze . . . Florence . . . It's small. The big towns in Italy, they are run by the politicians. The political parties split them up between them. But Florence, it's too small for the politicians. So instead it is run by the masons and the bankers and the judges.' She laughed a little. 'Often they are the same thing.'

Alex nodded. 'And the Joanna case is important to Florence?'

'Sure, for the judge it is like a government decision. They must make the city look good, especially to the foreign press. It's as Kelner said. They don't want to look like they do not care about the Joannas.'

Alex scribbled into his notebook. Then he settled back in

his seat, allowing the drone of the case to wash over him, the mutter and the grumble and the shout. His head ached less now than before, but still he was tired, in a way that he knew only another night's sleep would relieve. He slid further down in his seat, so that his buttocks stretched against its smooth plastic edge and looked over at the yellow glare of the nearest window, searching the dulled corners of his mind for a daydream or a fantasy, rich and wish-sodden, something to fill up the spaces in his head where it still hurt.

Real life as dreams. The backbone of time and order broken by bitter remembrance; on the road again, hot and dusty still, but moving. Rough now. Wheels hitting rocks. The Land-Rover rolls but always steadies, stays upright. Driving north to a place they've decided to call home, for the moment at least. Sun hot on their too-bare necks. Fatigue. On the floor, the body. One black hand sticking out from under the sack, now stained with blood, purple-brown against the canvas. In the corner the killing stick. Stark and black, barrel sharp, trigger hidden. It rattles against the metal sides. Rat-a-tat-tat. Metal on metal. A man's voice keeps saying: 'Alex you did all you could. Alex you did all you could. There was no more you could have done.' And he hears himself say: 'But he's dead and I was there.' The wheels bounce. The Land-Rover rocks but stays steady. The dead man stays still, attended only by the flies and the dust.

Dead people. You can't interview dead people.

'Ah, it is as I told you.' Isabella was nudging Alex. He sat up, shaking his head a little to clear his mind.

'What's happened?'

'This man here who is giving evidence now.' She pointed to a neat little man who was sitting on the witness stand. 'He is a professor from Padua, an art historian like Kelner. He wants to say that Joanna has been damaged but the lawyer for Conte, the one standing up, he won't let him. He says this is not what the case is about.'

'What does the judge say?'

Isabella leaned forward to listen. 'Oh. He says he will hear the professor for now.'

There was a shout and a gasp and a scuffle from behind them to their left. Everybody turned to look, flicking their heads round like the crowd at a tennis match following the ball. A round, middle-aged woman who had been standing up against the wall had fainted in the heat, her legs crumpling beneath her and throwing her back into the arms of the man who was standing behind. She lay there, grey-skinned and limp, his broad hands beneath her armpits the only thing keeping her from hitting the floor.

Isabella stared at the man. He was well built and in his forties, his hair cropped flat-top short and brushed through with grey. He wore a dark blue canvas jacket and jeans and he appeared to be chewing on something, but it wasn't clear what. He was turning round to the people behind, asking them to clear the way, to give him space, so that he could drag the unconscious woman out the door.

Alex said, 'Do you know him?'

Isabella slowly shook her head. 'I don't know. I know him from somewhere. He is so . . .'

'Familiar?'

'Familiar, yes. He . . . I saw him in Strossetti I think but I don't know where. Some time.' She followed his progress out the door with the body in his arms and when he had gone turned back to face forward. 'I will remember, I'm sure. These things return eventually.' She moved her small frame slightly in her seat. 'What did you think of Strossetti? It is pretty, up there in the mountains?'

'I wish I could see it,' Alex said. 'I'm afraid I haven't yet been able to get there. It's quite a drive and I haven't had time to leave Florence, what with all the interviews I've had, and . . .'

She looked at him. That face again, thought Alex, the one that said, 'You are an idiot.'

Suddenly Conte's lawyer was back on his feet, waving at the little man on the witness stand.

'What's going on?'

'He is objecting again.'

The judge considered the lawyer for a moment and then leaned down from the bench to consult with someone Alex thought might be the clerk of the court. Now there was a real silence, the crowd hushed by what they guessed was the first substantial development of the morning.

Isabella whispered to Alex: 'I think they will stop the hearing now and leave it for another time.'

'How long does it usually take?'

'A couple of months, maybe three.'

Alex shook his head and let out a loud hiss of breath.

'You might be lucky,' she whispered. 'It is an important case. Maybe just a month.' Alex shook his head again.

Finally the judge had spoken.

'Well,' Isabella said, her voice tinged with surprise. 'It is an important case. You are in luck. He will decide what evidence can be heard during the week and there will be another hearing next Saturday.'

Already the court was emptying, the herd shoving towards the door, desperate not to spend any more of a warm early summer Saturday locked up here, in the civic gloom.

'I think you should go to Strossetti,' Isabella said firmly, as they inched their way towards the door.

'I would like to,' Alex said. 'But I'm not even sure I'm staying in Florence. I . . .'

'You can stay long enough for this. What have you planned for tomorrow?'

'Well, nothing . . .'

'Good. Which hotel?'

'The Europa. On Lungarno delle Grazie. By the river.'

'I know it. You do not have a car?' Alex shook his head.

'Then I will collect you at nine. No, make that nine thirty. It is Sunday after all.' And with that she turned side-on to him, slipped her narrow shoulders through the cracks in the crowd and disappeared. By the time Alex had got out on to the gallery she had gone.

He didn't mind. Somewhere in the crush to get out, somewhere among the mess of sweaty flesh and damp clothing that had shuffled along the floor, Alex had already decided he would stay, for a little while at least. There was something about being here in Florence, among the old stones and dry bones that, for a reason he could not yet explain, he found comforting. It was as if the world had been put on pause; as if his life, with its strange memories and their dangerously sharp edges, had been allowed to stop, here among the battles over dead women and history.

A strange calm. He decided he was meant to stay. Why else would the case have been adjourned? They were pausing that too. Everything had stopped, at least for now.

And anyway, he had a date.

CHAPTER SEVEN

An hour's ride from the chamber where Bartolommeo first learned of his wife's betrayal there was another land governed by another Strossetti. Piero, the prince's younger brother, ruled his tiny world by delusion and sickness, a prince in his own poisoned universe; ministered to by neurosis, advised by fear. The sandstone walls of the fort, in which he had been incarcerated by his elder brother some thirty years before, were the borders to his country. The spartan room where he slept was his city, the small orchard and vegetable patch at the rear his lands. The well was his river and the wood pile his gold.

The world outside, he told his loyal subjects, was patrolled by demons, sharp-horned and hairy; terrible monsters who wanted nothing more than to own the souls of those inside so that they could be cast into the guts of hell. Serve him well, Piero said, and he would protect them. He listened to the rustling of the leaves on the lemon trees and heard what they said. He ordered the cicadas to be silent and the well to flow with wine. And then he settled down to discuss matters of philosophy and science with the chickens who pecked at shards of flint in the yard.

The three old monks who shared Piero's isolation, attending to his needs as best they could, had long ago stopped taking any real notice of the mad Strossetti's behaviour, even when he worked himself into a fury because the well insisted on flowing with water and the cicadas refused to be silent. In return Piero treated the monks as though they were imbeciles, sad souls who were too stupid to understand the complex workings of the world around them, more to be pitied than abused. The arrangement worked well. There was a rhythm to life in this fort, its familiar beat dictated by the twists and turns of Piero's deformed moods. Outside he had become a faint memory, a detail scrubbed out by time. Inside time had long ago been halted.

During the years immediately after Bartolommeo secreted his brother away, he visited often, riding down each Sunday afternoon to share olive bread and wine with the young Strossetti. But as time passed those trips became less and less frequent, the older brother finding the pressures of state duty and a heavy dose of guilt over Piero's imprisonment had robbed him of any desire to make the trip. Sometimes a year or more would pass between visits. Piero never seemed to mind. Isolated from the rest of the world, his madness was allowed to run whatever course it chose. The universe he had constructed around him expanded in size rather than shrank. There were always new messages to be plucked from the sounds in the gardens, new friends to be made among the trees and the bushes. Occasionally, whenever his mind overflowed with paranoid delusions, the utter certainty that those demons who stalked him from behind the walls were finally coming, he did become distressed. But he also took perverse pleasure in the battle between good and evil that raged inside his head. He was a warrior, duty bound to triumph. It gave him a sense of importance, a pride which made him feel he could greet his brother the prince as an equal.

'Come,' he would say. 'Prince to prince. We shall take a tour of my country and I shall show you the advances and developments we have made.' He would lead Bartolommeo around the ragged gardens, pointing out the piles of stones he had heaped up against the wall, his new armoury in readiness for the final battle. Or he would command him to look deep into the well to see the diamonds and emeralds that sparkled at the bottom as the sunlight flashed upon the water, his country's store of wealth. If Piero still remembered that Bartolommeo had determined, so long ago, to rob him of his chance to take the throne, he did not say. This was his life now.

When Brother Rubeo, the oldest and plumpest of the three monks, informed him this cold bright February morning that his brother was coming to see him, Piero nodded sagely. 'We shall have matters of state to discuss no doubt,' he said. Then he settled down on a garden bench, fell into a dead-eyed stare and waited.

The prince stood at the far end of the garden watching Piero in silence, studying the motionless figure, now slightly stooped by age. That the pustulant adolescent Bartolommeo had sent here so many years before should now be a man in his middle age, hair receding, brow lined, disturbed him greatly. When those who were your juniors become old men themselves is not the cycle all but complete? The younger man stared at the ground just before his toes, his shoulders slumped, a palm rested on each knee. There was normality in this quietness, the prince thought. All men can be still. Lord, if Piero could just be like all men. If the madness had left him, the poison been released. That would be salvation indeed. If Piero were well enough the younger Strossetti could succeed his brother. Find him a wife, pack them off to bed, and the succession would be secured.

On the journey from the castle Bartolommeo, his mind dulled by the rolling gait of the horse that carried him, had freed his thoughts to wrestle with each other. He had let hope be the master of his fantasies, dreams write fortune's script. After all, it had been more than a year since last he had visited his brother. What could he truly know of the man's condition?

With Lorenzo parading Joanna's betrayal before the world and laying claim to Strossetti from the mountain tops to the river beds even before Bartolommeo was gone, drastic measures were called for. If Piero could be trusted; if the man were strong enough, if he made even the slightest bit of sense, then there might just be a way.

The prince walked over to where Piero sat and touched him on the shoulder.

'Brother,' he said softly. Piero raised his gaze from the ground and looked at his visitor. He nodded slowly in recognition and then returned to intense contemplation of the ground before him.

'May I sit?' Piero said nothing. Bartolommeo studied the top of his brother's head, the patch of pink-grey scalp where the hair had fallen out, and decided he would sit anyway. For half a minute Piero did not move. Then he raised his head again, turned to his brother and said slowly: 'So, sir, how does fortune find you?' Bartolommeo smiled. A good, rational question. He patted Piero gently on the shoulder.

'Well, brother. Well,' the prince replied.

'That is good.'

'The weather has been fair.'

'Yes indeed, the weather has been fair. No disease among your subjects I hope?'

'None beyond the ordinary. And yourself?'

'We had trouble with aphids last summer. And the lemon trees were afflicted by black fly but that is gone. My subjects tell me they are strong now.' Bartolommeo chose not to try to make any sense of what his younger brother had said.

'They care for you well here?' he asked.

'They do my bidding.'

'That is good.' Silence once more. Bartolommeo looked around the small walled garden, turning his face up to the sky and enjoying the thin warmth of the late winter sun on his cheek. He turned to watch the three hens that strutted around the rough ground a few yards away.

'There have been events in Strossetti,' he said finally.

'Events?'

'An act of betrayal.'

'Ah, betrayal. Awful business. I know about betrayal. What has passed?'

'A Medici has come to court with a letter.' Piero looked at his brother.

Bartolommeo went on, dejectedly: 'It stated that Francesco is not my son.' Despite the fact that the younger Strossetti had, in all likelihood, no knowledge of either Joanna or Francesco, he still nodded. Such things as wives and sons were of another world. But Piero was ever biddable, a good listener, primed to respond as necessary.

'Joanna sinned with another,' Bartolommeo said, dropping his face into his hands, easing himself into his story. It was good to talk like this, to say these simple things; to speak where those that heard him could not pass judgement. 'There was an infection in Strossetti you see, a sickness that ate away at its very core.' He stopped for a moment. 'And its name was Joanna.'

Piero looked around the garden. 'Betrayal. Yes, I know about betrayal,' he said. 'Hm, just ask the pear tree over there, if the lying swine will say.'

Bartolommeo was closed in his own world now, his mind shuttered by despair. 'There was an illness I could not see. Eating away, burning away. It's a wicked evil thing, this illness. Silent and invisible. And when you see it, well then the sickness is complete. It's too late. But then I am no physician. I have given my life to Strossetti. Everything I have ever done has been for these lands, and then fortune plays it this way.' He sighed deeply. 'I should have killed the child. I should have known.'

'Oh yes, kill the child,' Piero said distractedly, in a low voice. 'You must kill the child. Cut its head off, so it bleeds. That's the best way. Slash it right across the throat. Lots of blood. Hang it from a tree so the crows can eat it and the blood will run into the ground. A prince has a job to do, after all. Hack the child limb from limb. That's what a prince has to do. I have to do that all the time. It's my job.'

Bartolommeo lifted his head from his hands and looked at his brother. Was this madness womb-made, soul half-formed in creation, or were these things he had learned here? The younger man held himself still, but he was panting now and there was a wildness in his eyes, as if the two sockets were waiting to burst and let free a stream of white-hot fury.

Piero went on: 'Flesh cuts well, doesn't it? Human flesh. Like pig. It's like cutting pig. Except pig squeals and people scream. Different noise: squeal and scream.' He stared deep into Bartolommeo's eyes. 'I prefer the scream. It's terrible work but we have to do it, don't we, us princes.' Bartolommeo shook his head slowly in disbelief.

Piero swung round to look at the three white hens. He jumped to his feet and pointed at them. 'Shut up!' he screamed. 'Shut up. Shut up. Shut up. Do not say these things, never say things. Oh, terrible blasphemy.' He walked in long bold strides across to where they stood and reached down to pick up the fattest of the three, wrapping his hands around its useless wings so that the bird could jut its neck but could not flap. He lifted the squawking creature up in front of him and stared deep into its eyes. 'You are in league with demons. I know it. We shall have no demons here.'

Then he brought the bird down, shoved it under his left armpit and squeezed it there. He turned to face Bartolommeo. Over the squawking he said: 'It's terrible work, isn't it, brother.' And he cackled, loud and hard. Then he wrapped his right hand around the bird's neck and, with his face screwed up in concentration, twisted until there was a sharp crack and the bird's screeching ceased. Piero dropped the dead animal to the ground, knelt down and placed his right knee hard on its body. He placed both hands round the shattered neck and continued to twist.

At first there was only a flash of blood, bright red against the white of the feathers, as the skin stretched and tore. But then, as the flesh beneath ripped and the animal's head came off, the blood poured out over Piero's hands, washing across his knuckles and on to the ground. When finally he had separated the head from the body, Piero, panting with excitement, looked at the mess of raw meat and feathers and tattered skin and said, between breaths, 'Who would have thought? So much blood from such a small demon.'

Bartolommeo looked at his brother with sad old eyes. This madman could never step outside the confines of the fort. That much was clear. There was too much sickness in his soul; the spirit was sodden with infection. Piero was now holding up the tiny, severed head, staring down the dead bird's beak into its eyes. He was saying: 'The demon has gone now. Don't you ever come back. Not to my land,' and swaying gently from side to side.

Suddenly the prince found himself overwhelmed by a powerful feeling of envy, a desperate desire to have the bird's warm blood on his hands. Oh to be insane, he thought, to be spared reality's troubles. What joys to be had from warped contemplation of the heavens. How much better to be a sick man with no cares than to carry the cares of the whole world on your shoulders and be well. How much easier to rip the head off a hen than to keep Lorenzo at bay. Far better a madman for a lifetime than a prince for a day.

A pot of ink to the right. A quill to the left. Between them the paper. The man leaned back, sat up straight and looked at the desk. He was not yet happy with the arrangement; something jarred. He placed the clean quill upon the paper to give him some space and moved the ink to the left. Then he moved it back again. Hell and damnation, how could the order of three things be so complicated? Perhaps it was not the arrangement but the deed they were meant for that was complicated. Where to start such a thing? How to start? So many ways. So many places.

Where does one find the strength to tell secrets?

He put the quill back to the left and picked up one of the pieces of paper. He leaned forward to the window and turned it to the sunlight so that its blank surface all but glowed. He liked the paper's emptiness. It was virgin territory, pure and unsullied. Clean. At the edges he could see where the delicate fibres met, twisting and turning around one another, clinging to each other for strength. What a glorious invention it was, so simple yet so powerful. The salvation of us all. Without paper where would the great city states and principalities have been? Were not riches born of these fragile strands? Could the Florentine Republic have grown so without it? Never. Paper made it happen.

Consider this: before paper a merchant had to accompany

every shipment, be present to see the deal done, or else trust to
memory and good nature. Paper put an end to that. It freed the
merchants to trade where they might. Suddenly he could make
his wishes known by simple strokes of the quill upon the page.
Orders could be drawn up, accounts kept. Paper made it just
like being there. So paper begat trade and trade begat money
and money begat art. And the art was made for the better
glory of God. Here were science and the soul working as one,
commerce and devotion intertwined, like the fibres of the paper
that had made it possible, to strengthen the spirit and make rich
the body. A rebirth indeed.

The only problem with paper was that it could not order
the thoughts you wished to place upon it. So where to begin?
He looked out at the view again, across the castle walls to where
the vines grew, in rough lines up the hillside, and remembered
an early meeting. A first sight. Perhaps best, then, to start with
what he could see.

He placed a piece of the paper in front of him, dipped the
quill in the ink, looked once more at the view and then began
to write:

> *Though the intellect be the centre of man's good*
> *government, charged to show us the path of life that we*
> *should follow, the heart shall tell us truths that can never*
> *be denied whether they prove good or ill. That I knew*
> *my Joanna as I did, that we shared a love born not of the*
> *intellect but of the heart, has shown me that truth can be,*
> *in unison, both good and ill. The heart and the intellect*
> *can work the one against the other. The day I walked to*
> *the vineyard and first saw my love, it was my heart that*
> *ruled my actions and which rules me still. Her body may*

be dead these four long years but her memory and the love it gives me live on.

The air was warm that day, as of summer in its youth, and she stood among the green vines, their branches weighed down in leaf, watching the birds who flew upon the air. I had heard tell of her beauty and had awaited her arrival in Strossetti with dreadful anticipation as any man told of great wonders should. But though there were comparisons with angels, and though it was said the lark would cease its chant when she chose to sing, none prepared me for what I should see. She was not of the blue heavens but of the red earth, as rich and brim-full of life as the very soil that fed the vines she stood among. There was a fullness to her lip and a roundness to her cheek that spoke of a warmth which I wished to reach out and touch then. I wanted to know her, from the first moment, there in the fields, upon the deep, dark sods of earth. I wished to feel the touch of her flesh upon mine and be granted the honour of a journey within.

But she was the wife of another, brought to court to provide the prince with an heir, and I but a mere servant of that court charged to do as I was bid or lose my right to stay. To beg such pleasures as her company would need cunning and resolve. Like the jackdaw who comes upon a lady's table to steal the brightest of her jewels I would need to pluck her away unseen. My own position in the household was neither high enough to allow me to walk freely unchecked, nor lowly enough that I should be ignored fully when I chose a path around the castle. And yet I knew that she should be mine and that we would, when fortune allowed, come the one unto the other.

*In the first days after I had met her in the vineyard
we would come across each other in the house and would
give our greetings in the way of court. But her eyes did
never stop their looking into mine and even when she
turned her body to go on her way still she would have the
delicate curve of her fresh face turned to me. I felt
the sadness of a young woman brought to be the wife of
an old man and wanted to reach out, but occasion did
not allow.*

*It was our good fortune, and great evidence for our
belief that fate played its part in our adventures, that in
those days the prince should still be firm of body enough
to ride out to hunt. When he was younger, so history told,
he would take to the mountains for the full seven days
from week's start to the eve of the day of our Lord. But
now, in fragile health, he would go for only one night.
Though I was charged on occasion to accompany them,
I feigned fever this day and did not follow.*

*At dead of night, when only shadows walked the
castle, I went instead to Joanna's chamber. I stepped into
her room and knelt by her bedside. There I touched her
so that she would awake. She gasped but did not shout
when she saw, by the moonlight, who had come to her.
She still called me sir in the way of court but she laid a
hot hand upon mine and said she had hoped I would come
and that the dark of night was a place for secrets.*

*I took her then, to my own chamber in the corner of
the house, a place so beyond the great halls that a horse
could hide unseen, and vowed that I would lead her back
when the sun next rose again in the morning. In my
chamber I put a flame to a candle and we sat the one*

before the other and looked. We did not speak. In those first minutes of silence, I thought true love need not say its name. But later when we would know who we were to each other, I saw that words too had their part, and that love must be spoken as much by the tongue as by the limbs. There was an ease to her in the quiet hours of the night that played not upon her place as lady of the house but something more. She could talk both as girl and as woman as those who bestride both ages can. There was the sound of a child at play in the way she threw back her head to laugh, and she did not wrap her arms about herself in shyness but was open to me.

We touched that night but did not come to each other. By day we would play our parts in the drama that had been chosen for us as long as there were those around us to witness. But we would choose our times and our places. When she should walk in from the gardens I should be by the door; when I had cause to be in the prince's chamber she would appear, as if by chance, beyond the door as I would leave. And if there was the moment, we would touch our warm lips together and laugh.

Though we were dedicated players, devoted to our charade as much as to each other, our passion brought forward pain from this performance. To want and not to have is agony beyond any the devil might design. It was again our fortune that the prince should choose to set off hunting once more, for the strain of our deceit would soon have made us leave the house, and run like fugitives to find protection elsewhere.

When, at last, by dark of night, we came to each other it was as if the very air we breathed were filled with burning stars that set a fire to our limbs and made our bodies tremble from the smoothness of our soles to the hairs of our head. We drank deep of each other, though that night thirst could not be quenched by a single draught. She was not bound by fear but welcomed in whatever passion I might find within me; she drowned the air with her calls, so that I feared the house might awake, roused by the sound of paradise made flesh. But her voice was as silk and though filled with strength floated off on the night air to join the music that the forest makes by dark. Only Bartolommeo had come to her in this way, but she showed knowledge beyond her years and had ways to bring on pleasure that in my greater age I had not found. That such joys should be there to take I had no doubt was a play of the Lord for nothing of such greatness could be in the devil's gift. If there is sin committed here it is sin in the Lord's name. Whatever fate awaits me I shall take, for heaven has been shown me already and time within the flame of hell could never such remembrance burn away.

There was a bawdiness to her which played against the life of court. She could find comedy in all, watching the carnival of rank and honour that attended the prince and laughing at those who would fight to have their place within it. Do not all men have water to pass, she would ask? Are not all womanhood made to press the wind from their bodies? Beneath those robes of silk and gowns of fine wool are we not all made of flesh that shall have need to speak? In the halls of state she was as heaven's gift to Strossetti and accorded devotion as though she were indeed an angel of womanhood. In the bed she could turn the ways of love to a game to be played with vigour and spirit.

When first she said she was with child a great sadness came upon me. She declared that it was made of our love and that the prince her husband could have no claim upon it. That this love should be given voice by the bawling of our child and not my own tongue pained me greatly. Where was true justice served? Again we thought to steel away. But where to go? A princess with child and her secret love, his place at court at odds with the calling of his heart? Where to hide? How to move, by day or night? We chose instead to live on as we had, wrestling fear of discovery against the warmth of our union, content that the child who rested now in her belly should be tasked with taking our devotion on into the world.

So it has proved. She has gone, her life taken for our sin in a night of rain and anger. The boy lives, the proof of what has gone before. Her death came to me, as an executioner with his blade newly sharpened, eager for his work. A limb has been sliced from me to leave a wound that bleeds into the barren earth. Even still I play my part in the carnival of court of which she made so much mock, but keep my heart hidden and my spirit locked within its jail. Shall it see release? I am not to know. Our son shall live in truth while I live in falsehood. By her actions she has seen to that, favouring the demands of honesty over those of diplomacy. In the words she wrote before her death she made plain the deed, playing the game of politics from beyond the grave. I may only stand and watch, a spectator at a game in which I have already played my part.

And now she has been made in stone, carved for an old man's misplaced admiration, a goddess to bare witness for eternity. Death's kiss has laid immortality upon *her, there in the sight of the Lord. May he be merciful upon her.*

I shall not be granted the right to lie beside my love as we did those dark nights; it is the holy spirit who gives her comfort now. In place of my flesh, instead I place my soul, held within these words. They shall be sealed beside her. There I shall know that the true strength of my love will be nearby to warm the cold marble, and give comfort to the stone lips that never shall pump with blood nor blow their tiny kisses on the wind.

To you, Joanna, I offer this, my heart and my last kiss.

If these words be seen take this to be truth: rare virtue is there in love found by chance.

He put the quill down and looked at the last word he had written. Was it really chance that they had met, or had there been some greater plan? Was he just a player in some larger game whose end would be the defeat of the principality? How could a singular love end in such crisis? Secrets had filled the castle for so long, rewriting its future in the blank hours of the night. And here they were laid out before him, each stroke of the quill so fragile upon the page but so powerful in the reading. And from his own hand.

Outside it was growing dark. He lit a candle, the yellow flame guttering in the gentle breeze from the open window and slamming broken shadows against the wall. He reached over the desk to pull it shut and looked out across the Strossetti mountains, the approaching night now smudging their sharp outline into the sky. Further down, just below the city walls, he could see the prince's horses as they rode back, Bartolommeo perched precariously on the largest of the animals. Around the castle they said he had gone out to the mountains for one last time, a tired old man making his final pilgrimage to see the lands from which his power had once come. Death would not be long now.

The man pulled the window shut and looked once more at the five pieces of paper he had filled that afternoon, the yellow flame spreading an arc of light across the desk. At the bottom he signed his name and beneath it he wrote the date. He folded the sheets over each other and sealed them with a lump of wax heated on the candle. He did not stamp it with a seal. Instead he scraped a crude drawing of a bird into the soft wax. Finally he placed it inside a long leather pouch, thick-stitched and heavy, which had been made for the purpose.

'Ah well,' he said to himself quietly, 'now that's done.' Then lay down on his bed and fell asleep.

CHAPTER EIGHT

They left Florence in the cathedral peace of an early Sunday morning, driving away to the west long before the sun had found the strength to heat up the cobbles or bake the lumps of chewing gum that had been spat mouth-warm on to the streets the night before. Isabella followed the road that led out from the clutter of the old town, through the wider boulevards of plane trees and apartment blocks that ring the city, to where the homes give way to scrubland and factories; the place where ragged sheets of corrugated iron lie long-forgotten, asleep in the brown grass, and breeze-block walls sit cracked and broken, the rubble scattered about on the dry earth, an industrial puzzle waiting either to be solved or thrown away.

The motorway lifted them clear of Florence's rubbish-scuffed fields, filled with the detritus that every city vomits out in time, and into a softer landscape of vineyards, olive groves and pine-covered hills; past the old towns of Prato, Pistoia and Montecatini and onwards towards the sea. At the village of Altopascio they came off the motorway to fill the car with petrol and drink thimble-cups of coffee that sat burning hot at the bottom of their stomachs. Alex smoked two cigarettes and Isabella told him he should give up. Across the coffee steam and tobacco smoke they made friends, in the quiet way of people who find themselves in each other's company for the fourth time in as many days and don't quite know why.

The car became their confessional, the rhythm of the motorway beneath its tyres underscoring their stories; it was a chorus, clanking and mechanical, there to fill the inevitable silences between them when they felt they had finally run out of things to say. Even Alex began to feel comfortable surrounded only by car noise. There was no order to their tale telling, just the unspoken agreement that they had little to lose from being frank with each other, that there was an indecent pleasure to be gained from such moments of honesty with strangers.

Alex went first. He admitted he hated covering stories about art. They were always soft, he said, even when the art was hard. Even if the art was about death or violence or anger, the story would always be limp, a clumsy examination of emotional responses to dramatic events. He preferred to be the one witnessing the dramatic events at first hand, to smell the death and see the violence. It wasn't that he relished these things, just that he didn't feel a painting or a sculpture or even a piece of music could really give you the truth. You had to be there. You had to see to understand. Normally he avoided art stories, left them to people who liked to live their lives at second hand. He went to cover wars. There was always a truth to be found in conflict, even if it wasn't very palatable.

Isabella frowned a little. 'Real wars?'

'Yeah, real wars. People killing each other.'

'Are there any other kinds?'

Alex laughed. 'Not that I know of. A war without dead people. That would be interesting.'

'Why come all this way to write about sculptures if what you really know about is blood and death?' she asked.

It was a negative decision, he said, not a positive one. A few months before, while on a story in Kenya, there had been an incident. That was the only way he could describe it for now. Somebody had died and Alex had been involved. It was complicated. Let's leave it at that. It wasn't that he didn't want to give her details. He did. It was just that he was still trying to get them straight in his own mind, to sort out exactly what had happened. In any case his newspaper had wanted him to stay in the London office for a while after that, to sit behind a desk and research his stories from there, a phone stuck to his ear. But he had needed to get away, to prove to the paper that he was still able to deliver the goods out in the field. If he hadn't got out, he would have been stuck there for ever, shuffling paper and dialling numbers. He had found the Strossetti story and the paper had agreed to send him. That was it. All he had wanted to do was sell it to them. He hadn't really thought much about the details of the yarn before he came, only that it was a route out of London. It had never been a way to get to Italy.

So it felt strange being there in Tuscany, going to Strossetti to visit a sculpture, watching the pine trees flick by and counting the ruptured animals that had been flung on to the hard shoulder by the traffic. He hadn't planned any of it. He almost felt like a fraud. It was all the more strange because, if there was one thing he hated more than stories about art, it was stories about history; stories where what had gone on in the past was more important, more dramatic even, than what was going on in the present. And this story was dripping with history. He could see that already. But that prejudice was a family thing, nothing to do with journalism. It had a long history all its own.

'My father,' he said, 'is an academic. His thing is the classics, Greek and Roman history. He always describes himself as a case of "the unsociable in full pursuit of the unfashionable".' Alex dropped his voice down into the lower registers for the last phrase, as if imitating the older man. Isabella looked blank.

'Sorry. It's my father's idea of a joke. He never was very good at them.'

Isabella said, 'What is bad about him?'

'He turned history into a competition. The whole of life is one big scholarly challenge to my father. Get this: he even named me after Alexander the Great.' The way Alex saw it his old man had set out to give his son something to fail against. It was an academic gag. The kid was doomed by birthright; he would never conquer.

He told her a story: when he was fifteen, angry and sullen and restless, Alex had been caught shoplifting. He had nicked some cigarettes from the newsagents near his school. 'My dad, he comes into my room and he says – and I'll never forget the way he said it – he says, "I didn't name you after Alexander the Great. It was Alexander the sixth. I had a premonition it would come to this." I have to go off and look up his insult in the encyclopedia. Even his abuse had to be scholarly.

'I sit in the school library, thumbing through the *Britannica* and looking up all the famous Alexanders in history until I get to Alexander the sixth. And I find out that he's the Borgia Pope. My dad is saying he's named me after someone who fucks his kids. I mean, how could I respect him after that? I'm a teenager, an adolescent, and he tells me he's named me after one of the most immoral people in history and he thinks I'll be offended? I've never been so proud.'

The two men's relationship had not improved much since; if Alex disliked historians his father now hated journalists. Part of the attraction of the classics, Fuller Senior had always said, was the lack of new documents. He didn't want to spend his time trying to authenticate texts that had been dragged out of the desert somewhere, just so he could catalogue them. If he'd wanted to do that he would have become a librarian. No, what he wanted to do was spend his time re-evaluating the old works. The fewer original texts the better. 'He hated journalists because he said they thought they were making instant history. You know, that someone like a war reporter now thought they were providing the only real first-hand account. He didn't think hacks should be allowed to do that, to produce original documents. Or, at the very least, he didn't think journalism should be thought of as historical record.' Alex didn't know whether he'd become a journalist to spite his father. He had never thought of it that way. The only thing he was sure of was that he didn't want to be like him. Perhaps, subconsciously, he'd decided to make sure that never happened, by doing everything his father hated?

Alex said, 'Who can tell?', and went back to looking for dead animals on the hard shoulder. He had said all he had to say, for now at least.

She had always been fascinated by history, Isabella said, but she was sure that was because she had never had to study it. For her history was a living thing, constantly impacting on the present.

'Then what Kelner said about you is true.'

'About me being a living exhibit?' Isabella shook her head. 'That is his way of saying I am only a bit of the past. He is too much in awe of the past. I am not.'

Some of the Italian aristocracy were like that, she said, strange in-bred creatures with poor eyesight and heart murmurs who insisted on marrying their cousins because that was the way it had always been done. That was the problem with being able to trace your family back a long way. It made it hard to look forward. To have an understanding of tradition, respect for what had gone before, was a good thing. But it was not good to be held captive by the past. Too many members of her family couldn't bear the idea of real change. True, they no longer married each other, but that was about the only real concession to progress. She was not like that. She agreed that being a Florentine banker seemed a bit of a cliché. But there was more to her choice of career than some mad desire to see history replayed on a continuous loop.

'What I do,' she said grandly, 'I do to break with the past.'

For close on 500 years the Strossettis had been involved in banking, sometimes for themselves, sometimes for others. Since 1877, when her great-grandfather had decided to go it alone, the family had been in control of their own banking house again. But the bank was old-fashioned and because it was old-fashioned it would always stay small. Claudio, her father, was a stubborn man, content doing a little business in France, a little in Switzerland and keeping the rest in Italy because that was how it had always been.

'But you cannot just stay with the old ways. Systems have to change. It is like all of Italy. It does not like to change the old ways because they look like they work. Why make waves? Why cause trouble when you can pay the bribes? A *pizzo* here, a *mazzetta* there. Things get done. Not well but they get done.'

'*Pizzo?*'

'Er, it means small bribe. We have many words for bribe here: *bustarella, spintarella, tangente* . . .'

'I wonder which came first,' Alex said, 'the Italian vocabulary or the things it describes?'

'Who's to know? Both are so old. Nothing ever changes here. My father, he does not like to change because he sees that the way things are is working well enough and when I tell him they could work better he does not want to hear. He does not understand that the bank will die if it does not expand. It is not enough to stay the same. The roots are weak. You cannot make good what already is dead. He will only see it when it is too late.'

Alex turned to look at Isabella as she talked, her eyes fixed on the road ahead. He felt something had changed about her. That Thursday afternoon, when they had met in the Boboli Gardens, she hadn't only been hiding herself behind her fine clothes. She had also been wearing a solid layer of emotional armour, an invisible suit as hard as tungsten. It was as if each twitch of her facial muscles, every lift of a finger, anything that might have given away more than she wished, had been kept firmly under control.

But yesterday, in the courtroom, that had started to dissolve. Now it seemed to have gone entirely. She was still tough. He could see that. But there was a softer side to her, an unwillingness to hide her feelings, however strong they might be. When she emphasized a word or phrase – 'the roots are weak' or 'the bank will die' – her nose wrinkled up; and when she talked of her family's history she would let the tip of her tongue just brush against the inner rim of her lip, as if in anticipation of what was still to come for the Strossettis. Kelner had talked about her 'exotic history'. Alex was beginning to get a sense of what those words meant, even if he didn't yet know the true facts of that history. There was indeed something exotic about Isabella, something desperately foreign and other, and he found it increasingly attractive. But then Alex had always found the unknown irresistible. He saw it as a challenge.

Isabella continued telling her story. After college her father had pleaded with her to join the family business but she refused. She already knew she could not change it from within.

'Instead you joined another bank?'

'Yes, and I went to Harvard to get my MBA and then I come back here and get my job in mergers and acquisitions. And when I am high enough there and my father is to retire the family will want me back and I will not just be working in the office waiting for marriage like a good Italian girl. I will be heading the board. It is simple really.'

She eased the car into the exit lane and off the motorway. 'So never tell me I am stuck in history,' she said, slipping down into second gear for the toll booth ahead. 'It is not how I am.' Alex said he wouldn't dare.

The Strossetti family villa, like the thick pine forests that surrounded it, had grown with the passing of the years. Once, Isabella said, there had been just a single rectangular house, low-slung and sturdy, built here to look out across the meadows to the river and the steel-blue mountains beyond. Over time, the family had added to it. Some Strossetti bankers, those unlucky enough to have invested in lost wars or merchant ships wrecked, had been less successful than others and unable to contribute. But those that did find themselves with spare cash in later life had always determined to leave their mark. It had become something of a tradition, a way by which the myth of the Strossettis, the idea that no individual was as great as the family they belonged to, could be realized in stone. They would erect large outbuildings, or add an extra room or even a whole new wing. Sometimes these grand developments were undertaken to provide space for their expanding families, at other times just to provide space for their expanding egos. Either way the building grew.

It was now less a house than a complex, although the seemingly random way in which it had been constructed – a piece here, a piece there – did not show. Each Strossetti had taken great care to see that the element they were responsible for, the bricks and mortar that they had designed to survive them, would not jar with what had gone before. The buildings of the main house now formed three sides of a square, with the original, 500-year-old villa at the top. To one side, facing the barn and the workshops, was the family chapel, a separate building with a small pink dome. On the other, there was a covered walkway from the main house, its ceiling decorated with frescoes, which led to the library.

Alex had been expecting something grand and imposing, a vast, turreted palace like the rotting, stately piles that belonged to the rotting aristocrats of old England, the dismal fortresses that he remembered traipsing around on trips with his family on damp Sundays. But this was warm and inviting. Ivy and honeysuckle scrambled up the walls and wrapped itself around the window frames; there were gardening tools laid out across the front step and two large white dogs slumbering in the sun. And when the wind blew through the trees that surrounded them, as it often did up here in the hills, there was a rush of noise like fine, white sand being poured across marble.

In the centre of the gravel courtyard was a circular walled flowerbed and, in the middle of the flowerbed, a walnut tree. There had always been a walnut tree there, Isabella said. It was another family tradition. Once every generation the tree would be pulled out, turned into a piece of furniture for the house and another walnut planted in its place. She led him inside to see the collection of Strossetti furniture: a walnut cabinet built in 1643, a bookshelf from the 1730s, a table completed in 1957. From an upstairs window in a small bedroom at the back, its walls covered with antique hand-painted paper, she showed him the present family's contribution to the house, a swimming pool they were in the process of digging in the back garden.

'My parents are arguing about this,' Isabella said. 'My father would like it tiled in blue. My mother, she says this is not *rustica* enough. She would like green. My poor father. In this one thing he tries to be modern but my mother will not let him.'

Beyond the treetops Alex could see the old brick towers and palazzos of Strossetti spreading away and across the valley, the heavy stonework shimmering pink and orange in the bright midday sun. The mountains that loomed over them seemed almost to have been placed there by design, a perfect crescent of jagged stone that stood proud, like ramparts, always ready to protect the people of the city from attack. Above the tree line, the peaks were stained a glowing white. In places the whiteness even extended below where the trees petered out, a vast bleached gash in the side of the rock.

Alex was confused. He said: 'Are we high enough here for there still to be snow at this time of year?'

'Snow?' Isabella looked at the view. She started laughing and let her fingers dance on Alex's arm for a second. 'No, dear Alex, that is not snow. That is marble. We are not far from Carrara here.'

He tried not to look as stupid as he felt. 'Do not worry,' she said. 'Many people make the mistake.' And then, 'Come. It is time you met the family.' Up until that moment Alex had assumed they were alone. Sure, the doors to the house had been unlocked and it did look like someone had been gardening but apart from their own footsteps creaking on the stairs he had not heard another sound. Of course, he said to himself, the house was big enough for an orgy to be in progress and they probably wouldn't have heard a thing. As she led him back down the stairs and into the entrance hall he began trying to tuck his shirt back into his jeans. If there were people to meet he wanted to be ready.

Alex stopped his tucking. There weren't going to be any

formal introductions, not to this bit of the family anyway. They were all two-dimensional. The walls were hung with a line of oil paintings, thick, dark portraits whose faces appeared to be glowering from out of the wood panelling, a welcoming committee of elders. She pointed out the portrait of Bartolommeo, the last Strossetti prince, with his square jaw and his thick black hair and his lips clenched hard together. Next to him was Francesco dei Strossetti, who had built the house. She showed Alex the paintings of her grandfather and her great-grandfather and his father before him. They stood together in silence looking at the pictures, the ranks of Strossettis, their varnished eyes turned to the darkness of a wood-panelled corner, the one looking back upon the other down the generations.

'You know,' Alex said, 'I find it hard to imagine you running around these corridors as a child. It's all too dark and depressing.'

'To live with pictures of your family is not a bad thing,' Isabella said. 'For me, my family's history is an old friend. Death stops being frightening because you know you always live on, here in the hallway. They have watched so many of us play as children. Maybe one day I will watch too.'

Alex felt desperately out of place standing there, being presented to the relatives. This was a world of which he could never hope to be a part; in the Strossetti house he could only ever be a journalist, the eternal spectator, trying to gain universal understanding from first impressions. Even Isabella was somehow different here, as though she too carried a layer of the thick varnish that gave the pictures their glow of antiquity. In Florence she was a woman of business. Here, in Strossetti, she was a woman of time. In these mountains she had the confidence of one who knows that the very thing which defines her has survived for the better part of a millennium and that nothing, save death for us all, could destroy it now. She had the confidence of one who knows that time is a commodity which can be made to work for you. She did not flinch before the portraits of these men with their dark eyes and their strong brows. She eyed them as equals, less members of a family than a board of directors, shrewd and calculating, each one determined to lead until they too became portraits, watchers in the hallway, and the next one takes over.

Isabella went and stood in front of one of the earliest paintings, a portrait of a young woman with long black hair and a tiny nose.

'And this is my naughty grandmother,' she said, with a giggle. 'Dead five hundred years and yet she is always my grandmother.'

'Your naughty grandmother?'

'Of course. This is Joanna, and you know her story.'

Alex said, 'Joanna. Ah yes. I know about her.' But there was something in the way Isabella had said 'her story' which made him uneasy. She seemed to be talking about something far more complex than just a death in childbirth or a statue made of marble; as though behind this simple painting there lay some huge joke, from which he was excluded. He waited for a second, summoning the nerve to admit his ignorance.

'Actually,' he said, 'I'm not sure I do know her story.'

'You do not know about her secret lover and the fall of the Strossetti princes?' He bit his lip and shook his head.

'Oh dear,' she said, turning away from the painting. 'I think it is time Alex Fuller had a history lesson.'

She took him to the library – built, she said, by Giovanni dei Strossetti at the end of the eighteenth century – and sat him down behind a small walnut reading table. It was a bright, airy room with an oak floor that reflected back the flood of light from two high windows in the back wall which looked down to the river. Isabella opened one out so that the gentle summer breeze and the smell of the meadow could come into the room. Two of the walls were filled floor to ceiling with books, some in cloth covers of deep red or green, most in leather of black and brown. Isabella went to a central block of three shelves protected by a glass door, which, she said, was the Strossetti family archive, chose two volumes and brought them back to the table.

One was a history of the family bank. The other was a biography of the artist Rafanelli, written in the late sixteenth century by Renaldo Nardi who had been a student of the great Giorgio Vasari, author of the *Lives of the Artists*. Yes, she said, casually turning the pages of the biography, it was a first edition. Most of the books in this library were first editions. What did he expect? Paperbacks?

Almost all of what they knew about Joanna came from the Nardi biography and that had been compiled almost solely from Rafanelli's letters. It wasn't much, but at least it gave the bare bones of what had happened. Using passages from the book Isabella told Alex the story: how important Joanna's child had been to the succession in Strossetti and how she had died in labour; of the commissioning of the tomb and its completion within the castle walls; of the letter that had been delivered to Lorenzo de' Medici after her death and Bartolommeo's discovery that the child was not his.

'Was the identity of the lover never uncovered?'

Isabella shook her head. 'No, but Rafanelli had his suspicions. In a letter he wrote to a friend in Florence he named, I think, four possibilities. Or was it five?' She flicked through the book. 'Here it is. I have always liked this passage.' First, Rafanelli said, there was Vincente, Joanna's sickly half-brother 'who was of such poor breeding, he would not have hesitated to father a child from within his own family'. Next came Father Roberto Corsano who was, in Rafanelli's view, 'a priest too prone to the temptations of the flesh to be truly in the service of the Lord and a man too handsome to be without willing admirers'. Then there was Cesare Scorza, 'but he was so burdened by a passion for duty and honour that it is inconceivable he could have made a cuckold of the prince unless there were an official text to tell him how such a thing should be done. And even if he were to have found this book it is certain the princess would have been asleep before the deed were finished, so lacking was this dour civil servant in spirit.' At one point, Isabella said, Rafanelli even goes so far as to suggest that the father might have been Lorenzo de' Medici himself. 'What better way,' the artist asked, 'to destroy the succession than to create your own bastard in the blood line?'

Alex had been scribbling in his notebook. He put his pen down. 'If Joanna's child was illegitimate, and the House of Strossetti fell as a result, how come there is still a Strossetti family here?' About that, Isabella said, there was no mystery. Up until Joanna's letter was discovered, the child had been known as a Strossetti. Even after his illegitimacy was discovered he kept the name, though he disappeared from the principality just before the Florentines arrived to establish their new government. No one knows where he went. Isabella opened up the second book, the history of the family bank, to the first chapter.

'Here it says that Francesco, Joanna's son, returned to Strossetti, with the agreement of Florence, in 1504, aged twenty, to start the bank.' She closed the book, her story told. She stretched her arms above her head and yawned, her head thrown back so that she could look up to the library's ornate ceiling. Alex liked looking at her in that position, her slender neck tensed, her small ribcage raised up so that her breasts were pushed forward. She looked both muscular and fragile like that, a lithe animal who could easily cross the room in one leap. And he liked being alone in the room with her, raking over the ashes of the family's history, with just the rustling of the trees for company. Sometimes, as she had told Joanna's story, she had reached across to touch his hand or leaned over the table to whisper an ancient family secret, though there was no one around to overhear. He knew that if, later, she reached out to him and touched his hand and didn't let go, or wrapped her arms around his waist and held him there, he would be able to trace it all back to those first, passing touches in the library. But these things could rarely be identified while they were happening and never with any certainty. It was not like a jigsaw puzzle where you could see the pieces fitting as you went along, a picture emerging from out of disorder. Sometimes it was only when you looked back that you could see how it had all snapped together. With hindsight you could analyse; in the present you could only dream.

She dropped her arms, picked up the two books and carried them back to the shelves. Alex followed. She slipped them back in place either side of a large volume bound in rich, brown leather. Alex took it down.

'What's this?'

Isabella looked at the spine. 'I don't know.' She read the title. 'It has the name *Lettere da uno scriba* . . . "Letters from a Scribe".'

Alex opened it. 'There are pages here dated 1508. And you have never looked at this?'

Isabella shook her head. 'There are many papers here that are not looked at. There are many papers in Italy. All the old families have archives. Some keep their papers in cardboard boxes. It is enough that we look after our papers well. We do not have to read them also.'

Alex was flicking through the book. The text was handwritten. Each line was sharp and spiky, the letters digging into each other from above and below, like thorns pushing for space. He liked the feel of the paper, its softness and the way the edges were ragged. But, while it was a fascinating object, it was still a dead thing to him. It was a fragment, a relic of something that was long gone, well buried. Joanna's story was like that. It had been interesting, enthralling even. And Isabella had told it as though it were something that had happened to a close relation only a week or so before. But it had never been alive for him in the way a murder story was alive or a war was alive. None of the participants was there to be interviewed. You couldn't visit the scene of the crime. There were no witnesses. They were all dead people.

Towards the back of the book he came across a poem in two parts: a verse of twelve lines and a verse of four. The text was in Latin but the title was in Italian. In the middle of the title he saw the word 'Joanna'.

'What's this?' He turned the book around for Isabella to look at. She squinted at the page.

'I do not know. It means . . .' She stopped and read the whole line. 'It means where the stones lie will Joanna be silent, or maybe that's be at peace. That's it: Where the stones lie shall Joanna keep her peace.'

Alex looked at the poem. 'It might tell you who her lover is?'

Isabella said, 'True. It might.' And she took the book from him and put it back on the shelf.

*

When Alex Fuller was fourteen years old he lost his virginity to a girl called Cassy Thompson at the back of St Cuthbert's church in Colchester, where he grew up. It was one of those damp, grey late autumn afternoons when the leaves on the ground are beginning to rot and the air smells of bonfires and stale cooking; the sort of afternoon when people do strange things to each other as much to avoid thinking about how gloomy the clouds look as anything else. For the better part of a year Alex had gone to church to look at Cassy, a strapping, breasty seventeen-year-old in the sixth form of his school and the only soprano in the church choir. He liked to watch the way her chest heaved when she tried to hit the high notes. For the better part of a year she had refused even to look at him.

Then suddenly, one Sunday after the service when everybody else had gone off to lunch, she changed her mind. Alex was collecting hymn books, working his way from pew to pew, piling the volumes up under his chin. Cassy went and sat on the edge of the altar, her feet dangling above the ground, and watched in silence for a while. Eventually she spoke. She asked Alex who he hated at school and who he liked. He told her, then he made a joke. She laughed and he flushed with pleasure and embarrassment. She told him to put the books down and come closer. He dumped the tattered pile and went to sit on the front pew facing her, like a child awaiting his first communion. She smiled indulgently and told him to approach the altar. He did as he was ordered. Then she took his hand in hers, pressed it against her breast and whispered, 'Don't be shy. You know you want to.' There were no other preliminaries; she showed him exactly what to do. There was, however, a price to pay: because of the height of the altar he had to stand on tiptoe just to reach her. Every time he thrust his hips, his knees banged against the cold stone.

The experience had left Alex with an abiding fear of churches which, though he knew it to be irrational, remained with him still. It wasn't that the experience with Cassy had been traumatic. On the contrary; she had been everything Alex had ever hoped for and more. Afterwards he even decided he had rather enjoyed bruising his knees. It had given him something to remember her by. The problem was it had all been too good; so fulfilling that, despite his devout atheism, he had never been able to stop thinking that the Lord had somehow been responsible for getting Cassy Thompson to be so obliging. 'After all,' he would say to his friends, 'it had happened on the altar.'

Since that day Alex had always wondered whether God – the God he really didn't believe in – might not feel that this heathen journalist owed him a favour; he wondered whether perhaps he had already been marked out to experience some huge spiritual awakening at a later date, a lurch of the soul that would leave him born again and helpless, in thrall to the ways of Christianity. He knew people it had happened to. His friend Nigel had been a four-pint-a-night man, crude and cynical and devoutly iconoclastic. Then he said God had come to him at the cooked meats counter in Safeways. He filled his house with images of Jesus, swore never to touch the demon drink again and promised to preach the gospel instead. And what about Ed? He claimed to have received his calling while on a cycling holiday in Ludlow.

Now, as a rule, Alex always tried to avoid places of worship. 'For Christ's sake,' he would say, 'if you don't want to catch leprosy you don't shake a fucking leper's hand, do you? So if you don't want to catch God you steer clear of churches. It makes sense. Doesn't it?'

Alex found it hugely disturbing that he should now be in a

Catholic cathedral, less than an hour after mass had finished, the air still thick with the smell of incense, tattered prayer books still scattered about the pews. Surely this was tempting fate? He closed his eyes and shook his head a little just in case his mind was becoming polluted by godly thoughts. There was an intensity to the atmosphere in here he found suffocating. He was weighed down by the idea that the edifice around him, this morbid sweep of shadowed arch and dome, with its stained-glass windows and its gold-leafed frescoes, had been built by people whose faith had been so absolute they would gladly have used their own hot blood to mix the mortar if that would have ensured its completion.

When Alex had first set eyes on the Cathedral of San Martino he had been surprised by its angularity. The outside of the building was clad in square slabs of aged coloured marble, as if it had been constructed from an enormous set of children's building blocks, in pastel hues of pinks and greens and greys. Save for the round, stained-glass window high above the cathedral doors, there were no soft curves or diagonal lines. The façade was almost entirely built on the horizontal and the vertical, a design which only made it appear even bigger than it really was. It was a looming monolith that demanded a sense of awe from all those who stood before it.

Inside, those hard lines were lost in the depths of the shadows, much of the ceiling obscured by blackness as the vault powered upwards to the heavens. Around the walls there were alcoves and compact private chapels with their own altars and their own pews, some in darkness, others with candles flickering a warm orange, a crowd of infant churches tucked beneath the hem of their obese mother's skirt. The only way Alex could get any sense of the building's true size was by staring down the aisles, as they narrowed almost to nothing along the lines of perspective on their way to the vanishing point.

Despite the cathedral's vastness he felt all but overwhelmed by black waves of claustrophobia. It was just too big, as if the whole building were weighing down on his shoulders. The sight of Joanna's tomb did not help. When Kelner had shown him the photographs of the sculpture he had been struck by the shape and the delicacy of the carving but he had not been struck by the person it was meant to represent. There was not a person there, just a lump of stone carved to look like one. It had been another work of art, emotions presented at second hand. But here he felt as though he was looking at the true essence of someone's humanity; not her flesh and blood, nor some mumbo-jumbo about her eternal soul or the gift of everlasting life, but the true idea of who she had been. He desperately wanted to know her story. He wanted to know what her thoughts had been, the sound her voice had made, even what she had smelled like. He gripped the iron rail that surrounded the tomb and stared.

Was this the feeling that had infected Kelner and Conte? Was this what was driving them on, some elemental need to protect that which they could not fully understand? They could touch the stone, run their hands along its curves; they could study Joanna's history and how she was carved. But they could never truly know her. By fighting over her they were able, at least, to declare publicly their commitment to the frozen princess, but that was all. Joanna would not hear them. Joanna would not know. But at least the words would have been said. Alex felt he understood. He could see how the sculpture could shape an obsession.

The marble seemed to glow in the dull cathedral candlelight, as if it were emitting its own kind of energy. She demanded you look at her. Suddenly Alex had a sense of what Isabella was, of how history was a thing she either had to fight or embrace. Joanna was a part of Isabella; they were a part of each other. If he wanted to know Isabella he knew he would have to understand Joanna as well.

Isabella spoke. Alex had almost forgotten she was standing there, facing him across the tomb. She said: 'I have remembered where I saw the man.'

'Which man?' He could not take his eyes off the princess.

'The man in court. The man I recognized, the one who caught the fainting woman.'

'Yes?'

'It was here. In the summer after I came back from Harvard. I spent the summer with my family and I came here to read, by Joanna. He was here too. He is an artist. He was drawing her from many sides.'

'Why? Did he say?'

'I can't rememb— No. He said something . . . I think he said it was a personal project. I think he was learning about Rafanelli or something. I don't know.'

Alex asked if Joanna had really been more striking before Conte had cleaned her. He found such a thing difficult to imagine. Isabella said yes, she had. She had looked her age; there had been a greater sense of depth and form. 'But there was damage. She was starting to break in some places. Something had to be done, though only to save her. Not to make her white and ill like this.' There was a gash across the belly of one of the cherubs, a rip in the smooth marble that, now cleaned, looked like a wound in bloodless flesh. How had it happened? Isabella said she did not know, save that, according to the books, it had been there almost as long as the tomb itself. 'It is called Rafanelli's Flaw. None of his other sculptures has such a thing.'

After a while Alex said: 'I learnt something last night.' He wanted to tell her new things now, as if the relaying of information could be a makeshift act of confession, a purging that would release him from a little of the anxiety that he felt standing here. 'I was reading some cuttings, some articles about Kelner. Ones I hadn't looked at before. You knew he had a son who died?' Isabella didn't look up from the sculpture.

'Yes,' she said.

'I found out what it was. What it was that killed him: muscular dystrophy.'

'What is . . .?'

'Ah, it's a wasting disease. A disease of the muscles. Very nasty. It's hereditary.'

'That is sad.'

'Yes,' Alex said. But the storytelling hadn't released him from Joanna's grip. He was still consumed by the idea of her and the story Isabella had told him and the secrets that were locked away within her tomb. He remembered the book with the poem. He asked if he could borrow it. Not for long. Just so that he could get the poem translated. There might be something in it, answers to ancient questions, hidden in the verse. He would look after it. He really would. He just wanted to know, needed to know. He couldn't explain it.

Isabella walked around to his side of the tomb and climbed over the barrier. She sat on the edge of the sculpture. 'You are that in love with my naughty grandmother?' Alex managed half a laugh. He said he was, deeply besotted, infatuated. He tried to laugh again but he couldn't make a noise. Isabella turned herself around, so that she could lie lengthwise along the tomb, thigh to thigh with the Strossetti princess, hip to hip, her hand resting on Joanna's rounded belly.

'This is how I would be when I would read here,' she said, looking at Joanna's sleeping face. 'My princess would never complain.' She wriggled a little against the smooth stone, until her body was tucked in perfectly against the statue. She turned to Alex. 'It is comfortable here,' she said. And then, 'You can touch her if you like.'

Alex stood, struck dumb. Her words were so unambiguous: she was daring him to say no, daring him to back away. Walk away into the shadows if you want to. Walk away if you dare. His lips were dry. His throat was tight.

She whispered, 'Do not be shy.'

Uneasily, Alex clambered over the barrier.

'You can lean over me,' she said. 'I do not mind.'

Alex reached across slowly as if scared he might frighten Joanna away if he moved too violently. He extended his hand and ran the pad of his middle finger along a crease of her stone gown, relishing the moment. His hand ran across her thigh, his skin barely dragging against the surface, and up over the ridge of her waist band. Isabella was tracing tiny circles with her fingertips around Joanna's belly. 'It is good to feel the smooth cold stone, isn't it,' she said. 'It is solid. You can touch her some more, if you like. She will not stop you.'

He had to lean up and across her so that he could move his hand on to the gentle rise of her marble breast, his belly brushing against Isabella's, her warm breath against his face. He felt her body tense beneath him, the muscles of her tummy go hard, as she leaned forward to press her lips to his neck, once, twice and then again, but so gently that they felt like butterflies' wings beating against him in a summer breeze. He turned to look, her breath moving across his cheek, hot after the cool stone of Joanna. He ran his fingertips around the marble as they touched, closed his warm palm around its curve as she bit gently on his lip, traced circles around the centre and bent to kiss her neck so that she let out the quietest of sighs. She let her hand come to rest upon his back.

'My princess always likes to make new friends,' she said, her eyes closed. 'Now there are three of us here together, you, me and Joanna. Perhaps it is right for you to find a way to read her poem, now you know her so well.'

'It's been a little ménage à trois,' Alex said.

'Two girls. One man.'

'My dream.'

'And she is family too.'

'Such decadence.'

'And we are in a church,' Isabella said, with a giggle. 'On a Sunday.'

Alex stood up suddenly, so that she almost fell back and over the other side of the tomb. She was left sprawled across Joanna's chest, her cheek against the statue's chin. He took a deep breath. Why the hell did she have to say that? Why? She could have said anything. She could have mentioned mammals, fish, reptiles. She could have gone on about broccoli, or the smell of petrol in winter. Anything. Instead she had to point out that they were in a church.

Isabella looked around. 'What? Who's coming?'

Perfect, Alex thought. 'Yes, I thought I heard someone too,' he said quickly, flicking his head around, from one side to the other, scanning the gloom. 'Come on. Let's go.'

He lifted her off the tomb and across the barrier in one smooth movement.

CHAPTER NINE

Antonio Rafanelli stood at the head of Joanna's tomb, leaned over her so that his open waistcoat dangled above her nose, and ran the hardened pad of his middle finger around the place where her right nipple should have been. 'Ah now my lovely,' he said quietly. 'Does that not thrill you? Shall your stone heart not go pitter-pitter-pat from my touch?'

He walked around to stand at her side and leaned down to peer at her face. 'No? Not a twitch? And I am so tender. Shame, poor lady. Made of rock and yet you cannot become hard as other women can. Is that not cruel?' He reached out with both middle fingers and tickled the left and right breasts at the same time, as if swinging tassels from his fingertips. 'Still no stirring? Nothing? What a dull life you do lead. But blame me, my princess. I am the one who has made you, am I not? Your flaws are all mine.' He leaned down and kissed both of the smooth marble mounds, first the left then the right. 'So cold.' He closed both hands over them. 'There. We shall warm you. Now tell me, dear princess, what is the point of these, hmmm? What purpose do these strange lumps serve? None now, that is certain, save to make your gown flow thus.'

He stood there for a few seconds, motionless, looking at the sculpture. 'I shall tell you a secret.' He leaned down to whisper into her ear. 'I prefer a bosom flat. Oh, and dressed with hair as well. Just a little. Black and curled. You will not tell? Promise me this? You will not say?' He stood up and patted her cold cheek. 'I knew I could trust you. Are you not loyal? You have not whispered a word yet.' Then he laughed, loud and sharp. 'I must say I do so enjoy these moments together.' He looked at her. 'But my love, you are so pale. Too wan, I think, too much as in death. This we must correct, for reputation's sake.'

He wandered over to the wall where his paints sat, looked at the freshly worked fresco that sat opposite the tomb and shook his head. 'Such childish daubings,' he said and turned to Joanna. 'But must we not work to eat? Well of course, you are no longer burdened by such worries.' He returned to the fresco. 'If he is happy so shall I be.' He examined a detail and shook his head again. 'So badly executed.' Then he bent down and picked up a stoneware pot of deep red powder, some of which had congealed around the edges where it had been mixed with water. He poured in a little more water and, as he walked back to the tomb, stirred it with one slim finger. Then he placed it on the edge of the sculpture and clambered up on top so that he lay, belly to belly, with Joanna. Finally he picked up the pot of paint and rested his weight on his elbows so that he could work.

'Now then,' he said. 'A little here . . .' The artist smudged red paint against her right cheek. 'And a little here.' He decorated the left. He arched his back so that he could put some distance between himself and his handiwork. 'There. Doesn't that feel better?' He ran his paint-stained finger around her lips, smearing colour all over her mouth. 'The finishing touch. The secret, my love, is all in the finish.'

He sighed and reached down with the cuff of his shirt to rub off the paint. 'Perhaps not. People will talk. They are already talking here, of course. They are talking all about you. Such a naughty one. Such a sinner. Such mischief.' He tutted. 'And so very young. And look, so brazen. You do not even blush.' He smiled broadly. 'Do not worry. I know you well enough. I shall carry your blushes on the cuffs of my shirt.' He shook his stained wrists at her. 'They are here for those who wish to see. Trust in me.'

A door slammed in the furthest recesses of the cathedral. Rafanelli slipped off the smooth marble and listened to the approaching footsteps. 'Now then,' he said, whispering in Joanna's ear again. 'You will not say, will you? We shall keep each other's secrets, shan't we? Of course we shall.' He wiped the last of the paint off her lips and scurried over to the fresco to stand in studied contemplation of his work, as if he had not heard his visitor approach. He even managed to jump convincingly when the man tapped him on the shoulder.

'Lord a'mercy, sir. You surprised me.' He feigned shock, drawing long, full breaths. 'No,' he replied to the visitor's first question. 'The work is completed as you ordered it.' And he waved one hand at the wall. 'But as I have said before, fresco is not where my talent lies. I can only try to serve as best I may.' The man stood back and considered the painting, slowly nodding his head.

'You are right,' Rafanelli said. The artist was more than ready to agree. 'The bird is somewhat large, but is it not in nature thus? I can copy only that which the Lord provides for me.'

He listened to his visitor again. 'To make the animal smaller? That may be possible, though fresco is notoriously difficult to adjust. Once the work is done well, it is as much set in stone as our dear Joanna here, may her soul rest in peace. I can attempt another layer to change the form, if you wish. It may take time to prepare but . . .' The man shook his head and told him not to bother. The fresco would do as it was. Time was in short supply in Strossetti at the moment. He handed the artist the heavy leather pouch containing the letter that he had written the day before. Rafanelli turned it over in his hands.

'Beautifully stitched if I may say so. A work worthy of the Etruscans.' And he smiled broadly. 'I shall do with it as you have bid. And yes, of course, no one else here need know of this. I presume you have the additional remuneration we discu— Ah, thank you, sir.' He weighed the bag of gold coins in his hand. 'Such generosity shall be met with equal measure of discretion. Yes, I shall complete the work this eve. Trust in me.' He walked over to where his tools lay, and stuffed the money into the bottom of a large leather bag.

'Dear sir,' Rafanelli said, rather formally. 'I wonder if you might now do me a service. It is small in nature and will be of interest to you, I think. There is an act I must perform that comes at the end of such a commission and to be complete it must be witnessed.' He stepped over to the next bench upon which sat a study of Joanna's tomb, perfect in every detail, only in miniature; it was just a foot and a half long, half a foot wide and modelled in terracotta. He picked up a number of tools from the floor, a selection of chisels and a large wooden mallet, and slipped them into his bag. Satisfied he had everything he now needed, he handed it to his visitor. Then he picked up the study and lifted it up in front of him with both hands, like a chef presenting a dish. 'Please, sir,' he said. 'It would honour me greatly if you would be so good as to accompany me outside.' The man pulled open the door to the west wing and they walked out, blinking, into the bright winter sunshine.

'You see the hills before us, Scorza? Do you see them?' Bartolommeo stood before the open window staring at the line of high snow-capped peaks. 'All this I took to be my armour. What need did I ever have of mercenaries eh? Why should I ever have had armies? Nature had bestowed upon me her greatest weapon.' He shook his head and turned away from the window. 'Close it,' he said, with a dismissive wave over his shoulder. Slowly, he shuffled to his seat, clearing a wide space among the cushions for his sagging buttocks, before dropping himself down between them, his flesh slapping against itself with a clump as he landed.

'They were my undoing, those hills, believe me. Because of them I attended only to what occurred outside. I did not think of what could come to pass within.'

'Sir, for what is happening here you cannot fault yourself . . .'

'Fault myself? Fault myself? I do not fault myself.' Bartolommeo spat a lump of sulphur-yellow phlegm on to the floor at Scorza's feet. It fell with a wet slap, like raw liver landing on a butcher's slab. 'Do you blame a man for falling ill by infection? Another's contagion cannot be your crime. But what defences are there to disease? How can you fight that which you do not see?'

'There could still be a cure, some remedy that could be found to satisfy all sides.'

Bartolommeo shouted at him. 'What remedy do you propose, oh great physician? Lorenzo holds the advantage, as he always seems to of late. The only cure that there was has now been revealed as a bastard, and no bastard of mine. My own bastard would be enough. That I could stomach. But Francesco, he is a symptom of the disease.' Scorza did not speak. His master stared into the middle distance with moist, rheumy eyes, red-rimmed and bloodshot. He looked up at his aide, like a child who has been thoroughly spanked for a crime he did not yet understand.

'Was I a bad man?' he asked pleadingly. 'Was I?'

'No, my Lord.'

'No.' He returned to staring at the wall. 'Could I have done other?'

'No, my Lord.'

'No.'

Scorza closed his eyes and listened to the silence. How to deliver more bad news when there was nothing good to sweeten it? He paced in a small circle around his corner of the room.

'Scorza, why do you fidget so?'

'My Lord, forgive me . . . I was deep in thought.'

'So then, share those thoughts with me. That is why you are in my employ. What do they gossip about beneath the stairs? Tell me, what do they say of Bartolommeo?' The prince settled back further in his chair and looked at the man.

Scorza took a deep breath. 'Of you they do not speak, except in honest anger at what has occurred here.'

Bartolommeo smiled weakly. 'How very loyal,' he said.

'But there is other news.'

'Yes?'

'Of a dark nature.'

'Get on with it, man.'

'Sir, Vincente is dead.'

'That little tyke? Dead?' Bartolommeo put his head on one side and giggled. 'In times of blackness such news can only be greeted as light relief. He gave nothing to the life of court. Only his going now is a gesture of virtue. It was by my foolish charity that he stayed here, in any case. You know, I think we could all do with a feast of some kind. Don't you? Perhaps Vincente's passing should be the occasion. How did the runt die?'

'By his own hand.'

Bartolommeo stopped his laughing and sat up. 'What?'

'He was found hanging in his chambers this morning, by the neck.'

The old prince trembled. 'So,' he said, 'do we have the end of our drama here? Is he the bastard's father? Oh gross sin; brother and sister, a match made by Beelzebub.'

'He says not. He left a letter in which he claimed to have taken his life because he could no longer face time on the earth with the knowledge of his beloved sister's adultery . . .'

The prince gripped both arms of his chair. 'Do we believe this devil when he lies?'

'Sir, I can only report . . .'

'Of course you can only report. That's all your sort can ever do. So report. Tell me, what other news?'

'Father Corsano . . .'

'Father Corsano? Sadini's junior? Should he be dead too?'

'No, my Lord. He was seen to flee the castle and Strossetti by darkness last. He gave no account of himself but went. We have no knowledge of where.'

Bartolommeo raised one eyebrow. 'A cast of suitors then, sickly brothers and errant priests. Did they all have the slut? And are there others? It must have been the vitality of her youth, that she could take so many while I slept on, old and spent. And what of you, Scorza? Were you tempted by the young flesh, to take that which was not yours? Did you have her?'

The younger man flushed red. 'Sir, please. Such things . . .'

'Shut up, man,' the prince said sarcastically. 'I do not care to hear your witterings.' He heaved up a little more phlegm and, with a full mouth, said: 'Leave me now . . . Have one of the boys come attend to me.' He swallowed and looked back over his shoulder at the view through the window, as though his thoughts lay out there somewhere, deep in the forbidding crags of the mountains. 'I have a task to perform.' Scorza left him.

The prince handed the youth that Scorza had dispatched to him a rod of thick, gnarled iron taken from the hearth where it was used to lift burning logs so that air might circulate beneath them. Then together, the boy's shoulder tucked beneath the old man's arm for support, they walked the few hundred yards to the Cathedral of San Martino and the place where his wife's body lay. The cathedral was empty, Rafanelli now fully paid and in his quarters gathering together his possessions. At the side of the tomb Bartolommeo asked the boy to give him the poker and then ordered him to wait outside until he was called upon.

The prince supported his weight on the thick end of the rod, as though it were a walking stick, and watched him leave. Then, when he heard the door slam and was sure the boy was now outside, he turned to face Joanna. He placed the palm of his hand on her cool forehead.

'Why should I not have trusted you?' he said quietly. 'What reason had I to doubt you? I have always believed in virtue before dishonour. Trust in a friend and a friend will trust in you. That has always been my code and it has served me well. Until now.' He ran his hand down over her eyes as though closing them one last time. 'Was your life taken for your sins, poor child? Was that it? Was it your adultery that has locked you in this marble shell?' He took his hand off and stepped back a foot.

'Do you know when first I saw you I could not have

imagined that sin was part of your lexicon. That such sin should now be immortalized here thus . . .' He looked at her closed eyes, the shape of her mouth, the bleached sweep of her neck. 'It is almost too much to bear.

'I weep for you now as much as I weep for me,' he said. Then he sneered: 'Oh Lord, how I weep for you.' He turned away as if to leave, the iron rod clasped in both hands. Then he swung back with as much force as he could muster. He lifted the lump of metal off the ground and turned to strike against the sculpture's head, trying to gain momentum as he moved, the blood rushing down his extended arms. But the weapon was too heavy for the weary prince and he was not able to get its tip more than two feet into the air. Instead of striking her across the bridge of her nose, as he had intended, he struck a glancing blow to the cherub that sat by it, sending dust and slivers of stone high into the air and leaving a huge marble gash across the child's rounded belly. It was as close as he would ever come to the act of infanticide he so yearned to commit.

He stood panting, one hand rested on the side of the tomb for support, and listened to the dull thud of his heart in his chest, beads of sweat breaking out across his forehead and in the dank creases of his jowls. 'That,' he said eventually, 'was for Francesco.' He gasped for air once more, trying to force oxygen into his tattered lungs and ease the ache deep inside him. Then he lifted the rod on to his shoulder and held it there with both hands.

'This', he said finally, 'is for you.'

He tried to swing the poker down but, as he started to lift the iron rod, a vast pain coursed through his left arm and he was forced to let it go. The weapon landed harmlessly on the floor behind him with a clatter. He reached for his arm and gripped it with his other hand to ease the pain; he clenched his teeth against the agony, all the time sucking for air. But nothing could halt it now, as it pulsed its way through his withered flesh. His chest lurched and he doubled up, holding on, with an ever tightening grip, to his arm. It felt as though the inside of his body had burst; that every organ, every vein, every cell and membrane that had ever kept his soul contained was haemorrhaging, one into the other, in some huge torrent of poisoned blood. He dropped to his knees and let out a low groan, the last sound he would ever make. Like a man who has clung too long to a rope to save him from falling into a bottomless chasm, he felt his grip on his left arm loosening, the weakened fingers scrabbling madly for anything that might just keep him held there, on life's fragile edge, for but a second longer.

And then he was gone, falling down and down and down until, at last, the noise in his ears had ceased and the pain in his head had gone and he could feel nothing more.

The boy sat outside on the steps of the cathedral for a good two hours, scratching his arse and picking his nose and huffing to himself and saying things like 'Oh, my lot is a poor one' and 'He should try his hand at the servants' life,' and throwing pebbles at the pigeons who flapped around the square before him. He had heard the two sharp cracks of poker on stone shortly after he had been sent outside but he had not thought to investigate. After all, was he not just a servant commanded to follow instructions? Was it his business to go about chasing after stray echoes? Not a bit of it. He would wait.

The body of the last Strossetti prince was discovered only when Father Sadini came to the cathedral to retrieve an aged volume of the catechisms, the Pope's encyclopedia of sin that the priest had felt moved to consult in light of recent events.

At first he just stood above the body, its eyes bulging, tongue lolling out of its breathless mouth, and stared, somewhat stunned by the fact that once more he had managed to outlive an elderly member of the household. Then he said: 'Oh, is it not a terrible thing that death should come so, here in the presence of a sinner. Believe me, it is. Such a terrible thing. The most terrible of all.' The body was moved to the great hall of the castle and then, with some insensitivity, it was taken to the crypt to lie on the same marble slab that had held Joanna's blood-drained corpse exactly four years before. Scorza came to look but did not stay long. He gave orders that preparations be made for the old man's burial as became a prince and said only, 'Mountains may stand, but flesh cannot endure,' before apparently disappearing to his chamber. Then, as the day drew on and night painted in the corners of the winter sky, Sadini ordered that the castle bell be rung, a single repetitive peal that would confirm the news of Bartolommeo's death which had been circulating around Strossetti as gossip for much of the afternoon. Soon the message was picked up by others and by nightfall bells were ringing all along the length of the valley and well beyond, a solitary mournful note, deep and menacing, that signalled the passing both of a principality and of the life that had tried in vain to guard it for so long.

Scorza was down by the stables when the bell first began to ring out across the castle courtyard. He started at the sound, turned to look to where the instrument swung at the top of its tower, and cursed it. If, as he suspected, Lorenzo and his party were still dug in at their hunting lodge over at Forno in the next valley, they would soon hear the news and be on their way; time was even shorter than he'd hoped. At least he had already ordered the nurse to have Francesco dressed and waiting in the courtyard. For the rest he would have to trust to the Lord. Scorza turned back to the open stable door, lifted up the lantern to peer through the gloom of dusk, pointed and said to the groom, 'Get me that one, the one at the back. He is bigger than the rest and it is strength I need now.'

The stable boy led the white stallion out and saddled him up. Scorza mounted the animal and trotted around to the other side of the castle where Francesco stood, bewildered, in the courtyard, the layers of clothes he had been wrapped in making him appear even more spherical than he actually was. He stood in the pool of light cast by the nurse's lantern, holding her hand, looking desperately confused, and wondering why he was to leave on a journey so late in the day. The child had not yet been told of the prince's death. What use, people said, was such harsh news to a child such as he. There would be time for real misery later. Let confusion reign for now.

Scorza tried to lean down from his horse to pull the child up, but Francesco was already too heavy for such gymnastics. He yelped when his arm was pulled and burst into tears, wrapping his fat arms around the nurse's thighs for comfort, even though he could barely bend them at the elbows on account of the thickness of his tiny cloak. Scorza shook his head, dismounted, picked the child up and heaved him into the saddle. Then he climbed up to sit behind him. 'It will all be all right,' he said quietly into the snuffling child's ear. 'You'll see. It will be much better this way.'

Sadini appeared on the castle rooftop above them. 'Scorza,' he shouted, in a painful rasp, rubbed raw by decades of profundity. 'Where are you to take the bastard?' The civil servant yanked his horse round so that he could look up to where the ancient priest stood, silhouetted against the smudge of early darkness.

'To Siena,' he shouted back. 'To the house of his grandfather. Florence can have no call on him there.' Then he turned the horse about to face the castle gate, dug both knees into the animal's ribs, and released a deep shout that came from the very pit of his stomach. The horse lifted his head, as though woken from a trance by the man's call, shook his mane and then, with a loud snort, broke into a gallop; out of the gates, across the cathedral square and away, at last, into the silent depths of a Tuscan winter night.

PART TWO

PART TWO

CHAPTER TEN

You will not find Tito Fossi's name in any of the Florentine guide books. There is no plaque to mark the place where he died, nor any official record to account for what happened save a few aged newspaper cuttings, now buried in the vaults of the national library on Piazza dei Cavalleggeri not far from where the accident occurred. Even his gravestone in the Cimitero Evangelista degli Allori on the south-western outskirts of Florence is coy about the cause of death. It says only 'Goodbye Tito, dearly beloved son and brother. You took to the waters and swam away from us for ever.'

But to Florentines of a certain age the name of Tito Fossi, the hot-headed philosophy student from Arezzo, will never die. It will always remind them of that terrible day in November 1966 when, after three days and three nights of torrential rain, the River Arno burst its banks and, like a crowd of drunk and angry gatecrashers at a society party, pushed its way through the narrow streets in a flood of truly grand proportions.

Tito shared a flat with two other students at the top of a house on Borgo Santa Croce less than a hundred yards from the river. On the morning of November 4th, a holiday, Tito got up late and, before he had even had his breakfast, stepped out on to the roof terrace into the wind and the rain to survey the scene. What he saw both thrilled and shocked him. The floodwater was swirling around the street below, and rising all the time. Though he could not see the road through the muddy waters he could tell by the level against the buildings on the other side that it was already at least ten feet deep. And as he watched it became deeper and deeper. And as it did so an idea began to form.

There were then, as there have always been, two cities in Florence. First there is the city of the pavements, where the tourists walk, for ever in shadow; a place of narrow alleys crowded with rusty cars and motor scooters in lines, the gutters running with foul water, the kerbs stacked high with rubbish. And then there is the city of the rooftops, with its balconies and terraces, a veritable Gormenghast that stretches for a good two miles in every direction from the centre, hung with white-flowered vines and purple wistaria, strung with washing put out to catch the hot sun that cannot reach the city of the pavements below. The latter is never visited by those who walk around the former, unless they are fortunate enough to befriend a Florentine who considers them worthy of the journey. The link between the two lies in the cool hallways of the old apartment blocks that honeycomb each of the buildings, dimly lit burrows that take you to the city's breezy red-tiled canopy.

For so long Tito, a resident of the rooftop city, had dreamed of finding a way from the one to the other which did not require him to go into the darkness of the hallways. It seemed such a gloomy way to get to ground, he said to friends. Once he thought of parachuting down. Another time he considered abseiling and even went so far as to find out how much an adequate length of good rope would cost, but abandoned the idea because of lack of funds. But here, in the grey-green floodwaters streaming through the streets seventy feet below, was an opportunity; a chance, at last, to make the leap that he had dreamed of for so long. He went inside and put on the wet suit that he wore to go water-skiing down at the coast and bid his two friends come and watch. By now the waters were fourteen feet deep.

They remonstrated with him but he wouldn't listen. What

was life if not an adventure, he asked. How could he ever hope to tackle the great questions of life, the very essence of philosophy, unless he was at least on nodding terms with death? No one could ever hope to do again what he was about to do, he said. And then, dressed in his tight black rubber suit, he clambered over the rail and leapt into open space. His two flatmates ran to the edge and got there just in time to see him enter the water with an almighty splash, legs flailing, arms in the air. Quickly he surfaced and waved up to them, smiling. He shouted something but, though they leaned far over to catch what it was, they could not make out the words on account of the wind and the rain and the growing distance between them as he was swept ever further down the street. He was still waving and smiling as he was pulled, out of sight, around the corner and on to Via de' Benci where the floodwater flowed towards the river.

They found Tito Fossi's body two days later, floating face down, bloated and blue-cheeked, by the water's edge not far from Empoli, some thirty miles down river. He was one of a miraculously small number of people who drowned during the great Florentine flood of 1966, but his story was the most talked about. Why, people asked, should anyone want to do such a thing when there are stairs to go by? What was so special about the roads? And who would want to venture out into such a storm? To this day parents still chastise their children when they lean too far over the balconies or from the terraces in the sky, by intoning the dead student's name. 'Be careful,' they say, 'or you will end up like Tito.' And the children always step away from the edge.

Isabella told Alex the story as they drove back from Strossetti, as much to fill up the electric silences as anything else.

Alex liked the tale. It was fully formed, one to be stored up for story-telling nights back in London. He said it appealed to his sense of the macabre. He had always been interested in dramatic death. Sometimes he blamed it on being a journalist, a product of his innate fascination with the newsworthy. But he had always been like that, even when he was a kid, perhaps because, in the quieter corners of his childhood, he had often planned ways in which a dramatic death might attend to his father. Alex said Tito's was the sort of end he would like. How much better that, than the mundanity of a life terminated by heart failure or a stroke. How much grander to die amid noise than peace. Isabella had shaken her head and said, 'I may never understand the humour of the journalist.'

He stood now, in the air-conditioned cool of the bar on the top floor of his hotel, looking out at the rooftops to the west. From what Isabella had told him he had to assume he was only a tourist. He could admire this other Florence, Tito and Isabella's Florence, from behind glass but he could not go there, not yet. He could marvel at its many levels and layers, the way the buildings seemed to tumble one upon the other, as though each new block were an organic growth. But he could not touch.

Maybe later.

'Alex, dear chap.' He turned away from the view, smile fixed in place, ready to greet his unwanted visitor. He had very little time for Richard Hawksmoor when they worked together in the London office; he had even less for him now he was striding towards him across the bar of his hotel in Florence.

'Richard,' he said brightly. 'The places you turn up.'

Hawksmoor was a man who had gone far on the strength of an interesting by-line and a talent for office politics. For a long time he had been the *Correspondent*'s diarist, living off the free gallons of champagne and the endless supply of goujons of plaice which have forever kept the wheels of media London turning. A few years before he had cost the paper somewhere in the region of £100,000 in libel damages for claiming a renowned Oxford history don was not just on the right of the Tory party, but an active racist as well. But Hawksmoor was not the sort to let a little libel stand in the way of a flourishing career. He had swiftly reinvented himself as a foreign correspondent, striding off around the globe, now buying on expenses the champagne which had once been his for free. He was famous among foreign correspondents for researching his stories from the confines of his hotel.

He called everybody dear heart or dear chap, talked in cricketing metaphors and, if he thought he could get away with it, wrote in them too. On Sunday mornings he played football with a bunch of fellow Wykehamists down on Wandsworth Common. Despite the desperately liberal tendencies of his newspaper it was rumoured that he harboured ambitions to stand as a Tory MP at the next election. Few, however, thought he had the guts to put his insidious personality to the test of democracy. He was tall and while he had once been well built he had recently developed an extensive paunch. His hair was a neutral brown and shaggy in a very studied way, as though he thought long hair marked him out as an amiable eccentric. Beneath the mop, however, he was just another uptight middle-aged public school boy, who feared women and drank just a little too much. Many suspected Hawksmoor maintained his standing on the paper because he knew dark secrets about Robert Hicks, the *Correspondent*'s equally Machiavellian editor and an Oxford contemporary. It was certainly not the product of any great journalistic talent. Among his friends and admirers he was known as 'The Hawk'; among his enemies and detractors he was known as 'that complete cunt'.

They found a table by the window so that they could at least look at the late afternoon sunshine even if they could not feel it. They ordered their drinks – an orange juice for Alex, a large vodka for his guest – and lit their cigarettes.

'Well,' Hawksmoor said after he had gulped down half his liquor. 'I was only passing through. Not queering your pitch or anything?'

'No, not at all. I'm glad you called,' Alex lied, without conviction. He rubbed the filter of his cigarette with the pad of his thumb, irritably. 'What are you doing here?'

'A little local trouble in Eritrea, dear heart. I'm off to Addis Ababa to report these great happenings for the *Correspondent*'s loyal readers.' He waved his glass in the air, as though toasting the city. 'Many of the Ethiopian charities and pressure groups are based here. Relic of the Italian Empire and all that, what there was of it.'

'I know that. When are you heading south?' Hawksmoor just couldn't help giving Alex reasons to hate him. Addis was his territory. Or at least it had been. Once.

'Dear boy, don't look so jealous,' the older man said, swigging his drink again. 'It's only going to be a short innings. And you know exactly what it will be like. Lots of meetings with UN people and Red Cross people and the towel heads from whatever tin-pot guerilla movement is making waves this time.'

Alex winced. 'Towel heads? Please.' He took another deep drag.

'Well for Christ's sake, you don't expect me to take the buggers seriously, do you? Frankly I think it very unlikely I will get a chance to go up country at all on this one. The way it looks I could do the job from behind the desk in London, but you know what the foreign desk are like. Don't like to fall short of their budget and all that.'

Alex nodded. So Hawksmoor was going to do another hotel bar special.

'And after all those damn meetings it will just be the standard piss-up: me, some sullen git from Agence Presse wanking on about his days in Algeria and the technical boys from CNN extolling the virtues of their new satellite phone. So that's why I'm here, old chap. And as there aren't any sullen French gits to have a drink with tonight I thought I'd give you a call.'

'Charmed, I'm sure.'

Hawksmoor looked down at the table and batted his now empty glass between his cupped hands.

'Actually,' he said after a while, 'that's a little white lie. The boys back on the desk asked me to seek you out. Not of course that I didn't want to . . .' A waiter appeared at their side and they ordered another round of drinks.

'Go on,' Alex said.

'Right. You see, I think they're a little pissed off. Particularly the boss.'

'Oh are they?'

'Hmm. He thinks you're swanning around Florence on expenses – his expenses – having a high old time and filing sod all. I'm sure he's only jealous of your enormous talents.' Hawksmoor spread his fleshy arms wide as he said it. Then he clapped his hands together. 'But it is also true.'

Alex smiled. Who was this man to lecture him on wasting expenses? 'There's a good story here,' he said. 'It's just going to take a little longer to nail down . . .'

'Dear heart, there's a good story everywhere. But couldn't you finish this one from London?'

'I don't need that much longer, just a little while.'

'It's not me you have to say these things to. Really. I am just the messenger.' He leaned across the table and punched him lightly on the shoulder. 'Just bringing you the news and all that.'

Alex smiled and turned to look out the window at the view. 'To be honest . . .' he said, his eyes fixed on the teat of the Duomo a little way over from the hotel. 'Well, you know how it is. I was starting to get things out of proportion back in London and . . .' His voice trailed away for a moment. 'And when you keep seeing stuff . . .' He turned back to Hawksmoor who had one eyebrow raised in expectation. 'I was beginning to find it hard to take normal life seriously back there and this place is being good for me.'

Christ, Alex screamed to himself, why am I spilling my guts to this complete cunt?

Hawksmoor patted Alex on the shoulder again. 'Nobody blames you, you know. A bunch of big black men with big black guns got shirty so you became a big white man with a gun for a while. You didn't kill anyone. You just lost it for a bit. Just think of it as a bad innings, a black mark on the score card. But it's all history now. On with the story eh?'

'I suppose you're right.' He looked back at the view again. 'Are they really getting shirty?'

'Do you know what they're saying?'

Alex shook his head.

'They're saying Mr Fuller, he dead.'

'Yeah, well you can tell them to paraphrase Twain. Rumours of my death and all that. Look, what about if I went for a cheaper hotel? I could change hotels. Do you think that would get them off my back?'

'Christ, dear boy. You can't do that. That's admitting you

were spending too much in the first place. You have the rest of the team to think of.'

Alex scratched his cheek in thought. 'OK,' he said. 'I'll deal with it.'

Before Hawksmoor left he dug into his briefcase and pulled out a wadge of photocopied cuttings. 'Geoff in the library asked me to give you these.' Then they shook hands. 'Don't forget to call the boss,' he said as he went. 'I'm sure he'd love to hear from you.'

Alex ordered another drink and sat down to look over the cuttings. The first few were dull: pieces about an international anti-restoration pressure group that Kelner had launched and some short news stories reporting the adjournment of the first court case that he had attended the day before last, taken from wire service copy. But halfway through the pile he came across something far more interesting. It was a picture of Kelner seated in an audience. Next to him was the flat-topped man Isabella had seen at the court case. Inset was another photograph: a miniature of Joanna's tomb, perfect in every detail but made in terracotta. Alex read the extended caption. It said:

Professor Robert Kelner of UCLA (right) watching the sale yesterday, at Carter's Auction House in London, of a study for the tomb of Joanna dei Strossetti by the Renaissance master Antonio Rafanelli. Prior to its discovery it was believed that the artist destroyed all his secondary works. After competitive bidding the study was bought by an unnamed Japanese financier for $8.5 million, almost three times the estimate. Professor Kelner, the art historian and Rafanelli expert who authenticated the piece, is rumoured to be receiving a 15 per cent share of the final sale price as commission. Seated next to him is the Tuscan artist Carlo Palecchi who first discovered the study in the monastery of Massarosa two years ago.

Alex blinked. He read the caption again. He pushed the cutting away from him and sat back in his chair.

'Christ,' he said to himself quietly, after he had done his sums. 'Kelner is rich. Seriously fucking rich.'

A few weeks before Lawrence Kelner's heart finally stopped, he said to his father: 'My first memory of California was the palm trees. They were so tall. I thought they meant we'd come to live in paradise. Then I found out that during the daytime that's where the cockroaches sleep, right up there at the top of the trees, tucked in among the leaves. Maybe they thought it was paradise too.'

Robert and Fiammetta Kelner went to Southern California less in search of paradise than the simple pleasures of family life. Back then Lawrence was a dour seven-year-old with much to be dour about. His future was defined solely by a pernicious disease which promised just two things: an ever increasing array of debilitating symptoms, and that the anguish caused by those symptoms would be relieved only by a premature death. They decided that if Lawrence could enjoy a better quality of life away from Princeton where the family then lived, they should seek it out, however short that life would be. In the first few months following the diagnosis, when they had just been made aware of the spectre of decay that had been appointed to haunt them and their lives were plunged into a kind of perpetual twilight, the idea of a life elsewhere seemed desperately appealing. It was as far as they could go in coming to terms with what had befallen them.

Thus, in the early months of Jimmy Carter's presidency, when America was itself searching for a new beginning, trying so hard to prove that it could at last dredge some form of redemption from the cesspit of political corruption into which the nation had been plunged, the Kelners decided it was time they too moved on; that they should abandon the smog-filled cities of the north-east coast, with their harsh winters and their burning summers, and go looking for something better. The up-and-coming art historian had little trouble finding a position in the faculty of art history at UCLA; his two published works – a study of the iconography of the Renaissance and a history of Lorenzo Il Magnifico's great art collection – had won him a growing if modest reputation among the etiolated souls who populated the world of art history, both for his rigorous research and his accomplished scholarship. And so, one cool and breezy Friday morning in March, the Kelners packed up their belongings, herded Lawrence and his older sister Giuliana into the car, hitched a wagonload of hope to the back and struck out west.

It was not the palm trees Kelner remembered so much from those early days as the sky, the sheer size of it, the forever-stretch of blue and the way it floated high above his head. Even the sky was emptier here. The constant sunshine and smell of damp pine in the mornings reminded him of Italy, which he had already visited many times; if he squinted at the view from his study on the sixth floor of the Dickson Arts Centre, across the tree tops of the pretty campus and up the hills which enfolded the tarmac scar of Sunset Boulevard beyond, he could even imagine he was back there, in the lush Tuscan landscape outside Florence. Though he had little interest in the wilder excesses of the Californian lifestyle – he had no time either for Eastern mysticism or the frugality of a macrobiotic diet – he did not, at first, allow such fads to irritate him. He had come here for other things, for the health of his son.

In Santa Monica, where they bought a house not far from the beach, the air was always sweet and fresh, scrubbed clean by the Pacific winds that blew towards them over 10,000 miles of unbroken water. They had three times as much space to live in as before, the roads in the Los Angeles basin were still relatively quiet and the pace of life was gentle. While every doctor they saw tried to warn them that the Duchenne Muscular Dystrophy from which Lawrence was suffering would inevitably prove fatal, the combination of the year-round sunshine and the lack of any major symptoms kept them from brooding.

But the warm sunshine which had at first given life its delicious syrup glow out there would later serve only to prove just how cruel a mother nature could be. Despite the unending summer of their honeymoon days in California the child's symptoms did not stay unpronounced for long. Within nine months of their arrival, he was stumbling and tripping and falling when he walked, his limbs turning in and under him and around him but never carrying him forward in the way he wished. His father shuddered every time he saw the boy go down, until he found it hard even to watch his pathetic attempts at guided movement. Soon his son was using crutches to pull himself forward, his wretched feet dragging behind him as he went. It was a development Lawrence tried to take in his tangled stride, but he barely had time to get used to it; the atrophy that had all but robbed him of the use of his legs soon spread to the muscles in his shoulders and he had no choice but to take to a wheelchair. Initially it was only a mode of transport into and out of which he would scrabble at the beginning and end of journeys using whatever reserves of control he had left. Later when he was no longer able to get himself into the wheelchair and he had to be placed there it became both more comfortable and more practical for him to remain in it. By the time he was ten years old Lawrence Kelner was confined to a wheelchair permanently, destined to spend the rest of his life in a prison of chrome and leather, his limbs becoming ever more twisted and deformed as the years passed.

And yet throughout it all, the stumbling and the falling, the withering of limbs and the loss of movement, the frustration and the fury, the Californian sun continued to shine, a blaze of light that seemed hell-bent on mocking them. You may have your agonies and your torments, it said, you may have your terrors, but the world will never stop turning.

'It's a biological time bomb, isn't it,' Kelner said to his doctor one morning.

'That's one way of looking at it, Bob.' The doctor always called the historian Bob, however much he winced when he did. 'Sadly, Bob, sometimes we don't know it's there until it's gone off,' he said.

'And the women are the carriers.'

'Well yes, Bob, that's the way it works. Women can only pass it on.'

Kelner repeated the last words. 'Only pass it on.' Then he turned to look at his wife and said, in a voice bare of emotion, 'Isn't biology interesting?'

Kelner felt so betrayed by biology. When he first met Fiammetta, at Ohio State, he thought she was the most beautiful woman he had ever seen, lean and dark and beguiling. He did not for a single moment imagine that she found him at all sexy, of course. Well, how could she? How could anyone? He had never imagined himself to be in any way physically attractive to anybody. That was not what Kelner was about. For an intellect such as his to be wrapped in a body which appealed to something as primitive as carnal instinct would, he always said, have degraded the power of the remarkable mind with which it had been blessed. No, he said, women would find him attractive because of the way he thought, not because of how he looked.

This argument, which often seemed to be little more than an excuse for the man's lack of social graces, hid another ideology which floated somewhere near the surface of his subconscious, theories which were, in their own way, more poisonous and infinitely more self-serving. Not only was Kelner confident of his intellectual abilities; he also had no doubt that as the years passed his mind would develop. Even if he became no better at the twin arts of analysis and deduction – and he considered that unlikely – even then, he would still gather more knowledge as he grew older. His brain would fill up. Thus the one thing that he thought made him attractive was the one thing that would, at least until the very end, defy the ravages of time.

But Fiammetta on the other hand, well, where would she be in forty years' time? Or just twenty for that matter? What did she have to look forward to? The things which Kelner thought made her attractive when they met – the turn of the lip, the curve of the cheek, the weight of an eyelash – all of it was essentially transitory, a trick of passing time. In the end it would just be a set of sun-bleached memories, held in curled photographs and nothing more. The way Kelner saw it, everything that gave his wife her virtue, her differentness, would eventually decay. That is what happens to the human body; it always rots in the end.

During the mid-eighties, whenever he sat looking at his son, so twisted and turned in his wheelchair that it seemed as if he were trying to return to the foetus position in which he had been made, the historian became quietly enraged. Fiammetta had not just saved her inevitable decay for herself. She had shared it with her son. She had foisted her own human failings upon their only male child. Here were the design faults of the flesh running at triple time, quadruple time; the movie of life rushing through the gate with indecent haste, turning the normal into the grotesque.

It was not a question of blaming his wife because, as he reasoned, the question of who to blame could only be posited where there was doubt over guilt. Without doubt, blame simply became absolute guilt. Here there was no doubt. The faulty gene was not his or he would have succumbed to its wicked fancies three decades before. Therefore the gene was hers. Fiammetta was the guilty one; she was responsible for Lawrence.

In his work he found purification. Renaissance sculpture was, he said, the perfect marriage of pure intellect and complete aesthetic beauty; in each curve of chiselled marble lay eternal truth, an investigation of man's relationship with the world in which he moved, over which he could at last be his own kind of god. And, of course, these glorious statues could not decay. Time did not drain them of their beauty. They were better than flesh. In these works the truth endured, forever outliving those who could only come to look and marvel and then wither up and die.

Kelner spent more and more time in Italy, embarking on his research into the work of Antonio Rafanelli which would eventually make him an expert with a world reputation. Fiammetta accompanied him on these trips once or twice at the beginning. But as both Lawrence's condition and their marriage deteriorated, they agreed it would perhaps be preferable if she remained in California to look after the child. To his colleagues, the once earnest and dry historian became simply pious and patronizing. The more he visited Florence the more dismissive he became of the Californian way of life to which he would always have to return. He would sneer at the campus and the students who would stride across it; he would forever interrupt seminars to deliver lectures on the evils of a culture of mediocrity that he said infected the American nation. 'Where is the heart?' he would say. 'The American heart is carved from stone and badly finished. That's the way it will always be, because those that carved it were incompetent. They were bad artists. And you cannot teach a bad artist to be a great one.'

Most of Kelner's colleagues forgave the man his pomposity, or at the very least ignored it. They knew about Lawrence and his condition; they had seen the kid rolling across the campus in his electric wheelchair, controlling his battery-propelled advance with one clawed and bony hand on the joystick. They would watch and feel pity. And then they would feel guilty for feeling pity. Finally they would turn away to go to the library or a lecture or a seminar or a coffee or a ball game or anywhere that Lawrence wasn't going.

'Does he love his son?' they would sometimes ask each other. And after a little thought they would shrug and say, 'Who's to know with Kelner? Who's to know what he feels?'

If they had asked, Kelner would have answered, 'Yes, I love my son,' though he could not have explained it. Every time he looked at Lawrence he was faced by the truth of his own failure; he had not been able to do anything about what had befallen his child. Throughout his life he had always been able to conquer through the power of his intellect. And yet here was something that could not be conquered, only observed. To be the spectator, he decided eventually, was the most painful thing of all. He buried the pain by doting on his son, attending to his needs, and continued the desperate search for a therapy that might reverse the condition or at the very least stall it for a while. His relationship with Fiammetta became just a murmur, as if the emotional volume had been turned down. If there were antagonisms they did not articulate them. They went through their marriage like two sailors who had capsized their boat far from land, and who were now clinging to the hull, dazed and exhausted, waiting either for rescue or death, whichever came first.

Even though, as the years passed, he spent more and more time away in Florence, researching and studying, the other academics still tried not to judge. He had to spend this time away, they said to each other in hushed corners, so he could research his books, so he could earn more money, so he could pay for the treatment for his son. Terminal illness was an expensive proposition, they said.

Thus, in the dog days of the Reagan presidency, when they heard that Kelner had been approached to authenticate a recently discovered work by Rafanelli, they were genuinely delighted for him. They all knew a successful authentication could mean serious money and they did not begrudge him it one bit. If there were riches to be made from academia, they said, it was only fair that someone like Kelner got them. He needed them. A few even went to his study to look at the pile of large colour photographs of the terracotta study of the tomb of Joanna dei Strossetti that had been sent over from Italy. They would flick through the pictures and then say, 'So, what do you think?'

Kelner would sit back in his chair, enjoying the glow of expertise sought. 'Of course,' he would say, 'it is impossible to judge from mere photographs, but the circumstances in which it has been found do seem promising. I will only be able to tell when I view the piece myself and consider all the facts.'

One was brave enough to say, 'But didn't you yourself write that Rafanelli never left any secondary works? Wasn't that one of the features of Rafanelli's art, that the few finished pieces are all that exists?'

The historian smiled indulgently, as a teacher smiles at a promising pupil who has reached the answer to a mathematical problem, but for the wrong reasons. 'Like a detective I can only make a case on the evidence I can dig up,' he said. 'If I failed to find all the evidence then of course I may have come to the wrong conclusions.' He folded his hands in his lap.

'In short, I may have been wrong.'

A lot of people found it deeply unnerving that Kelner should utter such a sentence.

CHAPTER ELEVEN

Alex didn't pull the flush after he'd pissed. Instead he waited, letting silence work the deception for him. What he was doing in there would be beyond the bounds of enquiry. It would give him a good two or three minutes to nose about, which was all he needed. This was hardly going to be a major investigation; it was more of a scavenging exercise, a quick rummage through the musty corners of a life for details of the kind only a week of interviews could otherwise get you. He had laid the ground well, claiming dire need as he stepped through the door after the long taxi ride from town. He hadn't even waited to find out who else was there, shuffling instead from foot to foot, dancing his way across the carpet, each step marked by a 'hello' or a 'nice to see you' or even a 'thank you for asking me' that took him, at last, to the exquisite solitude of the toilet.

Now, fully emptied, he zipped up and walked over to the medicine cabinet that sat above the sink on the other side of the bathroom. He slid the mirrored door across. The two shelves were full, as he had expected, stacked high with old bottles and tubes, jars and bandages. Alex studied the contents. He reached inside and took out a foil card of pills so that he could lift out the jar beneath.

At what point in a person's life does it suddenly become necessary to own all this paraphernalia, he wondered. When does the body maintenance business really begin, this desperate need for capsules and tablets and creams, some to help the ageing flesh sleep, others to keep it from creaking or leaking? His parents had owned a well-stocked medicine cabinet like this, smelling of dead flowers and disinfectant. There were always little brown bottles in there with typed labels that had names which ended in things like —oxin and —aldehyde, a code that he assumed was meant only for adults. The rest of the label was always written in imperatives, which he understood better: take three times daily. One after every meal. Finish whole course unless otherwise directed. He always liked that one. Even adults had their orders.

Later, in his early teenage years, he got hold of a pharmaceutical directory and cracked the code. That way he was able to follow the course of his parents' illnesses. It was the greatest insight he ever got into his parents; to be frank it was the only insight, a rare glimpse behind the door of adulthood, snatched from the silence of the house when they both chose to leave him there alone.

The habits of the young die hard; two decades on he still had a thing about medicine cabinets. He well knew that a single forage through someone's domestic druggery was a bit unscientific, even a bit random, and could never give you the full picture. If you rushed you could easily fail to spot a date on a bottle and drag some long gone illness into the medical snapshot, a pack of tranquillizers kept for nostalgia's sake, say. But it was still a useful way to discover secrets. It wasn't a polite thing to do. But, as he reasoned, he'd never seen it condemned either. And anyway he wasn't about to drop what he would find there into his copy, raw. But it did supply some invaluable background. A nice starting point.

The interesting thing here was the pretty even split between the two of them. Half of the contents belonged to Robert Kelner, the other half to Fiammetta. He turned the bottles around on the shelves to examine the grease-stained labels.

Many he didn't recognize because they were Italian or American brand names. But a couple were generic. The historian had a large supply of Terfanadine, a standard anti-histamine which suggested he was prone to allergic reactions. Behind this stash was an inhaler of the sort used by asthmatics. Did Kelner have some kind of breathing problem? It would explain his obsessive hatred of smokers. At the front of the top shelf in a corner where it could easily be reached was a large bottle of the sleeping pill Mogadon, recently dated, which Alex recognized from previous medicine-cabinet sorties elsewhere. So Kelner suffered insomnia too.

There were also a number of anti-depressants prescribed to Fiammetta. Apart from that there were no really dramatic finds, nothing like the supply of methadone he had once found in a German industrialist's bathroom or the bottle of oestrogen tablets that belonged to a rather butch game show host called Tamsin Wilde who, he noticed only after the discovery, had a pair of enormous, brittle hands. But it was interesting nonetheless. For one, he had found out that Kelner suffered from allergies. He wasn't just anti-social; his reaction against the world was physical as well.

Alex could now smell the ammonia from his own urine static in the toilet bowl. There was a sharp knock at the door. Quickly, he turned the pill bottles back to their original position and slid the medicine cabinet shut. Then he flushed the toilet and unlocked the door.

'Hello.' Isabella stood in the hallway, hands behind her back, ribcage forward, grinning.

'Isabella, the places you turn up. What are you doing here?'

'You are not pleased to see me?'

'Of course.' He placed both hands on her shoulders and

rubbed the top of her back with his thumbs. He was delighted to see her but, at the same time, uneasy. He was so unsure of what their relationship was, so nervous, that he had wanted to be prepared for any meeting. He had wanted to be armed with a set of sharp lines and ready-made gags. Now he felt completely defenceless. 'It's wonderful to see you,' he said lamely.

'You think only you shall get the invitations?'

'No. I already said: it's wonderful you're here.'

She narrowed her eyes. 'But you do not think I should be here, do you?'

'Not at all. I'd expect him to ask you; it was bloody obvious that first time you met him that he wanted to jump you. I'm only surprised you said yes. I didn't think you'd want to spend any more time with Kelner than you had to.'

'I was curious to know him.'

'Ach, there's not much to know. He's an asthmatic who sleeps badly. I've checked.' Isabella leaned round him to look into the bathroom, as if there were some list hanging on the wall in there which had supplied the information.

'Ignore me,' Alex said, finally leaning down and brushing her cheek with his lips. He whispered into her ear: 'Who's here?'

'People,' she whispered back.

'Really?'

Isabella nodded.

'Good. I always prefer having dinner with people.'

As well as Kelner there were two other guests on the terrace at the back of the old stone house, soaking up the last yellow flashes of evening sun and studying the view of the steep hills below San Casciano, pointing out a flower that had just come into bloom here, a vine that had spread across a garden there. The air was warm and still, exhausted after the exertions of the hot day just passed and the ever lengthening shadows of pine and cypress spread away over the house until the sun was gone altogether and the sky turned the deep blue of a calm summer sea.

A dapper little man, with receding white hair, well-oiled and slicked back, was introduced as Bucelli, a fellow historian from the Institute of Early Modern Sculpture. He apologized for his accented English with a sprinkle of tuts and shrugs and shakes of his head. And then, as he shook Alex's hand, said, 'The professor Kelner is a good man,' as if he thought the journalist might be trying to make up his mind on the matter.

Next to Bucelli stood another, as big as he was small, who, Kelner said, was Piero Gufarelli, his lawyer. The man's neck was as wide as his head. His heavy eyes and flat nose appeared to lie some three-quarters of the way up a fleshy column that emerged straight from the top of his bulky torso. His cotton-white shirt curved across his chest like a tarpaulin restraining goods on the back of a diesel truck and his shoulders trembled as he walked. When he grabbed Alex's hand he said something which sounded to the journalist like 'burgggnoo' but which Isabella later told him was simply a grand 'hello'. Apart from Kelner and Isabella the only other person there was Fiammetta, who drifted from the terrace to the kitchen and back again sometimes carrying empty glasses, sometimes a bowl of olives or a plate of paper-thin prosciutto. Kelner barely mentioned her. He waved at her back as she went into the kitchen and, with a mean smile, said, 'And she . . . well I'm sure you know who she is.' But they had not been introduced.

Fiammetta was small and round-hipped and while her

throat did not yet sag heavy with a gullet of flesh, there was a puffiness to her face which betrayed her age and suggested that it soon would. And though she smiled and offered drinks and food and tiptoed carefully through the language used with guests newly met, there was a deadness to her eyes that Alex knew all too well, from other less ordered places: it was the cold stare of those who have seen so much and so many destroyed and cannot quite understand why they are the ones who have been chosen to survive, to carry their scars only on the inside.

Fiammetta did not acknowledge Isabella. She seemed to avoid the younger woman, as if some terrible secret about herself lay within the clear line of her guest's youth.

Kelner snorted up the perfumed air in his glass of wine, exhaled and said, 'Mr Fuller. You have seen Joanna now. What does the journalist think? Tell us.'

The three men stared at him expectantly, eyes wide, glasses held still so that the surface of their wine did not ripple. Isabella looked at him too, an eyebrow raised.

'This journalist thinks . . .' But the only picture of the Joanna Alex could bring into his head was one in which Isabella was lying back across it, lips slightly parted, breathing deeply, candle-light flickering against her cheek. He swigged some of his own wine, rolled it around his mouth and then swallowed. '. . . thinks the Joanna is fabulous.'

The big man and the little man nodded their heads vigor-ously and would surely have applauded had their hands not been full. Of course she was fabulous. Who could say otherwise? Who would dare? Kelner dropped his head and looked at the ground. 'It is refreshing,' he said, 'to know that a man like you, who has seen so much, can still be such an innocent.'

'You don't need to be an innocent to be stimulated by beautiful things.'

'Forgive me,' Kelner said, rolling his wine around his glass. 'I'm sure your stimulation, as you put it, is genuine. However, if I had viewed the Joanna for the first time yesterday I would have been forced to respond differently. While I might have found it interesting in a scholastic way, I could not have described it as beautiful. My knowledge of sculpture would have made it impossible for me to be touched by the work in such a way because it is now so intrinsically lacking. You do not have that knowledge so, in your innocence, you still find it beautiful.'

'So very true,' said the little man, nodding vigorously.

Isabella scoffed and shook her head. 'It is only an expert who can judge? I cannot believe the arrogance . . .'

Kelner interrupted. 'It's not arrogance. It just happens to be the way things are. I'm actually rather pleased there are people like Mr Fuller here who can enjoy Rafanelli's work, despite what's happened to it.'

'So very, very true,' said the little man. And then, extravagantly: 'The professor Kelner is a friend of Italy.'

'And couldn't you see,' Kelner said, 'the likeness between Joanna and our Isabella here?' He looked into her eyes as he spoke and then reached out with one hand to brush a lock of hair off her forehead. 'Conte may have destroyed Joanna but time never kills a strong gene,' he said. She swatted him away, as if he were a wasp or a fly.

Alex said: 'I didn't notice any likeness at all,' and turned away to look at the hills.

In a corner of the terrace, away from where they sipped their wine and spat out their olive stones, a lizard scuttled, dark and fragile against the dust-grey paving. Alex watched the way it moved: a dash for a few feet and then a moment's rest. He liked its determination, the mix of speed and peace. For a few seconds it looked as though, if he were just there, just above it, he could close his hand around it and the lizard would be his, tiny claws scratching in the palm of his hand. But he knew that, should he reach out to touch it, it would be gone. This was the way of the lizard. He stepped away from the huddle and slowly walked towards the reptile. It paused again, as if aware it was now being followed. Then it was off again, dashing over the terrace, tail stuttering across the even ground. Alex advanced some more. The lizard stopped. Alex stopped. Stand-off. He waited.

'What are you doing?'

Isabella was beside him. He turned to her. 'Chasing lizards.'

'Where?'

He looked over to where it last sat, but it had gone. 'Nowhere.' He sipped his wine and felt in his pocket for his cigarettes but thought better of it. 'Why did you come? You so obviously dislike him.'

'He asked me.'

'Not a good enough reason.'

'I thought it would be good for you to be here.'

'But I was invited as well.'

'You weren't going to be.'

'What?'

'He invited me, I think, because he wanted to show me to his friends. I said I would come only if he invited you.' She tapped her glass against his. 'You do not have to thank me.' She ambled back to join the others.

At dinner Kelner insisted Isabella sit beside him. He said: 'I want you to tell me all about your family. I want to know what they think of what has happened to Joanna.' She turned to Fiammetta, who was holding a large terrine of thick white-bean soup that she had just carried from the kitchen. The older woman said only, 'Please . . .' and nodded Isabella towards the seat at Kelner's right hand. Alex was placed at the other end of the table, with Fiammetta to his left.

When they were all seated, and the first course had been served out, the bread had been passed around and the conversation had started to flip-flap its way between them, he said quietly, 'What do you think of your husband's battle?'

She let the soup that she had just scooped up slip from her spoon and studied the bowl as if the answer lay deep in there. 'I have lived with my husband's work a long time, Mr Fuller,' she said eventually. 'I have always known there are some parts of it he loves more than others. And if you love something you must fight for it. This I understand.' She looked to where her husband sat. He had one hand placed on Isabella's forearm, to emphasize a point. Isabella shook her head at whatever it was Kelner had said and lifted her arm away to continue eating.

'Who knows if he will win,' Fiammetta said. She turned back to Alex. 'In such a battle I may only watch.'

Isabella and the lawyer were talking now, in Italian. At the end of each point the big man waved his spoon at her, like a baton, which caused her to flinch slightly. As his voice dropped so did the baton. And when he finished he banged the spoon on the edge of the table and let out a huge, rolling laugh that made his belly shudder beneath its tarpaulin shirt. Isabella replied with something which, from the curl of her lip, Alex took to be sarcasm but, though he strained to catch a word or a phrase or a sentence, he could not understand. On home territory banter was a game he understood perfectly, with complex rules and hidden challenges that usually he could navigate by instinct. But deprived of his own language, his own tongue an inconvenience to those around the table, he became little more than a spectator. He sat there feeling clumsy and inarticulate. But he wasn't just inarticulate. He was practically mute, the mummer in a play fair bursting with words.

And yet all he really wanted now was to sit beside Isabella. He wanted to let his hand brush against her thigh or the side of her breast and see if she would mind. He wanted to touch her hand with his to see if she might hang on, entwining her slender fingers with his and throwing back her head and laughing. But here that was impossible. He couldn't even understand what she was saying. His exclusion was total.

After their time in the cathedral this new watching game was uncomfortable, too much like the drone of his last few months in London, from which he had been trying so hard to escape. Since his return from Kenya he had stumbled through life dead-eyed. It had felt as though he had left a vital part of himself back there, buried in the brown desert scrub to shrivel up beneath the glare of the sun; as if he were somehow no longer properly equipped to do the job of living. In London his feelings were like shadows of themselves cast upon a wall. They were the right shape and they moved in the right way, but they lacked form or detail and could all too easily merge into each other or fade away to nothing.

At a newspaper for which he once worked there was a glass-walled lift that rose up through the building past the news desk, the business section and the magazine. If you took it to the top floor you could watch the paper being produced: you could see people making decisions, editing copy, writing headlines, heads bowed before their terminals. But you couldn't be a part of all that because you were in the lift and only passing through. They were out there where real things were going on. Occasionally someone might join you in the lift but after a casual smile or a chummy wink, they would avoid eye contact, searching instead for something to watch while they too passed through. In London he had been riding that glass lift for three months, unable to clamber out, separated from where the real things were going on by glass walls of his own design.

He had not intended to kiss Isabella in the cathedral though that didn't mean he was unattracted to her. He was, but in a way that he thought would have made any progress seem impossible. If he had only wanted to have sex with her, to see her naked and have her supple limbs wrapped around him, he might have been able to make it work. That required the deployment of crude tactics, manoeuvres which were only to be used if, in the morning, he had intended to walk away. But he had wanted far more than that. He had wanted to spend the day with her. And the night and the day after that. He had wanted comfort and reassurance and knowledge. He had wanted Isabella to show him who Joanna was. But he hadn't for a moment considered himself capable of making such a leap.

And still, in the cool of the cathedral, with Joanna lying there and the candles burning all around, and the early-summer Sunday heat locked away outside, they had grabbed for each other and it had felt right. Or had she grabbed for him? Was that the way it had happened? Had she turned him round and pulled him down on to her and around on top of her and forced him to play the game her way? He couldn't remember now.

Afterwards they had driven back and spoken little about it.

Occasionally her hand had drifted over from the steering wheel to his leg which she stroked, grinning broadly all the time. And when she left him at his hotel she had kissed him on the cheek and told him to stop looking so serious. She had been busy the whole of Monday and he had been called to meet Hawksmoor a few hours earlier. Finally, though, they were together and she was talking and he couldn't even understand a bloody word.

'They are discussing corruption in the Soprintendente's office,' Fiammetta said, baldly. 'They believe Conte gave him bribes to get the work on the Joanna.'

'Do they have proof?'

Fiammetta shook her head. 'No. You cannot prove these things, though that does not mean it is not true. It is more likely true than not true. Or it is more true than not true. It is always hard to tell.' She looked at Isabella again, then she turned and whispered conspiratorially to Alex. 'Do you think she looks like the Joanna?'

Alex studied Isabella who turned and threw him a wink from the crossfire of her conversation. The way the jaw cut square, the small mouth, the full lips, it was all there. But in his mind now, Isabella and the Joanna appeared together, the one atop the other, warm skin on stone, her hands gripping the marble for support.

'Maybe there is some likeness,' he said quietly. 'But I don't know the Joanna well enough to judge,' and returned to his soup.

The conversation clattered on inconsequentially: a little talk of government and corruption, of civic duty and self-interest. A little talk of nothing in particular. Later, as they passed a plate of parmigiano around the table, Bucelli said to Alex: 'Could the attack on Joanna have happened in England?'

Kelner replied for him. 'The details of this case are Italian,' he said theatrically. 'But the conflict that caused it is universal. Joanna is a victim of the battle for a New Renaissance, nothing less.'

Bucelli shovelled a few lumps of cheese on to his own plate and said, 'So very true. In what has happened to her is the essence of this conflict.' He popped a piece of cheese into his mouth and chewed slowly.

'What,' Alex said to Bucelli, 'is the New Renaissance?'

Bucelli looked at Kelner who pushed his chair back from the table, crossed one leg over the other and gestured to his guest to continue.

'As the professor has passed to me the floor I shall explain. A little lecture?'

Alex said, 'If nobody else minds, I'm willing.'

Bucelli ran his tongue around his teeth to clear them of any cheese that had got stuck there, and then laid one index finger against his puckered old lips in thought.

'The Renaissance that began here – ' he pointed with his outstretched index finger to the hills beyond the terrace – 'in the early fifteenth century was, as its name tells us, a rebirth. It was a rediscovery of Greek and Roman thought, of the writings, of the sculptures. This we know. And from this came new art. But money had to pay for this. Without money there would be no Renaissance. You understand? Money is the key.'

Alex laughed. 'I understand all about money.'

'Good. But where does this money come from? I will tell you.' He swung his outstretched index finger around to emphasize the point, as though he were balancing a spinning plate upon it. 'Before this time man's world was dominated only by God. It was the church that gives the meaning of the life. Then man develops trade. There are better boats and they have paper to keep records, and so on. Through trade they make money. This means that man has discovered his place in this world. You see what I mean? He is discovering his potential. There is not just God in this world. There is man too.'

Alex settled back in his chair; Kelner picked lazily at some crumbs of cheese on his plate.

'You understand me?' Bucelli said. 'You understand that there were these two things: there is the church with all its laws and its devotions. And then there are the merchants who make money by trade and by banking, by collecting interest. But to make money through interest is a sin to the church. It is usury. And the merchants still care about their sins. Now the church says you may atone for your sins by paying for art. And in this we have the root of the rebirth. Not just that the merchants are working outside of God but they are paying for art. And also there is the conflict: God on one side and money on the other, or man if you wish, and his own power over his world.'

'OK,' said Alex. 'It's man versus God. So what's the New Renaissance?'

Before Bucelli could explain further, Kelner uncrossed his legs, pulled himself to the table and began talking, his tight American accent jarring uncomfortably with Bucelli's smoother Italian. 'This century has seen another great moment in our development, just as the birth of trade was a great moment.' He was in control now, the academic in full plumage.

Bucelli grinned. 'Listen to the professor. He is the one who knows.'

Kelner went on: 'Today we have technology. Our ability to

make and build has not just changed the way we see the world. It's actually changed the world itself: the car needs roads to run on, the train needs rails, the factory needs somewhere to put its waste. This technology is a product of the same belief in man's limitless ability that came from trade which in turn created the Renaissance five hundred years ago. You're with me?'

Alex said, 'Yes, of course. I'm with you.'

'The conflict now is between what you can do with technology, what you can invent, and what the invention will do to the world it has to exist in. Do you see that?'

'Are we on to eco-issues?' Alex said.

'If by this you mean is it to do with the planet, then yes. You see, technology has no spiritual element. The act of invention is not a philosophical one; it is purely practical. The question is simply can we do this? Ecology, on the other hand, does have this philosophical element. It is all about how we view our world and the impact we make upon it. And it raises this one question and this is the question which will create the New Renaissance.'

Alex had pulled his notebook from his inside pocket and was scribbling, partly because he wanted to have a record of what Kelner was saying and partly because he was sure the historian would be flattered if he did so. Kelner stopped talking for half a minute while Alex wrote, the silence around the table broken only by the scratch of pen on paper.

Alex looked up. 'Go on.'

'The question,' Kelner said, 'is this: just because we have the technology to do something is it a good thing to do it? We already have this debate with the bomb. Why create a machine like an atom bomb when you would never want to use it?'

'Because some people do want to use it,' Alex said.

'We all know there are insane people about,' Kelner said dismissively. 'But we can agree that for the common good exploding the bomb would be a disaster. We have seen this, yes?' Alex agreed.

'So why make one? Why do it? I will tell you: you do it because you are able to and once you have made it you can't unmake it. You have to decide what to do with that knowledge and that is the most difficult thing of all. The tragedy is that so many of the scientists who worked on the bomb project in the last war understood this. But, of course, the politicians were paying the bills so they made the decisions.' Kelner pulled a few grapes off a bunch in a bowl before him and threw a couple into his mouth.

'Here is the new conflict, between man or technology on the one side and the planet on the other. And from this there has to come a completely new way of looking at the world. A New Renaissance, a rebirth. It is logical.'

Alex rubbed the back of his neck. 'What form will this rebirth take?'

Kelner took a deep breath, turned to Bucelli and said, 'I have no idea.' Bucelli laughed, loud and long, his little body bouncing in his chair. They were like two wicked children sharing a joke.

'OK. How does this New Renaissance apply to the Joanna then?'

'Ah. This is simple: they used technology to clean her up because they knew they were capable of doing it. A hundred years ago someone like Conte couldn't have damaged Joanna in the name of restoration because they didn't have the know-how to do it. But just because they are able to do it now doesn't mean it was a good thing. Strictly speaking, therefore, she's a victim of the conflict that will lead to this . . .'

'Rebirth?'

'Yes. Rebirth.'

'Are you against all restorations then?'

Kelner pushed his plate away from him and leaned forward over the table. The academic games were over now. This was serious. 'I'm against interfering for purely aesthetic reasons. If it's in danger then do something, but don't clean it just because you like your marble white rather than grey. When I look at a painting that's five hundred years old I want it to look like it's five hundred years old so that we understand its context. It's like getting a face-lift. Why would you want to look forty when you're really sixty? What's the point? There is none. It is truly pointless.' And then Kelner grinned, as if the utter futility of it all somehow pleased him.

Before he left, Alex told Kelner there was something he wanted to show him in private. The historian said, 'I'm intrigued,' and took him to the clutter of his study at the top of the house, up a narrow spiral staircase laid with deep red tiles, and away from the sluggish noise of chatter below. Alex took the book he had borrowed from the Strossetti library out of the plastic carrier bag in which he had been keeping it and handed it over. Kelner turned it over in his hands, inspected the spine and then opened it to look at the title page.

'Where did you get this?'

'Isabella leant it to me,' he said. 'I found it in her family archive. Have a look at the poem I've marked.'

Kelner shook his head as he turned over the heavy pages. 'Isabella obviously trusts you, perhaps a little too much. A book like this should not be carried around as if it were some pulp novel. It's a precious object, to be cared for.' He read some more. 'Good God, there's sixteenth-century material in here. Do you have no sense of responsibility? I suppose you convinced her that it was the right thing to do. The charm of the hack.' Did Alex detect a strain of jealousy in the older man's words? Did the historian want to be the one to have received the loan?

Alex said: 'Can you read Latin? Do you understand it?'

Kelner peered at the verse, leaning the hard edge of his nose ever closer to the page, his lips moving as he worked. Soon he gave up. 'My Latin really is not good enough.' He closed the book and handed it back. 'Probably of little interest. There are books like this all over Tuscany.' He turned to leave the room.

Alex felt his guts drop with disappointment. He wasn't sure why, but he felt he had a duty to find out about Joanna, one that was growing. It was as if there was the promise of redemption in this search; that even just by trying to solve the mystery of her lover's identity, by attempting to put that story to rest, he would be able to exorcize the demons of his own past. He was sure his relationship with Isabella, whatever that might be, depended on it. So did his sense of himself. 'But the name Joanna in the title, and the date . . .'

'Probably nothing.' Kelner walked away towards the top of the stairs. Alex stood holding the book in both hands, staring at the leather cover, willing it to give him an answer.

'Do you know anyone else who could translate it?'

The historian turned back to look at him, his face caught in a scowl, as if outraged that his judgement should be questioned. 'If you insist on pursuing this,' he said sharply, 'try David King-Thomas.'

'I know the name . . .'

'So you should. He was once the director of the Courtauld Institute.'

'And he lives here?'

'He's been in Florence for the past twenty years. He lives somewhere around the Forte di Belvedere. His number is in the telephone directory.' Alex scribbled the name down in his notebook. Kelner turned to leave once more.

'Professor Kelner, there's one other thing.'

'What?' he said, turning back to face him again.

'After you made all the money from the auction of the Joanna study – hope you don't think I'm prying – but after that did you ever think of leaving academia? You must be a rich man by now.'

For ten seconds Kelner said nothing. He stared at Alex, as though the journalist were some grimy squatter who had forced his way into his home and who now refused to leave until he had been allowed to scramble through every last detail of his private life.

'I had a son, Mr Fuller,' he said finally.

'Yes, I know. You told me. I'm very sorry about his dea—'

'A son who died. It costs a lot to care for a dying son.'

'Ah, I see. I . . .'

'I was never rich, Mr Fuller.' His surname had become a term of abuse. 'I had a lot of money for a while. But I needed that money to care for my son. I spent it all, every last cent and then some. Is that all right with you?' Alex was silent. 'Is it?'

'Yes, of course. I didn't mean to . . .'

'No. Nobody ever means to.' Kelner turned and walked away. This time Alex did not call him back.

CHAPTER TWELVE

David King-Thomas, stooped by age but dressed in suits of finest silk, moved about his septuagenarian world with perfectionist rigour, drank absinthe once a week and took tea every afternoon at four. He hated the English for their philistine ways, and detested the Scots. Of the Irish he thought rarely and of the Welsh not at all. He could not abide the French, nor the Spanish nor the Greeks and the only German he had ever liked was Richard Wagner. The Dutch, he said, did not demand of one an opinion and for this he admired them, though not for much else. He had met an American gentleman who once had amused him but had little time for those of his countrymen he had been unfortunate enough to come across since, and no time at all for those who had the cheek to walk below his window, clad in plastic dresses of fluorescent pink and green. As to America itself, that was a place one must say one has visited but not somewhere to which one would like to return. New York in the early forties he had found stimulating but, he had heard, it had become somewhat less sociable of late.

For Italy, where he had made his home, he had only praise. Here he considered himself to be a guest and thus to say otherwise would hardly have been good manners. In Italy, he said, they cared about art. They understood its place in the greater scheme of things. In Italy life itself was an aesthetic feast, each aspect of the daily routine tailored to the needs of beauty. Was this not the birthplace of the Renaissance, where Michelangelo and Donatello literally carved their reputations in stone for all to see? Did not, from here, come all of Western civilization?

What more delightful city is there in the world than Florence, he would ask of visitors, what greater natural jewel than the Tuscan hills?

If he missed anything of his former life in England he did not say, though occasionally he could be heard to reminisce about Anthony Blunt, and to bemoan his old friend's cruel treatment at the hands of those shadowy figures who do the dirty work for the overlords of the British establishment. But now Anthony, like so many of his close circle, was gone and from his past he was left only with his memories and his learning. In keeping with his devotion to Italy he had long ago converted to Rome, and though he could not claim himself free of the need for confession, he attended mass every Sunday without fail. Such was the exile life of David King-Thomas.

In the Florentine world of art history he was known, sometimes even to his face, as 'The King' which he rather liked. Behind his back, however, he was known as 'The Queen' on account of his predilection for pretty rent-boys, purloined from the Cascine Gardens down by the river who, to his intimates, he insisted on calling his 'part-time catamites', in knowing tribute to his classical education.

Despite his august career his departure from England had not been a happy one. Outraged that he had not been plucked from the Courtauld Institute to head the British Museum, a job he considered to be his by right, he flew into a rage, throwing abuse at whoever would listen, proclaiming loudly that he was the victim of a hate campaign of monstrous proportions; once, in a vast fit of pique, he was heard to say that the English art history fraternity was now 'a nest of vipers, grown weak from the effort of poisoning each other'.

'Good old King-Thomas,' his admirers could be heard to

say, after that. 'He could always turn the phrase.'

Soon afterwards, he sold his flat in Kensington, packed his bags and went, by train, to Florence where he determined to live on the proceeds of his writings and a small legacy he had been left by an aged aunt some years before. Journalists called to see him often back then, making the pilgrimage to his grand apartment overlooking the city on the Via di Belvedere, in search of the customary diatribe about the parlous state of English art history which, of course, they would get. King-Thomas did not like to disappoint. He would sit on the edge of his seat, flick specks of his own cigarette ash from his lapels, and say: 'My dear, most of them would be better suited to judging the exhibits at a bring-and-buy sale.'

But eventually the pale youths who once came, notebook in hand, to record the great man's thoughts grew tired of his rantings and went elsewhere for their quotes. The publication of his autobiography – entitled, with customary vanity, *Impeccable Provenance* – had occasioned another rash of newspaper profiles on account of the vitriol he made a point of heaping upon his contemporaries on every page. But that had been some five years ago. These days he spoke to few outside his immediate circle – those he called his 'new friends' even though he had known most of them some twenty-odd years – and was rarely, if ever, disturbed by enquiries from the press.

And so, when he had received the phone call from the man who introduced himself as Mr Fritter or Mr Filter or perhaps it was Mr Flower (the hearing was no longer what it once was, though the eyes, praise be, were holding up) and requested an audience, King-Thomas sighed, said to himself, 'Perhaps, old chap, you should take one last walk around the Daffodils,' and gave his assent. Now he sat by an open window, a volume of Petrarch – in the original Italian, of course – laid upon the table before him, though only for effect. He studied his watch and sighed and waited for death to carry him off, or for his visitor to call, whichever happened first. Sadly, he suspected that, as always, it would be the latter.

King-Thomas huffed, and shuffled in his seat. The man was late. Five minutes late. So ill-mannered. Why make an arrangement if you could not keep to it? This wouldn't do at all. He folded one leg over the other, inspected the creases of his trousers, brushed fluff from his ancient crotch, and settled back to wait a little more.

Alex stood in the shadows of the hallway outside the old man's door, trying to stem the flow of sweat from having walked up four flights of stairs, shook both arms to try to get rid of some of the creases in his jacket, tucked the shirt into his trousers and knocked on the door.

'Mr Flitter, I expect.' King-Thomas stood in the doorway, coiffed and thoroughly preened, well ironed and bone dry. Sunlight flooded out behind him. Alex did not correct the man's mistake.

He smiled broadly and said, 'Absolutely. So sorry I'm late. Got a little lost.'

'Indeed.'

He was led into the airy lounge with its rococo-framed mirrors and its oakwood floor. King-Thomas said: 'It is too early for tea. I may offer you only mineral water at this time of day. Tell me, Mr Flitter, will a mineral water suffice, or shall you be awkward?' Alex said yes, a mineral water would do fine, and found himself bowing his head ever so slightly as he said it. King-Thomas returned with the glass of water, placed it on a coaster before the journalist and then settled back in his chair on the other side of the room.

Alex pointed at the book on the table in front of where the

old man sat. 'I hope I'm not disturbing your reading.' King-Thomas sniffed, picked up the volume, flicked through it and said, 'Just revising, my dear. At my age one has to remind oneself of these things. The mind is less retentive than once it was. I read Petrarch for exercise.' He reached around, put the book on the window ledge behind him and then folded his hands in his lap. 'You suggested, during our conversation early this morning, that there was a matter you wished to discuss with me on behalf of your paper – the *Chronicle* did you say, Mr Flitter?'

'The *Correspondent*. The *Daily Correspondent*.'

'Indeed. A paper of which I have no knowledge. I suspect it is garbage, like most of that which passes for the press in England these days.'

'It would not be for me to say.'

'No indeed. It would not.' King-Thomas placed one hand on the carved wooden arm of his chair so that the sunlight sparkled off his perfectly manicured fingernails. 'What, Mr Flitter, is the nature of your enquiry?'

Alex opened up his leather side-bag and pulled out the plastic carrier holding the book. He unwrapped it, saying, 'I have a sixteenth-century poem in Latin which I thought you might be able to help me with.'

'I do not run a translation service.'

'No, sorry. Of course not. I know that. But it was Professor Robert Kelner who suggested I come to you. I think he thought you might be interested.'

'Kanter? Never heard of the man. Who is he?'

'Kelner. An American art historian from the Institute of Early Modern Sculpture.'

King-Thomas snorted. 'An American? Not the sort I would chance to come across.'

Alex screwed the plastic bag into a ball and pushed it hastily into his pocket. He sat with the book on his lap and quickly explained the background to the poem: the story of Joanna, which King-Thomas said he knew, and the impending court case, which he said he had also followed with a little interest, though not obsessively.

'I was taken by the poem,' Alex said, holding up the closed book, 'because of the date and because the name Joanna appears in the title. It's not much, I know, but . . .'

'I suppose then, as you have come this far to see me, I should do you this service.'

Alex got up and walked over to where King-Thomas was sitting, handed him the book and said: 'I've marked the page.'

'So I see.' With his thumb and index finger, he picked up the piece of paper, a page torn roughly from one of Alex's notebooks, and laid it on the table, as though it were a piece of rotting meat. He looked at the poem and then lifted the book up and away from him. 'My eyesight is perfect,' he said, without looking up. 'But I do find a little distance always helps.' Alex returned to his seat.

The historian looked at the page for a moment. 'First we shall do as the poem demands. We shall read. Oddly the title is in Italian while the verse itself is in Latin. The title reads "Where the stones lie shall Joanna keep her peace".'

'Yes. I know that bit.'

'What?' He cupped one hand behind his ear.

'I said I understand the title.'

'Why have you come to me then? Are you wasting my time?'

'It's the verse I need help with. The verse.'

'Very well.' King-Thomas pulled a yellow silk handkerchief

from his jacket pocket and dabbed at his upper lip, though it appeared already to be dry. 'As I have said, a poem is written to be read and so we shall do.' He sucked his teeth for a moment and then began:

> 'Columba quiescit ubi miles est; non excaecata
> prae belli igne, mendico suum pallium dat.
> Nunc amor meus quietus erit.
> Statio nigri phaseoli
> intra pacem robusti receptaculi sui
> rationes putaret,
> cupiditatis saevium pretium hoc est. Illa non Laura,
> sed collum est albi alabastri. Hebes filia
> Thalia cliens, mortis aeterna persona.
> Adspice cum columba corvum pictum
> super lapides spectat, ubi nigrum et album
> idem erunt.
>
> Preme locum positum sub unguibus suis,
> rupes illa occulta sua aperiet,
> et amoris veritas perspecta erit.
> Hec verba aperta exprime, non retine in pectore.'

King-Thomas placed the book in his lap and bowed his head. Then he said: 'Let us begin as the poet began: with the form. It is a rare verse type, in two parts. It is called a *Dodici-Quattro* or, quite literally, a twelve-four, for no other reason than that that is the number of lines in each part. But this does have its own significance. The first twelve lines are to represent the twelve tribes of Israel of the old testament. The last four are the four evangelists of the new testament – Matthew, Mark,

Luke and John, though I do not suppose you know your bible, Mr Flitter.'

Alex had his notebook out and was writing. 'I've never heard of that verse type before,' he said.

'No indeed. One would not expect you to. Such things are for true scholars only. A journalist would have no interest.' He said this as though it were merely a statement of fact rather than a judgement. 'The form is rare because it was so cumbersome. One was expected to use the last four lines to deliver something of a moral on that which lay in the first twelve and doing this with any grace was beyond the wit of most of its proponents.' He dabbed at his upper lip again. 'But the form is only the walls of the building. We must find what treasures lie within.' He pointed to a bookshelf against one wall to the side of the room. 'At the far end of the third shelf you shall find a dictionary of Latin bound in red. Bring it to me.' Alex did as he was asked.

King-Thomas pointed to a Japanese lacquered box on the table between them. 'Can I interest you in a cigarette?' He leaned forward and flicked open the lid. 'Davidoff's finest. I have them sent from Geneva. There is no substitute for fine tobacco.'

They each took one. Alex lit up from a box of old matches he had in his pocket, and sucked down the smoke hungrily. King-Thomas tapped his on the back of his hand, took a flame from a heavy silver lighter and then settled back. He smoked as though he were sipping from the cigarette, which he held between the third and fourth fingers of his left hand, just below the first joint.

'To work.' King-Thomas read the first two lines to himself

again. Then he consulted the dictionary. He looked up. 'What relevance would there be in a dove?'

Alex looked confused. 'Sorry?'

'There is a dove mentioned in the first line. What relevance would that have? Do your ears need waxing?'

Alex closed his eyes for a moment. Then he reached into his bag and pulled out a guide book. He flicked through to the page on the Joanna that he had marked.

'Bingo,' he said.

'I beg your pardon?'

'So sorry. A dove is part of the tomb of Joanna. It's down here at the end by her feet.' He turned the book around to show King-Thomas, his finger pointing to the relevant part of the picture.

The old man ignored him. 'Good. This is useful. Am I also correct in remembering that the tomb lies in the Cathedral of San Martino in Strossetti?'

'Yes.'

'Now we may make some sense of your poem. It does indeed refer to the tomb of Joanna dei Strossetti. The first lines read, "The dove rests where the soldier, not blinded by the fire of war, gives the beggar-man his cloak." ' King-Thomas looked up to the ceiling, and put his hands together as if he were delivering a sermon. 'One of the few acts for which Saint Martin is famous is the giving of half his cloak to a beggar-man during a war at . . . I believe it was Amiens. We can check. In any case the reference to our sculpture is clear. Let us read on.'

He studied some more, looking from poem to dictionary and back again. He worked like an archaeologist, eagerly scrabbling away at the mud of centuries, searching for the truth that lay hidden below. 'Look here. More evidence. Just look. There is a reference to the dropping of a bean into a box. In just such a way did they record the birth of a child, by placing a bean in a box. White for a girl, black for a boy. Certainly it was the case in the Florentine Republic of the fifteenth century and we can suppose the practice existed in Strossetti as well. Again you may check, Mr Flitter. In any case as we know, Joanna died in the process of birthing a bastard son.' Alex nodded vigorously and scribbled. He shifted to the edge of his seat, anxious for riddles to be solved, codes to be broken.

There was silence now as King-Thomas worked. He uncrossed his legs, placed both books on his lap, and bent his head low over the pages, so that the normally slight curvature in his spine became more pronounced. Suddenly Alex felt like an interloper sitting there, as the old man attended to the text, sniffing around its twists and turns, burrowing between the letters. King-Thomas straightened up. 'The next four lines would seem to be a protestation of love.'

Alex leaned even further forward: 'Do you think it was written by the father of the child?'

'That I cannot tell. You have no knowledge who wrote it?'

Alex shook his head. Of course he hadn't. That was why he had come to see King-Thomas. Couldn't the old man see that?

'You see here, the Latin could suggest the author were someone of an ecclesiastical bent. A priest perhaps. If he were the father – and this is distinctly possible; the priesthood, though large in those times, was still recovering from the great schism and had no discipline – he would, indeed, seek anonymity for such a terrible sin. But there are also interesting images. He says she is no Laura – *Illa non Laura*. Now, as I'm sure you know – or perhaps not; one must never assume – Laura was the idealized woman in Petrarch's love poetry, of which our love-struck versifier would have known. Here he says she is no Laura. Therefore she is not idealized but real. And yet he says she has a neck of alabaster white. A rather nice little joke. Petrarch was forever describing Laura's alabaster skin and her flaxen locks. And yet Joanna has a neck of white stone because she is now dead and made of marble. Do you see? It's almost clever.

'Then he follows this with two classical references. *Hebes filia* – daughter of Hebe. Hebe was the goddess of eternal youth. Joanna is now captured in stone and therefore in eternal youth. And then a little flattery: *Thalia cliens*. Guarded by Thalia of the Three Graces; she it is who bestows grace and charm. Our poet believes therefore that Joanna has been endowed with charm. It is all rather neat.' For the first time since he had arrived there Alex saw David King-Thomas smile. The old man was pleased with himself.

'Either the author is the father or he worshipped Joanna from afar but I suspect not. If he had, she would have remained idealized and within this verse she does not.'

He pursed his lips. 'As for the rest I am really not so sure. It talks about doves looking at ravens – do you know anything about a raven?'

Alex checked his guide book. 'No, nothing in here I'm afraid.'

'No indeed. Those books are dreadful; they will tell you nothing at all. But then, in this line it states that black and white shall be the same to one another.' He took out his handkerchief once more and rubbed the smooth yellow silk between his thumb and forefinger in thought. 'It could be an early denunciation of the doctrine of original sin, I suppose . . .' He looked at Alex. 'Have you found yourself to be directed by the innate desire to sin, Mr Flitter?'

He shrugged, irritably. 'I suppose so. These things are all relative. I once got done for shoplifting and I was also caught for drunk driving a while back.' All he wanted was King-Thomas to complete his translation.

'Dear boy, that would strike me as rather unoriginal sin. A half-hearted effort.' Alex sighed with frustration. The old man continued his speech. 'Original sin is of an earthier nature altogether; it is the best kind of sin there is. I am well practised.' His gaze drifted off to a distant corner. There was silence in the room for a minute, broken only by the rumble of traffic and a bell pealing far away.

'Do forgive me,' he said eventually. 'At my age one has so many memories and they do tend to impose themselves on one occasionally.' Alex tried to smile convincingly.

Finally King-Thomas turned to the last four lines, or the evangelists, as he called them. But, he said, if these evangelists had a word to spread, he wasn't at all sure what it was. 'It is all about rocks yielding secrets. It says only "if one presses beneath the claws". What can that be about, I wonder? It is proof, if we needed it, of the flaws in the verse form. If this is meant to be a moral then it is one of great idiosyncrasy. And the last line: speak these words clear and not as of the heart. What on earth can that mean?'

Alex had been drawing spirals in his notebook again. 'Perhaps,' he said quietly, 'it's an order. Perhaps we're being told to take those lines literally. Like when they use the word "confused" in a crossword clue to tell you it's an anagram. Here we're being told not to get too spiritual about it – "as of the heart" – but to speak the words clear.'

'In other words, my dear, you must seek out a place to press upon and great secrets shall be told unto you. You could indeed be right. Heaven knows there are enough secrets to be told.'

King-Thomas wrote out an English translation of the poem in perfect copper-plate. He handed it to Alex and said: 'Occasionally I have had need to correct the language. The author's Latin was good but not perfect. Of course, I have kept the sense.' Alex went over to the window, where, with the rooftops of Florence laid out before him, he read through the verse:

Where the Stones Lie Shall Joanna Keep Her Peace

The dove rests where the soldier, not blinded
by the fire of war, gives the beggar-man his
cloak. Now shall my love be still.
That the laying of one black bean,
within the peace of its case,
should bring a life to account,
is passion's cruel price. No Laura she,
but neck of alabaster white. Daughter of Hebe;
guarded by Thalia, in death's eternal mask.
Look then as the dove looks upon the raven
painted to the stones, where black and white
shall be the one to the other.

And press upon the place beneath his claws
that rock shall yield up its secrets
and truth of love be known. Speak these words
clear and not as of the heart.

Alex patted his jacket pockets, found his own cigarettes and lit one, cupping his hands around the match to keep it from flickering in the breeze. He offered the pack to King-Thomas, who was browsing through the Strossetti book. 'No thank you, my dear,' he said, with one upraised palm. 'I prefer to keep only to that which I know.' Alex turned back to confront the view of the city: those old stones and dry bones again, always old stones and dry bones. But now the stones had secrets and there was flesh on the bones.

He thanked King-Thomas for his time, reclaimed his book and said he had to go. The old man stood up, straightened the line of his jacket and walked him to the door, in carefully placed steps. 'It has been a curious pleasure,' he said quietly. 'I shall be most interested to know of your discoveries.' Then he opened the door just wide enough to allow Alex space to slip out sideways and said: 'Well, goodbye then.' And with a solid clunk the door closed on the twilight world of memories and bitterness that had become death's waiting room for David King-Thomas.

Down on the road by the river, overlooking the loaf of grubby sand that marked out the south bank just below the Ponte Vecchio, Alex stopped and watched the fishermen. They sat, motionless on their little aluminium stools, dragging their lines across the smooth waters of the Arno. The peace was broken only by the noise of motor scooters, spluttering along over on the north bank, the riders' bodies obscured by the river wall, so that only their heads could be seen skimming, like bowling balls, along its length. He watched them for a while until he grew bored. It was hot now, and the air smelt only of the Arno: all damp, musty weeds and resting water off the back of the weir. He lit another cigarette and dropped the dead match on to the sand twenty feet below, watching it turn and flip as it fell. Then he held his arms out in front of him so that whatever breeze there might be would dry out his armpits, and recited the last words of the poem quietly to himself:

'Speak these words clear and not as of the heart.'

He hated being excluded from a secret. Here was a tale to be told. He was sure of that now. A grand tale, rich in detail and intrigue. The answer to a mystery. Just his kind of yarn. Who was the child's father? And where had he signed his name? And how, damn it, how? The truth lay somewhere in the cathedral, near Joanna. It had to. Of that he was sure. Or why else would the poem bear so many clues? Why would it direct you there? A game? A little conceit? Unlikely.

And the dove. Why mention the dove if it didn't have anything to do with it? Of the raven he could make no sense at all. That was a mystery within a mystery. He brought up his right arm to drag on his cigarette.

He wanted something to look at, a visual reference to help him think. He wanted to be able to walk around Joanna's tomb so as to understand her shape and her position, to get a full sense of how she lay in relation to the world about her. He wanted to look her in the eye and ask her for clues. Alex dug into his side-bag and pulled out the collection of cuttings he had been given by Hawksmoor the night before. He laid the pile on top of the wall and flicked through until he found the picture of the auction with the small inset shot of the study for the tomb. He turned over to the next cutting, which was also a story about the auction, but illustrated by a single picture of the tomb itself. This would have to do. He stared at it, following the line of the stonework from one end to the other. For the first time he noticed how the body sloped down to the toes. They did not stand vertically, but were flexed as though Joanna were a ballerina, limbering up to go on point; he noticed how the shape of the dove followed the same line so that its beak seemed to turn towards the same vanishing point, which lay somewhere outside the frame of the picture. And that line began with the tip of Joanna's nose, her head raised upon its cushion, so that the whole sculpture almost had about it a sense of direction and geometric purpose.

Casually he began to skim-read the story alongside the picture, essentially the same as the photo caption, but with a few more details. One caught his eye. The date the study had been discovered. Alex read through the paragraphs again. He reached inside his pocket and pulled out his notebook. He shuffled through it and found the page where he had jotted down a few points about Isabella, background stuff for his story, or a crib sheet for seduction. At the time he hadn't really been sure which it was. Now it was proving useful.

There was something curious here. A problem with dates, a piece of the jigsaw puzzle of recent events that wouldn't quite go into place. If his memory served him right Isabella said she had seen the man that she recognized from the court case, the same man who had discovered the study of the Joanna which made Kelner all his cash, in Strossetti the summer after she finished Harvard. For some reason he had scribbled the year down in his notebook. She said he was sketching the tomb. If his notes on Isabella were correct, the artist – what was his name? He looked at the first paragraph. Carlo Palecchi, that's right. Palecchi. If he'd got his notes right, then Palecchi had been sketching the Joanna the year before he discovered the study in the monastery of Massarosa. Wasn't there something odd about that? A coincidence maybe? Sure. But real coincidences are rare. Alex knew that.

He sucked hard on his cigarette again, burning it down close to the filter. He would have to ask Isabella, the next time he saw her, whenever that was. He stubbed out the cigarette on the wall and, when he was sure nobody was looking, released it to join the match on the sand. Maybe he was just trying to read more into all of this than there really was, he thought. Maybe he just wanted a reason for staying, a reason to avoid going back to London and all the unfinished business there? He had more than enough material to finish his piece. The court case would end on Saturday. He could take the verdict from agency copy and just work it in.

He walked east along the river, crossing by the grey, post-war Ponte alle Grazie and doubling back on himself to reach his hotel across from where he had been standing. At reception there was a message from the paper. It said: 'Mr Fuller, he dead? Please advise.'

'Sarcastic bastards,' he muttered under his breath. He screwed the note into a ball and threw it away. Up in his bedroom he phoned the foreign editor and told him he wanted to take a few days' holiday. He would charge no more expenses to the paper.

'Don't go native on us, lad,' the foreign editor said. 'We'd hate to lose you.'

Next he called reception and told them he would be checking out and asked for a porter to come up to help him with his bags in a few minutes' time. Finally he dug through his notebook to find Isabella's work number and called her.

'I'm afraid I need somewhere to stay.'

'You do not have the hotel?'

He liked hearing the soft tones of her voice, the gentle vowels oozing their way down the line. 'Because I went to Strossetti with you they think I've stayed too long.'

'You are trying to blame me?'

'No. I was trying to be funny. The thing is I want to stay for the case but they want me home. I've taken a few days' holiday.' He stopped and looked around his hotel room: the vast expanse of parquet floor, the chandeliers and the thick linen sheets, the mini bar and the bathrobe. 'But I can't afford to stay here.'

'OK,' she said slowly. 'I shall do my work for the homeless today. Meet me at my apartment at six o'clock. Eleven, Borgo degli Albizi.' She hung up.

Alex sat on the edge of the bed, rested a hand on each knee and slowly slid his feet forward along the polished floor. He turned and looked at the rich blue stain of sky out the open window behind him.

'Christ,' he said to himself quietly. 'I hope I'm not about to make a complete idiot of myself.'

CHAPTER THIRTEEN

Alex was leaning far out of Isabella's window, watching a dead match float to ground on evening thermals, when he heard the shout. It was thick and belly-loud, like a cry of pain or an expletive. He shoved his cigarette into his mouth to free his hands and leaned further out to see where the noise had come from. Down in the square that opened off the road far below Isabella's window were three young men. He had seen them standing there, all bad teeth and attitude, some two hours before when she had brought him up here to her apartment, a lung-busting climb to the very top of the building. Now they were closing around an old man. From that distance all Alex could see was his balding pate and his caramel mackintosh and the shine off his big, black leather shoes. He was poking one of the younger men in the chest and shouting, a fiery stream of words. The square, which earlier had been crowded, now seemed to have cleared. There were just these four angry men, one old, three young, shouting at each other.

One of the lads, the tallest of the three, smacked the old man in the shoulder, a real thump, packed full of bodyweight, so that he rocked on his heels and groaned. Alex called out. 'Isabella. Come here. Come see what's going on.' But he couldn't make much of a noise because of the cigarette stuck there in his mouth. He called again. 'Isabella.' This time he parted his lips to shout and the cigarette dropped out, following the path of the match to the ground. Alex didn't bother to watch it fall. There were more interesting things going on down below. The old man was being hit again, as though his assailant had need to perfect his technique. And again, knuckles to the chest and cheek, that pushed his whole body up and around and back. And then again. Finally his frame refused to soak up any more of those clenched fists and tensed biceps and he fell backwards on to the ground, landing just out of sight of Isabella's window with a heavy clump. Now all that could be seen from up there was the assailant throwing his weight behind a right-foot kick, both arms raised for balance, jaw jutting forward for direction.

Alex pushed himself away from the window and ran from the apartment, almost tripping over Isabella as she came out of the bathroom, rubbing her wet hair with a towel. He managed only a breathless 'I'll be back,' before storming out the door and down the dimly lit stairs. As he came out on to the square, into the stinking fug of early evening heat, he could hear the thud of each kick to the gut and the old man's weak cries. Alex shouted as he ran towards them, 'Get the fuck off him. Get away.' The three men turned to look at him, lips caught in a sneer, hair razor-cut and spiky. The two shorter men decided to run, one to the left, one to the right. The last of the three, the one on kicking duty, stayed still for a second, foot lifted off the ground and held well back, as if lining up for a shot on goal. He had the English word 'spider' tattooed in sludge green right around his neck, as if marking the place for a first incision, and a large gold tooth at the front of his mouth. He grinned at Alex, so that the metal flashed, flicked his tongue out like a lizard lapping up the air and then threw all his weight behind the toe of his shoe. He cracked it into the old man's ribs, who crumpled around the impact into a tight foetus position. He tried to groan but his strength had gone. He could manage only a faint wheeze. Spider smiled proudly at his footwork and then turned and ran too, skipping over a loop of thick chain that separated the square from the road, and down the long, red-brick arch that led through to the next street.

Alex began to give chase but gave up before he had even made it into the tunnel, stumbling to a halt by the chain barrier. He watched the crowd of people huddling around the kebab shop in the archway separate to let Spider through and close up behind him when he had passed. Alex could see the man was taller and thinner than he was and that he lifted his legs high as he ran, slapping the soles of his shoes down hard on to the cobbles with a sharp echoing crack. The journalist knew he didn't have a hope in hell of catching him. He shook his head and turned to see how the old man was, but already people were wandering back into the square, shuffling out of doorways and from narrow alleys to check the drama was over. Some crowded around the victim, holding a handkerchief to a bloody gash in his forehead or tucking a blanket around him to keep him warm. Others set about preparing the shops and bars for the evening's trade, switching on lights which cast a glow of undisturbed normality over the cobbles. Alex walked slowly to the door of Isabella's block. She was standing waiting for him, hair still damp.

'This was not clever,' she said.

Alex coughed loudly. 'Please. Don't lecture me.'

'They are not nice people.'

'Now you tell me.' He leaned back against the wall by the door. He realized for the first time that he was shaking a little. 'Do you know who he is?'

Isabella said, 'I know too well. Come with me.' They walked twenty yards down the street to an empty shop unit, a bare concrete shell, its open front guarded only by a heavy metal grill. Scattered over the bare stone floor just behind the grill were dozens of tiny syringes, the needles sometimes bent, the bodies spotted with congealed blood, dark brown against the grim yellow plastic.

Alex studied the mess; the debris left by so many nights in desperate pursuit of narcotic oblivion. 'I don't know why, I didn't expect smack here. It doesn't seem the place . . .'

'Just because we have our marble madonnas and a pretty bridge with houses on it does not mean we do not have this as well.' She slipped the fingers of one hand around the grill and pointed at the syringes. 'Firenze is a city, like London or Roma.'

'I know that.'

'And the narrow streets hide secrets better than wide ones. It is not just a place with memories. It has life. Which means having this as well. Having life means having death too. The boy you chased away, he is a heroin dealer. They come here to make the sale. The old man was telling them to go. You were brave to stop the attack.'

'I can feel a big "but" coming.'

Isabella touched her fingertips against his lips and laughed a little. 'But you should not have followed. There was no point to this. It is for the police.'

'Perhaps,' he said quietly. 'But I'm afraid I have a thing about running after people.'

Back in her apartment Isabella opened a window to let in the sweeter evening air that floated around up there and poured him a large glass of wine. She sat down next to him on the couch, curling her legs beneath her like a cat, stroked the back of his neck and said, 'Why did you do that? It was like you were chasing after your own shadow, running into the square like that. Why did you go? I think you want me to know. I think it is Kenya that makes you run.'

Alex held up his glass so he could look at the old city, refracted through the piss-yellow wine. He took a large gulp, swallowed and turned to look at Isabella.

'I will not judge you,' she said.

He lit up a cigarette, ran his hands through his hair and looked at the view through his wine again.

'You do not have to say if you do not want to.'

'No,' he said quietly. 'No I don't. But I will have to some time. Maybe I should tell you now.'

They had been driving since well before the Kenyan dawn. Tooley, the Irish photographer with a suitcase full of newspaper commissions, was at the wheel of the jeep, being his usual misanthropic self, moaning about the car and the rocks on the road and the sun, because he knew his professional reputation allowed him to. Carla Stropp, the American reporter from Associated Press, was sitting next to him, shielding her eyes against the glare and chipping in with a few complaints of her own; being bitchy about rivals from other news outfits who were all, she said, 'incompetent cunts. Present company excluded. Sometimes.' Alex sat in the back with Mantu Kiango, their Tanzanian fixer who was short and bony and never complained because he said time spent saying bad things only reduced the amount of time in which you could talk of good. He called the journalists 'my pupils' and pressed one hand against his cheek whenever he laughed, as if he suspected the side of his head might fall off if he wasn't too careful. He had an immense capacity for beer and could squirt it through a gap between his front teeth in a constant stream sometimes of ten feet or more, though he wouldn't perform the trick often because he said it was a waste of good ale.

They were driving through the Chalbi Desert in northern Kenya, towards the Ethiopian border, when they were stopped. As Tooley would later say: 'It was the fuckin' Ethiopian guerillas we were after. We just hadn't thought we'd find them that fuckin' quickly or on that fuckin' side of the border.' There were two battered old jeeps, one parked on each side of the deserted road, back wheels sunk into the sand. A couple of soldiers were slumped, apparently asleep, in the back of each, caps down over their eyes, feet laid lank over the seats in front. Three others were leaning against the vehicles, tired defenders of a Marxist regime now in tatters, desperately looking for action. They had their Russian automatics slung around in front of them, and a holstered pistol at the hip. As the journalists approached, one of the men lifted his weapon up in front of him horizontally, to bring them to a halt.

Tooley said: 'I don't fuckin' believe it. It's a checkpoint. In a fuckin' desert.'

Carla began scrabbling around in her bag for her ID. 'Who the hell are they?'

'I don't fuckin' know. They look like the Ethiopian lot but I didn't think we'd crossed the border yet.' Alex picked the map off the floor of their jeep and started folding it over to find their location.

He scanned the flat, heat-stained horizon. 'There's not a single point of reference out here,' he said. 'Not a fucking thing.' He passed the map forward to Tooley who said, 'Kiango, I think we may need your services.' The mood in the jeep stiffened. They had all been stopped at checkpoints before. All of them had felt the cold stare of a boy soldier with a new rank and a new gun, both of which he wanted to use. But however many times it happened, however many occasions they were forced to ride this emotional roller-coaster, its carriages powered by adrenaline, its rails greased by fear, it didn't become any more comfortable. For many it became worse. The poker players, the ones who knew about these things, said the odds on them getting away unscathed shortened with each new encounter.

At every checkpoint, they said, death was always standing there, dressed in regulation fatigues, trigger-happy, hungry for blood. A checkpoint, usually little more than an attempt by the relevant armed militia to prove they have enough guns to control a worthless strip of tarmac, was not an ideal place to be.

Tooley stopped the jeep and smiled at the soldier with the greatest number of steel stars stitched to his cap. They handed over their laminated press passes and their passports, as requested. The soldier studied each one in turn, looking from the photographs to the owners' faces, as if searching for some wicked deception, staring into their eyes so that they could not shake his gaze. He handed them back, except Kiango's, whom he ordered out of the jeep. The Tanzanian stood to attention in the harsh sun, while the soldier shuffled through some more of his papers. The sleeping Ethiopians had now woken and were standing a few feet away, gripping their guns, chewing and watching. Silence. Only the sound of sand flies and papers being flicked over. The glare of the sun and the white blur of the horizon.

The commander started shouting at Kiango, pointing at documents.

Alex said, 'Oh shit.'

Tooley said, 'Shut the fuck up and we'll all get out of this.'

Alex gripped the side of the jeep and said, 'Oh shit. Oh shit. Oh shit.' The soldier was now stabbing a finger in Kiango's chest and screaming at him. The Tanzanian had his hands up to defend himself.

Carla could understand a little of the local dialect. She said: 'Oh Christ. I think he's accusing him of being a Tanzanian spy.'

Alex said, 'Oh shit.'

Tooley said, 'Shut the fuck up.'

Later Alex would say he couldn't actually remember making the decision to get out and plead. There wasn't a thought process as such, he would say. He just did it, took hold of the metal sides of the jeep and jumped over. He grabbed Kiango's arm and started shouting. 'He's with us. He's press. He's nothing else. Press. It's all fine. We'll just go and it will all be fine.' The rest of the soldiers straightened up and moved towards them. But Alex didn't stop. 'Just let us go. We'll be fine. No problems. No nothing.' He didn't even stop when the men slipped the safety catches on their rifles, a loud chorus of gunmetal cracking against itself in the stillness of the afternoon. Kiango moved forward, to put himself between Alex and the guns. The journalist tried to pull him back again as if he wanted to get to the men's weapons first, shouting all the time. But all he did was pull Kiango over so that it looked like he was going to lunge at the shortest of the soldiers.

Alex heard the gunshot and felt the hot slap of blood and tissue against his chest almost instantaneously. It was as if Kiango's head had exploded from the inside, a spray of raw meat and bone. The fixer crumpled to the ground. Alex stood stunned for a few seconds, staring at the blood on his hands and his forearms and his chest as though trying to work out why he could feel no pain from such a bloody wound. A little more of Kiango's blood dribbled down his chin and on to his collar. Then he screamed.

'Baaaastaards!'

Behind him he heard Tooley shout, 'Fuller. No. Oh fuckin' Christ, no.'

The soldier who had fired the shot was standing a few feet away, stock still, staring at the bloody mess on the ground, as if amazed by the power of his weapon. Alex staggered over, grabbed the gun and tried to pull it away from him, screaming, spitting, shouting. A second shot went off which hit the dead body on the wrist, almost severing Kiango's useless hand. The soldier let go of the gun and stepped back. The commander backed off too. There was a strained silence again. The journalist slipped the rifle strap over his shoulder, put a hand around the trigger and walked over to Kiango's body. He could smell his friend's blood and brains drying on his denim shirt. He turned the man's head over to look into his eyes. But he only had one eye. The other had gone. He only had half a head. The rest was blood and meat and the buzz of flies.

Tooley jumped down to put the shattered remains in the back of the jeep. He folded a canvas sheet over the body which quickly soaked up the blood. The photographer told Alex to 'get the fuck back into the jeep'. He did as he was told, climbing over the side backwards so he could keep his eyes fixed on the Ethiopians all the time, his rifle pointed towards their knees.

As they accelerated off down the road towards the border Alex stood up, lifted the gun and sprayed the sand with bullets, forcing the soldiers to dive behind their own jeeps for cover. Then he dropped the gun and fell down sobbing on the back seat. Ten minutes later he was violently sick over the side of the moving vehicle.

They didn't stop in southern Ethiopia as planned but drove straight on to Addis Ababa. For three days Alex lay on his bed in the Red Cross compound muttering to himself and sweating and reliving the events in slow motion: the shot, the blood, the despair. Despite Carla and Tooley's advice he did not contact the paper to tell them what had happened. In the end Carla did it for him, telling the *Correspondent*'s foreign editor that he was in no fit state to be out in the field. The paper took her advice; they ordered their blood-stained reporter home.

Isabella refilled his glass. 'And the worst thing about it,' Alex said, 'was the way they treated me when I got back. They didn't give a fuck about Kiango. They kept talking like it was me who had died. They'd come up and they'd squeeze my shoulder and say, "We were so sorry to hear about what happened to you," like I was both the bereaved and the corpse all at the same time. In a way they were right of course. I should have been the one who got his head blown off. If I hadn't behaved like such a complete prick it wouldn't have happened.'

'If you go to wars such things will happen.'

Alex slumped forward and put his head in his hands. 'Isabella, please don't start.'

She said, 'I was not telling you off. I mean it. You cannot blame yourself for someone dying in a place where there is war. People die in wars. You know that. Your friend knew there were risks. It is right that someone goes to be a reporter in wars. It is an important job.'

Alex scoffed. 'I'm not so sure. I haven't met a single journalist who's done it for any length of time who isn't fucked up in some way. Not one. They've all got screwed up marriages and screwed up friendships and screwed up kids. All of them. What's the point of doing a job if it fucks you up?'

'You seem OK.'

'Only here,' he said, turning to look at her. 'In London I was twitchy after that shooting. If I heard a car horn I jumped.

239

If a burglar alarm went off I got ready to take cover. And I couldn't take anything seriously. Nothing. As far as I was concerned there were just wars and then there was all the other shit which was of no consequence. Why bother to pay the gas bill when there are people blowing each other up? It was like they were fiddling while Rome burned.'

'Who is this?'

'That's the thing. It was everybody. Everything.'

'And here?'

'And here? Here, well, I don't know. I don't get the anxiety attacks and stuff. My stomach used to tie itself in knots, you know. It was horrible. I kept feeling like I was going to cry, all the time. That's stopped.'

'This is good.'

'It's strange. In London I couldn't even take normal life seriously and here, I'm doing this story about princesses and sculptures and poems and . . .'

'And?'

'And it all makes sense. Somehow. I want to know what happened. I want to know what the poem means. All of that.' He drained his glass. 'I actually give a damn. It's like I've been numb for a long time and now all my reflexes are coming back. It's like I'm putting myself back together again.'

'So now you even like history.'

'Yeah. I just don't like my own history.'

Later, after they'd drunk the wine and talked the night to a candle stub in a smooth puddle of wax, Alex showed Isabella the translation of the poem and told her he wanted to go back to Strossetti and the cathedral the next day. She agreed to take the day off work and go with him. She had turned herself around on the sofa and was sitting with her legs across his.

She said: 'It is late. We should go to bed.'

Alex rubbed his hands along her calves and, without looking up, said, 'This, I think, is a good idea.'

Isabella swung her legs down to the floor, and then put her arms around his neck and kissed his cheek. 'You will be sleeping here on the sofa.'

Alex feigned outrageous disappointment to mask his outrageous disappointment. 'I knew I should have had a shower after all that running about,' he said. 'You probably think I stink.'

She pinched his cheek. 'Only a little bit. The smell I can live with. Some of it I like. But the rest of your body is not ready to go to bed with me.' She kissed him again, brushing her soft lips against his. Then she kissed his forehead. 'That bit is not ready. Not yet.' She stood up and went into the next room to get him some blankets.

CHAPTER FOURTEEN

Just past Massarosa, where the road to Strossetti turns towards the Apennine mountains, he told her to turn off the motorway. 'It won't take long,' he said. 'We're just going to drop in on someone for coffee.'

'Are we invited?'

Alex said no, Signor Palecchi had no idea they were coming. 'But it won't be a problem. We won't be staying.'

They found the low-slung house easily enough, down a quiet dirt track off the road to Valpromaro, just as the gallery owner had told Alex he would when the journalist went sniffing around the streets of Florence for information the day before. 'Palecchi can be a bit prickly sometimes,' the dealer had said, after agreeing he knew the man. 'Don't be put off. It's just his way.'

Before they knocked on the door Alex told Isabella she would have to translate. 'It should be all right. You did meet him once before. Back in the cathedral a few years ago, sketching the Joanna. Remember?'

The artist took a long time coming. When finally he did open the door he looked like a man who had just woken from a deep sleep, his eyes wide and bloodshot. His grey, closely cropped hair was even spikier than it had been when Isabella had first recognized him in court, and he was chewing on a wooden toothpick. He had a stack of them tucked in behind his ear, a Lilliputian quiver of arrows. Isabella told him who they were. He grunted, mumbled a few words and walked away up the corridor through the house, like a huge, dopey bear stumbling back to his cave.

Isabella was a little startled. 'I was telling him who we are but he says he knows. He says he knows who you are. I think we are meant to follow.' The corridor opened out to a wide artist's studio. Half the roof was made of glass and the room was filled with bright, white sunlight. A pair of doors were open, letting in a cool breeze to take the edge off the glasshouse heat. There were plan chests against the walls and a vast hinged drawing-board in one corner. In the middle of the room was a pedestal on which he was building a clay sculpture around a chicken-wire frame. It was of a woman, naked, legs bent. She was curled over, gripping her knees, her head laid along one arm. In one hand the artist held a lump of thick, brown clay. With the thumb of the other hand he would scoop off a little and press it down on to where her back curved away from her spine, first to the left then to the right, gradually building up the heavy muscles of her shoulders. In front of him stood two screens hung with charcoal studies of nudes. He didn't look at them.

Alex said, 'Ask him how he knew who we were.'

Palecchi carried on working as he talked. He would only stop to spit out a splintered toothpick and replace it with another from behind his ear.

'Kelner told him.'

'They're still friends then?'

Palecchi raised one thick eyebrow. 'He says they keep in touch.'

'Ask him what he thinks of the restoration of the Joanna.'

Isabella said, 'Is this what we are here for? More opinions?'

'Just ask him.'

Palecchi picked a new ball of clay off a lump in the corner and kneaded it with his left hand. He turned to Isabella and stretched out the hand, showing her the lump of mud turning over and over on itself in his palm, folding in on top of itself, his long, heavy fingers pressing down upon it as he talked. Then he squeezed it back into a ball. 'He says ... he says sculpture is about the hand, about touch. If Conte ... if he had been a sculptor he would have known this. Even if the stone is hard you must be careful with your touch. Conte ... he was not careful.'

'Does he think it has been ruined in the way Kelner does?'

Isabella translated. 'What Conte has done, this is not good.' Palecchi shook his head slowly. 'But ruined? No, not ruined. The Joanna, it ... the form, the essence. It is there.'

'Does he support Kelner's fight then?'

Palecchi sniffed. 'Kelner, he likes to make a noise only about Kelner. He has his own reasons. Sometimes ... sometimes it is not so good to make a noise. Sometimes it is better to keep quiet.'

'Tell him you remember meeting him when he was drawing the Joanna. Tell him you would like to see those drawings.'

Isabella turned to Alex. 'Tell him that *you* want to see them?' she said.

'No, no, no. That you want to see them.' She looked at him quizzically. Alex said: 'I'll explain later. I promise.' The artist didn't look up from his work as they talked. He just carried on pressing scales of clay down on to his lady's naked back. Isabella made her request. He put the piece of clay down on the side of the board and pulled a damp cloth over the top of the unfinished work. He did the same with the pile of clay in the corner. Then he wiped his hand on a muddy rag and walked over to one of the plan chests in the corner. From the top drawer he pulled a four-foot-square, clear plastic envelope, stuffed full of sheets of paper, which he heaved on to the worktop. There was a whoosh of air as it landed.

Some of them were small pencil drawings, built on a grid, more like draughtsman's studies than sketches, which considered Joanna's tomb from every elevation. Others were in charcoal, big, bold works which gouged out their image in stripes of thick blackness, smudged grey to give form and dimension. There were a number of drawings that concentrated on the profile, on the smooth curve of her forehead and the rise of her lips, the turn of the dove's head and the fold of its wing. Others were more general, almost impressionistic sketches of the tomb that played upon where the shadows fell, between her legs and behind her hands and beneath her head; pictures where the eye was drawn more to the patches of dark than to the light. On one of these there was a large, muddy-red stain, which covered almost a quarter of the paper.

'These are beautiful,' Isabella said in English. And then: '*Signor Palecchi, l'ha colta in tutti modi.*'

The artist put another toothpick between his front teeth, bit upon it so that they could hear the wood crack and said only, '*Grazie.*' He started piling the drawings back up on top of each other to put them away. At the bottom of each one was a date, all of them from August and early September of the same year. Alex looked at them as the works were heaped up.

'I was certainly right about that,' he said under his breath. And then, 'Tell him it was an amazing coincidence that a few months after he was doing all these drawings he should go to Massarosa and discover Rafanelli's study for the tomb.'

They both heard the wood of his toothpick crack again as he bit down hard. He began working faster, shoving the drawings back into their envelope.

'He says he's sorry but we have to leave now. He says he's busy. He has no more time.' Palecchi left the drawings on top of the chest and herded them out of the studio and down the corridor. On the wall, by the front door, was a watercolour painting of a beach. It was a wide view, taken from a distance, of a long curve of sand-fringed coast disappearing into the blue haze where the sea met the sky. Palecchi had signed his name in the bottom right-hand corner, a careless scrawl, executed as if he had been desperate to get rid of his name by scribbling it on to the paper. In the left-hand corner it said only 'Santa Monica'. There was no date. Alex stopped and looked at the picture. He said to Isabella, 'Find out when he was in California.'

'I lived there for five years in the eighties, Mr Fuller,' the artist replied in perfect English, before Isabella could translate.

Alex spun around. 'You speak English. I didn't know.'

'You did not bother to ask, Mr Fuller.' He grinned. 'Good day to you. And to you, Signorina Strossetti.' Then he shoved them out the door and closed it behind them.

For a while they stood blinking in the sunshine, staring at the door, as if expecting it to reopen, as if it had all been some peculiar joke. But it didn't.

'He's right of course,' Alex said eventually. 'Next time I must remember to ask.'

Later, when he recalled his stay in Italy, it would be the time spent in the cathedral Alex would mention first. He would say: 'A part of me always used to die when I went into churches. It was as if the corpses buried under the flagstones and in the walls were sucking a little bit of the life out of me for themselves.' Then he would lean forward to confide. 'But after that first time in the cathedral it was different. Once I had the poem, once I knew that there were secrets in there, it all became so unthreatening. I realized that the corpses didn't need to take away any of my life; you see, they had already been through lives of their own.'

When they got to Strossetti later that Wednesday the cathedral square was busy, more crowded than it had been the previous Sunday. Teenagers sat in rows on the steps of San Martino, leaning forward over a friend's shoulder or across a lap for team photographs, as eager to cop a feel of each other's pubescent flesh as they were to get within the frame. Vicious toddlers chased pigeons into the sky while their parents bought postcards and guide books to remind them of their memories. A couple of exhausted hikers, fresh off the mountains, sat in the shade of an awning, spooned ice cream into their mouths and stared at the heap of polished marble before them, all of it so finely worked for the better glory of God.

From a distance the cathedral could be seen to sparkle in the sunshine. Close to, however, it was a grubbier proposition altogether: the cracks in the stonework now clogged by dust and grime, the panels of green and pink discoloured by age. Time had signed its name on the Cathedral of San Martino. But this, said Alex as they made their way across the square, was all to the good. 'You only have to look at the building to know how much it has seen,' he said. 'All the births and deaths and marriages. Centuries of funerals. This building has outlived ninety-nine per cent of the people who have ever been in it. Just think about that.' In front of the main doors he stopped, looked up at the stone façade that weighed down upon him and said, 'It's only a pity that it was built in the name of God. Why couldn't they see it? Why didn't they understand? God's the ultimate conman. Life's just a wicked cosmic joke.'

Isabella said, 'You do not know this.'

Alex laughed. 'Tell me, do you believe in fairies?'

She shrugged. 'Sometimes.'

'Ah well, that's where we differ.'

Inside the cathedral a small herd of German tourists was being led around by a guide with a high-pitched voice which grated like an old squeaky gate banging open and closed in the wind. A solitary woman, greying and saggy in plaid skirt and thick glasses, wandered up the left aisle with her nose buried in a guide book, as if terrified to look up in case someone would notice just how alone she was; a young priest with a heavy brow and sensible shoes worked his way around the walls pulling spent candle stubs from their holders and straightening those that still burned.

Alex and Isabella padded up the central aisle towards the west wing where the tomb lay.

'Where will we begin this search of yours?' Isabella said.

'It's not my search,' Alex said, defensively. 'I just happen to be the one who's doing it.' Couldn't she see he was doing it for her?

She said, 'Why do you believe this verse? Why are you so sure?'

Alex stopped. He reached into his side-bag and pulled out the piece of paper bearing the translation of the poem. He opened it and looked at the words. ' "Look then as the dove looks upon the raven . . . press upon the place beneath his claws . . . rock shall yield up its secrets . . ." See? There's just too much in this. It's telling us something, I'm sure. It's telling me something. And – oh, I don't know – I can't believe someone would write a poem like this about the Joanna, make most of it completely intelligible and then make the last seven lines read like a riddle unless . . .'

'Unless what?'

'Unless . . .' He folded the piece of paper again. 'Look, nobody's followed up this damn poem before. The least I can do is give it a try.' He turned away and carried on walking.

'You want to believe,' she said as she followed after him. 'You want it to be special.'

He waved the paper above his head as he walked. 'Maybe,' he said. 'Maybe you're right. But I can take the disappointment. I'm a big boy now.' He stopped and turned around and said to her, 'You'll thank me in the end.'

Isabella pursed her full lips and shook her head and said, 'Don't confuse me with Joanna.'

There was nobody by the tomb. Alex paced out a careful circle around it. Each curve of stone was so familiar to him now, each crease and tuck and cuff; the way the collar folded at her neck and the tension in her ankles that made her toes point to the wall; the softness of her skin and the lightly lidded eyes. They said she was ruined. They said she was half the woman she once had been. But this was the only Joanna that Alex had ever known. This was his Joanna. He walked over to stand beside where her head lay. 'Sorry,' he said quietly, 'that I didn't have the chance to know you in better days.'

Isabella was standing beside him now. He said: 'When you first heard her story, when you first heard that she'd had a secret lover who had been the father of her child, didn't you ever want to come and ask her? To find out who that man was? I would have done.'

'For a man who will not believe in fairies, you are senti-mental.'

'Thank you,' he said. 'I'll take that as a compliment.' He unfolded the poem and placed it on Joanna's chest. 'If those marble lips could move this would all be so much easier, wouldn't it?'

Alex went down to where the dove sat, its head turned forward towards the wall. He bent down and looked into its blank marble eyes. 'Look then as the dove looks upon the raven painted to the stones,' he muttered to himself. He looked back over his shoulder at the wall behind him. On a heavy stone shelf six feet up was a marble bust of a man, with a narrow chin and pinched lips and pointed nose. Beneath it was a plaque with a passage in Italian. He walked over and stood beneath it, squinting at the bust.

'You know, in any newspaper story the problem isn't actually finding your source. That's easy. Almost every time you know who it is who has the information you want.' He was almost enjoying the intensity of the cathedral this time. It was helping him to think. He turned around to Isabella and said, 'No, the real problem is getting that person to tell you the things you want to know. It's getting the source to speak.' He looked up at the marble bust. 'That's the problem here. The source on this story is people like him. It's this building. It's the cathedral itself. The question is how do we get the stones to tell us what we want to know?'

He asked her to translate the plaque. She read it and said there was nothing there of interest, certainly no references to ravens or any other species of bird for that matter. She said: 'He was just another Strossetti who said his prayers and gave money to his church. Anyway he died in 1760, too late for your poem.' Together they worked their way along the walls, translating plaques, studying busts, examining large stained-glass windows for any signs of bird life that might lie within their designs. There were numerous passages on the walls in Latin, which Alex tried to check using the King-Thomas translation of the poem against the original to work out what the word for raven was in Latin. He had no success. Either ravens weren't mentioned in there or he was looking for the wrong word. He looked down at the flagstones on the floor, to read the gravestones that had been set among them, and walked in ever-tightening circles around Joanna, studying her tomb from every possible angle as if he thought that, with enough concentration and enough effort and enough commitment, he might just get those marble lips to twitch.

'We must be the only architectural ornithologists in the world,' he said as a joke to keep their spirits up. But Isabella didn't understand what he meant and Alex was too consumed by his search to explain. And yet for all his concentration he could find nothing in there, not a single bird, not even the smallest of sparrows, or the daintiest of thrushes. Apart from the dove at Joanna's feet, the bird proved to be a somewhat less than popular image in the iconography of the Cathedral of San Martino. Thin bearded men with nails through their hands, yes; birds, no. Eventually, after an hour of looking and studying and examining and scrabbling, save only for a five minute break when the German tourists came to admire the tomb, Isabella said, 'You will not find it here. Whatever it is.'

'Maybe we're missing something,' Alex said. 'Just some obvious point which we don't know about.'

'Like?'

'Well I don't know. If I knew what it was that I didn't know, then . . .' He was getting irritated. He rubbed the bridge of his nose in thought and said, 'The person who would know most, other than Kelner of course, is Conte. He spent weeks here with Joanna. He'd know every inch of this place. You could call him.'

'He is not at home.'

'How do you know?'

'He told me.'

'You've spoken to him?'

Isabella laughed. 'Of course. He has called me, many times. Well, three times. No, it was four. He called me to apologize about the night in the bar. There is something wrong in this?'

Alex didn't answer. He was thinking. His mind was working overtime, cranking this new piece of information around, turning it over and over, trying to work out exactly what it meant: four times? Conte had called her four times? He felt his guts harden, and his heart start to pump a little faster. He felt his face flush red. It was obvious Conte's persistence didn't bother Isabella or she would have said. She would have said: 'It's a bore but what can I do?' or 'I want to tell him to go away but I feel sorry for him.' And why hadn't she mentioned this before, her quiet little chats with Conte about this and that, at dark of night or at the office or maybe even early in the morning?

Did it show? Did this jealousy thing show? Was his face giving him away? Could she see what he was feeling? It was clear Conte had taken a liking to her that night in the bar. Anybody could have seen that. A blind man led by a myopic guide dog could have seen that. Conte had tried to wrap her in his words, as if he thought she could only truly understand what he was saying if he had a hand laid upon her. The man had seemed to need a point of physical contact, so he could try to pump his energy into her, fingertip to fingertip. But Alex hadn't for a moment imagined the man would follow it up. He was old enough to be her bloody uncle. It was obscene. Who was he to go calling her up like that, oozing charm, talking to her in her own language? Who was he to go around being tall and broad-chested and rich and . . .

Alex said: 'So he called you up four times to apologize?'

'No, don't be silly.'

'Then he called you up to check things about the tomb? Is that what it was? He wanted your family knowledge.'

'No, of course not. He called me to be friendly.'

'I wouldn't trust him if I were you. Bit highly strung.'

Isabella shrugged. 'Oh sure, but I have known men like him before.'

'Oh yeah?'

'Yes.' There was silence between them. 'Alex. Is there something wrong?'

'Wrong?' He tried to look as relaxed as possible, face clean of emotion. He was sure his bottom lip was trembling. 'No, nothing's wrong.' He started pacing around the tomb again. 'So you say he's not at home. Where is your friend Conte then?'

'In Massa.'

'Massa?'

'Yes.'

'That's conveniently close to here. What's he doing in Massa?'

'Restoring a sculpture. Alex, are you sure you are all right?'

'Absolutely. I'm fine.'

'He is a friend. He called me to be friendly.'

'I know that. Sure, I know that.'

'You don't believe me.'

'I do.'

'You think it is something else.'

'I don't.'

She walked over to Alex, forcing him to stop his walking, and fixed her eyes on his. 'I tell you what: we shall now go to Massa and we shall find Signor Conte so that you can ask him your questions. And I promise you, on Joanna's grave, that when we meet him he and I will not have sex on the floor in front of you. Is that OK?'

Alex closed his eyes. He said, 'You're telling me not to be such an idiot, aren't you?'

'This,' she said, 'is the polite way of putting it.' She wrapped her arms around his waist. 'And anyway it is not me he is interested in. You know that. It is my grandmother here that he wants to make love to.'

As usual, Joanna said nothing.

Conte, on the other hand, said a lot. He gripped Isabella by both shoulders, bent down to slap his puckered lips across her cheeks and babbled his joy, his unending happiness, his complete and utter honey-coated, sugar-frosted, love-drenched delight that they should have chosen to visit this poor, humble artisan while he was here in Massa – of all places – going about his labours. He shook Alex's hand, kissed him too, told him what a wonder it was to have the chance to meet him once more and slapped him on the back in a big, hearty, six-foot-five sort of a way.

And then he kissed them both all over again.

Finally, when all the kissing and hand-shaking and hugging was done with, he picked up a glass bottle and a wad of cotton wool, kneeled down on an old leather cushion, and returned to dabbing at the piece of mottled stonework he had been working on when they had arrived. It was a small frieze: the three wise men, bearded, their faces drawn down by time, draped in flow-ing robes to hide their skeletal bodies, delivering their gifts to a deeply sour Madonna and child. It was not the kind of art one would ever describe as witty or moving. It was just gloom and piety and devotion from one end to the other.

Conte rubbed his moist swab gently along one of the men's arms. Occasionally he would examine it to see just how much dirt he had removed, turning it over and holding it up to the light to get a really good view of the grime. The blacker the cotton wool came up, the happier Conte would be, shaking his head and drawing in deep breaths and presenting the soiled pad to Alex and Isabella so that they could agree the work really was desperately mucky and in need of his services.

'What's the liquid he's using?' Alex said.

The restorer sniffed a damp piece of cotton wool and, with a grin, said, '*Acido solforico.*'

'Sulphuric acid? Is he serious.'

'No, Alex,' Isabella said. 'He is not serious. It is a joke.'

'Oh.'

She spoke to Conte quickly. 'He says it is just alcohol. It is what he always uses first.'

'Sure,' Alex said. 'I knew that.'

Isabella explained why they had come. Conte said, 'For five hundred years people have wondered about the name of the man who fathered Joanna's child. And now this Englishman thinks he can solve the mystery in a week. What is his secret? Can he speak to the spirits?'

'Tell him I don't know if I can solve it. But he might be able to help us. Ask him about the raven.'

Conte shook his head and pulled off a clean piece of cotton wool. 'He says he can think of no bird like that around the tomb. He says he could go and look. But if we have already looked and there is nothing there . . .'

'Yeah, you're right.' The journalist took the translation of the poem out of his bag and read it over. ' "Painted to the stones",' he said under his breath. He turned to Isabella and said, 'Ask him what "painted to the stones" could mean.'

Conte sat up and studied the frieze before him. He rubbed the piece of cotton wool between his fingers and looked around the walls of the small church. Finally he turned to Isabella.

'He says it could mean fresco. That is painting on stone. Or it is painting in plaster. But . . . but there is no . . . he says there is no fresco by the tomb either.'

'Sod it.' Alex folded the poem up and put it in his bag. He looked down at the ground. 'One last question,' he said eventually. 'Ask him, have the walls been changed? Maybe there was a fresco there and it's been covered up or something.'

'Alex, this is becoming silly.'

'Ask him. It's the last question. I promise. Then we can get back to Florence.'

Conte stopped, turned to Alex, looked up and smiled. 'He says . . . well I . . . Alex, I think you have been lucky. I think you have asked the right question.'

'What is it? What does he say?'

'He says it is not the walls of San Martino that have changed. He says it is the tomb. The tomb was moved.'

'Moved?'

'Yes, moved. At first . . . at first he says it was in the east wing. That is where Rafanelli put it. And then . . . and then, after the war, the second war, it was moved to the west wing.'

'Why?'

'He says they thought it would be safer. There are no buildings around the east wing. There are buildings around the west. It would be safer if another war happened.'

'Because it's not so exposed?'

'Right.'

'We've been looking in the wrong place.'

'That is what he says.' Isabella looked at her watch. 'It is too late to go back and look now. They will close the cathedral before we are there. We will have to look in the morning. We can stay at the Strossetti house tonight.'

After Conte had kissed them and shaken their hands and patted them on the back and generally taken as long to say goodbye as is humanly possible, Alex said, 'I've thought of something. We now know the tomb was once in the east wing. The question is, where exactly was it? I mean, how was it positioned?'

Conte pointed to a stained-glass window high above their heads, the coloured panels now glowing in the late afternoon sun that streamed through from outside.

'He says there is a window in San Martino. It is a long window. He says ... he says that it was made so that in the afternoon when the sun shines it leaves a *pista*, ah, I see, a path of light along the tomb. Now the tomb is not there. But when there is sun there is still the coloured light on the floor.'

Alex said: 'Joanna's tomb has left its scar.'

As they were opening the door Conte shouted after them.

'He wants to know if you will be at the trial on Saturday,' Isabella said.

Alex laughed, as if suddenly reminded of an old joke. 'The trial? Of course. That, I wouldn't miss for anything. It's what I came for.'

CHAPTER FIFTEEN

During the night vast herds of bilious storm clouds swept off the Mediterranean Sea and lodged themselves in the mountains, slicing their bellies open on the jagged peaks and drenching the valleys below. Alex was woken, just before dawn, by a clap of thunder so loud it made his teeth clatter together and the old wooden frame of his bed rattle. Even the rain seemed desperate to take refuge from the noise and the flashes in the sky that accompanied its descent, attempting entry by throwing itself against the window in wave after wave of shattered water.

He lay awake in his room high up in the Strossetti house for an hour or more, watching the dawn battle its way over the mountains to bring a tombstone greyness to the clouds. For a while it looked like dawn would not come at all that morning, the malarial sky to be left balanced on the cusp of daylight until the clock said it was time for night to smother the clouds black again. That, he decided, would be typical. He had spent the better part of a week chasing history's shadow, building his own pathway to the answers as he worked. Today, if the sun would prove biddable, a little bit of that path might be laid out for him, the colours of the window in San Martino dancing across the floor and telling him where the tomb had once been. But instead the sun looked as though it would not appear at all; as ever, Alex would be left feeling his way through the darkness, reaching out for answers which, like a rat scurrying by on hot stones, would not stay still long enough to be caught. But soon he lost those thoughts, swept back to sleep on the waves of water and noise and wind, powering into the deep red earth outside.

When he woke again a few hours later the clouds still hung low over the valley, grey and bloated, their sulphurous intestines impaled on the mountain tops so that only the lower slopes were visible. Rain lashed against the windows and lightning flashed through the air once more. 'We should wait a while,' Alex said, as he stared out of the old kitchen window, his hands stuffed deep into his trouser pockets. 'It's filthy out there.' Isabella agreed.

'It will pass,' she said. 'Summer storms do not stay long.' They spent the morning drinking coffee and foraging through books in the library, looking for any other information about Joanna that might be hidden away in there between the soft leather covers, but found nothing of any worth that they hadn't seen the weekend before. By noon the rain had stopped and the sky was beginning to brighten and though there was no sun yet the air was warming too. They decided there was little to be gained from leaving it any longer. The sun would only have been a bonus, Alex said. They could do without.

Strossetti was all but deserted that Thursday lunchtime, save for a few damp tourists who sat beneath sodden restaurant awnings, watching steam float off the puddles in the cathedral square. Though the rain had washed some of the grime from San Martino, its smooth marble front reflected back the dismal tones of the sky making it appear even more subdued than ever. Alex looked up. Between the clouds he saw what he thought might be a patch of blue, a little burst of colour from out of the grey. 'Perhaps the weather's clearing,' he said hopefully. 'We all deserve a break.' But then it was gone again, swallowed up by the bruising sky.

After the mediocrity of the gloom outside it was a relief to get into the solid uncompromising darkness of the cathedral. The bold colours of the stained glass in the windows filtered out more of the weak sunlight than they let through, and the shadows around the dark wood pews swallowed up most of what was left over. The only real illumination came from the candles that burned this day, as every other, along the walls. It was, Alex said, like wandering into some monstrous cave, a walk into the belly of a mountain to where the sunlight never reached. He liked the feeling of a journey into the unknown. They walked up the aisle, holding hands. At the altar, instead of turning left to the west wing where Joanna's tomb lay, they turned right. Alex felt a little disloyal turning his back on her like that. It was as if he were suddenly forsaking the Strossetti princess. War had forced her from her home and now here he was, ready to loot the place of whatever family treasures she had left behind. He was scavenging around the tattered hem of her history. Isabella told him not to worry: 'You are doing this for her as well.'

The east wing was exactly like the west, save for the tomb. It was like a family home that had been abandoned for somewhere bigger, somewhere new. Empty of furniture the familiar was rendered foreign. All the dimensions were wrong, all the shapes. There were too many spaces that they'd never had the chance to move about in and too many corners that they'd never looked at. Without Joanna lying there, without her elegant marble face turned up to the roof, the east wing really was a dead place, a space to be filled only by dust and memories.

Isabella said: 'What do we do now?'

Alex squinted through the darkness at the high stained-glass window over on the other side. It was where Conte had said it would be. The design was not particularly original: Christ rising to heaven, rigid and skeletal, borne up by a troop of tiresomely loyal angels. Some of the smaller details Alex couldn't make out because of the lack of light coming through from outside. The wall below was so shrouded in darkness he couldn't tell if there was anything there at all.

He handed Isabella his side-bag and said, 'I'll go over there and start looking beneath the window. I promise you if I can't find anything I'll give up.' Though he wasn't sure he could.

Slowly he began to pace out the thirty feet to the wall. After a few steps he stopped and looked around him. He could have sworn it was getting lighter. The atmosphere seemed to have lifted a little. Not much. Just a little. It was as though a corner of the blanket that had swathed the place in darkness had at last been raised. He could almost see the outlines of the bricks now; he could just make out the place where the wall met the floor. But the change was so small he could barely tell whether it really was getting lighter or whether it just seemed that way because he had moved closer to the window. He turned back to Isabella and said, 'Is it me or . . .'

But Isabella was looking up and away and over him. She pointed to the glass and said only, 'Look.' Outside the sun had at last fought its way free of the clouds. The magnesium beams of daylight were spreading from the very top of the window down, as though brilliant torches were being set aflame behind each lead-rimmed panel in turn; the sunshine streamed through the tinted glass and on to the floor, dragging the glowing colours with it as it came, a pyrotechnic damburst that illuminated the cathedral vault from the very top to the very bottom.

And there, marking a pathway along the floor before him, was the scar of Joanna's tomb, the colours shimmering in the afternoon sun against the grey flagstones. The wide beam of light from the window could even be made out now, caught on specks of cathedral dust that floated gently in the air. Alex stepped into the column of light, the colours sparkling against his white shirt and across his pale flesh and dripping down on to the ground around him. When, at last, his eyes had adjusted to the change, he squinted at the wall ahead of him. ' "Look then as the dove looks upon the raven painted to the stones",' he muttered to himself. ' "As the dove looks upon the raven . . ." ' He took a few steps forward along the path of light and leaned towards the wall. He stepped forward again. He began to laugh. Then he thrust one fist into the air and said, 'Yes!'

He strode away into the shadows. Isabella came and stood beside him. 'What?' she said. 'What is it?'

Gently Alex touched the fresco with his fingertips, as though unable to believe it was actually there. A little of the black plaster from the bird came off. He spread his fingers wide and held up his paint-stained hand for Isabella to see. 'Tell me this is a coincidence.' He rubbed some of the colour between his thumb and forefinger. 'I come looking for a raven and this is what I find. There's no such thing as a coincidence. Never.'

It was a small fresco, only a foot square, some of the pigment now cracked and broken by age. In the middle of the picture were two people, standing before a range of mountains. One was a grand gentleman in a heavy scarlet gown. Next to him was a much younger woman who, if you wanted to see it that way – and Alex certainly did – could be construed to be Joanna, though the representation was desperately poor. Behind them both, in one corner, was a third figure: a man, in simple black robes, his face obscured by a hat pulled down low on to his brow. He was bending over a book or a ledger. It was not clear which. In the foreground, so large that it almost filled the bottom third of the picture, was a vast black bird with a quill held in its shiny beak. There were no identifying marks in the picture, nothing to tell you who the people were or who the artist might have been.

Alex started thumping the wall beneath the fresco with one clenched fist. 'It's got to be here somewhere,' he mumbled. 'Somewhere.' He worked his way from the left to the right and then moved down a little and came back again.

'Alex, what are you doing?'

The journalist pulled the crumpled translation of the poem out of his bag and passed it to Isabella. 'Read the last four lines to me,' he said.

She opened out the ragged piece of paper and, in a voice full of rounded, floating vowels, began to recite: ' "And press upon the place beneath his claws that rock shall yield up its secrets and truth of love be known. Speak these words clear and"—'

Alex interrupted. 'See? See what I'm doing? I'm looking for a place to press . . .' He gritted his teeth as he banged his fist against the wall. 'A place to press upon.' Now he was on his knees, banging his hand into the wall, as though trying to punch a hole through to the daylight beyond. Suddenly he stopped, his punch pulled. He was looking at a small marble plaque, a foot long and half a foot wide, raised just slightly from the rest of the wall. 'Give me the book,' he said. 'The original. It's in my bag.' Isabella dug it out and handed it to him. He opened it to the poem and scanned the lines, running a dusty finger down the page.

'Yes!' he said again. ' "*Nunc amor meus quietus erit*".'

'Now you speak Latin?'

He looked up. 'What? Latin? Fuck no. Not at all. See this line?' He held the book up to Isabella with his hand obscuring the words he wanted her to read. Before she could have had any chance to look, he put it down again. 'Well it's here. It's carved on this plaque. Look.' Isabella got down on her knees beside him.

'It means "Now shall my love be still". Two coincidences. But coincidences like this don't exist.' He started whacking the plaque with his fist.

'Alex. Stop. You will hurt yourself.'

'Bollocks to that.' He braced his knees against the wall and punched the ball of his hand into the plaque, throwing his body weight behind each punch, a slap of flesh on stone that echoed around the east wing. The battle was between himself and the cathedral now, as though the echoing chasm were a prison cell from which he had to break out. Until this point he had been driven on by the imperative of the search, more by the need to have a trail to follow, however faint and random that trail might be, than the desire to reach conclusions. The narrative of his own investigations had been as enticing as the 500-year-old narrative he was trying to uncover. He had come to understand Joanna just by asking questions. But now he needed answers. He felt he would not be able to leave the Cathedral of San Martino until he knew the truth.

'Alex. I cannot watch this. Please.'

He carried on thumping, changing hands, grazing his knuckles on the cold marble until a little blood dribbled down his fingers and printed itself on to the wall with each new contact. Isabella flinched at the sound of his bones smacking into the wall. But the plaque would not move. Nothing he did would make it shift. It just stayed there, immovable stone. He stopped punching and fell silent, panting for breath, disappointed. 'Fuck this,' he said quietly. 'Fuck all of this.'

He scrambled to his feet and turned away, brushing the dust off his knees. Isabella watched him get up. She stayed stock still; she said nothing.

Alex took a few deep breaths. 'Why did I come?' he said through his gasps. 'Why?' He spun round on one foot and with a huge, bellowing scream of 'Fuck it all,' threw the toe of his shoe into the marble plaque. He turned and wandered away into the darkness to stand, hands on his hips, like an athlete after a heavy race, dragging oxygen into his smoker's lungs. He stared into the west wing where Joanna lay.

At first he ignored Isabella's calls. She was saying: 'Alex, I think you should come and look. I really think you should.' But he was far too embarrassed by his own performance to turn and face her. All the violence had got him was a bunch of bruised and bloodied knuckles. He stood staring at the milky white line of Joanna's carved body, over on the other side of the cathedral. He hated her for causing him so much frustration.

Isabella called again: 'Please, Alex. You must come. I cannot move this by myself.'

Eventually he walked back over to where she was kneeling. He stopped and stared. 'You did it,' she said. 'That last kick did it.' The plaque was hinged into the wall down the middle, like a revolving door. The very last kick had pushed the left side in just an inch, so that the right protruded a little. They could not yet see the space behind it. Alex told her to sit three feet away with her back to it and brace herself against the floor. He pushed his back against hers, put his left foot up on the wall and with a loud grunt, thumped his right heel into the plaque. The first time he kicked all they heard was the crunch of stone scrubbing against stone as the dust between the two edges began to move for the first time in half a millennium. But it only went in another half inch. The second kick forced it an inch further. 'We're getting there,' Alex said. 'Just one more.' He lifted his foot high and beat it into the stone.

It was the searing pain, as the back of his ankle cut against the edge of the brickwork, which told him they had done it. His foot was now lodged inside a hole in the wall; the slab of marble stuck straight out of a perfectly square cavity at a ninety-degree angle.

Alex said: 'Bugger me.'

Isabella turned round to look. She squeezed Alex's shoulders from behind and bent down to rub her cheek against his. 'Whatever this is,' she said quietly, 'you have found it.' Alex pulled his foot out of the hole and scrambled over on all fours, like a toddler chasing after scattered sweets. He looked inside. 'There's something in there,' he said. 'Something flat. But it's quite a way back.' He reached in with one arm right up to the shoulder, leaning back against the part of the plaque sticking out of the wall. 'Got it,' he said after a few seconds. He pulled his arm out.

It was a long, heavily stitched leather pouch, closed tight with a buckle. Hidden away in there from light or heat or fresh air, it had not been able to decay. The smooth hide was in pristine condition. Alex turned it over in his hands. 'Should I open it?' he said.

Isabella looked at it and said: 'You have come this far. Why not?' Alex was still not sure. 'You have the permission of a Strossetti,' she said.

He pulled the strap out of its buckle and drew back the

cover. Inside there were two letters, one much heavier than the other, both folded over and sealed with a lump of red wax. Into the seal on each was scraped the image of a slightly ill-shapen bird. Alex picked up the heavier of the two and slipped his thumbnail under the edge of the wax. 'Birds again,' he said. 'Always bloody birds.' He looked up to the roof, as if scanning the airy vault for a shimmer of black feathers in among the shadows, the flap of a raven's heavy wing; the birds once trapped within the poem and the fresco, were now to be released to fly free among the grey stone arches of San Martino.

'My father would have a fit if he saw me opening a letter as old as this with my thumb.' He considered what he was about to do and then said: 'Ah, fuck it. Fuck him.' He snapped the thick lump of wax up, cracking it across the middle of the drawing. The letter fell open.

There were five sheets in all, heavy, yellow paper, filled with thin and wiry writing, that seemed to have been scraped into the page. The hand was familiar. They compared it to the poem; it was the same. Alex passed it to Isabella.

'You'll have to read this,' he said. 'Funnily enough it's all in Italian.'

'The language is difficult,' she said after reading the first few lines to herself. 'But I will try. We should go to the tomb. Joanna should hear this too.'

And so, for the better part of an hour, they sat on the floor of the cathedral, slumped against the cool white marble of Joanna's tomb, and learned the story of the Strossetti princess and her secret lover: of how he first met her out in the fields where, he soon decided, she was 'as rich and brim-full of life as the very soil that fed the vines she stood among' and how he fell in love with her there and then; of how bawdy she could be, so foul-mouthed and dirty, forever ready with a pin to prick the pomposity of courtly life; of how, when they made love, 'it was as if the very air we breathed were filled with burning stars that set a fire to our limbs and made our bodies tremble from the smoothness of our soles to the hairs of our head.'

First the author rejoiced in the love they had found, so rich and strange and fulfilling. And then he mourned the secrets that they had to keep, their real lives tucked away behind the cape of their charade, the more so when she became pregnant with their child. Finally he talked of the pain of her death in childbirth, how it came to him 'as an executioner with his blade newly sharpened, eager for his work'.

In a low voice Isabella slowly translated the very last words: 'I shall not be . . . given the right to lie . . . to lie with my love . . . my lover as we did those nights. The holy spirit . . . he is there now. In place of me . . . no . . . that's my flesh . . . In place of my flesh I put my soul, held within this word . . . these words. They shall be sealed with her. There I know the strength of my love will be close . . . will be nearby to warm the cold . . . the cold marble, and comfort her stone lips which will not . . . will never pump with blood nor kiss the wind again.

'To you, Joanna, I offer my heart and my last kiss.

'If these words be . . . if this letter be read take it to be true: precious is it to find love by chance.'

Isabella put the letter down in her lap and looked at it. There was something intensely brazen about those pages. She felt guilty for having even seen them, let alone for having been fascinated by their meaning. It was, she said, as if she had gone scrabbling through the man's private diaries, searching for the rawest of his emotions, the most naked of his desires, more out of sport than pity. She felt like a spectator at a bloody car crash, standing there beside the splattered tarmac and envying the injured for having known the pain of life on the fringes of death, for being able to carry the memory of ultimate fear away from the pile-up.

Alex said: 'But he wanted us to see the mess that love affair made of his life. He wanted us to know.'

They fell silent after that, neither of them wanting to break the spell of the lover's words. Eventually she picked the letter up again. The bottom of the last sheet had folded back on itself after so many centuries curled up inside its leather sheath. She opened it out flat.

It was dated February 15, 1487. The writer's name was Cesare Scorza.

Alex gasped. 'The dull civil servant who was obsessed by duty and honour,' he said.

'Not so dull after all, it seems.'

He got up and rested his hand on Joanna's forehead. 'Such a clever one,' he said. 'To take your husband's right-hand man as your lover. You went to the one place he would never think to look, didn't you: right on top of his desk. And because of that a government falls.'

'I do not think you can blame her for this.'

'No,' Alex said. 'But it does make her slightly less of the goddess Kelner and Conte seem to think she is.' He traced a finger across her lips. 'She was only human. She wasn't some sweet, naive little girl who accidentally got herself in the club: she knew what she was doing. If we're to believe old Scorza, she adored sex. And she was beautiful to boot. A lot of men today would find the combination uncomfortable. Believe me. They don't like the idea of a woman wanting it as much as they do. And they certainly wouldn't expect it of a fifteenth-century princess. Kelner would be desperately depressed to hear that she was so great in the sack, really he would.' He giggled. The mood had lifted a little. He looked up and said, 'Do you want to tell him or shall I?'

Isabella laid her hand on Joanna's. 'My grandmother was a liberated woman. I like that.'

'Perhaps,' Alex said. 'Or maybe dull old Scorza was hung like a donkey and knew how to use it. What woman could resist that?'

Isabella punched him playfully. 'Alex, sex and love are not like a trip to the butchers where you must always weigh the meat.'

'Perhaps not to you,' he said. 'But personally I've always been fascinated by statistics. Maybe Joanna was too.'

Isabella chose to ignore him. She folded up the letter and put it back in its pouch. Then she cracked open the second. It was just one page long. She read it out loud quickly. When she had finished she looked up, an eyebrow raised, and said: 'What can this mean?'

Alex grinned and slapped out a drum roll on Joanna's belly. 'My dear Isabella, it means two things.' He raised a single finger. 'Firstly, it means that I am a superb journalist, and that whatever might have happened to me in the past I have not yet lost my touch.' He raised another finger. 'And secondly it means that our friends Kelner and Palecchi have been rather less than true to the memory of poor old Joanna here.'

He hitched his side-bag up on his shoulder. 'I think it's time I went and asked the dear professor a few pointed questions.'

CHAPTER SIXTEEN

Kelner was away from Florence the rest of Thursday and Alex wasn't able to contact him by phone until late that evening. When they did eventually speak, their conversation was formal and abrupt. Kelner said the only time he was available was before breakfast the next day. He could see Alex then or not at all. And it would have to be at his house in San Casciano. Nowhere else. Alex agreed.

The historian had a sheaf of documents in his hand when he opened the front door, their corners tattered and torn from too much handling. He looked up from the top sheet reluctantly, as though afraid that if he took his eyes off the words some of them might escape from the page. He said, 'Oh it's you is it? Well I suppose you better come in then,' before retreating back into the house. Alex found him stooped over the kitchen table, arranging his papers into neat piles. After he had laid a new sheet down he would flatten the sides of the heap with his hands, patting the edges straight, first top and bottom together, then left and right. Alex remembered their first meeting in the Piazza della Repubblica more than a week before. The historian was building blocks of ideas again, page by page, thesis by thesis; he was creating academic bricks that would eventually be cemented together to form a wall of learning behind which he could shelter while fighting his case.

'I am in court tomorrow morning, Mr Fuller,' he said, as he distributed another set of papers on to their relevant piles. 'I do not have much time.' He patted the piles square. 'Therefore I suggest you tell me what is so very pressing, and that you then depart.'

'Fair enough.' Alex pulled the longer of the two letters they had discovered the day before from his bag, unfolded it and placed it on the table in front of Kelner. The historian picked it up, his hands clasped around its edges like claws.

'I found it yesterday. Or I should say we, because Isabella helped. We found it in the Cathedral of San Martino.'

'What exactly is it?'

'It's a declaration, a confession maybe, of love for Joanna. It was written by the father of her child.' Kelner began flicking through the pages, scanning lines, mumbling words.

'Have you been robbing graves?' he said. 'Have you been digging around inside the tomb? I wouldn't put it past you.'

'Not at all. It was hidden in the wall, opposite the tomb. It was the poem that led me there.' Alex walked around to the other side of the table from Kelner, pulled out a chair and sat down. He was comfortable here. He knew exactly how this game was to be played. He had written the rules, drawn up tactics. He rested his head on his hands and watched. Kelner read in silence.

'You may not have been robbing graves but you have certainly been disturbing the dead,' he said, after a few minutes. 'Tell me, exactly how did you find this?'

Alex explained. When he had finished Kelner closed his eyes and reached beneath the frame of his glasses to pinch the bridge of his nose. He said, 'Lord help us.'

Alex grinned. 'Don't you think it was worth finding then?'

Kelner turned to the last page and read the name at the bottom. He shook his head. 'You kicked a hole in the wall to get at this? Lord Jesus mercy, do you know what damage you could have done? These things should only be dealt with by people who have a legitimate interest. Not thugs with heavy-heeled boots.'

'People like you?'

The historian started thumbing through the pages again. 'Of course people like me,' he said. 'I think one could fairly describe my interest as legitimate.'

'Define that legitimate interest.'

'I beg your pardon?'

'Explain your feelings for the Joanna and why they are so much more legitimate than my own.' He took his notebook out of his inside pocket. 'I don't doubt that they are, but I would like to understand the distinction. For example, do you like reading the details of her love affair? How does it make you feel, finding out what she was like in bed? Does it thrill or disturb you? It thrilled me. Does it arouse you or does it turn you off? Would you like to have been Scorza? Would you? And please keep it simple. Not too many long words. I'm not good with long words.' Alex scribbled each question into his notebook as he asked it.

Kelner put the letter down on the table and stared at the younger man. He folded his skinny arms across his chest so that they lay in front of his vital organs, as if for protection. 'The difference, Fuller, is this: it is clear from the way you phrase your questions that you are only interested in an insignificant sexual relationship between a girl barely out of puberty and a man of middle age that lasted little more than a year. And you are so fascinated by the details of her affair that in your eagerness to find out answers you would willingly kick holes in churches.

'I, on the other hand, am concerned with a greater history that goes beyond the base sensations of the flesh. The history of

Joanna which concerns me extends to the present day. That obviously requires a far greater investment of intellectual energy and commitment.'

'Obviously. So your interest is even more enduring than Scorza's.'

Kelner ploughed on. 'In terms of time, undoubtedly.'

'And as Scorza was the adulterer we can presume he had an illegitimate interest in Joanna. Whereas yours is pure and unsullied.'

'What exactly are you getting at, Fuller?'

'I'm only trying to work out just how much of a damn you give about Joanna.'

Kelner rested his weight on his hands and leaned forward over the table. 'Look at these papers, Fuller, look at them: hundreds and hundreds of sheets.' He stood up straight and waved one hand across the table, as though it were a feast he had prepared for his guest. 'This is my commitment to Joanna, here, laid out before you, stacked up, aligned, ordered and counted. Thousands of dollars worth. One does not make this kind of effort on the basis of salacious interest.'

Alex dug around in his bag and pulled out the second letter. 'Of course not. And a very reasonable answer, if I may say so.' He held up the folded sheet of antique paper. 'So now, tell me this. Considering the huge emotional and intellectual investment you have made in the Joanna, how much soul-searching did you have to do before deciding to employ Carlo Palecchi to fake the terracotta study of her tomb?'

Kelner did not blink. He did not gasp, or wince or snort. He gripped the edge of the table, forcing the blood from his knuckles, and said: 'What in God's name are you talking about?'

'Professor Kelner, before you say anything more, I suggest

you read this.' He passed over the letter. 'We also found it yesterday when, as you put it, I kicked a hole in the wall.'

Kelner took the letter from Fuller and unfolded it. It too was signed by Scorza though it was dated a day later than the first. The writing was less controlled, some of the strokes running across each other and into each other, as though the writer had needed to dash his thoughts off quickly. However, it was legible. Kelner pulled out a chair and sat down to read:

Though her soul has been taken for judgement by the Lord and her body is now but dust within its linen gown, the memory of my Joanna has remained within me as clear as were she here at my side these four years. And though remembrance may be a virtue, designed to allow the spirit of those we love to live on with us through life's single course, so too can the grief it brings hold back progress on that journey. Thus has it been with my Joanna.

And yet this very day have I been released from the shackles of my past to pursue my future alone. Before noon, by the Cathedral of San Martino, did I bare witness to the destruction, by the artist Rafanelli, of a study made in terracotta that he had created as a guide for the tomb of my Strossetti princess. There are no other models by which she may be judged, no drawings or death masks. For these, he has said, are the relics by which one may recognize a person newly dead and a tribute half made. Now there is but Joanna's tomb. It is this which may stand for my love, perfect in its completeness, as she was in life.

And still Florence waits on death to come visit these lands, that it may bring a new history to those who have been protected from the ways of politics for so long, by the mountain

*peaks that are the Lord's gift. But that which is new need
not, at once, bode ill. It is certain that an age concluded is to
be mourned, but new beginnings bring with them cause for
celebration. The breaking of Joanna's study heralds, too, a new
beginning, where only her tomb may bear witness to what
has gone before. There shall be nothing on this earth to detract
from its beauty.*

*So shall it be with my dreams. Beneath those hammer
blows did Rafanelli crush my grief so that I too am whole
again, enriched by her memory, as one with my own spirit to
face my own new beginning.*

I do not fear the future. I have found my peace.

Cesare Scorza

This 16th day of February, in the year 1487

Kelner folded the letter up and, with an indulgent smile,
handed it back. He seemed to have gathered himself together
while he had been reading. He showed no more interest in
it now than one would in a holiday postcard from a friend.
'Interesting,' he said. He sat down, crossed one leg over the
other, folded his hands in his lap and said, 'I think perhaps you
ought to give me your version of my activities. As you have
gone to so much trouble.'

Alex was thrown. Kelner was too comfortable, too relaxed.
The man was like a village doctor, limbering up for a consul-
tation. Already the journalist was beginning to feel like a hyp-
ochondriac. Perhaps he had misread the symptoms? Perhaps he
had misunderstood? No. He had the letter. It was enough.

Step by step. That was the way to do it. Take it point by
point.

Alex sat up in his chair. 'The first thing is, I stumbled across a coincidence.' He was shuffling around in his seat. It had been so long since last he had been forced to prove himself like this, so long since he'd allowed himself to be this exposed.

Kelner said, 'Go on.'

'I believe that coincidences, real coincidences are so rare that each time you think you've come across one it's far better to ignore that possibility and work on the assumption that there's something else behind it.' Coincidences, he said, were just hidden connections.

'When we were in court for the first trial last Saturday, Isabella recognized a man who turned out to be your friend Palecchi. She didn't know why she recognized him at first but eventually she remembered. He had spent a week in Strossetti, sketching Joanna's tomb. Then I noticed him in a newspaper photograph from the auction of the study. I went back through the cuts and found that Palecchi had discovered the study at Massarosa only a few months after he'd done those sketches of the tomb. So there's a coincidence.'

'But coincidences don't exist,' Kelner said.

'Exactly. Next we go and see him and we find out three things. One, that you had told him we might be coming – not revelatory but interesting. Two, that they weren't just general sketches of the Joanna but full plans – you have to ask yourself why? And three, that he had lived in Santa Monica for five years while you were there. That is yet another coincidence. But, as we know, coincidences . . .'

'. . . don't exist.' Kelner finished the sentence for him. Alex was beginning to feel confident now. All the pieces were falling into place. But it was unnerving that Kelner kept nodding and smiling at every point. He seemed to be trying to help him along the way.

'And then we find the letter which tells us categorically that there were no secondary works by Rafanelli.'

Kelner spread his hands wide: 'All your suspicions confirmed.'

Alex nodded, slowly. He would finish his story. 'I thought maybe it had been Palecchi who'd done the forgery and then dragged you in as an innocent to finish the scheme off. But I junked that idea. He would have got very little for just finding the thing. He would have needed to split a large authentication commission with you to make it worthwhile. You had to have done it together. And he needed you more than you needed him. Good forgers are rare but findable. There's only one Robert Kelner.'

The historian gave a little bow. 'Of course.'

'I didn't reckon I was home and dry yet though. I wasn't worried about how you could age a new sculpture. That's been done many times before. Bake it out in the sun for a few months, that sort of thing. An object can be as old as you wish to believe it is. No, the one element that bothered me was the question of authentication. You would have been the most important historian, the one they needed. That's obvious. But you wouldn't have been the only one.'

Kelner gave him a slow hand-clap. 'Very good indeed. Most people would have missed that.'

'Because I couldn't get hold of you yesterday I had some time on my hands so I made a few calls. And I discovered that all three of the other academics consulted, at a flat fee, were former students of yours. You supervised their Ph.Ds. And which one of them would have been brave enough to disagree with you?

'Finally there was the question of motive and you certainly

had that.' He spoke quietly now. 'You needed the cash to care for your son.'

Kelner got up and walked over to the French windows that looked out over the valley below the house. He stood with his back to Alex and said, 'How right you are.' He shoved his hands deep into his trouser pockets. 'You do not have any children, do you, Mr Fuller.' Alex said he didn't.

The older man let out a hiss of air, like a punctured tyre deflating. 'If you are able, like Rafanelli was, to create with your hands then you may leave your mark upon your world through lone endeavour. That is the privilege of the artist. But if, like myself, you are not gifted in that way, then you must trust to your loins. Parenthood is the closest those of us who are lacking the talents of the painter or the sculptor can come to understanding the joy of an artist.' He turned to Alex. 'It is all we have.

'But then to see that which you have created, your own son, wither up and die, to see his flesh become so degraded, it's hard to describe the agony.' He pulled the French windows wide open and sucked up the fresh morning air. 'Unlike Rafanelli, I could never carry out repairs. I couldn't patch up the canvas or cement the marble back together. I could do nothing. I could only watch my son succumb to his own form of decay.

'And yet I was the great academic, a man who believed himself equal to any of the great intellectual challenges of our age. But still I could do nothing. I didn't even have the money to care for him as I wished to.

'So, yes, I had the motive. And yes, I took the opportunity.'

Alex had been scribbling in his notebook. He said, 'Professor Kelner, I have every sympathy for you over the death of your son. But I have to say I'm surprised. You seem so willing to admit everything.'

Kelner walked back to the table, sat down and yawned. 'There's no doubt your explanation is well thought out. But I suspect I do not have to worry about you turning the whole thing into some journalistic grand opera. You will not be writing a story about myself or Signor Palecchi.'

'I won't?'

'No.' Kelner shook his head. 'You see, you understood the motive and the method so very well but you have not understood why I was able to do what I did. You did not understand the context. One should always study the context. I shall explain.' It was impressive. Even while being accused of international art fraud, Kelner could still play the part of the academic, breaking life down into carefully phrased paragraphs and clauses and sentences, picking arguments apart point by point, cross-referencing as he went. The historian settled back in his chair to give his lecture. 'A decade ago a study for Joanna's tomb would never have sold at auction in the way it eventually did. The only takers would have been museums and galleries and they would have paid very little, relatively speaking. It would also have been too much of a risk to try and sell a fake to them.' The world art market, he said, was far too wise in those days.

But then the Japanese art market was born, and that was a different beast altogether. Conceived to serve the demands of mammon, birthed on the altar of eighties excess, it was a cultural feeding frenzy in which provenance was far less relevant than profit.

'During that decade,' Kelner went on, 'in an attempt to stop the country's economy from overheating, the Japanese government introduced regulations designed to limit the size of financial deals. But this didn't stop the deal makers. Oh no. There was far too much money around for that, so much liquidity flowing around the streets of Tokyo, flushing through the gold-trimmed boutiques, into the real-estate markets and out again, that a few flimsy laws were not about to stop people charging what they wanted to charge or paying what they wanted to pay.' Alex watched the historian shape his story, banging a clawed hand against the kitchen table to emphasize a point. Kelner was revelling in the idea of untamable excess; it was as if he felt the seething rivers of gold were cascading towards him.

'All that was needed,' Kelner said, 'was a way to move the cash about. The vehicle they chose was art.

'A company would buy a painting by, say, a minor Ecole de Paris painter like Marie Laurencin, and then another company would buy it from them for 30 per cent more. And they could be sure that soon enough someone would come along who would buy it from them in turn for 30 per cent more than they had paid, as a way of making payments off the books.'

Between 1985 and 1989, he said, the price for a Laurencin went from $100,000 to $1 million. It no longer mattered whether the art was of good quality or not. All that was important was that it looked like a reasonable work for the company to buy; that when it was hung on the boardroom wall or behind the chief executive's desk its neutral shades and bland composition did not attract too much attention. These were not works that one was meant to look at, save on a balance sheet. The art market no longer had anything to do with art. It was all to do with the market.

'Frankly, by introducing a fake into that market I think I was being a good deal less cynical than the buyer. The study was bought for $8.5 million. Three months later it was sold on for $10.75 million. It was sold on again for $12.2 million, and once more after that. Now it sits in a bank vault in Osaka valued at

$14.35 million.' Kelner settled back, satisfied. Finished.

Alex rubbed the side of his face. His cheeks were warm. He had flushed with excitement as Kelner had continued his explanation. The story was becoming better and better the more the man said. It was grand stuff now. It wasn't just some everyday tale of individual corruption. It was bigger than that. It was cultural corruption too, a whole society debasing art for financial gain. Perhaps Kelner didn't understand what a story was. Perhaps that was it: he just didn't understand how journalism worked. Alex was confused. 'Why won't I be writing this story?' he said.

'Because since then the art market bubble has burst and the piece is now worth around a third of what the buyers paid for it on the open market. If you wrote your story its value would fall to nothing. The bank could not afford that. It wouldn't just be me that would sue you. It would be me backed by the bank.'

Alex still didn't understand. 'My paper's been threatened with writs before. I've been threatened with writs before. We're insured.'

Kelner smiled his indulgent smile. 'Tell me, just how far do you think you would get? How far do you think your paper would take it, faced by a bank with millions of dollars to spend on a legal battle? All you have is a letter, pulled from a hole in the wall, written by an adulterer dead for five hundred years. It's hardly much in the way of evidence, now is it? And if that weren't bad enough there is the character of the man who found it to think about.'

Alex leaned across the table. 'What are you getting at?'

'Well you wouldn't be the best person to have in court as a star witness, now would you? I'm sure you would agree. A man with a past. A journalist who reacts badly under stress, recently responsible for the death of a colleague, blood on his hands, desperate for a good story to restore his reputation.'

'What the fuck is this?'

'Mr Fuller, did you think I would talk to you without first checking up? It didn't take much to find out what had happened to you. Everybody in London seemed to have heard.' He grinned.

Alex laughed. 'Do you really expect me to roll over just like that? After all the effort I've put into getting this thing together, you expect me to surrender?' He shook his head in disbelief. 'Forget it.'

Kelner pressed his fingertips together. 'I believe you had one witness to this discovery, and that was Isabella?'

The journalist pulled a face that said, 'So? What's your point?'

Kelner was calm. 'Thus your one witness was herself a Strossetti, not exactly impartial. Neither of you have any formal historical training. And, to cap it all, you rip the letters open, thus destroying the seals, one of the few things which might have provided definite proof of their origins. It's a very sorry tale, isn't it, Mr Fuller?'

Alex narrowed his eyes and said nothing.

'And also,' Kelner said, 'what if I was now to tell you I too had a fifteenth-century letter that I had recently found hidden in a little known archive, a letter that said the exact opposite of yours? That the study had survived?' As he spoke he stood up. 'Please wait one moment.' He walked out the kitchen and went up to his study. When he returned he was carrying a large flat leather box. He put it on the table and opened it up. 'I bought this at an auction last year,' he said proudly. 'It cost me a lot of money but I do think it was worth it. There aren't many pieces of five-hundred-year-old paper left these days.' Alex had only a few seconds in which to peer at the thick yellow sheets before the historian closed the box back up.

'So let us recap,' Kelner said, as if concluding his tutorial. 'On the one side there is yourself: an unfortunate young man, unhinged by recent events, clutching a piece of paper he says he found in a wall. He has no expertise and no independent witnesses to back him up. On the other side, however, there is myself, an internationally respected expert, with my letter, accusing you of being the forger. Think about it, Mr Fuller. I would be more than willing to go through with such a court case. I would stand to make a vast amount of money. Sadly, you would come away with nothing. Not even your job, I suspect. As I say, it is up to you.'

Alex patted his jacket pockets. Where was that packet? He needed a cigarette. Now. Something to calm the blood bubbling in his chest, to slow the pulse in his head. The game hadn't worked out the way he'd planned. None of it had. He had been outwitted by his own history. He found the packet, shoved one in his mouth and took out a match with which to light up.

Kelner said: 'I would prefer it if you did not smoke.'

Alex laughed, ironically. 'Do you think I don't know that?' And he sparked up. Kelner watched the first exhalation fold out across the kitchen table, weaving its way between the blocks of tattered documents, a carcinogenic smog floating in a city of paper arguments. He grimaced and pushed his chair away from the table. Alex liked the power the cigarette gave him. A little strength at last. He took another deep drag and exhaled straight at Kelner. He was relaxing. He realized he had nothing to lose now.

'One thing, professor,' he said, between slow, heavy puffs. 'You failed to answer my first question. You say you care about

Joanna's tomb so very much and yet it was easy for you to betray her. Why?'

Kelner got to his feet with such speed that his chair toppled over on to the floor behind him. 'I'm fighting for her now, aren't I?' he shouted. 'I'm defending her. That's all that matters: me and Conte and Joanna and that courtroom. Nothing else. I'm making my stand now.'

Alex blew on the end of his cigarette, sending sparks of flaming ash out over the table. 'I'm sure Cesare Scorza would have been very relieved to know just how much you care about his princess.' Then he dropped the cigarette on the kitchen floor and crushed it beneath his heel.

Isabella was rubbing the crevices between her toes, a slim finger pulling back and forth, and wondering whether the thin rolls of black that she had rubbed out of there were more dead skin than dirt or dirt than dead skin, when she heard the bell ring. She pressed the button to release the front door to the apartment block and waited, listening for the uneven beat of Alex's footsteps on the stairs. It didn't come. She stepped out of her apartment, turned on the light in the hall and looked down the narrow flight of stairs that led up to her door. She could just hear someone approaching now, a low shuffling from down inside the guts of the building. If it was Alex, it sounded like he'd had his knees stapled together. The hall light flicked itself off, plunging her into darkness. She thumped it again and started with surprise.

'Signora Kelner,' Isabella said. 'Are you all right?'

Fiammetta was standing on the bottom step, holding on to the banister, trying to get her breath back.

'I am so sorry to bother you, Signorina Strossetti,' the older woman said, in Italian. 'It's not my way to arrive unannounced.' She took a lace handkerchief from her handbag and dabbed the sweat from her upper lip. 'But I was wondering if by chance my husband is with you?'

Isabella said no, he wasn't there. 'Please, come in. Let me get you a cold drink. I know how hard the stairs can be. Come in and sit down.' Fiammetta refused. She really didn't want to be any trouble, she said. She would not dream of disturbing her any more on this, a Friday evening, of all evenings. But Isabella insisted. She sat Fiammetta down on the sofa, took her jacket and gave her a glass of water.

'How did you mislay your husband?' she said.

The woman sat on the edge of her seat, twisting her handkerchief in her fleshy hands. Her calves were large and round, shiny grand piano legs in their fine black tights, and she kept them clasped together beneath her, as though she were preparing to stand up at any moment. 'Oh Signorina Strossetti . . .' she said. And then she began to sob. Tears dribbled down the creases of her jowls and on to her top lip. Her double chin folded up as she dropped her head low on to her neck, her shoulders rocked and her hands trembled.

She had arranged to meet her husband for a drink in the Piazza della Repubblica, she said, a relaxer before the next day's trial. Gufarelli, their lawyer, was to join them as well. But Kelner was late and when he did arrive it transpired he was already relaxed. Indeed, he was drunk. He began shouting expletives at the waiters because they were slow with his gin. He bawled at the other drinkers for staring at him or for smoking or both, and swore at passers-by for walking too close. He even barked at the pigeons for flapping above his head. And when he had done with them he turned on Fiammetta, accusing her of all manner of trivial things: mislaying his papers, not taking phone messages, throwing away his magazines and newspapers.

When she tried to calm him down, he became even angrier, spitting gin-soaked abuse at her. She knew nothing of the case he was about to fight, he said. And she didn't care. She never had cared. Ever. His whole life was on the line, everything he'd ever worked for, his entire reputation. And she didn't give a damn. His lawyer tried to remonstrate with him but Kelner would have none of it. According to Kelner, Gufarelli was useless; a Neapolitan whore, a dirty, back-street tart who would claim devotion to a case just to get the cash at the end.

Eventually, when Kelner had drunk his fill and exhausted the supply of people to abuse, he announced he was going off to find someone who really did care about the Joanna, who understood what he was talking about. He got up, almost overbalancing the table, and stumbled off in the direction of the Duomo. 'I came looking here,' Fiammetta said, 'because he has talked about you so much and it's obvious that you do care about the Strossetti case.

'As for me, well, he's right of course. I don't care. To me it's all just an argument over old stone.' Her sobs seemed to be easing at last, the effort of navigating her explanation having taken her mind off her misery. The restoration of the tomb had occurred just three months after Lawrence Kelner had died, she explained. Her husband had felt so helpless, so utterly impotent while their son had dwindled away before their eyes, that the defence of Joanna's tomb had offered him the chance of redemption. It was something else he loved, and it was also in peril. 'I don't suppose he meant to go to court over this at first, but when they served the writ he was delighted,' Fiammetta said.

'He could have settled it all with an apology a year ago, but he believed he had to take it the whole way. Me, I just wanted to be left alone to grieve for my son.' And she sobbed a little more.

Isabella went to sit beside the older woman. She caressed Fiammetta's rounded back and looked at the grey strands of hair that she knew would soon appear on her own head and said, 'It will all work out. Once tomorrow is over, it will be fine. I'm sure it will. Just get the court case out of the way.'

After a few minutes Fiammetta seemed to pull herself together. She sat up and dried her eyes with the corner of her handkerchief, which she then tucked away neatly into her cleavage. She took a deep breath and said, 'That, I'm afraid, is unlikely.' She stood up and walked to the window to look at the city below. 'Please forgive my tears. I am so embarrassed for coming here like this and . . .'

Isabella told her not to worry. 'You made it sound like you see no future for yourself with Professor Kelner,' she said.

Fiammetta tapped her fingers against the glass, as if the city behind were some sleeping creature in a zoo that she wished to waken. 'I'm afraid we have had little past to talk of either. I've known for a long time that we only stayed together for Lawrence. It may sound wicked but a part of me hoped that once he was gone, once he was dead, the pressure would lift and we could start again. But it didn't. Our son's wasting disease affected our marriage too. That's the problem with marriage. If you don't take care of it, it rots. We took care of our son. We had nothing left for each other.

'Afterwards I thought Robert might show some passion for me. But in the end he kept it all for the Joanna.'

As she talked on Fiammetta relaxed. Her broad shoulders

dropped and she was willing at last to allow her arms to hang loose at her side, unoccupied. She had begun to say what she had once thought unsayable. Words and phrases that had been so laden with dread they were too heavy even to escape her mouth, were now floating off and away across the rooftops of Florence, like so many soap bubbles on a spring breeze. And as they went they carried her anger with them. The emotion she recognized most now was relief, a sense that she was at last beginning to understand what had befallen her. She had resented Isabella at first, she said, for her youth and her confidence and for being a Strossetti. She had even found herself resenting Joanna, for much the same reasons. But those feelings had gone too.

Instead of resenting others she was now able to feel sad for herself, as though she were at last in mourning for all those things she had lost: for Lawrence and for her marriage and even for that part of her life when she had thought it would all be different. But sadness was not like anger or hate. Sadness didn't sap your strength. She had been happy before. She would be happy again. 'You know, you don't become any wiser as you grow older,' she told Isabella. 'You just get better at recognizing things because you've seen them so often.'

When the doorbell rang again and it was Professor Kelner who stood at the bottom of Isabella's stairs, clutching a large bunch of flowers, rubbing the sweat off his upper lip with his sleeve and swaying ever so slightly, Fiammetta was ready for him.

She said: 'You are far too predictable. Leave the flowers on the stairs. Signorina Strossetti deserves a little present from the Kelners for the trouble we have caused tonight.'

Kelner lifted his foot to advance further up the stairs but

then thought better of it. He looked at the bouquet that he held in his arms as if trying to work out how it had got there. 'I didn't mean anything by it,' he said feebly, though it wasn't clear who he was addressing. Then he put the flowers down on the floor as he had been ordered, turned around and wandered off back the way he had come, his scrawny, drunken frame making him clatter down the stairs like a string puppet whose wires had gone slack. Fiammetta followed after him. 'We will see you tomorrow morning,' she said before she left. 'Things will be resolved then.'

Alex returned an hour later, smelling of beer and old cigarette smoke. He had been walking around Florence and doing some thinking, he said. He had decided that he didn't mind not being able to write about the art fraud after all. Sometimes, he said, it was good to be forced to keep a few secrets. He had needed to solve the puzzle of Joanna's lover, more for himself than anybody else. The search had been his way of moving on, of leaving the past behind. He had done that now. Kenya was just another bunch of dog-eared cuttings, old stuff, long out of date, to be filed away and forgotten.

But before he could turn away from history and face the future he had to pay his dues. His past had claimed the story of the art fraud. That was the pay-off, the one part he had to leave behind in the desert with the sand flies and the blood. It had been extra anyway. It wasn't much to give up. It seemed sort of right this way.

Isabella said, 'You will always know you were right.'

'So will Kelner, and that's even better.'

Alex turned to look out at the view of Florence, the white

streetlights shimmering through the heat of another close summer night. The floodlit Duomo, dominating the city skyline even more than it did during the day, looked like a vast galleon rising above a churning sea of light and dark, ready to lift on its moorings and sail off down the valley. Isabella walked over to Alex and stood behind him. She wrapped her arms around him, kissed the small of his back and said, 'I am proud of you.'

He said, 'Thank you.' And wrapped his arms back behind around her, letting his hands come to rest on her hips. She kissed his back again. He laughed. 'You are trying to take advantage of me because I am a touch drunk,' he said, a little sleepily. Isabella mumbled a denial, her face buried in the folds of his shirt, as she laid more kisses upon him. Alex stroked her legs and pulled her closer in against him. He could feel her hot breath against his back. She reached up and felt her way between the buttons of his shirt to the warm skin beneath and started stroking his chest. He giggled and rested his forehead against the window as she nuzzled his back and found his right nipple. She squeezed it gently.

'I'm not this much of a pushover,' he said between shallow gasps, as she bit his back lightly. 'You'll have to talk me out of my clothes if you really want me.' He gripped her thighs with both hands and squeezed. 'It takes more than a little nipple stroking – ' he gasped again as she pinched it between her thumb and forefinger – 'to get me to come round.'

She said, 'Oh really?' and swapped to the left nipple. He let his hands rise up to stroke the gentle curve of her buttocks beneath her jeans.

'Yes,' he said, his voice trembling slightly as she carried on biting him. 'Christ, yes.'

Suddenly Alex let go of her, reached up and dragged her

hands out from under his shirt. He turned around to face her, and tried to look as dignified as was possible with a fast emerging erection beginning to strain his jeans. 'No,' he said with a half smile. 'I insist upon a little subtlety.'

Isabella put her hands on her hips, looked down at his tented trousers, and raised an eyebrow. 'You call that subtle?'

Alex looked down as if he hadn't even known it was there, shrugged and said, 'I can't answer for him. He has a mind of his own.'

'Oh yes?' Isabella reached down and stroked his crotch. Alex closed his eyes and let a smile stretch out across his lips. 'This is very subtle, isn't it,' she said.

Alex slowly began backing off. 'No, really,' he said, trying not to laugh. 'We are going to be adults about this.'

Isabella tickled him between the ribs. He backed off some more. She went after him, backing him around the room as he tried to protect himself from her probing fingers.

'Honestly,' he said. 'I think you should treat your guests with more respect.' He tried to tickle her back but she was too quick for him, swerving out of the way of his cumbersome hands.

She stopped and stood, fingers poised, flexing in the yellow lamplight. 'I always make sure my guests are comfortable,' she said. And she pushed him so that he fell backwards on to the sofa that he hadn't even realized was behind him. Then she jumped on top of him, pulled open his shirt and lightly bit his nipple. 'Are you comfortable now?' she said. And she did it again.

Finally, there on the sofa, with the city flickering through the darkness around them, Alex and Isabella made love.

And it wasn't smooth as Alex had imagined it would be. It

wasn't delicate, or slow or gentle or soothing. It was raucous and noisy and funny and sweaty and hungry and extremely dirty.

And, as it happens, it was also over a damn sight faster than he'd imagined as well.

CHAPTER SEVENTEEN

True, it didn't have the intrigue of the Nude Contessa trial, but then few did. The Contessa, a compulsive coke-head, was famous throughout Florence for the effort she had made to snort the entire family fortune up her nose. Discovering one day that she was broke, she determined to be rich once more and so set about insuring herself against kidnap. She then staged her own abduction to claim the cash. While the police searched for her across the Tuscan hills, she was having a fine time of it in a Corsican nudist colony, where nobody could tell her from Eve. She was eventually spotted by a Milanese genealogist who happened to be holidaying in the same resort and recognized the family birthmark on her left hip.

Nor indeed did it have the novelty value of the Transvestite Hooker case, in which a Florentine businessman brought a private prosecution against a local prostitute for gross misrepresentation because, when they finally got down to it, he discovered that Carolina – or Carlo as his parents called him – had more than the businessman had bargained for: to whit, a penis. Carolina was 6 foot 4 inches tall, had continental size 49 feet and a fetish for wearing taffeta. The judge decided it was physically impossible for Carolina to misrepresent himself – taffeta or no – and dismissed the case.

But whatever Conte versus Kelner lacked in intrigue or novelty it made up for in glamour. It was the trial at which to be seen. It had class. It had style. The previous day's announcement that the judge would take statements from only one person for each side – and both of them little more than character witnesses at that – had made it certain that a verdict would come today. Thus, where the first trial had been purely an exercise in procedure, a time for experts to mingle in the dusty corridors of the courthouse and heave their learning high upon their shoulders, this was an occasion for grand display. The old families who, like the Strossettis, had centuries of great art to care for in their villas and palaces, and the new families who had recently bought all the art that they now intended to pass on for centuries to come, had both decided the case of the Joanna's restoration was of direct interest to themselves. And so they came in their suits of silk and dresses of satin, in their hand-made shoes and monogrammed shirts and stood, scattered about the gallery outside the courtroom, talking of duty and honour and shares and investments.

It was grander even than a society wedding. Lord, it was almost as grand as a society funeral.

Isabella excused herself from Alex's company soon after they arrived. 'It is a bore,' she said, 'though necessary. I am afraid I must mingle.' But Alex doubted she found it a bore. She looked at ease here, slipping from one clutch of proffered cheeks to the next, throwing kisses to the air and offering the sort of flattery that only those truly confident of their own position can muster. Kelner stood with his lawyer at the far end, his nose buried in a sheaf of documents, complimenting no one, the shrivelled wallflower at his own party. Fiammetta was there too, though she stood with her back to her husband, looking out over the courtyard as if she would have much preferred to be down there in the sunlight where there was space to breathe.

Conte was at the other end of the gallery, a vast heap of a man rising head and shoulders above his friends and family, propped up against the wall on one arm. He looked more nervous than he had been before, tired and a little drawn, though he was trying to force a smile at each of the soothing words offered by those who surrounded him. Suddenly he hooted with laughter at a joke or a quip or a cutting remark chucked up at him from below. He threw back his head and directed the noise at the ceiling so that it bounced along the archways. But it was only a louder shout among a crowd of many and was no more obvious than a large wave crashing over an already churning sea.

A dark, squat figure emerged from out behind the restorer, saluted Alex with one bold upraised palm and bumbled across to him, all hair and truncated thighs. Raisa Sharpe slipped her bag off her shoulder and dumped it between her splayed feet as though she had just given birth to it.

'Fuller. You came back,' she said.

'I never left.'

'Hey, that's what I like to see. Commitment.'

'Oh sure,' Alex said. 'I never give up.' He knew that she wanted to spar again. He could see it in the way she held her mouth open, her tongue primed to shower him with questions; questions which she reckoned she could answer better herself. She wanted to drag him into a game of note-swapping just so she could prove how much more on top of the story she was. But he was ready for her this time. He had all the answers. He would get in there first.

'So, who you got?' he said.

Raisa Sharpe knitted her brow. This, she hadn't expected. 'What do you mean?'

'Who have you spoken to?'

'Oh right.' She pulled a ring-bound notebook from her bag and started turning pages. 'Kelner and Conte of course, and Bucelli, the historian from the Institute . . .'

'Yeah. I know who you mean.'

'. . . and Falchi, Soprintendente for art in Strossetti. I got Falchi.'

'Have you tracked down Cesare Scorza yet?' Sharpe looked blank, as if Alex had suddenly lapsed into another language. 'You haven't got him?' he said. 'Really?'

'Who's this Scorza?' she said.

'An adviser to the Strossettis. Retired now. And old, very old. But still lucid.'

'Does he give good interview?'

'Dynamite. But I'm afraid you'll have to talk to him yourself.'

She was scribbling this new name into her notebook. 'That's fair. Do you think he'd give me an interview?' she said.

Alex shrugged. 'If you approached him in the right way. He's a bit of an elusive character.' He picked his bag off the floor. 'Anyway it was good talking to you. See you later.' As he walked away up the gallery he could hear her muttering under her breath: 'Scorza. Gotta get Scorza. Hmm, Scorza. Why ain't I heard of him before?'

Isabella slipped out of the crowd and walked up to Alex. Had he heard the news? she said. Had anybody told him? Falchi, the Soprintendente, had been arrested. The day before. He had been under investigation for months, apparently. Now he had been charged with corruption. Local magistrates had suspected him of taking bribes in return for handing out the biggest restoration jobs in Strossetti. Conte wasn't under investigation, they said. Conte was clean. But other restorers were in serious trouble. There were rumours of a Mafia connection too. Politically it was a mess, Isabella said. And, of course, politics counted for more here than just about anything else.

'You know what this means for Conte?' she said.

Alex laughed. 'It means he's like we were last night.'

'I do not understand.'

Alex leant down and whispered in her ear. 'It means he's completely fucked.' She punched him in the stomach.

The trial, when it started, was short. Had it been a long-drawn-out affair, a significant proportion of the great and good of Florence might well have died from asphyxiation, crammed in there together like that, an ignoble way for a collection of nobles to die. As it was, a number of people did faint from the heat and had to be passed over the heads of the crowd, hand over hand, because there was no room to carry them through it. Fiammetta had tucked herself into a corner down by the barrier separating off the public area near the door, Isabella noticed, and seemed to be managing well enough. Alex found himself having to clamber up on to a high window-sill so he could get a proper view. He pulled Isabella up beside him so she could watch and translate. Nobody appeared to mind.

The two witnesses were predictable. Bucelli, so tiny that he looked like a polished toy soldier standing there in the dock, delivered a cloying speech about Kelner's impeccable scholarship, his devotion to art history and his intellectual commitment to the works upon which he chose to comment. The Deputy Soprintendente for art in Strossetti, who spoke for Conte, could manage nothing more spectacular. The restorer, he told the court, was a master craftsman. He had executed over a hundred major restorations and not one had given cause for concern. To question his handiwork now was, he said, little short of ludicrous.

The judge scribbled during the speeches, looking up to nod occasionally when a nod seemed appropriate, and staring at his pad as he scribbled when it did not. He continued to write for a few minutes after the Deputy Soprintendente had finished his speech. A hush settled over the crowd. All that could be heard was the panting of the elderly, their blood pressure rising with the temperature, and the shuffling of tired feet across the polished parquet floor. Kelner examined his nails. Conte rocked back and forth on his chair and stared at the ceiling, a look of grim determination dragging his weighty features down.

Finally the judge put away his pen and arranged his papers in a neat pile before him. He leaned back in his chair, clasped his hands together over his belly and took a long, deep breath. This was his moment. This was his show. Let them wait for it. Finally, he began:

'Italy,' he said grandly, 'is in a state of flux. The challenges it faces now are greater than any since the end of the Second World War. No longer can the drawing up of plans for the future be put off until tomorrow. Those plans have to be made today, and for plans to be made requires debate. Without debate we cannot decide what is in need of change and how that change should be made. These things are obvious.

'But for that debate to be of any value,' he said, 'it has to consider all sides of the argument. It has to be full and open.'

By his comments, the judge went on, Professor Kelner had initiated debate on the future of art restoration in Italy. He had not been subtle in his choice of words or even polite. The judge could well understand the very real hurt Signor Conte had felt when he had read of Professor Kelner's outburst. He picked up a sheet of paper that lay in front of him: 'Professor Kelner admits to having said, and I quote, "It looks like he plunged her into an acid bath. The Joanna looks like it has undergone an industrial cleaning. The man responsible should be ashamed." ' The judge put the sheet down again and turned to Conte.

'Any man who had dedicated his life to one cause would be well within his rights to be aggrieved at having his work described so and might well be able to argue that such comments had been detrimental to the pursuit of his trade.' Conte nodded his thanks to the judge.

'If Professor Kelner had restricted his comments to Signor Conte's work on the tomb of the Joanna then I would indeed have been duty bound to find in favour of the restorer. However the professor made other statements.' He shuffled through his papers in search of another sheet. 'I quote again: "We must beware the evils of restoration. We cannot replace these works of art. Once they are gone they are gone." '

He turned now to address the whole courtroom. 'Undoubtedly these words place Professor Kelner's comments about Signor Conte's work in a very particular context. They make them part of the general discussion on the future of art restoration in this country, rather than just a personal attack. While there may be those who would disapprove of Professor Kelner's approach to the issues it would be wrong to disapprove of his motives, which this court believes to be entirely virtuous. It would therefore also be wrong for the law of this country to be used to smother debate which will prove vital for its success in future years. Thus, from this court's assessment of the words as spoken by Professor Kelner and those statements made by witnesses here before us, I am bound to find the professor not guilty of the charge as brought by Signor Conte.'

The massed ranks of the aristocracy in the back of the courtroom, a fickle sort who had long ago learned not to support any side in a battle until the battle had been won, now started whooping and cheering and applauding. It was, they said to each other, a great day for Italy. It was a victory for free speech and reasoned argument, for art criticism and debate. Conte shook his head as if trying to wake himself from a long sleep, gathered his papers together and took the apologies and condolences of his lawyers with a heavy shrug. Then he walked across the court to shake Kelner's hand before leaving the room. When Conte had gone Kelner stood up and turned to his lawyer. He said something which made Gufarelli raise both hands as if to say 'it doesn't matter'. The historian sat down again.

Isabella shouted to Alex above the noise. 'Do you know where Fiammetta is? I cannot see her.' Alex was reading back what he had just finished writing in his notebook. He did not look up.

'She's over there by the door,' he said, pointing with his pen.

'I still cannot see her.'

Now Alex looked. Kelner was sitting in his chair staring at the space where Fiammetta had been. All around him people stood chattering and shouting and slapping each other on the back. But Kelner didn't move. He didn't even acknowledge them. He just stayed sitting there. Motionless. Blank.

It was true. Fiammetta had gone.

Late that afternoon, when the day's heat was at last beginning to dissipate and most of the tourists had drifted away to smother their blistered shoulders in calamine lotion, a thin man of middle years stood in the west wing of the Cathedral of San Martino, staring at the tomb of Joanna dei Strossetti. He wrapped his fleshless hands around the bars of the wrought-iron barrier that surrounded it and squeezed until he could feel the metal biting into his skin. It was peaceful here in the dark with

Joanna, he decided. It was so peaceful it was almost as if the outside world no longer existed, as if he no longer existed. He needed the pain of the metal against his hand to tell him he was still alive. He gripped harder.

Here it was just him and Joanna. No court cases. No confrontations. No strife. Here it was just the princess and her defender, both wrapped in shadows. Not much of a defender though. That was clear. Not much of a knight errant. He'd got there too late. By the time he'd arrived the damage had been done. Not much of a princess any more, either. He let go of the barrier and leaned across to stroke her marble hand.

'Sorry,' he said, 'that I wasn't able to do more.'

He stood in silence, staring at Joanna's scrubbed face, trying to remember what she had been like before. He heard footsteps in the further recesses of the cathedral but he didn't look up, not even when it was clear they were heading towards him. Only when Conte began shuffling his bulk from foot to foot and cleared his throat and said to him in Italian, 'Professor Kelner. I had no idea you were here. If I had known I would have waited,' did the historian take his eyes off Joanna.

'Where else would I go?' he said quietly to the bigger man, as though he were not at all surprised to see him.

'I'll leave,' Conte said. 'It's obvious you want to be alone here and I have no wish to disturb you further . . .'

Kelner raised a hand to stop him talking. 'Stay. I will not be here much longer.'

So they stood there in silence, facing each other across the tomb, staring at the marble and trying not to move for fear of being the first to make a sound. Eventually Conte gave in to the temptations of silence and said, 'She's beautiful, isn't she?'

'She was.'

Conte scoffed. 'Professor, it is obvious you still think her beautiful. Otherwise why would you be here?'

'Please let's not argue about this,' Kelner said, dismissively. 'We've both wasted far too much money arguing about it already.'

Conte agreed. 'May I congratulate you on winning then?'

'You may, but I don't consider it a victory.'

'You have been proved innocent. I have lost my case.'

'Is it a victory,' Kelner said, 'when a murderer is found guilty of his crime?'

'Professor, can you never stop?'

Kelner continued staring at Joanna's face. 'Forgive me,' he said in a monotone. 'I did not mean to offend . . .' His voice trailed off. 'What I meant was that this was never personal. It wasn't about my victory. Nobody seems to understand this. I did it for Joanna. Not for me. I had nothing to gain. Personally I had a good deal to lose. As it turned out, even if I won I had a good deal to lose.'

'I don't understand. The judge praised you.'

'Ignore me,' Kelner said with a wave of his hand. 'I'm being a self-indulgent old man.'

'Please. Explain. I think I've gone through enough to deserve an explanation.'

Kelner shook his head and huffed. He would give the man his explanation, if he insisted, but he would deal only with the facts. Fact was all the man deserved. Fact was all that remained. He had nothing else to offer now. 'If you must know,' he said, 'my wife did not want me to go through with this case from the beginning, but I felt I had to. Last night she told me she wanted a divorce, whether I won today or not. She has left me. My marriage is over.'

'I'm sorry.'

'I suppose I am too. In a way.' He looked up and said, 'You see, though you have lost your case, you still have your marriage and you still have your career. The judge didn't chastise you for bringing the case. You haven't even lost face.'

'Perhaps,' Conte said. 'But things are still going to be difficult. I was told yesterday that I had been rejected for a major restoration job in Siena. They thought I was too controversial to employ at the moment.'

Kelner was satisfied at last. 'We have got something in common,' he said. 'We've both lost out over her.'

Conte agreed. 'And of course we have the same taste in women.'

Kelner shook his head and sneered. 'Perhaps that was true before you went to work on her, my friend, but not any more. I could no more love this Joanna than I could my own infections. She's yours now.' He turned and wandered away into the gloom of the cathedral, his feeble outline soon engulfed by the shadows, until all that remained of Professor Robert Kelner was the distant sound of tired shoes brushing against the floor.

There are many copies of Michelangelo's David in Florence: there's the full size one that stands, grey and dusty, outside the Palazzo della Signoria for the tourists who can't be bothered to drag over to the Galleria dell'Accademia to see the real thing; or there are the little ones, just a few inches high, sold from the barrows outside the Uffizi or in front of the Duomo. Sometimes, if you look carefully, you will even see bits of him hurtling around the city, safety-belted into car seats for the journey from one apartment or hotel to another, a blank-eyed head here, a rippling torso there.

But the grandest David of them all, the David who has the best view of his city, is the one who stands oxidized green and caked in guano in the middle of the Piazzale Michelangelo high above the south bank of the Arno. Lightning may strike him and the vicious winter winds nip at his ankles, the air may eat away at his bronze skin and the birds may defecate upon his head, but David will never cease his vigil. He looks away over Florence to the hills beyond the red-tiled roofs, his sling laid slack across his shoulder, and waits, impassive, with the gaze of one who has seen it all before and knows he will see it all again. He waits and he waits and he waits. He was waiting for Alex and Isabella that evening as dusk fell, waiting as they clambered up the hill, bottle in hand, waiting as they wandered across to sit beneath his sea green feet, there to eat chocolate ice cream, swig champagne from the bottle and watch the sun drown itself in the tepid waters of the Arno.

They sat with their backs against David's plinth, looking out at his view, and said nothing. It was good to be silent together like this, to know they didn't have to speak. They had listened to so many words that day. Even Alex was comfortable with a little peace at last. He spooned some ice cream into his mouth and then gulped champagne from the bottle. He closed his mouth and held the mixture there for a minute, his head tilted back to look at the fading sky.

Isabella said, 'What are you doing?'

Alex swallowed. 'I'm making a champagne float. You should try it. It's nice.' He kept his head tilted back. 'You know,' he said. 'They're wrong.'

'Who is wrong?'

'The people who say you can tell the size of a man's penis from the size of his hands. Look at David. He's got enormous hands but his dick's tiny.'

Isabella turned around to look at the sculpture. 'It is the cold,' she said. 'You would have a small one if you spent all your time naked here.'

Alex said, 'True,' and made another champagne mouth float. He was still rolling the ice cream slush around his mouth, enjoying its smooth texture against his tongue, when Isabella said, 'Now your story is finished you will be going home, I suppose.' She didn't look at him.

He emptied his mouth. 'I'm not sure,' he said. 'There's no rush.' He tapped his feet against the step and watched a moped skim along the bank of the Arno far below.

'Your paper will be wondering where you are.'

'They're already wondering. Let them wonder.'

'Is that wise?'

'Perhaps not.' He swigged some more champagne and passed the bottle to Isabella. He lit a cigarette. 'Actually,' he said quietly, 'I was thinking of staying for a while. I like Florence. Things seem to have worked out here for me. I'm more myself. More in control.'

Isabella took a large gulp. 'I do not think you should.' She turned to look at him. 'I really do not think you should.'

'That's nice.' And then, 'I thought you liked me.'

'Oh Alex.' She cupped her hand around his cheek. 'I do like you. I like you a lot. You are fun. You are funny. But this is not about me. This is about you.'

'I thought this was about us.'

She shook her head and laughed. 'Do not be so dramatic. We have known each other a week, Alex. There is no us. And anyway, this is not your city. You only want to stay here because it is easier that way.'

'That's great. I tell you I like your town and you tell me to bugger off.'

'I am glad you like Florence.'

'Is this because it was all over so quickly last night?'

'Alex? Please.' She stroked the back of his head. 'It was fun last night. Quick, but fun.'

'If I stayed a little longer,' he said with a grin, 'I could work on my timing.'

'Alex, go home. Your life is not here. Whatever you have to deal with is back there in London.' She kissed him gently. 'If you feel stronger that is good. But you will not really be you until you go back.' She kissed him again. 'I think it is best this way.'

He threw his half-smoked cigarette on to the ground and said, 'I know you're right.'

They finished their ice cream and drank their champagne. They talked some more and then, as the night sky swept in along the valley, they kissed. Before they went back down to town Alex said, 'Let's leave the bottle here. I want to mark the spot where we sat on our last night.' He climbed on to the sculpture to prop up the bottle in the crook of David's left arm, so that it looked like he'd been swigging from it. Isabella applauded.

'At least he will know we have been here,' she said and Alex laughed.

He said, 'He could probably do with a drink.'

They put their arms around each other's waists, turned their backs on David's indulgent gaze and started walking back down to town, a little bit drunk and a little bit tired and just a little bit sorry that it was finally all over.

EPILOGUE

Francesco dei Strossetti never did discover his father's identity, though the desperate need to know the truth remained with him until his death. The gaping hole in his life story became a fixed piece of his emotional furniture, his emptiness the only thing he could ever truly be sure of. He spent his days in pursuit of something with which to fill the chasm, forever sniffing around the fringes of his life for answers to the strange questions that had nagged at him since before he was old enough even to know about the fall of the House of Strossetti, or to understand the part that he had begun to play in it while he still slumbered in the womb.

As a child growing up in his grandmother's house in Siena, the memories of his early life in the mountain principality now but the faintest of murmurs, Francesco was haunted by a recurring dream. It was always the same: he was on a white horse galloping through the night, the stars in the sky dancing before him as the animal lurched. He could hear its hooves clattering against stony ground, smell the sweat rising off its neck; he could see its mane blowing towards him in the wind and feel its muscles heaving as it charged on to the horizon. Francesco's chest and belly were cold, wind-chilled and tired, but his back was always warm because there was somebody sitting up there behind him, a man who was leaning down over his shoulders, hunched against the wind. He could not see the man's face but he could see the hand that held the reins. Francesco would always remember that hand when he awoke, the way the veins stood up as it gripped the narrow strip of leather, the knuckles tensed.

When he was ten years old he asked his grandmother about his dream. She hugged him to her saggy chest and stroked his hair and tutted and said it was time he knew as much as there was to know, although, she confessed, that was not very much. She explained how he had been brought to the house, delivered to them from Bartolommeo's court by a stranger who told them only that the prince was dead and the child now in need of protection. Then, she said, the horseman had dug his heels into his animal's ribs, cracked the reins and disappeared back into the night. The details of what exactly had happened in Strossetti they discovered later. She said she could tell him nothing more about the man who had accompanied him, and she certainly couldn't say whether he was the boy's father. This, she said sadly, was all there was to tell.

That night, when the dream came to him again, Francesco tried to turn around in the saddle to look at the man's face but he could not move. He was held there, facing forward, allowed only to watch the stars leap about the sky. The man was saying something, the same thing over and over again, his breath warming the edge of Francesco's ear as he spoke. He was saying: 'It will be better this way. It will be better this way. It will be much, much better.' On and on and on. After that, if any man was ever to whisper to him during his waking hours, Francesco would feel their hot breath against his ear or across his cheek, and he would turn to look at them and wonder, just for a second, if they might be the one, if they might be his father.

The child was advised by his grandmother never to talk to her husband about these things. She said, 'Your grandfather has dreams about Strossetti too, but his are nightmares. Do not trouble him.' The old man had never been able to accept the truth of his daughter's adultery. Instead he chose to believe a different story, a dark tale of Medici conspiracy and deceit. He told the boy that he must one day return to Strossetti and reclaim the throne, if not for himself then for his dead mother. Francesco would always agree but only because he had no desire to offend his grandfather. He did not for a moment believe this to be his destiny.

As he passed into adulthood the idea of returning to Strossetti, to the city whose name he still held, became ever more appealing. He had no desire for power, he said to himself, only answers. There, he was sure he would find them. That was where it had all begun; there too must it end. All he needed was a route by which to return. Eventually it was the family's expanding business which took him back to the mountains. Towards the end of his grandfather's life the old man found, much to his surprise, that he had been so successful as a goldsmith he was wealthy enough not just to work the metal but to lend a little as well. Though he maintained a sentimental attachment to the craft that had been the source of his power, he became, in effect, a banker, providing modest funds to a select group of Sienese merchants.

On his death Francesco's uncles, unburdened by sentiment, determined to abandon their father's workshops and to concentrate on the investments. Francesco, by then a bright twenty-year-old and well tutored by his late grandfather in the ways of finance – he thought a trainee prince should have a proper grasp of matters fiscal – suggested the family business expand. He gained the approval of the two brothers and entered into negotiations with Florence for the right to establish a branch of the bank in Strossetti. In return for providing funds for the various military adventures the city still seemed intent on pursuing – at preferential interest rates of course – Florence agreed to allow the last Strossetti to return to the city of his birth. What meagre profits the bank would see from that deal, Francesco said, would more than be recouped from the trade that would come their way through their close proximity to the coast.

A few days after he arrived in Strossetti, Francesco paid a visit to the east wing of the Cathedral of San Martino and the tomb of his mother. He stood before it trying to imagine this young girl, with her taut marble skin and flowers in her hair, caring for him, suckling him, enfolding him in her arms and promising to be his protector. But he couldn't see it. He was already older than Joanna when she died. The only thought that came to him was that, had they met when she was eighteen and he twenty, he would have been the one to enfold her, to wrap his arms about her narrow waist and bring her up to him so that their lips might touch. He had a strong desire to run his fingertips across her marble thighs, so smooth and round, to reach down to the hem of her flowing gown and lift it up so that he could look at the hidden flesh beneath and run his hand across her warm skin, up to the place below her waistband where her body dipped. The sudden remembrance that the woman he was having such thoughts about was his mother so disturbed him that he immediately turned and fled from the cathedral. He never returned to look at the tomb of Joanna dei Strossetti.

Though he still thirsted for information about his father it was difficult for Francesco to make too many enquiries about the town in case the Florentine bureaucrats, who sometimes visited, got wind of what he was doing and suspected him of harbouring ambitions to see his family restored to the throne. Instead, for the most part, he buried himself in his work, allowing the pressures of business to distract him from those questions that still tugged away at him in the silent hours just before dawn. Happily during the day he had enough distraction. As he had forecast, the bank was a great success and within a few months the Strossetti villa became the centre of financial power in the town, staffed by a team of eager clerks who passed their days calculating rates of interest and return, checking accounts and advising Francesco on investments that were safe and those that were not.

Two years after his arrival in the mountains, an elderly man with piercing grey eyes and sunken cheeks came to the door of the Strossetti villa and offered his services as a scribe. Francesco asked his visitor his name and where he had come from. The man answered both questions at once: he said he wished to be known only as Signor Cortona, after the town that had been his home for the last five years. Of his past he would say nothing save that he had spent much of his life in the service of others and that he hoped to end his days that way. 'Men untouched by greatness must depend on memory to provide the text of their history,' Signor Cortona said, by way of explanation. 'But with age one's memory falters and one's history becomes confused. I thus prefer not to dwell too much on the past. One can never know whether what one imagines to be there is truth or just a trick of passing time.' He stared at the ground and dragged a line in the dust with his stick, a deep groove that firmly underlined his words.

Francesco employed the stranger to take on the burden of the letter writing that had, until then, consumed so much of his time. He also commanded him to keep a daily record of events within both the house and the town.

'Then, when I wish to look back,' he said, 'I will not have to trust to my memory.'

'No indeed, sir,' Signor Cortona said. 'You will have to trust to mine.'

Francesco liked the man. As a child the only elder there had been in his life was his grandfather, but in the early years he had been too busy and in the later years too eccentric to pay the boy much attention. The other old men who came and went from his grandfather's house seemed to think Francesco essentially foolish, an innocent who had little of worth to say, even when he entered his late teens. At best they ignored him, at worst they subjected him to ridicule. But Cortona was different, and not just because he was now in the Strossettis' employ. He had a way of listening without judging. He would sit there and stare away into the distance as Francesco spoke, his eyes fixed on a point of nothingness just above the horizon, jerking his head occasionally to reassure his master that he was paying attention. And yet he would not shy away from giving his opinion where he thought his opinion necessary.

In the evenings they would sit, young and old, on the terrace at the back of the villa, watching the sun go down behind the mountains and they would talk, of business and of faith, of art and of philosophy. One evening, some six months after Cortona had come to Strossetti, Francesco told him about his quest for knowledge of his father.

When he had finished he said: 'Do you think I should assume my father to be dead? If he were alive surely he would have shown himself to me by now.'

Cortona closed his eyes and tapped his stick against the ground. 'Sometimes,' he said, 'men must hide their lives behind secrets. Sometimes knowledge is not in their gift. But trust in me: if he were to meet you now he would have good reason to be proud.' They sat in silence after that, watching the last of the evening sun leak from the sky.

There was nobody in the cathedral the day the old scribe went there. He stood by the tomb, resting his weight on his stick, and stared at the marble princess. Here she lay, caught in youth, not a feature out of place. But he had aged so much since last he had seen her. Would she have recognized him? He suspected not. His heart no longer pumped hard and proud but mumbled erratically at him, a shattered rhythm that had drained the colour from his aged flesh. His joints ached, and his spine was curved. Each breath was so shallow now, so weak that sometimes he thought he was about to stop breathing altogether. That last breath would come soon, he was sure. But the prospect didn't frighten him; he knew now that he would welcome it. The passage of time was slowing down for the old man; for Joanna, time had already come to a halt.

'I will be with you soon,' Cesare Scorza said quietly. 'There is not much longer to wait.'

He shuffled over to the wall opposite the tomb and looked at the fresco. Rafanelli, he thought to himself, was a gifted sculptor, of that there was no doubt. But he could not paint. Look at the bird, just look at it. He had asked for a jackdaw. A jackdaw was appropriate. They steal things from under people's noses, take away their prized jewels. It takes skill and cunning to commit such larceny, subtlety and grace. A sense of timing. He'd always rather fancied himself as a jackdaw. But what did Rafanelli give him? What did the man do? He painted some huge, lumbering animal, which had little more in common with a jackdaw than wings and a beak.

So instead he had to be a raven. Not much subtlety in a raven. Its blackness did give it a certain mysterious quality, he supposed, but that was about it. Ah well, he thought to himself, everything else had gone to plan. Everything else seemed to be in order. He looked at the plaque beneath the fresco, read the Latin inscription that stretched across it, and remembered another time, some twenty years before, when his joints had not ached and his lungs had been powerful. He remembered Rafanelli kneeling there before the plaque, making a great display of the slab of marble and the way it was hinged down the centre, demonstrating how, once it was closed, it would take significant effort and determination to open it again. He remembered having to return the leather pouch. He had taken it back from the artist that afternoon so that he could add his account of the destruction of the terracotta study to his earlier description of his relationship with Joanna.

As he handed it over he had said: 'You swear that you will not breathe a word of any of this?'

Rafanelli had grinned. 'I keep so much of my nature hidden, sweet sir, that another secret will not burden me. You have paid for my services and I have promised to provide them. I shall keep my promise.'

The scribe shook his head at the memory of his earlier life. So much deception, so much intrigue. It would be good to die knowing that those secrets need not be kept for ever, that the pieces were in place. There was the poem, written shortly before he had departed Strossetti for Siena two decades earlier, and carried with him so carefully throughout the intervening years. If Francesco had inherited as much of his parents' natural cunning as he believed, the lad would have no trouble finding the answers he seeked. The old man had thought it all through. Originally he had planned to leave his writings so that they would be discovered after his death. But now he considered that too risky. There was so much paper about the Strossetti household these days, so many letters and bills of sale and accounts, that a few more sheets could easily be lost. He knew he would have to find another way.

Two days before he finally died, the frail scribe called Francesco to his bedside and directed him to a cabinet on the far side of the room. Inside, he said, he would find some papers. 'It is not much to show for a life,' he said, 'but it is the only legacy I can muster. There are a number of dramas and some sheets of verse. Please see to it that they are cared for.' Francesco held the dying man's hand and promised that he would. It was, he said, the very least he could do.

Three months after the death of the man he had known as Cortona, the banker sat down to study his dead servant's papers. The experience was less than gripping. He found the plays tedious, their long, tortuous dialogues on duty and honour lacking either wit or drama. Indeed, he was rarely able to advance much beyond the first act before becoming so bored he had to move on to the next script. One of the poems, however, did intrigue him. The title, written in Italian, he could understand. It said: 'Where the stones lie shall Joanna keep her peace.' The rest, unfortunately, was in Latin, a language he could not read. Desperate to find something of worth within Cortona's papers, to have his faith in the man restored, he found a priest to undertake the translation, and waited, eager to know what thoughts the wise old scribe had placed on paper about his mother and her mysterious lover.

Francesco was thoroughly disappointed by the results. The poem made no sense at all. Some of it amounted to nothing less than a declaration of love for his mother, which seemed a little peculiar. And those were the bits he understood. But the rest? Well, it was nonsense, convoluted rubbish which bore no relation to anything he knew about his mother or remembered about the tomb. Perhaps, Francesco thought to himself, the poor chap had started to lose his mind as death approached. Such things were not uncommon. He had seen it happen to his grand-father. Why should it not have happened to Cortona?

Despite his conviction that his old friend had gone quietly mad in his later years Francesco did not break his promise. He had sworn to see to it that the papers would survive and so they would. He ordered that a box, just large enough to contain the pages, be made of chestnut. It was given hinges of silver and a clasp of iron. The wood was rubbed with wax to seal it and then its lid decorated with the words 'Letters From A Scribe'. Finally it was placed on a table against a wall in Francesco's study, across from his desk where he could see it and remember the man whose counsel he had so respected. And that was where it remained until he, too, died, and his sons inherited the family business.

In truth the box became little more than just another Stros-setti family heirloom after that, passed down and down through the generations, its value defined neither by the contents of the pages within it nor even by the way it had come to be there, but by its age. It became a symbol, a fragment of family history that was regarded as important only because it had managed to survive. And the longer it survived the more important it became. Like the portraits in the hallway and Joanna's tomb in the cathedral, it provided this wealthy tribe with a sense of continuity, fed their unshakable belief that no one Strossetti was as great or as important as the self-perpetuating myth of the Strossetti family itself. But while, as an object, it carried such intense significance, none of them ever thought to read the papers inside it or to try to work out what they meant.

It survived intact for nearly 300 years. In 1798, driven by a conviction that the aristocracy had a great responsibility to record history, Giovanni dei Strossetti set about building his library, part of which would be the family archive. He took the heavy sheets of antique paper from the box where, hidden away from light and damp, they had remained beautifully preserved, arranged them in what he considered a logical order – plays at the front, verses at the back – and bound them in rich brown leather. He had the words 'Letters from a Scribe' embossed in gold leaf on the front, and slipped it on to the shelf, between a history of the family's bank and a biography of the artist Antonio Rafanelli. And then, like so many of the Strossettis who had been there before him and so many of the Strossettis who would come after, he never bothered to look at the pages again.